Shadow Council Series Omnibus:
Money Makes it Deadlier
Revenge Makes it Sweeter
Christmas Makes it Chaos
Treachery Makes it Tense

By Julie C. Gilbert

Aletheia Pyralis Publishers

http://www.juliecgilbert.com/
https://sites.google.com/view/juliecgilbert-writer/

Love Science Fiction, Fantasy, or Mystery?

Choose your adventure!

Visit: **http://www.juliecgilbert.com/**

For details on getting free ebooks.

Shadow Council Series Book 1: Money Makes it Deadlier

By Julie C. Gilbert

Dedications:

Money Makes it Deadlier:
To the many editors and proofreaders, especially those I met at BookExpo America. You're all awesome.
Side Note: This is a work of fiction; no actual banks were cased in the creation of this story.

Revenge Makes it Sweeter:
Thank you to S. of SAL Media Group for another spiffy cover.

Christmas Makes it Chaos:
To Scott Bury and David Schoonover for editing.

Treachery Makes it Tense:
To my very own Special Agents. Thanks for being a great source of encouragement.

Note: A variant of each story was previously published as a Kindle Worlds novella.

Table of Contents:

Prologue:
Hotdogs and Homicide

Martin Cantrell listlessly swirled the ice cubes drowning in his lemonade. He'd much rather be drinking a Scotch on the rocks, but he was scheduled to meet his cardiologist in a week and wanted to go with a clear conscience. Dr. Victoria Drake's *frown of deep disapproval* was not something he wished to face. Originally, he had gone to her out of desperation, but he continued to see the brainy beauty because she was nice to look at. Plus, he didn't have to write her an alimony check every month. He had not yet convinced her to go out on a date with him, but he enjoyed keeping his game skills sharp. Once he settled things with the ex, he could think about making a serious move on the good doctor.

His watch alarm beeped, startling him from his reverie. Letting the sweaty glass drop onto the coaster, Martin hauled himself out of the lounge chair and rushed to the grill to turn the hotdogs. They were plumping up nicely but not quite done yet. He added a slice of cheese to the first two in line and shifted the hotdogs to bring the ones that looked the least done over the hottest part of the grill.

"Am I late?"

A dazzling flash of lightning and the crack of thunder that followed prevented Martin from answering Max's question immediately. Watching the surf kick up in the distance, Martin glanced at the hotdogs again and decided they were done enough.

"Not at all," said Martin. "You're just on time. Grab my drink there. We're going to have to take this party inside." Expertly snagging two hotdogs at a time, Martin had them safely tucked into warm buns in a matter of seconds. Then he turned off the grill and double-checked

1

that the propane valve was shut off. Taking care not to tip the plate filled with hotdogs, Martin grabbed as many condiments as his left arm could hold and rushed inside.

As he crossed the threshold the skies opened up, announcing their assault with more angry flashes of lightning and chest-rumbling peals of thunder. Shuffling over to the table, Martin dumped the condiments onto the edge and carefully placed the hotdogs in the center. Snatching up one without cheese, he shoved half of it in his mouth before turning to watch nature's fury thrash his palm trees. The lemonade glass caught his eye. Rainwater rapidly filled the glass to the rim then over the top. The delicate lemon slice hung on desperately. When the lemon finally lost, Martin could only glare at his protégé since his mouth was still too full of hotdog to speak.

"It was the lemonade or the beer, Mart." Max held a bottle out as a peace offering and proof. His expression flickered from apologetic to sheepish to defiant.

Martin grunted and snatched the offered drink. Opening it, he drank deeply to wash down the hotdog.

"Don't call me that," he grumbled. He'd always hated that nickname.

Maxwell Nicholson grinned in response.

"Ah, it's the tenth of the month, isn't it?" said the young man.

A quick check of the date on his watch confirmed it for Martin. "Yes. Why?"

"Because you're always touchier after paying your divorce dues," Max explained. His dark eyes bore into Martin and the boyish grin faded away. When he spoke again, his voice was softer and more serious. "Maybe someday you'll let me take care of that for you."

A long moment passed while Martin weighed that statement. Both the respected city councilman and the lawyer in Martin told him to steer clear of his godson's business. The boy's history was a riches-to-rags-to-riches-of-a-different-sort kind of story. The Nicholsons had been quite prominent until Max's father made a few catastrophic financial blunders. The sudden setback changed everything but only fueled Max's ambitions. He'd all but disappeared for four years before emerging as a new man. Martin didn't question it, but he was curious. He wasn't sure how he felt about Max walking on the dark side, but he'd dealt with enough shady individuals during his career to know that they had their uses. He had sources he could turn to if he really wanted answers, but he wanted to maintain plausible deniability. This wasn't the first time Max had hinted that he could solve the ex-wife problem. Before Martin's mind could conjure delightful *deal with the ex* scenarios, he reined in his thoughts.

"Maybe." Martin put enough inflection into his tone to let Max know the offer was noted and appreciated. "Let's devour these dogs first. Then we can see what the weather's like. If the rain stops, we should take a walk." The suspicious gene in him got kicked into overdrive several years back when Lynn had tasked her seedy lapdog of a private investigator with digging up dirt on him. Since that time, he could never hold a serious conversation in the confines of his own house. The term *walk* had become synonymous with *business discussion*.

Max's smile bounced back. He went to the table and arrayed three hotdogs in his left hand. He then drenched them in mustard, ketchup, and hot sauce before adding a dash of relish. The chopped onions had suffered the same fate as the lemonade, but they probably wouldn't have fit on Max's hotdogs anyway.

Martin envied the younger man's appetite as he polished off his first hotdog and reached for his second. He had ambitiously grilled three hotdogs for himself but knew two would sufficiently fill him.

The storm made conversing without shouting impossible, so the rest of their quick meal was spent watching the driving rain pound the back deck. Max finished his third hotdog about the time Martin started chewing the last bite of his second. Max's eyes flicked over to the last hotdog. At a dismissive wave, Max scooped up the last hotdog and further claimed it with a broad red blob of ketchup.

The delight in Max's eyes made Martin feel old. He only vaguely recalled enjoying such simple pleasures.

Kenny's eyes used to light up like that. The thought doused the remaining good feelings. Here he was enjoying a leisurely evening meal with his godson while his own son avoided him like a plague. *It's not the boy's fault.*

True. Fault rested largely on Lynn. Kenny had always been a bit of a momma's boy, so when Lynn fought like a demon to keep Katelyn but not him, it destroyed something in him. Still, that was ages ago. It was high time the boy became a man. Perhaps Max could break Kenny out of his listless state.

By the time they'd finished eating, the storm had mostly abated. To further stall for time, Martin washed the rather large collection of dishes in the sink. The maid could certainly do all that, but it was the one household chore Martin had never minded. It had always allowed him some thinking time. After carefully placing the last plate in the drying rack, Martin wiped his hands on his pants and nodded to Max who'd spent the last fifteen minutes nursing another beer.

Martin considered grabbing another drink, but he didn't want to carry anything on their walk. The sun had already set by the time the storm clouds left, but a cool, gentle twilight settled. Martin sniffed at the clean, post-rain air. A stiff breeze ruffled his thick white hair. He glanced over his left shoulder to make sure Max was following. Then he set off at a brisk pace until they reached the tiny patch of sand that marked the far end of his property. Reaching the water's edge, Martin stuck his hands in the pockets of his chinos and waited. He considered starting the conversation but decided to let Max take the lead. He couldn't remember when they'd last had a true gentleman's conversation.

"How much do you know about what I do?"

Max's opening question was one Martin had anticipated but still had no good answer to, so he stuck with the truth.

"Not much."

"Good."

The swish of the waves hitting the shore was the only sound for several seconds.

Despite his good intentions, Martin couldn't let the lapse stand for long.

"Are you in trouble?" he asked.

"No. I think I'm the answer to your troubles," said Max with a chuckle.

"How so?"

"How much would you pay to make your Lynn problem disappear?"

"I guess that depends on what you mean by disappear," Martin answered carefully. His mind raced over the possibilities.

Would Max wear a wire? Would Lynn set me up like this?

"I'm a Fixer, Uncle Martin. Do you know what that means?" Max's thick, wavy hair yielded to the wind's playful batting. The effect contradicted the calm set of his jaw.

"Speak plainly," Martin said. Max hadn't called him *Uncle Martin* in ages.

"It's simple. You're a rich, powerful man with a problem, and I can fix it. That's what I've been doing all these years." The young man's chest swelled slightly but a guarded look crossed his face, as if to ward off possible disapproval.

Why didn't Jackson tell me?

A small memory fought to the surface and exploded in Martin's mind. About six months before, His Honor, Judge Clarence A. Jackson did sing the praise of an up and coming Fixer. Martin had simply never connected that to Max. Officially the organization didn't exist, but those with enough money and power learned about it when they needed its services. Completely modular, the organization either had no name or many names, depending on who you asked.

"Assuming I was in the market for your skills, what do you propose?"said Martin, deciding to humor the boy.

"First, we talk money. Then we talk services," Max insisted.

"All right, ten thousand."

Max shook his head and turned away.

"Wait!" Martin laughed as he waved Max to come back to the water's edge.

At least he knows the business.

Martin had put out some delicate feelers a few years ago, but he didn't know what the going rate was for a permanent solution to a messy divorce.

Max's features were stiff with anger.

"Make me a real offer. If you can't take this seriously, then I've misjudged you. If so, I apologize. We'll never speak of this again."

"Ten thousand now and another twenty when the life insurance payout comes through."

"Ten thousand now and fifty when the life insurance comes through," Max countered.

"Forty thousand's my limit. Anything more and it would be cheaper to let the alimony bleed me for the next ten years."

"You can easily do fifty," Max argued. "The life insurance policy on Lynn is two hundred and fifty thousand if she dies on a plane and two hundred thousand if she has a motor vehicle accident. It's only one hundred and fifty-five thousand if she dies by any other means."

"How do you know all that?" Martin's jaw almost hit the sandy beach. He felt violated.

"You're not the only one with powerful friends," Max muttered. He sighed. "I know because I have to know to be good at my job. Let's skip to the point. Even if I can't arrange a plane accident, you won't see a dime until she's dead."

I can't believe I'm even considering this.

"I could cut her brake lines myself for that price." He would never dare, but the idea of paying somebody fifty or sixty thousand dollars rankled.

"You can't go anywhere near her. You'll be the prime suspect, whatever happens. The less you know the better. Just say the word, and I'll make it happen." Max held out his right hand.

Martin stared at the hand like it was a viper, but he slowly took it and shook firmly.

"All right, Maxwell. Agreed," said Martin. "The less I know for now, the better. Let's leave it at this. Should something unfortunate happen to my dear ex-wife, I'm due a nice chunk of change. I can be very generous when things go my way. Do you follow?"

"Absolutely. I'll be in contact when I have a plan. I may need you to pull a few strings for me."

"One more thing," said Martin as Max turned to leave. "It's got to be soon. That policy expires at the end of the year, and I have no way of renewing it."

"No worries. There are almost two full months left in the year. We'll make it."

Chapter 1:
Righteous Takedown

"Relax." Special Agent Daniel Cooper drew out the one-word piece of advice and smiled at his partner. "Glaring at that screen won't make the warrant come through any faster." His Texas drawl gave the words an almost hypnotic cadence.

"I hate stakeouts." Special Agent Megan Luchek's muttered declaration almost disappeared in the hot, sticky air. Long strands of light brown hair were escaping the pins and ties she'd used to contain them. They fell onto the back of her neck, making her miserable.

"What's that? You love this? I'll let SAC Maddox in on that little secret."

"You heard me." She lifted her glare from the tablet screen long enough to bestow part of it on her chipper partner. Her neck started to itch, so she took a few seconds to fix her hair. "I swear the more miserable the conditions, the cheerier you get."

"This state ain't got nothin' on a good-old Texas meltdown," Cooper replied. "Besides, it's kinda fun watching you squirm."

"I do not 'squirm,'" Megan protested, shifting uncomfortably in her seat.

Cooper lifted his eyebrows in an I-told-you-so expression.

"That one was your fault. Power of suggestion." Just to give her hands something to do, Megan fixed the wilting mass of hair she'd bullied into a half-ball, half-bun-like thing at the back of her head. She tended to think of her days by how many twists she put in her hair. A three-twist updo was reserved for meetings with the boss-man, court, and other such confrontations. Stakeouts rated two twists. Casual occasions warranted a single or a half-twist.

Her personal cellphone beeped from the center cup holder where she'd thrown it hours ago at the start of this hurry-up-and-wait exercise. Seeing that the caller ID said *Mom*, she grunted and took the last bobby pin out of her mouth to tell Cooper to let it go to voicemail.

Too late.

"Hello, Mrs. Luchek," Dan greeted, ignoring a frustrated stare from Megan. "Why yes it is a fine day here, ma'am. It usually is in Hawaii. No. She's right here, but I'm afraid y'all might get cut off. We may have to move at a moment's notice. All right, will do, ma'am. Here she is."

Even as Megan's eyes widened in alarm, Dan triumphantly stabbed the button to place the call on speaker.

Her mother's voice filled the car.

"Maggie! What gives? Your father and I haven't heard from you in days!"

"Hi, Mom," Megan said, trying to rub away a tension headache. She reached for the volume button since conversations with her mother tended toward the loud side. "I meant to call yesterday."

And the day before. There just wasn't much to say. And I didn't—

"What could be more important than family?" The question held the warning signs of a prelaunch into a well-loved lecture.

Suppressing a sigh, Megan weighed the options of protesting her innocence and settling in for the scolding.

"Do you have a boyfriend yet?" asked her mother. "That is the only good reason a girl has to forget to call her mother."

Dan's face twisted as he tried to keep from laughing aloud.

"What? No!" Megan sat up straighter, shocked into better posture. "Mom, I don't want a boyfriend. I have a job, a very busy one. I don't—"

"Tut-tut. You must make time for such things, Maggie! You're almost thirty. It's about time to be making babies ..."

Where is that blasted warrant?

"Danny!"

The laugh lines disappeared from Dan's face, and Megan was pleased to note he too straightened in his seat.

"Yes, Mrs. Luchek?"

"You must help my Maggie. She needs a man! Hawaii is a beautiful place. It's not right for her to be alone there!"

"Oh, I don't think Megan needs any help from me, ma'am. It's all I can do to keep the fellows at bay out here."

"Thanks for calling, Mom, but we're working. I've got to go. Love you. Kiss Dad for me." Before her mother could respond, Megan ended the call.

As blessed silence fell, Cooper blinked at her.

"Did the warrant come through?" he asked.

"Not yet." Megan's eyes dared him to question how she handled the conversation. "But it'll be here any second. I can feel it."

Her phone binged, announcing a text message from her mother.

"Did you just lie to your mother?" Dan's voice was incredulous.

"Not exactly," Megan muttered, checking the text. "We *are* working."

The message read: **Call me regularly, or I will sic Tara on you.**

"Megan—what's your middle name?"

"That's irrelevant." She swept the message aside, but made a mental note to call her mother more often. Megan liked chatting with her older sister in small doses, but Judge Tara O. Sidell slipped pretty easily into lecture mode.

Dan shrugged. "I'll look it up later."

"If you've got enough time to poke around in my file, you clearly have more time than I do, so you should write up both reports for this takedown."

"Nice try. I—"

The tablet in Megan's hands pinged and flashed with the warrant and confirmation from their boss that they could make an arrest. Megan let a war whoop fly and reached for the door handle.

"Nobody should be that lucky," Cooper mumbled. "Do you play the lottery, *Maggie?*" He tossed the question over the car as he tightened the straps of his bulletproof vest.

"No, and if you call me that again, I'm giving Mom your personal cellphone number, *Danny.*"

Deepening his drawl, Dan said, "All right. Steady on there. Take the bee outta yer bonnet and gimme a hand with this here vest thing."

Sniffing with amusement, Megan slipped on a vest and tightened the straps with a sense of purpose. Technically, they should have been geared up in the car the whole time, but Megan didn't know of a single agent, save maybe by-the-book Bryan Maddox, who didn't bend that rule from time to time to save a few gallons of sweat.

Megan's steps hitched a second as her mind checked and rechecked that they had everything in order. There was no way this weasel could wiggle out of the net. James Edson Turner's fancy lawyers might cry foul, but as far as she could tell, they had a mountain of embezzlement evidence against Mr. Turner.

"It'll be different this time," Cooper whispered, appearing at Megan's left elbow. "He's not Cantrell, and the evidence is rock solid."

Megan bristled but nodded, encouraged by her partner's subtle support. She had recently made the biggest mistake of her career by trying to take Councilman Martin Cantrell down on fraud charges. The case had been shaky to begin with, but every sense in Megan screamed that something about Cantrell was off. Long story short, Cantrell had survived the scrutiny and come out smelling like freshly picked roses while Megan earned her first official black mark and Special Agent in Charge Maddox's personal ire. She would have to keep her nose clean for a while to come back into his good graces.

Turner might not be a crooked politician, but he made a convenient target for her frustration.

"Let's get in there," Megan said impatiently, checking the straps on her partner's vest. "He's probably shredding more evidence as we speak."

"That's fine. We can have a nice paper-pasting party later. I'll bring the scotch tape if you sneak in the Scotch."

Megan reached for the door handle and swung it open to let her partner take the lead. She threw him one last quick smile before donning her *official business* look. Her left hand found her badge and her right hand rested on the butt of her gun.

"FBI. We have a warrant for the arrest of James Edson Turner." Cooper flashed his badge at the woman behind the impressive front desk. "I have to ask you to put down the phone and step away from the desk, ma'am."

"What do I do?" hissed the woman into the phone.

Spotting the number for Turner's office suite behind the receptionist and the doorway to the stairs, Megan shouted, "Fourth floor! I'm on it!"

Heart beating between her ears, Megan burst into the stairwell and practically flew up the four flights of stairs. Dan's indistinct shouts cut off abruptly as the door slammed shut in her wake. She chose to believe his shouts were encouragements. Training kicked in as the door to the hallway appeared before her. Megan paused to cautiously open the door and peered around carefully so as to not get her head blown off by a desperate, overweight suit jockey.

The quick look revealed her quarry hard at work shredding sheaves of paper. Turner's entire office had glass walls. It was like a giant fish bowl. In the second Megan took to gauge the situation, another three papers were reduced to confetti. Betting Turner was more interested in destroying papers than fending off invaders, Megan drew her gun and sprinted down the short hallway to his office.

"FBI. Step away from the shredder. James Turner, you're under arrest—"

Megan broke off and ducked as a dark, heavy object slammed into the glass wall a foot from her head. Luckily for Turner, Megan had kept her finger outside the trigger guard or the reflex pull might have put a hole in the man. She didn't like having a stapler thrown at her head. It made her cranky. Megan was already hot, tired, and fired-up from dealing with her mother. She did not need an inconsiderate suspect too. Holstering her weapon, Megan leapt up and over Turner's desk and pinned the man against the back wall.

With her face inches from his, Megan growled, "Let's try that again, shall we? This time without the stapler. James Turner, you're under arrest for embezzling from your own company. Anything you say can—"

"And *will* be used against you in a court of law. Do you understand these rights?" Dan Cooper finished.

Turner slumped in Megan's grasp. He looked ready to weep.

Megan always found that part interesting. Once people understood that there was no escape, they either turned belligerent or sullen. Turner was going for sullen, which didn't surprise her.

When the suspect was safely turned over to local law enforcement officers, Cooper turned to Megan and whistled.

"Nice work, partner. If the FBI doesn't work out, my vote's on action movie stunt double."

They started to meander toward their car.

"You saw that?" asked Megan.

"I was right behind you. I wanted to catch you and say the LEOs were a minute out and that we should probably wait for them."

Call me skittish, but I never fully rely upon local law enforcement officers.

Upon reaching the passenger door, Megan asked, "So, what are your thoughts on the takedown?"

"Cleaner than a—uh, really clean place. Whew, that sentence didn't work out so well. It's been a long day."

Chuckling, Megan agreed.

"Yes, it has."

"Anyway, it was a righteous takedown. Turner might fuss about the rough treatment, but he clearly fired the stapler first. I'm glad you've got a good duck reflex."

"Me too. He's lucky I pulled the heck out of the trigger guard instead of the trigger," said Megan.

"Him? You're the lucky one. Can you imagine the paperwork if you shot the guy? Maddox would bury you in it for weeks."

"Too true." Megan shivered at the thought. "Get me to the nearest coffee joint. We're going to need it."

Chapter 2:
The Substitute Second Man

A sense of déjà vu tackled Martin Cantrell as he looked out at the relentless ocean waves making their way toward the shore. Fluffy white clouds decorated the heavens, and the afternoon sun glittered off the clear blue waters of the Pacific Ocean. The scene was undeniably peaceful, but Martin couldn't quite tap into that serenity. Max had called an hour earlier requesting an emergency meeting. Since they'd reached early December already, Martin had been getting anxious to read of his wife's unfortunate demise, but an impromptu meeting didn't bode well. He expected much better of Max. Midway through rehearsing a fine speech about expecting some progress, Martin heard footsteps approaching. Twisting around he was surprised to find two young men approaching. Mental alarms rattled his composure, but he put on his unflappable politician's gaze.

"Who is this?" Martin demanded. He drilled half a dozen additional questions into his godson with his eyes.

"Uncle. I'd like you to meet my associate, Alexander Spiros," said Max. "I've worked with Alex several times, and I find no fault with his results."

The way Max phrased that last sentence made Martin's blood pressure spike again. He would have to have a private word with Max about discretion, caution, and surviving this dangerous game.

"Mr. Cantrell," Alex acknowledged.

Stiff nods and awkward handshakes were exchanged.

"Alex is going to be point man on the actual bank job, and his girlfriend works as a teller there. But we still have a problem. Alex's usual second man got busted on an unrelated job." Max spoke slowly like he wanted each word to sink in fully before uttering the next one. "I have an idea for a substitute, but I told him we'd need your permission first." He looked at Martin expectantly like he should know exactly who ought to be the substitute.

I don't know any criminals. Not ones who do this sort of work anyway.

"Who did you have in mind?" Martin asked, getting the inkling that he wouldn't like the answer.

"Kenny," said Max.

"No." Martin's answer was instantaneous.

"Just hear me out." Max obviously anticipated an initial protest.

Martin pointedly looked at his Tag Heuer watch.

"You have two minutes to convince me. Go."

"Kenny has a legitimate reason to be in the bank. He could go there to speak with his mother."

Martin's incredulous look let Max know that his opening argument was weak.

"He hates her. She practically threw him at me so I wouldn't fight for Katelyn. Why would he go to see her?"

A vision of Lynn on the night they had made that bargain came back to him. She'd looked so gorgeous in that heartbroken state, begging him to let her keep Katelyn. Martin mentally shook off the image.

Max shrugged off the point.

"I have an idea for why he should go there, but that doesn't matter right now. Besides, his hatred for her is the perfect reason he should be in on it. Payback."

"He's not going to kill his own mother."

If this is the best he can come up with, I'm surrounded by idiots.

"We're not going to kill her at the bank." Max's tone added: *that would be stupid.*

"You're not?"

"Of course not. We're just going to rip the bank off so badly they fire her or put her under so much pressure she snaps."

"There's a suicide clause in the insurance policy," Martin said, shaking his head. "If she kills herself, I get nothing. If I get nothing, you get nothing, so if that's your plan, it's rubbish."

"That is *not* the plan," Max said. His jaw clenched with the effort to contain his temper. "The bank robbery is going to shake things up. I'll finish the hit later. Whenever there's a major incident, it's standard practice to place the management on administrative leave until the investigation is done. Once we're certain your ex will be home, I'll take care of her myself."

"What about Katelyn? I don't want my daughter anywhere near Lynn when this happens."

What if she's not my daughter?

Martin brushed the disturbing thought aside. It wasn't the first time the ugly thought had materialized, but he couldn't deal with it right now. He needed to focus.

"That's Kenny's role, and the real reason he should go to the bank," Max explained. "He's going to ask Lynn about taking Katelyn for the day. On the day I plan to kill Lynn, Kenny can take Katelyn to the beach, see a movie, whatever. It'll keep the kid away from Lynn long enough for me to complete the task."

"And if Lynn says no?"

"Then Kenny takes his sister out for the day anyway. The kid doesn't have to know what her mother says." The answer came from Alex. His smooth, detached way of speaking was chilling.

Martin had to admit the plan held some promise, but several things bothered him. There were too many people, too many unknowns, too many moving parts to track. A bank robbery could conceal the real plan, but what would they do if something went wrong? Having forgotten his sunglasses inside the house, Martin squinted at both young men for several seconds. They looked so earnest standing there in their khaki pants and polo shirts. Their nearly identical mirrored sunglasses made them fit in with the white sand. Martin felt very out of place in his business suit. His only concession to the beautiful place was his beach sandals.

Realizing they were waiting for him to speak, Martin cleared his throat and voiced his main concern.

"I don't want my son involved in any of this. He'll feel awful once he realizes the truth about his role in this."

"He doesn't need to know about that part," Max said.

"He's going to figure it out," Martin noted.

The boy is lazy, not oblivious.

"Not necessarily. Separate the two incidents by a few days and he'll never know," Max argued. "Press home the point that he saved his little sister by keeping her out of the house. In fact, the idea of visiting with Katelyn should come from you. That way it'll seem more natural." He frowned in thought. "Yeah. I like this idea even better. We don't really need Kenny on the bank job. Just have him concentrate on getting Katelyn out of the picture at the right time. Alex should be able to handle the robbery on his own. Right?"

"Is this a real robbery?" Alex demanded. "You said I could keep seventy percent of the haul. I'm out if it's seventy percent of nothing, man. I need two people minimum to make a real robbery work. Three would be ideal."

"I think something of value has to be taken for the mandatory leave to kick in anyway." Max shrugged. "And we're back to needing Kenny to do double duty. He'll be the getaway driver."

"Will he even want to help with the bank job?" Martin wondered. He couldn't believe he was seriously considering letting Max talk him into this madness.

"If I frame it right, I think he'll go for it," Max answered. "He'll like the idea of getting back at his mother, but I'll keep that reason in reserve. He should agree because of the money and the thrill."

"There's the small matter of successfully pulling off the bank robbery without going to prison. How do you intend to do that?"

"Leave that to us, Mr. Cantrell," Alex said.

This time the young man's confidence struck Martin as a good thing, but he couldn't simply leave it at that.

"Not going to happen. I have a lot to lose here," said Martin. "I want to know for certain my son's future is in good hands. I need to know."

"What happened to the less you know the better?" Max raised an eyebrow to further ask if Martin *really* wanted to know the details.

"There are too many moving parts in your plan. Either it gets my approval or I'm pulling the plug on the whole thing. I can afford to pay the witch her blood money for a few more years. I'll just hate every moment doing it." The thought of continuing payments twisted his stomach. It was more than just the injustice of the judge's unfair terms, though that itself was a travesty. He felt like he couldn't move on with his life until the issue was resolved.

"Let me talk to Kenny about the job," said Max, holding both hands out in a placating gesture. "If he's in then we're good to go. I'll tell him only what he needs to know. Alex is handling the disguises and other logistics. Even I won't know everything. That's for everyone's protection."

Alex nodded.

"I have some people I contract regularly for jobs like this. We've never met in person, but they're all very good at what they do. Once I get the go-ahead, I'll alert my contacts. When they're ready, I'll coordinate with Max about a specific date."

"This might take some time, but I'm guessing we could be ready by the end of this week," said Max. "Do we have your permission to proceed?"

The close timetable hit Martin in the gut. He opened his mouth to cancel the job completely then stopped himself. The plan was highly risky. Martin had no delusions about loyalty among conspirators. If either Max or Alex were caught, they would cut a deal to implicate Martin. His friends would likely get him off without a hitch, but most of the damage would be done. His reputation would never be the same. That smoking-hot FBI kid who'd taken an instant dislike to him would never stop digging if she caught wind of the plan. He had gotten lucky in the first battle, but the fall-guy he'd cultivated for years had been sacrificed on that silly fraud charge. He wouldn't get that lucky the next time.

On the flip side, nearly three years had passed since the disastrous divorce. He had delayed dealing with the Lynn Problem for far too long. The potential rewards were plentiful. He'd get the insurance payout and custody of his daughter. Lynn would get what she deserved, and the job might even make a man out of his son.

Feeling the need to be extra formal, Martin said, "You have my permission to proceed."

Martin half-expected Max and Alex to bow before leaving. Instead, they simply nodded once, reversed direction, and retreated as swiftly as the thick sand would allow them. Martin knew he ought to get back to work soon. His lunch break was long past over, but he wanted to cling to this moment a little longer. He couldn't even tell why for almost a full minute until the power of what he'd done seeped into his bones.

Enjoy your last days on Earth, Lynn. The thought mingled with the warm, salty breeze, making Martin giddy with the euphoria of being alive and holding another's life in his hands. He felt like the pair of scissors held by the Fates. Martin drew in a deep breath and held it until he could feel his heartbeats slowly thumping within his chest.

Snip. Snip. Snip.

Chapter 3:
Picture Perfect Loneliness

After several hours of mind-numbing paperwork to make sure Turner's lawyers had zero wiggle room, Megan had a moment of weakness and let Dan Cooper invite her to dinner with his family. They would have to return for a few more hours of report writing fun later, but the prospect of a home cooked meal—or anything that wasn't originally frozen—held a lot of appeal. She had wavered until he'd dropped the information that sealed the deal. Dinner would be fried chicken, mashed potatoes, and sugar snap peas doused in butter and garlic. Megan couldn't care less about the vegetable, but fried chicken was not something to be refused lightly. She couldn't remember the last time such greasy goodness had crossed her lips. If she had to endure some semi-awkward conversation with her partner's wife to earn the boon, then so be it.

When they pulled up in front of the Waikiki house the Coopers rented, Megan disembarked and unconsciously squared her shoulders.

"It's not going to be that scary, but I do have to ask for your gun," Dan said.

Megan did a double take, trying to gauge whether he was serious.

He took off his suit jacket and undid the straps of his shoulder holster before holding out his hand to take her gun. His tie had been a casualty of their first hour of paperwork. He'd left it draped over his chair back at the office.

"Sorry, Bethany's first rule: no gun or no food."

Megan stopped short, tempted to climb back into the car and

wait it out while Dan ate with the family. Her breaths came a little quicker at the strangeness of it all.

"You'll get it back the second you step out of the house. I promise." Dan spoke gently, and his eyes twinkled with amusement.

"I don't want those things around the girls. It's bad enough y'all have to wear 'em for work," said a pleasant female voice.

I thought guns never bothered Texans.

Megan peered past the screen door, looking for the voice. She'd only met Dan's wife once at a Bureau holiday party, and she couldn't exactly swear by her memories of that night. Despite the strict no-alcohol policy, the eggnog had been particularly potent during that party. Megan thought it odd that Dan didn't keep photos of his family on his desk like most agents. She'd have to ask him about that someday.

The screen door swung open and Megan's eyes fell upon the lady of the house. The tips of her light brown hair barely brushed the thin straps of her red sundress. A line of large buttons marched down the center of the dress, and a broad brown belt wrapped around the waist. Her expression said the no-gun rule was nonnegotiable but managed to be simultaneously hospitable. A slumbering infant rode in the crook of the woman's arm, and she stood at an angle that didn't quite look comfortable. In another second, Megan spotted the reason why. Two tiny arms wrapped around the woman's left leg, and a blond head cautiously peeked around that same leg.

Feeling like she was chopping off her arm, Megan reluctantly handed her partner the small backup piece she always carried around with her.

Snatching the gun before she could change her mind, Dan said, "Megan, you've met my wife, Bethany, but I don't think you've met the girls. The lurker is Giggles and the sleeping one is Sweet Pea."

"Daniel, they have real names," Bethany protested. Smiling at Megan, she added, "Call me Beth."

"Yes, dear," Dan replied. Holding the offending weapons behind his back, he closed the distance between himself and his wife and greeted her with a lingering kiss, careful not to disturb the baby. Turning to Megan, he said, "She wouldn't let me call the baby 'Stinker,' but I'm pretty sure that's the most accurate description."

The comment earned him a playful swat.

"You are a horrid man sometimes. That's an awful thing to say about your daughter!" Beth turned to Megan. "Don't mind him. This one in my arms is Carolina Michelle and the one wrapped around my leg is Ashley Ann."

"She also answers to 'Giggles,'" said Dan in a stage whisper. He smiled down at his wife and planted a kiss on her nose. "Admit it. I have my charms too." He brushed the baby's fuzzy head with his fingertips, then said, "Now where'd that Giggles get to?" He made a show of searching high and low and not finding anything.

"This is a daily ritual, Agent Luchek," said Beth. "Ignore him. Come on in and wash up. The restroom's right down that short hallway over there. You can't miss it. Dinner would go stone cold if he had his way."

"Please, call me Megan. Dan's told me so many wonderful things about you and the girls." Megan squeezed past Bethany Cooper and went to give her hands a good scrub before dinner. She couldn't recall much about what Dan told her about his family, but she assumed it would be good things.

Upon returning to the front room, she saw how Giggles had earned her nickname. The child was riding high on her father's shoulders, laughing, occasionally squealing and/or shrieking, and covering Dan's eyes with her small hands. For his part, Dan was stripped down to his white undershirt for the role of horsey. The tattoo souvenir from his marine days poked out from beneath the t-shirt. He stumbled around the room pretending he couldn't see. Megan spotted the safe over by the door and felt better for knowing where her weapon was located. She watched the show for another minute before Bethany intervened.

In short order, they were arranged around the dining room table, which appeared to be the kitchen table relocated into the family room. The chairs they sat on were metal folding ones, but Megan decided not to judge. If she'd been hosting the gathering they would have been eating off garage sale tray tables. One could hardly afford a sprawling estate on an agent's pay. Megan couldn't remember what Mrs. Cooper did for a day job, but she wanted to say it had something to do with a hotel gym. Whatever it was, the job probably didn't net even as much money as Dan's meager paychecks. She remembered Dan saying his wife liked being home with the girls most of the week. She went to work a couple of hours three times a week to keep sane.

It took several minutes of observations before Megan felt at ease as a guest. She was sadly out of practice. The food was well worth the brief period of awkwardness. The mashed potatoes would probably cost her an extra half-hour of cardio tomorrow, but it seemed a fair trade. The chicken was crispy on the outside, hot and juicy on the inside, just how she liked it.

As they finished the main meal, the baby woke up and voiced her discontent with an ear-piercing shriek. Bethany slipped out long enough to tend to her needs. Dan got up and started the coffeemaker. Megan was left alone with Giggles which could have been bad, but the child entertained herself by squeezing small bits of chicken between her fingers and laughing at the results. Occasionally, the girl would shove a fist into her mouth and drop off a bit of chicken. Megan found herself fascinated.

"She definitely likes to play with her food," Dan remarked.

"The messy parts are all you, dear," Bethany said, sweeping in with a hot apple pie cradled on a dishtowel.

Giggles babbled something Megan couldn't decipher, stabbed a finger in her direction, and laughed.

"Yes, love. That's daddy's friend." Bethany set the pie down and expertly served it onto plates Dan retrieved from the kitchen.

He disappeared then reappeared a few seconds later with three large mugs of coffee.

"Dig in and enjoy," he advised. "It'll probably be the last bit of fun we have tonight."

Unfortunately, he was right. Once they finally pried themselves away from Dan's family and headed back to the office, Megan really didn't want to fill out paperwork. Nevertheless, she forced herself to deal with the unpleasant task. Word by painful word, the report on the Turner case emerged from her mind. By the time Dan stopped by to kick her out of the cubicle she called an office, the clock said one-thirty.

"Quitting time," Dan announced. "Come on. I'll drop you off before I head home. I got a message summoning me to a seven o'clock meeting with Maddox and Oldwick. I'm assuming you got the same."

Megan's eyes fixed on the ancient phone in the far corner of her desk. A piece of paper had fallen over half of it. When she knocked it aside, the blinking red light glared at her accusingly. She groaned then fumbled for her work cellphone. A few deft keystrokes confirmed it. Maddox had heard the good news about the Turner case, was delighted—or at least as excited as the man got—about them being suddenly free, and wanted to see her at 7 a.m. sharp.

"I wonder what he's plotting now. He hardly ever calls for

official powwows. Did we break any rules lately?" Megan wondered.

"Not that I know of, but let's not jaw about it now. The mystery will solve itself on the morrow."

"I think you mean today," Megan lamented.

"To me, 'on the morrow' means after I sleep," Dan clarified.

"We could just sleep here." Alarm jolted through Megan as she caught the possible double meaning in her wording. "I mean on the couch. Separately!" She blushed fiercely. "Oh, just take me home." It wasn't getting any better. She sighed. "I'm going to stop talking now."

Dan chuckled.

"Your carriage awaits, ma'am."

The drive to Megan's apartment passed in silence. She thanked Dan for the ride then stumbled up the stairs. Her feet felt like they had dried concrete on them. She dropped her keys in the bowl by the door and took a moment to absorb the emptiness surrounding her. On another night she just might care, but right now she was too tired to think beyond passing out for a few hours. Mindful of her important meeting, Megan set her alarm then flopped onto her bed.

As the darkness slipped blissfully over her, she thought, *Maybe Mom's right. It's not right to be alone in such a beautiful place.*

Thoughts of Derrick and handcuffs tried to intrude, but Megan was too tired to wrestle with her usual demons. For now, she'd fought the good fight, dodged a stapler, put one bad guy in his place, and finished her reports without a paper cut.

Time to call it a day.

Chapter 4:
Cold Pizza and Clandestine Contact

"Mom! We're out of milk!" Katelyn Cantrell shook the very light box of cereal, opened it up, and overturned it above the table. A dozen stale cereal fragments tumbled out. "Mom! The cereal's gone too! What am I gonna eat?" Desperate, she plucked up a piece that looked like it might have been a marshmallow once upon a time and tentatively stuck it on her tongue. It didn't taste half-bad but it certainly couldn't satisfy her hunger.

"Stop shouting! I'll be down in a minute!" Thanks to a quirk of the house her mother's exasperated cries floated down to the kitchen through the light fixture above the table.

"But there's nothing to eat!" Katelyn repeated, staring up and addressing the ceiling lamp.

"Eat the pizza," Lynn Berkley calmly instructed. "There should be four slices left."

"For breakfast?" Katelyn whipped her head around and looked to see that the woman coming up behind her really was her mother.

Lynn shrugged.

"Sure. Why not?" She finished clickity-clacking her way into the kitchen as she donned her second best pair of earrings. "I don't want you to make a habit of it, but once in a while won't kill you. You're on vacation this week anyway."

Katelyn leapt from her chair and scrambled to the refrigerator before her mom could change her mind.

"Katelyn Amelia Cantrell. Look at this mess!"

Aware her mom had just used her full name, Katelyn cautiously ducked from behind the refrigerator door.

"What?" Her question came out muffled due to a large bite of cold pizza still mostly filling her mouth.

"Young lady, we do not speak with food in our mouths, and this table has crumbs all over it." Lynn waved at the kitchen table. "Please rectify the situation." She placed hands on hips and waited.

Rolling her eyes and groaning, Katelyn trudged from behind her shelter, threw the remains of her pizza slice onto a napkin, and wiped the cereal crumbs and dust from the kitchen table into her hand.

"Use the washcloth and make sure you don't miss anything."

"Mom." Katelyn managed to make the word last two full seconds. Snatching up the washcloth, she did as bid.

"What?" Lynn waited until the table had had a nice thorough scrubbing before cheerfully matching her tone to the whiny cadence Katelyn had used.

"You're doing it again."

"Doing what, dear?" Lynn retrieved a slice of pizza from the refrigerator and took a delicate bite.

"Giving orders," Katelyn complained.

Lynn laughed, laid the pizza on a paper towel beside Katelyn's, and brushed her hands off over the sink. She moved over to Katelyn, placed both hands on her shoulders, and drew her back into a tight hug, pinning Katelyn's arms in place. She lowered her voice like she had a deep secret to share.

"I hate to break it to you, Little Miss, but I am your mother. I *get* to give orders. And kisses." She planted a big kiss on Katelyn's right ear.

It earned another long, multileveled protest from Katelyn.

"Mom!"

"That's my name, don't wear it out." Lynn tightened the hug before letting Katelyn squirm free.

"You're so weird."

"Why, thank you," Lynn said. She returned to the cold pizza slices and picked up both. Holding Katelyn's out to her, Lynn held her own slice up in a toast. "Here's to lovely leftovers. May they not clog our arteries on the way down."

Katelyn decided she liked this odd side of her mom. She didn't get to see it often. Mostly she seemed to worry about money, but Katelyn guessed that was a job hazard from managing a bank. Today, her mom had chosen a navy blue skirt with a white blouse. Katelyn studied her critically.

"Do I pass inspection?" Lynn turned to the side so Katelyn could get the full effect.

"You look ..." Katelyn struggled to find the right word. She scanned the word magnets covering the front of the refrigerator. She sometimes looked up random definitions to stave off boredom or pass the time waiting for her Candy Crush lives to regenerate. Her eyes found just the right word. "Competent."

"Thanks for the vote of confidence, love."

They settled into their respective kitchen chairs and each enjoyed a full slice of cold pizza. They also split a slice before Katelyn's phone pinged, destroying the comfortable mood. Her heart fluttered, going up with joy and sinking with sorrow for the lost moment. A quick glance at her mother reinforced the icky feeling she was getting.

The expression Lynn wore couldn't be read easily. It was a carefully contained neutral thing, but child's intuition told Katelyn, her mother wasn't happy.

"May I answer the message?" Katelyn knew her mom hated the fancy smartphone because it had been a surprise gift from her dad. He'd programed it with his number and Kenny's number. She had since added a dozen friends and her mother to the contacts list.

"Go for it," Lynn said, attempting a smile. She got up quickly and cleared the napkins. "I've got to go to work soon, but Mrs. Ting will be here to stay with you."

"I'm in seventh grade. I don't need a babysitter," Katelyn muttered absently. Most of her attention went into entering her code to unlock the phone.

"She's not a babysitter. She's a housekeeper who happens to be here when you are. Don't stay on that thing too long, okay?"

"Okay." Katelyn's chirruped response didn't satisfy her mom, so she flashed a bright smile. "Have fun at work."

"I'm serious. Get some fresh air today. Try not to give Mrs. Ting too hard a time. She has enough to worry about with her own family."

Katelyn's hands froze, poised over the button to see who had sent her a text message. She looked at her mom expectantly. When no further information was offered, she demanded, "What's wrong with Mrs. Ting's family?" Her tone said there shouldn't be anything wrong. Mrs. Ting was the nicest lady ever.

Lynn was silent, and Katelyn knew that meant she was

measuring how much to say.

"Her mother is dying from cancer." Lynn's soft tone couldn't take the sting out of the announcement.

Katelyn sucked in sharply, not sure how she should feel about that news.

"Poor Mrs. Ting." It wasn't her mother after all, but it was somebody she'd met.

Lynn placed a hand over Katelyn's wrist and squeezed, initially saying nothing. Then, she cupped Katelyn's head between her hands and kissed her forehead.

Katelyn was too lost in thought to protest.

"Don't worry about it, baby. There's not much we can do except be understanding. Hug her for me when she gets in, all right?" Lynn released Katelyn and grabbed her purse. "I'll pick up milk and cereal on the way home. Remember to set the alarm after Mrs. Ting gets here."

Katelyn waved to let her mom know every instruction had been received. Her mood stayed melancholy until she remembered the unread text message. She'd waited so long her phone had gone to sleep, so she woke it up and accessed the message. She smiled half-evilly when she saw who it was from.

KDCbuttmunch (Cell): Hey shortstuf call me

Katelyn wrinkled her nose at her brother's misspelled words and complete lack of proper punctuation. She doubted he'd even have the first letter capitalized if his phone didn't do that automatically. As a condition of being allowed to text people, her mother insisted she use complete sentences and spell things correctly. At first it had been totally annoying, but by now, it was second nature. Katelyn wished her mom could make Kenny follow the texting rules. She hit reply and scrolled down to call. Her brother answered on the second ring, which was unusual for him. He must have been waiting for her call.

"Yo."

"Yo?" Katelyn repeated dubiously. "You texted me, Buttmunch, and now 'yo' is all you can say? How about 'Hi, Katelyn. Long time no talk. Thanks for calling.'"

"Whoa. Tone down the snot level, brat." Despite his words, Kenny sounded amused. "I wanted to know if you would like to hang out sometime, just you and me. It *has* been a long time since I've seen you."

The invitation stunned Katelyn into silence. She'd hardly seen

Kenny since the divorce hearings. Her mom wouldn't let her go to many of them, but she'd wanted to go just to catch a glimpse of him. They'd traded a few barbs by text message in the intervening years, but even calls were rare things.

"Did you ask mom?"

"No. I'm asking you, dumbbell. It wouldn't make sense to ask her unless you wanted to hang out with me."

That actually made sense, so she forgave him the arrogant tone.

Now fully recovered, Katelyn's response gushed out.

"Of course I want to see you. When can we meet? What will we do? I don't have much money because of Christmas. There were a few gift exchanges at school I had to join."

"Cost don't matter," said Kenny.

"Doesn't," Katelyn corrected instinctively. She bit her bottom lip. Mom said that was a bad habit.

"Are you always this annoying?" Kenny wondered.

"Yep."

He chuckled at her honesty then settled into a rare moment of seriousness.

"Dad says, 'hi.' I'll give you his gift when I see you."

"I hope he didn't spend a lot of money on it. Mom hates it when he does that. I think she feels bad that she can't …."

"Compete," Kenny finished.

"Yeah, compete. That's it." The iPhone was only the latest in a long list of gifts. Katelyn had mixed feelings over the pricey offerings. Of course, she loved getting things from her father, but she didn't like the strained expression they always conjured in her mother. She was old enough to understand this was just a different way for her parents to fight. Mom had once explained that part. Since her dad wasn't around her, he sent things so she wouldn't forget him, which was stupid. He was her father and an important man. Katelyn could never forget him even if she wanted to.

A sad beat passed between the siblings.

Kenny cleared his throat.

"Yo. I've got to split, but now that I know you're in, I'll talk to mom and let you know more details when I get them. Think about what you want to do."

"Thanks, Kenny. I mean it."

He grunted and ended the call.

Katelyn stared down at the phone. She smiled then frowned,

suddenly having the urge to cry. She killed the urge with a dose of anger. She shouldn't have to miss her brother this much. Truth be told, she missed her dad too, but at least she got to see him on TV late at night on the boring channel that replayed city council meetings. Why couldn't her parents act like adults and work it out? They'd loved each other once upon a time.

What happened? The question was quickly followed by another. *What will happen?*

Katelyn couldn't predict which way her mom's decision would go. Mom was often lingering up in her bedroom staring at the framed high school picture of Kenny, but the topic was strictly off limits. Katelyn would bet her iPhone her mom would do just about anything for Kenny, but then why didn't he live with them?

Chapter 5:
No Rest for the Best

Megan Luchek slept right through her alarm, but two minutes later, her partner called. She didn't bother answering but woke up enough to notice the time. Panicked, she sprang out of bed and rushed about like a madwoman until she was somewhat prepared for work. For one crazy moment she considered wearing the clothes she had yesterday, but then she remembered the important meeting with Special Agent in Charge Bryan Maddox. Besides, her mother might disown her for such a fashion offense. Once Megan wrestled on new clothes, she raced down the treacherous stairs, flew out the door, and sprinted to her partner's Explorer since they'd left her car in the sweet parking spot she'd found across from the Prince Kuhio Federal Building the previous morning. She spared a thought to hope she didn't have a parking ticket she'd have to fight.

Slamming the passenger door closed, Megan tossed her purse to the floor and dumped hairbrush, pins, and a handful of ties into her lap.

"You're really going to use all that?" Dan Cooper asked skeptically.

Megan eyed her partner as her hands got busy beating her hair into its proper place.

He redeemed himself from the stupid question by holding out a large cup of coffee.

"You're a life-saver, and I think I love you," she mumbled around the bobby pins she had clenched between her front teeth. With a delicate pfft Megan spit the bobby pins into her lap and grasped the giant coffee cup in both hands. She drank cautiously because she could see the steam billowing up. As much as she needed the coffee, she didn't fancy burning off every taste bud within the first second.

"That's the pre-coffee fog talking, and you're welcome," said Cooper, having the decency to let her enjoy the first sip.

"Drive slowly, please," Megan placed the cup back into the holder and returned her attention to her hair. "I forgot to re-pack the go bag at work, so this is my only shirt. If I have to meet Maddox wearing a coffee stain, you're dead meat, mister." As she spoke, Megan made good use of the things she'd dumped into her lap.

"Can't. We're late. Somebody overslept." Nevertheless, Cooper carefully turned around and started down the road toward the office.

By the time they reached Punchbowl Street, Megan had miraculously transformed her bedhead into a passable triple twist and put on enough makeup so as not to scare people. It certainly wasn't as good a job as she would have liked, but since she was set to meet Maddox anyway, she figured minimal makeup was the way to go. Learning how to conduct herself around her boss had taken the better part of four months. The man seemed to scrutinize everything she did three times as hard as any of her male counterparts. On the other hand, he wasn't exactly a fluffy teddy bear to anybody.

Grizzly with a hernia would be a better description, Megan thought, mentally measuring the SAC.

Cooper found a place to park and they headed in to do the morning security ritual. As they walked toward their side-by-side cubicles, Special Agent Samuel Chang nodded and waved.

"Congratulations on closing the Turner case."

Special Agent Oldwick also passed by and called, "Congratulations."

This time, Megan detected a smirk that made her uneasy. She glanced at Dan who was staring after Oldwick with a thoughtful expression.

"Did that second congrats strike you as weird?" Megan inquired, hoping her senses were just slowed by a lack of caffeinated brain cells.

"Yes, ma'am, it did, but if it makes you feel any better, I believe we're about to find out why."

"Not very comforting," Megan muttered. She reluctantly surrendered her coffee to the Star Wars coaster on her desk and grabbed a notepad and a pen for the meeting.

Each step toward the SAC's office felt longer than the last. For some reason, Megan felt eyes upon her, as if every agent in a twenty-foot radius held their breath for what was about to come. They stopped outside the door, but before Megan could knock, Oldwick swung the door open and beckoned them in.

"Nice work on the Turner case," Maddox said. He waved them into seats and skipped other pleasantries.

Megan wished she'd brought her digital recorder to preserve the praise.

"Thank you, sir." The acknowledgement came simultaneously from Megan and Dan.

Maddox leaned back in his large leather chair and regarded each of them in turn, first Dan and then Megan.

"I have a new case I'd like to assign to you, but first, I want to know if you can handle it."

Mentally counting to five prevented Megan from blurting out assurance that they could handle anything.

"What does this job require, sir?" asked Cooper.

"It's actually the tail end of a case I've been working on and off for about a year now," said
Oldwick. "Somebody's been stealing identities from inside Bank of Hawaii branches. The most recent ones are here in Waikiki."

Maddox picked up the briefing.

"The case goes beyond identity theft. Credit card numbers and bank information are also being stolen. As a last insult, the perpetrators forge and cash a few checks that clear out the victims' accounts."

"I finally have everything in place. I just need the bait," Oldwick said.

Megan indulged in a private ah-ha moment but didn't let her features broadcast the feeling.

Maddox opened his center desk drawer, reached in, and took out something Megan couldn't see until he plunked them in the center of his immaculate desk.

Wedding bands?

"What are those for?" The question slipped out even though Megan knew the answer.

"I want you two to go undercover as a couple looking to line up a high-end housing loan," Maddox explained. He smoothed out his black tie with blue stripes.

"There have been five thefts in total." Oldwick spoke

unhurriedly, but there was fire and determination in his eyes. "Each time, there was an insider working from the bank and a separate individual forging checks. We've statistically narrowed it down to three local branches they'll hit next."

"There's a distinct profile for victims, so we'd like you to become the ideal target for this group," Maddox finished.

"What profile?" Megan eyed Oldwick suspiciously.

"Rich man with a trophy wife," Oldwick supplied.

Megan nodded slowly, finally understanding the reason for them handling this with kid gloves. In the politically correct era in which they lived, being cast for a trophy wife in a sting could be taken the wrong way. Megan decided to wait them out a few more seconds to see what sort of verbal hole they'd dig for themselves before she graciously accepted the role.

"Given the good working relationship the two of you have, plus your background, I feel like you're the right people for the task," Maddox said. He straightened in his chair, indicating that was all he would say on the matter.

"What did you have in mind for the character?" Overcome by a fit of generosity, Megan decided to let them off the hook. She knew the oblique background reference was to her early experiences overseas, including training as a spy and a pole dancer. One didn't gain either brand of expertise without also acquiring a serious confidence boost and a fair amount of acting skills.

"The details are in the file, Agent Luchek." Maddox hefted a thick beige folder from the left side of his desk and held it out to Megan. "You'll have some leeway with how you interpret it, but the name and basic information are already established in case the thieves can run a moderate background check."

Accepting the file, Megan barely resisted the urge to dive in and devour the contents.

"The assignment's not without its perks," Oldwick said, waving to the folder. "Inside, you'll find a gold credit card. It's been specially made for this task, but do not lose it. It's live. The backstory is that you just arrived in Hawaii, but you're looking to buy a summer home. Your characters are staying in the presidential suite at the Trump International Hotel Waikiki Beach Walk, so you'll have to do a minor shopping spree tonight to show some activity on the card."

"Do not lose the receipts," Maddox cautioned. "Everything goes right back as soon as the case wraps up."

"What do you say?" Oldwick asked, needing verbal confirmation.

"I'm in," Megan said. The case offered a nice change of pace. Besides, she'd never again get Maddox to tell her to go shopping as part of her job. This case aside, life as an FBI agent wasn't always glamour and guns.

"And you, Agent Cooper?" prompted Maddox.

Dan hesitated but nodded.

"I'll do it, sir." To prove his words, he leaned forward and picked up the larger of the matching wedding bands sitting on Maddox's desk.

"Better go warn your wife about the assignment, Cooper," Maddox suggested with an understanding look. "Read the guidelines on what you can and can't say first, but you could have some late nights this week."

The remark made Megan consider that perhaps she didn't give SAC Maddox enough credit. For a DC transplant, he almost seemed human sometimes.

The nod was much more vigorous this time. Dan rose then paused waiting to be dismissed.

"That's all I have for you now," Maddox assured them. "Use the remaining morning hours to do what you need to do, and then spend the afternoon studying those files. Tomorrow you'll have to visit each of the target branches. Get some rest. It's going to be a very busy few days here. Tell your families not to expect you around for the week."

"We'll do that. Thank you, sir," Megan said. She rose gracefully, cradling the bulky file, and led the way to the door.

Dan was a few steps behind because he had to retrieve the folder prepared for him.

"Here, you forgot this." Cooper's grim expression seemed out of character.

"Thanks." Megan accepted the wedding band she'd neglected. "What's the long face for? This case is going to be great."

"What do I tell Bethany?"

"Uh … the truth. That usually works well," said Megan. "What's the problem?"

Dan plodded into his office and slumped onto his chair, tossing the file onto a semi-clear spot on the desk. Running a palm down his face, he said, "If Bethany finds out about the couple we're portraying, she's going to kill me … or you … or both of us."

"The sweet lady I saw last night? The one who hates guns? That one?" Megan quirked an eyebrow at Dan as she fired questions. "I don't think we're talking about the same person here."

"That 'sweet lady' hates guns *in her house*," Dan clarified. "She's actually a crack shot on a range, and she has some self-image issues which lead to irrational fits of jealousy. The therapist is working on it with her, but she's still got some ground to cover. It took her months to accept the fact that I can work with you and leave it at that. Let's just say pretending to be your husband isn't going to sit well with her."

"She thinks we're sleeping together?" Megan struggled not to laugh out loud.

"Don't laugh."

"Would it help if I called her to explain the assignment?"

"Heck no. There's probably a nondisclosure paper to sign. Maddox and Oldwick will douse you with oil and breathe fire in your face if you ruin this case. Besides, I need to handle this delicately."

"I can do delicate when necessary," Megan insisted.

Her partner shot her a knowing look.

"All right, so it's not my strongest trait," she admitted.

He blinked at her.

"Or even near the top of the list."

"Try, 'tact equals dead last on your list of attributes,'" Dan suggested.

"Ooooh, ouch. I think we just had our first official fight as a married couple." Megan tried and failed to contain a wicked grin. "See you later, pumpkin-poo."

Chapter 6:
Shopping Spree

Megan Luchek spent twenty minutes proofreading her Turner case report then turned it in. Next, she grabbed the file for the Bank of Hawaii case and told Dan she was going to find a more comfortable spot to read before embarking on her shopping spree. He hummed a distracted acknowledgement. She felt bad for the guy. No doubt his mind was occupied concocting the right balance of truth and white lies of omission. The assignment might call for some late nights and sudden departures. Bethany deserved some explanation beyond the usual "can't talk about work" line.

The first thing Megan did when she got home was take a very long, piping hot shower. If she was going to go on an officially sanctioned shopping spree, she would need to be well-rested to do it. The non-work side of her wardrobe could probably handle the rigors of the assignment, but fate and fortune had placed a gold credit card in her hands. She was definitely going to give it a good workout today.

Ensconced in a silky robe, Megan decided to read the file while she mulled over what to wear shopping. A white towel held her hair until she summoned the energy to deal with it. She made a pot of strong coffee in anticipation of the reading marathon. FBI briefing files weren't exactly known for their moving prose. Nevertheless, true professional that she was, Megan forced her eyes to absorb each and every word at least once, often twice.

She would play the part of Teresa Maria Antonelli, a graduate of the California Institute of Arts who specialized in local theater work in the greater Los Angeles area before meeting the love of her life.

Megan thought they might have gone a tad overboard with the name. The vaguest details of Teresa's life mirrored Megan's early background. She grew up in New Jersey, attended a private school through eighth grade, and graduated near but not quite at the top of her high school class. That's where the similarities ended. Teresa was a middling college student, whereas Megan graduated from NYU magna cum laude with her prelaw degree. Teresa loved golf, tennis, hiking, and collecting jewelry, while Megan preferred martial arts, cardio fitness routines, and collecting tech gadgets.

The love of Teresa's life—to be played by a reluctant Special Agent Daniel Cooper—was one Collin Avery King, a stock trader who'd made some very risky, yet lucrative moves that paid handsomely before the job stress gave him health problems. They met during his two months of prescribed rest when King, a theater enthusiast, saw Teresa playing Olivia in the little known romantic comedy: *Spies, Lies, and other Highs.* There was even a note about the play which featured a high school English teacher at the American International School in Vienna who wanted to be a writer and thought the wrestling coach was a Russian spy.

The notes about Teresa's character were short and to the point, which suited Megan. She could play the part of a well-dressed, sophisticated woman of leisure who possessed a dramatic flair and expensive tastes. She was all those things, albeit on a tighter budget.

A quick search through her closet revealed several possibilities for appropriate shopping attire, but eventually, Megan chose a sleek, ribbed, black mini dress that showed off her well-formed legs. The ability to maintain a good tan was something one could take for granted working in Hawaii. Megan contemplated herself in the mirror, mentally trying on different accessories to enhance the dress. She finally settled for a glossy black clutch, white sunglasses, a teal bracelet, and some small diamond earrings. If the purpose was simply looking good, she would have gone for bigger earrings, but small worked better for shopping excursions.

Once the clothing issue was settled, she tackled the hair issue. She found having quality hair time a refreshing switch from rushed variations of haphazard twists. Megan could be very inventive, but there were only so many quick, functional hairstyles able to deal with a healthy volume of hair. She decided on a casual look that took forty-five minutes to arrange. First, she dried her hair thoroughly, which created unsightly frizz. Next, she selectively dampened sections of hair, wielding a straightener against the stubborn sections as necessary. Finally, she used a curling iron and some hair gel to strategically place fun waves.

A little lip gloss and the barest hint of eyeshadow completed the effect she'd aimed for. The results were stunning. Megan wanted to pretend she forgot something at the office just to see what the boys would say. Perhaps they wouldn't recognize her from the buttoned up version she usually presented.

After a quick stop for a light lunch, Megan freshened her makeup and set about doing her shopping duties. At the Salvatore Ferragamo store she bought several pairs of pumps that tallied about two thousand dollars. On a whim, she also bought some shirts for Dan. She didn't know if the thieves would be true fashion police, but it didn't make much sense for her to be dressed in a few thousand dollars while Dan wore Walmart specials. Nordstrom and Neiman Marcus were fun to wander around. She bought several dresses at each department store so she'd have many choices when it came time to visit the banks. To be fair, Megan bought a few more possibilities for Dan as well. She found a cute purse at Chanel Boutique then went to the Tiffany and Co for the appropriate jewelry.

By the time she made it back to her car, Megan was exhausted. She made a mental note to clear a high class rental car with Maddox. There might have been a note about that in the file, but she couldn't recall one. It wouldn't do for them to show up at the bank in a government issued sedan, and neither her personal car nor Cooper's Ford Explorer would do either. She remembered the card that had opened so many doors today. Her black dress had garnered her some sales people's attention, but not even the dress could compete with the power of the gold card. After catching sight of it, they waged polite wars with each other to wait on her.

Megan knew she'd need permission to rent a luxury car because there wasn't any return policy on such things. Maddox wouldn't like it, but he was a practical soul. He would understand. The Bureau had a limited number of luxury cars available for special cases, but even those wouldn't work here. She called her boss but got shuffled to voicemail, so she left a detailed message and bought a venti shaken sweet tea lemonade from Starbucks to ease the wait for a callback.

Twenty-three minutes later, Special Agent Ophelia Pitman called her work phone.

"Hi, Lady O. I hope you have good news for me," Megan

greeted.

"I do, Maggie dear. At least I think I do." Ophelia's deep, sonorous voice rumbled like a bulldozer, softened a bit by the Georgian accent. "SAC Maddox has approved the delivery of a red, two seater, Viper SRT-10 to your apartment tomorrow morning, but mind you, honey, this baby comes with some caveats."

"What kind of caveats?" asked Megan.

"You'll need to check her into the garage at the hotel listed in the file every night. I've made arrangements for the nice young gentlemen there to watch over her in the evenings."

"Sounds reasonable."

"I'm not done yet, sugar. Here comes the un-fun parts. There is to be no joy riding, no excessive risks taken, and no other drivers or passengers besides yourself and S.A. Cooper. You'll also need to keep track of the gas receipts and mileage and file them as per usual procedure. Do you understand these conditions?"

"Yes, ma'am," Megan said, swallowing a snarky response.

"Good. Then I hope you enjoy this fine set of wheels."

Ophelia disconnected before Megan could respond, but her last comment brought on a broad smile. The mental image of the large black woman crammed into a Dodge Viper was amusing. She had never had the pleasure of actually working with S.A. Pitman on a case, but Megan had many an occasion to get briefed by her about borrowed equipment. If you wanted something strange, expensive, obscure, or quick, you asked Lady O about it.

When Megan returned to her car, she found the police scanner sputtering with indignation. She hesitated only a split-second before turning up the volume so she could hear the alert. It pertained to a robbery in progress happening a mere five blocks away. As she reached to put her black Honda Accord into drive, her personal cell rang.

Cooper. How did he know?

Megan considered not answering. She already knew he would tell her to mind her own business and get on with the shopping. There was no reason to get involved. Getting mired in a Honolulu Police Department matter on the eve of a big undercover operation would not please Maddox. Though she knew how the argument would go, Megan sighed, turned down the scanner, and accepted the call.

"I'm here."

"In case you just received that armed robbery alert, Maddox says to leave it alone. If you have no idea what I'm talking about, great.

I repeat: leave it alone."

"But I'm so close!"

"You're probably also dressed to kill and wearing six inch heels," Cooper fired back.

He had a point there.

She heard sirens in the distance, closing fast.

"They're headed this way."

"Megan. No. Let the HPD do their job. We've got our marching orders. Go home."

A gray car blasted past Megan. In that brief moment, she formed an impression of the driver: young, male, blond, thin. She mentally filed the information away, though the likelihood of that becoming useful was next to nothing. Her right foot itched to stomp on the gas pedal and join the chase, but she couldn't bring herself to willfully disobey the direct order coming from Maddox through Dan. She was already on thin ice with the SAC. This assignment had the potential to move her closer to Maddox's *nice* list. She drew a deep breath and blew it into the phone.

"All right. You win. I'll let the HPD do their thing, but they're probably going to lose him."

The sirens sounded closer but hadn't quite reached her yet.

"What makes you say that? And how do you know it's a 'him?'" asked Dan.

"Woman's intuition, basic math, and twenty-twenty vision. They're more than thirty seconds behind him. With the number of side streets around here, all he has to do is stop driving like a maniac and he'll lose them." The idea latched onto her mind and refused to let go. "In fact, we're near enough to the Ala Moana Center that if I were him, I'd grab a parking spot and head for the tourist hotspot."

"That's a great idea, and I'll pass it along to Sergeant Kawai. Under no circumstances are you to check out that hunch."

"I hear you loud and clear." Megan was starting to get annoyed with her partner, but she couldn't exactly blame him for the constant reminders. She *had* been getting the urge to re-visit the Ala Moana Center.

"Put me on speaker in your car."

"Why?"

"Because then I'll know you can't leave the car as long as we're talking."

Rolling her eyes, Megan did as instructed.

"Done. Now we both get to sound like we're talking from a fishbowl. Are you satisfied?"

"For now."

Two seconds of loud, static-filled nothingness ticked by.

"Well, this is stupid," said Megan.

"Tell me what you bought today," Dan prompted.

Figuring she'd have to tell him anyway, Megan described each of her treasures in detail. By the time they reached the new shoe acquisitions, the scanner and Dan's HPD contact confirmed that the suspect had gotten cleanly away.

Megan voiced her discontent with an unladylike growl.

"It happens. Every day in fact. You can't catch them all." Dan's philosophical encouragement offered little comfort. "Especially not wearing impractical shoes."

That earned a small sniff.

"Well, since I won't need to chase any robbers on foot today, I guess I'll head home." A thought snuck up and bit her. "Oh, did you get to talk with Bethany, yet?"

"Yes, that's what I've been doing most of the day. Maddox let me have her sign a non-disclosure agreement and receive the barest of debriefings. She knows less than we do, but it helps that she has proof it's an official case."

"Great. Glad that worked out. I wasn't looking forward to life on the run. Guess I'll take this loot home to sort, use once, and sadly return."

"You do that. And, Megan? You did good today, really. We'll grow a level head on you yet."

Megan highly doubted it, but she didn't want to burst his bubble.

Chapter 7:
Casing the Banks

Special Agent Megan Luchek expected to have a long day, but she was not prepared for the level of mind-numbing boredom banks could conjure. The closest comparison she could make was to buying a car, but even that pain ended after one round. This job required the same charade three times in a row, specifically at Bank of Hawaii's Keeaumoku, Ala Moana, and Waikiki branches. The only fun so far had been the short morning drive to Dan's place. Lady O hadn't been kidding about the rental car being a *fine* set of wheels.

Mid-way through the second bank on their hit-list, Megan's jaw started aching from smiling pleasantly.

By the third bank, she was ready to shuck the heels and sprint out of there barefoot.

The briefing had been very detailed about what Megan should look for. At each location she mentally took inventory of who noticed them but didn't interact with them, who spoke with them, what was said, approximately how long it took for them to get shuffled around to the right people, impressions of the managers, and stock of every employee in view. The parallels between their approach and bank robbers casing the place were not lost on her.

Megan let Dan do most of the talking, figuring that was the most logical move for a trophy wife fishing the bank waters for a fat loan with which to buy a summer house with her hubby. He'd thickened his Texas accent for the part of Collin Avery King. She found the effect charming. He also looked good in black designer jeans and a black Armani Collezioni sport shirt. She kept that thought to herself, though she did enjoy making adoring moon eyes at him. To his credit, her partner did a credible job of pretending to be fully love-struck.

The first thing Megan did after climbing into the Viper after the third bank was toss her shoes to the floor. The second thing she did was grab her notepad and scribble a few impressions before the memories dulled. To keep their cover intact, Dan started the car up immediately and drove toward the federal building. Since he didn't have the luxury of taking his own detailed notes, he dictated a few things for Megan to list so he could write his notes up shortly. By mutual agreement, they did not otherwise speak of the case in the car. They wanted to come up with detailed preliminary reports before comparing notes.

After a quick stop to pick up sandwiches, they made it to the office, commandeered a conference room, and settled in to work the case. For a time, only the crunching of chips and crisp pickles and the tapping of laptop keys could be heard as Dan split his time between eating and writing. Megan couldn't bring herself to eat until every impression was scrawled out in full. She liked to think the hunger motivated her to work faster. Her hand started cramping. She could have retrieved a laptop to work on, but she liked the organic process of physically penning her thoughts. It slowed her down enough to let her consider the words that emerged.

An hour and a half later, as Megan's stomach started protesting the neglect and her head started to feel very light, Dan said, "You should eat something."

"I will when I'm done," Megan replied. To prove a point, she jotted down one additional note before making a show of carefully placing her pen on the table. "There. Finished for now. Tell me what you've got while I deal with the monster trying to eat me from the inside out." She reached for the bag of sour cream and onion chips and squeezed it until it popped.

"That's an interesting mental image." Dan watched her curiously. "Doesn't that break the chips into crumbs?"

"That's the point." Megan continued reducing the potato chips to fractions of their former selves. She rolled the bag into a small funnel and drained the crumbs into her mouth, careful not to let any fragments escape.

Judging by Dan's expression, the chip-eating exercise was fascinating. He waited until she finished the bag, balled it up, and tossed it at the garbage can across the room. The bag bounced off the wall and in.

"Does your mother know you do that?"

"Absolutely not."

"I didn't think so. Where did you learn that ... artistic way of eating chips?"

"Necessity. Greasy fingers and expensive clothes don't mix well."

Dan Cooper shook his head, clearly bewildered by the inner workings of the female mind. To keep from staring as Megan started on the turkey and avocado sandwich, Dan started talking about what he'd gotten out of their long morning of stalking banks.

"The terms offered on the loans were standard across the board. The manager of the Waikiki Branch seemed eager to see what special rates she could get for us, but the Keeaumoku and Ala Moana managers seemed content to apologize and stick to the policy."

"Uh-huh," Megan said to let him know she was listening.

"Tellers were largely unremarkable and indistinguishable from branch to branch. Keeaumoku happened to have two male tellers and only one female. The others had a reverse of that ratio this morning."

Megan nodded.

"I wrote that down too, but I doubt it means anything." She took another deep bite of the sandwich and waved for him to continue.

"The layouts of the physical structures varied widely. Waikiki stands out to me as the most robbery-friendly, but they each have decent street access. Having the parks near it isolates the Waikiki branch a little more than the others. Do you agree?"

"Yes, it's definitely the loner of the bunch," said Megan. She thoughtfully licked a glob of spicy mustard that painted her left pinky finger. "Did you notice the middle teller at BoH Waikiki? Ali-something or other. She definitely noticed us."

Dan searched through his file for the profile on the branch in question and scanned until he found the appropriate name.

"Ailani Kahele," he reported.

"That's the one. She seemed very interested in our clothes. I could almost feel the sparks of interest flare from her."

"I think you're being dramatic, but I get the point," said Dan. "You got a vibe from her."

"You didn't?"

"No, but that doesn't mean it wasn't there." Dan made a ball

43

with his sandwich wrapper and rolled it back and forth between his hands. "I was concentrating on the mortgage officers and managers."

"Let's consider them individually. What do we know about each of them? Start with the Keeaumoku branch." Megan unconsciously started with the bank they had visited first. She ate the last bite of her delicious sandwich, moved the white paper aside, and started digging for the employee files.

Since Dan had the files already arrayed in a system, he found the correct paper first.

"Kamea Carter. Hawaiian mother, English father. Married to Leon Carter. Finances are in order. Reasonable amount of debt." He shook his head. "Nothing jumps out at me as a great motive to help the thieves rip off her bank."

Megan wasn't ready to render a judgment one way or the other yet, but she did find the correct sub-file for the Bank of Hawaii Ala Moana.

"What did you think of Cameron Dent?" she asked.

Dan executed a one-shoulder shrug.

"He had pictures of his wife and kids all over his desk. If I were a mystery writer going for perfect patsy to pressure through a kidnapping, he'd be my number one pick, but I'm betting these thieves are lazy, which moves him down the suspect list. The only manager with a realistic financial motive would be Lynn Berkley."

A few quick flips and Megan had Lynn's profile cradled in her hands. It was thicker than the others.

"Divorced. Unhappily, it appears." Megan leafed through several newspaper clippings the background agent had attached. One name halted her skimming cold. "Wow. Did you see who the ex is?"

"I was wondering how long it would take you to notice."

"Darn it. Divorcing Martin Cantrell makes me want to root for this woman." Megan pressed her lips together and quickly re-read the first page of the file. "But she does make a nice prime suspect. Financial troubles. Custody battles. I don't know what the going rate is for betraying a bank, but given the expensive taste this group has in targets, it's probably attractive."

"Most factors point us toward Waikiki, but we should stop by all the branches tomorrow to do some follow up and open personal accounts. Should we travel together or separately?"

"Separately," Megan answered almost immediately.

"Which branch do you want?"

"I've got a quarter. We can settle that issue later."

Cooper shrugged and made a few adjustments to his computer notes.

"It might be premature, but if we're going to order detailed work-ups for each employee at any of the banks, we should do it soon," said Dan. "If the thieves are going to strike during this calendar year, it'll have to be soon. We're only going to get one shot at this. Can you think of any other reason to concentrate on Waikiki?"

"Location's the biggest reason for me," Megan said. "The other places simply have a lot more shopping going on around them. They're practically surrounded by stores and businesses. The downtown Waikiki branch has resorts, which are probably abandoned in the daytime, and some parks near it. A bigger crowd might make the other places more attractive if the thieves intend to strike unseen and disappear on foot. But that's much riskier. The high volume of tourists around might even work against them?"

"I don't follow," Dan admitted.

Megan scrambled to articulate her thoughts.

"We're assuming the thieves snag the credit card information with a card reader. Human nature. If they gather more numbers than they're interested in they'll be tempted to use them. If they're truly targeting certain rich people, then it follows that they'll want to minimize snatching collateral numbers." She shuffled papers looking for one particular note but gave up after a few seconds. "Somewhere in here, there was a note about card readers having a small chance of completely ruining cards. It's a numbers thing. If that happened on a crowded day near Nordstrom a careful investigation would be launched using the security cameras."

"I'll buy that," Dan commented. "But the banks are going to have top of the line security cameras both inside and on the buildings around them."

"It's not about the cameras," said Megan. "It's about the attention drawn to each bank if and when the card reader is unleashed. And about how quickly the alarms are tripped. We're expecting high tech here, not the masks and hit-and-run tactics of a traditional bank robbery."

"Cyber-crimes are so impersonal," Dan complained. "There's practically no risk involved."

"Would you rather be in the Wild West trading shots with robbers decked out in sweaty bandanas?"

45

"You do have a point about the clothes," Dan noted. "Nice dress."

"Took you long enough to notice, but thanks." Megan had chosen a stunning, strapless blue dress with a floral pattern, but this was the first compliment it garnered from Dan. "I could get used to this dress code."

"Where do you keep your gun?" Dan wondered.

Since his shirt was incapable of hiding a gun, Dan wore only a backup piece in an ankle holster. They had special permission to not carry their guns on this phase of the assignment, but both preferred to have a weapon close at hand.

"Wouldn't you like to know?" Megan raised her eyebrows at him. She hit him with a seductive smile until Dan blushed, before waving vaguely to the floor. "It's in the clutch purse."

Chapter 8:
It's Only a Few Hours

Bracing for a battle of wills, Lynn Berkley knocked tentatively on her daughter's bedroom door. As expected, nothing happened. A short pep talk later, Lynn tried again, pounding on the door with more force.

"Katelyn, get up. You need to come in to work with me this morning." Lynn halted her explanation. She would likely have to explain again in a moment. No sense in delivering the whole message to deaf ears.

A muffled mumble told Lynn she was making progress, so she made a fist and thumped the door three more times with purpose. For good measure, she repeated the order to get up and the reason for the intrusion.

More stirring from within encouraged her, but five seconds later when the movement ceased, Lynn said, "Now, Katelyn. I can't be late. It's my early morning. Remember? This happens every week."

The door opened and Katelyn peered out with sleepy eyes. Lynn had to concentrate to keep her features passive. Her daughter's short blonde hair was frightful. It looked like a bird had tried to make a nest and given up halfway through the process. The scent of stale room seeped out and assaulted Lynn at the same time as her eyes registered the mess beyond Katelyn.

"Open a window." Lynn held up a hand to forestall a protest. "I know. I promised to let your room be your inner sanctum, but it's not supposed to rain and the place could do with a little fresh air."

Fumigation followed by aeration is more like it.

Because of its prime location on the end of the house,

Katelyn's room boasted two windows. The pre-teen tried to stomp over to the nearest window but tripped on a shirt that spilled over from the laundry basket. Young, quick reflexes saved her from a fall. She finished the trip to the window and opened it a few inches.

"Why do I have to go to work with you?" asked Katelyn. She kicked the offending shirt aside and started rummaging in her closet. "What's wrong with Mrs. Ting?"

"Nothing's wrong with Mrs. Ting herself, but she just called and said she couldn't make it this morning. She had a late night at the hospital. We can visit with her and her mother after work if you want. She'd like that."

The reminder of Mrs. Ting's family situation mollified Katelyn. She chose a white T-shirt with tropical flowers and a pair of jean shorts.

"You might want to wear your khaki pants," Lynn suggested. "The bank is pretty cold. Besides, the pants are fancier."

"Nobody's going to see me," Katelyn grumbled. This wouldn't be her first extended visit to the bank. "You make me stay in your office. It's so boring."

"It's only a few hours, dear. I can leave early on days I go in early. We'll be out by two."

"Six hours is not a 'few' hours, mom."

Lynn silently conceded the point, but she wasn't about to admit that to Katelyn. She decided to attempt bribery.

"If you hurry, we might have time to stop at the 7-Eleven for a breakfast sandwich. Otherwise, you'll have to make do with a multigrain bar from my emergency stash at the office."

"Can I get a large Slurpee too?"

At least she knows how to negotiate.

"If you're in the car in five minutes."

"Deal! Got to go!"

Lynn didn't get to add anything else to the conditions because the door closed in her face. She glanced at her watch and noted the time. She doubted Katelyn could cram the morning routines into the tight deadline, but it should be interesting to see her try. Before waking the girl, Lynn had already packed the bank survival kit. It contained her iPad, a word search and puzzle book, a paperback book, her Kindle, and a pack of cards. Despite Katelyn's claim that nobody would see her, she occasionally convinced employees on break to play an abbreviated game of Rummy. As long as the bets consisted of gum, mints, and bragging rights, Lynn turned a blind eye to the *gambling* in her bank.

Five minutes and thirty-five seconds later, Katelyn thundered down the stairs, raced out to the car, jumped inside, and slammed the door.

Lynn winced.

"Easy on the door, girl. I can't afford a new one."

"Did I make it?" asked Katelyn.

"Thirty seconds over, but close enough," Lynn reported. "Let's go get junk food for breakfast. You're a bad influence on me, my dear."

"Yes!" In her excitement, Katelyn raised both arms in victory then yelped as her knuckles rapped the ceiling.

"Be careful, baby." Lynn put her aging, green mini-van into reverse and backed out of the driveway.

Letting her arms drop, Katelyn asked, "Did you grab my bag?"

"I did. It has all the usual supplies plus a book you should try. It's called *Ashlynn's Dreams*. It sounded mysterious. I was going to give it to you for Christmas, but you might get more use out of it today."

Katelyn twisted around until she could haul the stuffed backpack up to the front seat. She found the book almost immediately.

"What's it about?"

"The back cover description sounded like something you'd enjoy: adventure, kidnapping, scrappy teens with cool powers surviving hardships. You love that stuff. Your brother did too. No glittery vampires, sorry about that."

Grunting, Katelyn said, "That was one book, one time, and I didn't even like it, mom."

"I know and it gives me hope."

"Hope of what?" Katelyn asked the question delicately.

Lynn shot her a teasing grin.

"Hope that you inherited my good sense, love."

Katelyn didn't respond right away, but Lynn felt the mood shift. She pulled into the parking lot and slipped the car into a spot near the door but made no move to turn off the car or get out. She could feel Katelyn gathering her nerve to open a serious conversation, so she waited.

"Mom?"

Lynn's turn to hesitate.

"Yes, my love?"

"Why doesn't Kenny live with us?"

"That's between your father and me," Lynn replied, falling back on her default response. She turned off the car and got out, hoping that would end the conversation.

"You always say that!" Katelyn emphasized her point by slamming the door.

Lynn looked at her daughter sharply but decided not to comment. She didn't want to spark a fight in the 7-Eleven parking lot.

"Go get your breakfast and drink. We can discuss this when we get to my office."

Brightening, Katelyn dashed inside.

Knowing she'd have to follow through on that, Lynn went inside and ordered a breakfast sandwich. She usually skipped breakfast, but if she was going to be drawn into a serious discussion, she wanted to focus on something besides her daughter's accusing eyes.

They finished the trip to the bank in silence. Now running a few minutes behind, Lynn sent Katelyn ahead to her office with instructions to clear a space for the food. Then she hurried to check the security system on the vault. The rest of her morning tasks could wait until after breakfast.

When she entered her office, Lynn noticed Katelyn sitting in her large, comfortable chair, spinning around in circles. She paused in the doorway and watched. Part of her wanted to tell Katelyn she was getting too old for that, but mostly, Lynn wanted to preserve the carefree moment.

Katelyn made it three complete revolutions before she realized she had an audience. She stopped spinning and leaned forward eagerly.

"I waited for you." She motioned to the two sausage, egg, and cheese sandwiches sitting on Lynn's desk. "You should eat. You've got a lot to do, I'm sure."

How generous. Lynn kept the comment in as she settled onto one of the two guest chairs. She un-wrapped the sandwich and took a careful bite. She didn't want sausage grease dripping onto her light gray suit jacket.

Heedless of the grease, Katelyn immediately devoured half her sandwich in a series of ravenous chomps.

The sight slowed Lynn's breakfast consumption even more.

"Do you always eat like that?" Feeling a pang of guilt, Lynn knew she ought to know the answer, but sharing a meal with Katelyn didn't happen often.

"Like what?" A partially chewed sandwich fragment sailed free of Katelyn's mouth and landed just shy of Lynn's stapler.

Lynn was appalled by her daughter's lack of manners.

"Like somebody's going to steal the food out of your mouth." Lynn took another delicate bite while waiting for an answer.

"It's 'later' and you're stalling," said Katelyn. She air quoted the word later then grabbed a napkin to wipe grease from her fingers. "You don't want to keep your promise to answer my question about Kenny."

The girl's tone was even, but Lynn saw her jaw jutting forward, a sign of the struggle to contain her emotions. Lynn felt a surge of compassion for her daughter. The last few years felt like a black blur. In her own struggles and concerns, Lynn had forgotten to wonder how everything was affecting Katelyn.

"I *can't* answer your question about Kenny. He's old enough to make that choice, but I don't think he wants to live with us."

"Why not? Doesn't he love us anymore?" As Katelyn grew more upset, her tone turned childish.

"He loves you. That I'm sure of. Otherwise, he wouldn't have asked permission to see you. And I wouldn't let you go with him if I wasn't a hundred percent sure he loves you dearly." Lynn felt like a giant fly swatter had just flattened her. The next words out of her mouth were barely audible. "He loves me too. He's just … upset."

"Why?"

Lynn's mind raced, trying to predict which way the news would strike her daughter. Their gazes locked and held. The moment was broken when Lynn blinked, suddenly fighting tears. Drawing a quick breath, she spoke before she lost the ability to do so. "Because he thinks I didn't fight for him." She blinked rapidly to keep from releasing the tears.

"*Did* you fight for him?" Katelyn asked with the innocent relentlessness of youth.

"Not like I should have." Lynn's voice was haunted.

"Oh." The honest answer stunned Katelyn, but she recovered in short order. "I could tell him you did. Then he'd come home, right?"

"I wish it were that easy." Even as Lynn dropped that reality, she hoped Katelyn clung to the sense of invincibility for a long time. Wearily, Lynn rose. "Would you mind cleaning the desk? You can throw my sandwich in the refrigerator. There are some bottles of water if you get thirsty."

"I should be good for a while," Katelyn said, waving toward the large Slurpee sweating all over Lynn's desk.

Convinced Katelyn would at least be well-hydrated, Lynn headed for the door. Once there, she couldn't help giving some last minute instructions.

"Use the coaster so you don't ruin the desk. Don't play too many games. And—"

"Mom! I'll be fine. You're going to be like two steps away."

For some reason, Lynn found Katelyn's indignation comforting.

"Be good. Love you. Keep the door closed, and don't make too much noise, you're right near the guests here."

She chose to interpret the eye roll as an I-love-you-too gesture, pre-teen style.

Chapter 9:
Much More Exciting

For round two of bank surveillance, Megan Luchek chose a simple, sleeveless light purple blouse and a stylish jean skirt with a cute belt. She took special care to make sure the messy waves in her hair gave off a girlish vibe. Since the outfit didn't reek of money like the dress she'd worn the previous day, Megan accessorized with a seven hundred dollar purse she'd picked up at Nordstrom. She'd have to let the agency return it as soon as the case ended, so she might as well get some enjoyment out of the expensive toy. The purse also fit her gun well, a bonus she appreciated.

Megan and Dan had discussed the suspects and bank branches in great detail throughout the previous afternoon and decided to check them out individually today. They assumed the bank employees might react differently if they were alone rather than together. Side conversations could be very revealing. By quarter flip, it was decided that Dan would go to the Keeaumoku branch first and Megan would visit the Waikiki branch. Whoever finished most efficiently would peek in on Ala Moana a second time.

There's motivation to be slow, Megan thought as she parked the car and strode briskly up to the bank door a few minutes after ten. She wanted to arrive early to check out the morning regulars. Her original intent had been to arrive before the bank opened, but she'd needed to drop Dan off at the Keeaumoku branch first.

Noticing the Financial Adviser was not in his office, Megan waited in the short line until one of tellers waved her over.

"Aloha. Welcome to the Bank of Hawaii, how can I help you

this morning?" The young woman's nametag read Ailani.

Megan smiled at her luck. She'd been meaning to speak with this teller anyway.

"I'd like to speak with Mr. Sims, please. Do you know when he'll be in? I'd like to open a few accounts."

"What kind of accounts?" Ailani's manner brightened at the prospect of a new account. "I can open a checking account for you right now. I'd just need proof of identity and a hundred dollar deposit." Her expression said she knew the deposit would not be a problem.

"That's all right. I have some other questions for Mr. Sims. He's the Financial Adviser, right?"

"Yes, ma'am, that's correct, but if you'd like, I can call the manager for you. Ms. Berkley can probably answer most of your questions."

Megan processed the offer. She'd walked in intending to have a nice chat with Mr. Sims. Her interviewing skills were sharp, but she always found it easier to question men. They were much easier to distract. Still, Sims wasn't here and she would need to speak with Ms. Berkley anyway. She decided to roll with the change.

"Thank you. That's so kind of you."

Summoning Ms. Berkley took longer than expected, so Megan wandered over to the complimentary coffee station and used the time to make some simple observations. The bank shared the building with Longs Drugs, 7-Eleven, a café, and an English school, but it was still attractive and well-spaced. The bank manager's office was next to the coffee station. The other three tiny "offices" were created with cubicle partitioning. Next to Ms. Berkley's office was a short hallway that led back to the vault and the Employees Only sections. A few steps led up to the area Megan mentally dubbed the "teller bullpen." Local potted plants were placed at strategic locations as expected.

Megan paced enough to let her eyes wander in many directions. As she turned toward Ms. Berkley's office again, her eyes caught a brief fluttering movement of the shades. Before she could investigate, clicking heels announced Ms. Berkley's imminent approach. Megan finished the turn and sipped the coffee she had prepared.

"Ms. Antonelli?" The approaching woman wore a white blouse, light gray suit jacket, and a matching gray skirt. Everything from her thin silver watch up through the simple bun that contained her hair screamed bank manager. But for those whose powers of observations weren't sharpened by life in the FBI, there was a nametag that spelled out the woman's name and title.

"Yes. That's me. You must be Ms. Berkley."

"Aloha. Ms. Kahele tells me you have some questions for Mr. Sims. He'll be in later today, but perhaps I can help you now." She gestured toward Mr. Sims's cubicle. "Step right this way and have a seat. My office is currently occupied, but we can borrow Chris's."

Megan wanted to ask why Ms. Berkley's office was occupied, but the moment passed. Once settled in Mr. Sims's office, Megan ran through the list of prepared questions about various bank loans and conditions. The coffee lasted through only half the questions. Megan learned much about the different types of accounts one could have but not much concerning her case. She inserted personal queries wherever possible, but Ms. Berkley remained coolly distant. As Megan let the conversation wind toward a close, she concluded Ms. Berkley possessed more than enough information to make her attractive to the thieves. However, Megan's suspect senses were still reading green light.

"Thank you so much for answering my questions. I think I've taken up—" Megan didn't even get to finish the pleasantries before a man's voice made the morning much more exciting.

"Everybody remain calm and nobody gets hurt! Tellers, fill the bags before you. You know how this works. Silent alarms get people killed. Ink packs get people killed. Delaying us gets people killed. Somebody get me the manager!"

Sitting in the guest chair closest to the wall in Mr. Sims's office, Megan was in a terrible position to gain tactical information, but she read Ms. Berkley's growing alarm easily enough. The general gist of the situation could be catalogued in microseconds.

"Stay right there," Megan whispered, instinctively freezing.

Ignoring the warning, Ms. Berkley launched from the chair and stepped to the threshold.

"What's going on here?" she demanded.

Stupid question! Stupid question!

Megan mentally bound and gagged the brave, yet not so bright bank manager. It didn't do any good, but it made her feel better. Sinking lower in the chair, Megan frantically ran through her options. Adding her gun to the mix out there would probably not end well for anybody. Calling 911 would bring the police and likely spark a drawn out hostage situation. The option with the highest survival rate was to let the robbers take what they wanted and leave, then call the police. It was a plan of non-action and devilishly hard to enact with this many other people involved.

Megan did a quick rundown of the people present. She'd only seen two tellers this morning, but there could be a third in the back somewhere. Ms. Berkley and two, maybe three customers plus Megan put the number at six people minimum. The robber and at least one more to make an "us" brought the approximate total up to eight people. Lynn Berkley had mentioned her office being occupied, so Megan added one more to her tally.

Nine. Even if that count was completely accurate, it still translated to way too many people.

While deep in thought, Megan ignored the chaos raging behind her, but she snapped her attention back when the voice sounded a lot closer. Maddox was going to blow a fuse when he learned about this.

"You! Get out here!" shouted the robber.

Ms. Berkley disappeared from the doorway, protesting all the way.

"You too!" barked the voice. "Keep your hands in sight."

Megan showed the man that both her hands were empty, making sure her expression exuded the sort of numbness typical of a lady facing the wrong end of a gun for the first time. If the robbers sensed *fed* from her, the excitement might end painfully and abruptly.

"Please. Please don't hurt me," she whimpered, letting the man haul her out of the chair. She had to work hard not to let her Tae Kwan Do training take over.

"Shut up." The man dragged her out of Mr. Sims's cubicle and flung her toward the center of the room where they'd herded everybody.

She used the momentum to stumble to a spot next to Ms. Berkley and took quick stock of the company. An elderly Asian woman sat farthest from Megan, weeping softly and clutching her arms around her thin knees. A pair of young tourists clung to each other looking dazed. The poor suckers probably just had a lousy sense of timing about checking out the ATM. Right next to Ms. Berkley sat a man wearing black dress pants, a white shirt, a colorful tie, and a nametag that read: Christopher Sims. The two tellers were at their stations filling black duffle bags with cash. On Ms. Berkley's other side stood a young man wearing a straw hat pulled low to prevent security cameras from capturing his features. His gun was pointed in the manager's direction.

"Throw your purse over there," he ordered Megan.

A quick glance confirmed that the other robber also wore a

straw hat. Both young men appeared to be late teens, early twenties. The leader had short cropped dark hair and the second guy had longer dark hair. Both seemed fit and wore aviator sunglasses, plain T-shirts, and nondescript beige shorts. After absorbing what she could of their descriptions, Megan reluctantly followed the order, but instead of tossing the bag as instructed, she slid the purse toward the growing pile of cellphones, purses, and other goods building up near the door. It wouldn't do to have her gun give itself away with a loud thunk.

"All right. I think that's everybody. Get her up and over to the vault," said the leader. "I want to be gone in ninety seconds. Go!"

The second robber reached down and yanked Ms. Berkley to her feet. As she was dragged past, she locked panicked eyes with Megan. The look gave the agent a sinking feeling, for she had seen similar expressions before. It wasn't fear for self, it was fear for another.

"Just do what they say," Megan encouraged. She'd ceased caring about staying in character. If she couldn't knock the panic from Ms. Berkley's eyes, odds were good the lady would get herself killed in the next thirty seconds.

"Leave her alone," Mr. Sims said. He started to rise but stopped when the lead robber's gun swung his way.

Stop talking. Right now. You'll only make it worse for her.

Megan caught his arm and eased him back down, shaking her head no. She tried to subliminally beam the message into Mr. Sims.

"Get up again and I'll shoot you." The leader held his gun with both hands now, settling into a comfortable stance. "That goes for the rest of you too."

The other man had disappeared into the back room with Ms. Berkley, presumably to collect valuables from the vault.

Everybody settled in for a tense wait.

The female half of the young couple started babbling in a whisper. At first, Megan couldn't make out the words, but eventually, she deciphered the meaning. The girl was saying, "I want to go home" over and over on loop.

Her significant other held her tightly, frantically trying to quiet her.

The old woman was also murmuring. Megan couldn't understand the words, but the cadence was appropriate for some sort of prayer. Mr. Sims's disgruntled silence was almost palpable.

The tellers finished their task and received orders to come

around and load the personal belongings into the duffle bags. As they started to comply, Ms. Berkley and the second robber emerged from the back rooms.

So far, so good.

With luck, the robbers would be gone within the minute, and Megan could commandeer a phone and kickstart a manhunt.

That's when she heard the police sirens.

Chapter 10:
Bad to Worse

Each of the robbers cursed aloud.

Megan cursed silently.

Could this day get any worse? Even as she thought it, Megan hated herself for tempting fate to throw more wind at the sails of this ship headed to Hades.

Almost in answer, the bank doors crashed open.

"Let's go! Let's go! Cops are on the way!" The new young man wore the robber's uniform of T-shirt, shorts, aviators, and straw hat.

Ms. Berkley gasped.

"Kenny?"

"Mom?" The newcomer's attention riveted upon the bank manager. He took off his hat and glasses.

Megan punctuated each title with a silent, *Oh, crap!*

"What are you doing here?" Ms. Berkley's voice was shaky with shock mixed with anger and bewilderment.

"What are *you* doing here?" Kenny retorted. "I thought you worked at Ala Moana."

"I transferred last year," Ms. Berkley answered, as if she wasn't standing next to an increasingly agitated bank robber.

"Enough already!" shouted the gang leader. "Grab what you can and get back to the car."

"I didn't sign on for this," the man with Ms. Berkley said. "I'm out."

The leader trained his gun on his wavering help.

"You'll pull your weight here, or I'll kill you where you stand."

For a second, Megan thought the threat would be enough to bring the second robber to heel, but then she caught the determined flash in his eyes. Hefting the large duffle bag, he sprinted out the door.

The first robber uttered a wordless roar and fired three times. Two shots missed completely and the third slammed into the black bag, knocking the robber off balance. Abandoning the bag, he quickly righted himself and sprinted away.

Spotting her chance, Megan leapt up, closed the distance, and stole the gun from the distracted robber.

He blinked down at his empty hands like he couldn't fathom what had just happened.

"Get down on your knees and interlock your fingers behind your head," Megan instructed. Feeling the stares from the entire set of hostages, she shifted back a step so she could keep an eye on Kenny and the leader. "Kenny?" Getting no response, she spared a glance at him, but his attention was locked well to her left.

Ms. Berkley inhaled sharply.

Somebody from the crowd groaned.

"Give him the gun, or she dies." The voice sounded nervous.

"What are you doing?" Kenny demanded. "Stop that."

The first robber gave Megan a million dollar smile and held his hand out for his weapon.

Megan shifted position again until she could take in the drama unfolding to her left.

Sweet, little Ailani Kahele had a small gun pressed hard into her boss's side.

I did not see that coming.

"Don't stand so close to her, baby," the leader coached. "Make her kneel down then point the gun at her head."

Ailani followed the directive and looked at Megan expectantly.

"Give him the gun," she repeated.

The audience added their commentary as Megan tried to think.

"Don't do it!" hissed Mr. Sims.

That's cold with your boss's life on the line.

"Do it!" That came from the young man of the tourist couple. "You have to. She's gonna kill her!"

The other comments piled up on each other and didn't make much sense.

Unfortunately, the tourist was correct. Straightening out of her shooting stance, Megan reversed her hold on the gun and held it out toward the leader. She imagined a tiny timer happily ticking away the last seconds of her life.

The man snatched back the gun and pointed it at her face.

Amateur. She could have the gun back in a hot second. However, since that wouldn't improve Ms. Berkley's situation, Megan kept her hands raised in a non-threatening manner.

"Who are you?" he growled.

Before Megan could answer, yet another new voice spoke.

"I've called the cops. You'd better run." The young voice wavered with false bravado.

"What's she doing here?" Kenny's question held a lot of righteous indignation. He'd fired the question at his mother.

Ignoring him, Ms. Berkley waved both arms frantically. "Get back inside, baby! Lock the door and stay there!"

"Don't go, sweetie. Stay." Ailani spoke in a sugary, sweet voice. "I insist." The last statement was decidedly darker and emphasized by the gun tapping the top of Ms. Berkley's head. "Come over and give your mother a big hug."

"What? No!" Kenny looked ready to explode. "Katelyn, get out of here!"

Megan's vote was with Kenny's suggestion, but she couldn't blame Katelyn for following the crazy lady's instructions. After all, she had done just that a few seconds ago.

In another moment, Katelyn was wrapped in her mother's arms, muttering, "I'm sorry. I'm sorry. I'm sorry."

Ms. Berkley couldn't even reply with words. She wept into her daughter's hair, trying to shield her as much as possible.

Megan wondered why the police hadn't shown up yet. Surely a few years must have passed since they'd started hearing the sirens.

"Get that gun off my mom! Alex, call her off." Kenny took a step toward Ailani and his family before the leader's words stopped him.

"Do your job or I let her cap them both right now!" Alex's gun remained on Megan but he glared at Kenny.

"This has gone too far." The young robber looked stunned.

"It hasn't gone far enough until we're away. Now grab those bags and get in the car. We've got to move." He softened his tone when he addressed Ailani. "Baby, knock out the woman and take the kid to keep Kenny-boy in line."

"I can't do that!" Ailani's voice practically squeaked as it sailed high.

Yes, because hitting her is so much worse than pointing a gun at her.

Much as Megan had done earlier, Kenny used the distraction to his advantage. Though she wanted to stop him, Megan knew that shouting to Kenny would alert the robbers to his movements. The best she could do was wait for him to make his move and recover the gun trained on her.

"Kenny," Alex called. "Don't do something you'll regret."

Despite the warning, Kenny made his move. His tackle caught Ailani around the waist and drove her toward Megan.

The teller went down with a shriek and dropped her gun.

Megan wanted to grab it but instead, she snatched back the gun that had so recently been staring her down. Unfortunately, at that moment, Alex pulled the trigger. He'd been in the process of redirecting the gun at Kenny. The bullet caught Ailani in the right ankle. Her scream was more of a squeal because Kenny's tackle had knocked the breath out of her.

By this time, the other hostages were on their feet ready to lynch their tormenters. As Megan gained a firm grip on the gun, Alex scrambled away.

"Stop! FBI! You're under arrest!" It felt great to say those words, but as usual with guys like Alex, they didn't work.

He paused only long enough to scoop up Ailani's abandoned gun.

Kenny too had repositioned himself, only this time it was in front of the door.

"It's over, man. Give it up." He stood with his arms out in front of his body like he meant to literally catch Alex on the way out.

The gun came up at the center of Kenny's chest.

Kenny's jaw tightened with determination. His eyes dared his former comrade to shoot him.

"No!" Ms. Berkley's strangled cry ended in a sob. She clutched Katelyn's head so tightly to her chest that Megan feared the child might not be able to breathe let alone shift her head to see anything.

"Move or die." The order was delivered in such a calm, cold manner Megan had no doubt Alex would pull that trigger if the instruction wasn't followed.

"Step aside, Kenny," Megan urged. "He's not worth dying for. I can track him down later."

"Your choice," Alex said.

Megan readied herself to fire on Alex before he could shoot Kenny, but somebody jostled her from behind. Her heart slammed up into her throat, preventing the frustrated cry that wanted release. She saw a muzzle flash and the tiny gun bucked in Alex's hand. In beautiful, slow motion the smoking gun pointed upward as Kenny dropped to the ground.

Alex barreled through the double glass doors and out onto the street. He glanced in both directions then sprinted off to his left.

The crack of the gunshot smacked Megan's ears, striking her like the sound of a starter pistol.

The sight of Kenny's body lying across the doorway made her pause. Grabbing Mr. Sims's arm, Megan yanked him around so that he faced her squarely.

"Call 911. Try to stop the bleeding and get him an ambulance. And tell the police the suspect fled on foot down Kalakaua Avenue. He's armed and dangerous. Got that? Armed and dangerous." Noticing Sims had glassy eyes, Megan addressed the crowd of recently liberated hostages. She tried to make eye contact with each of them, but time was not on her side. "Somebody follow those steps: 911. Ambulance. Police. In that order."

She used the seconds it took to deliver those instructions to kick off the three hundred dollar sandals. Running down the streets of Waikiki barefoot wasn't ideal, but at least Megan wouldn't risk breaking an ankle or destroying the sandals. She headed toward the door.

"Wait! Go out the side," the other teller said. Her nametag read Elizabeth Mullins. She pointed at the Employees Only door. "There's a corridor that leads through to the park."

Nodding thanks, Megan changed the direction of her sprint. As promised, a corridor ran behind each shop in the complex and led directly to the street facing the green running along Kalakaua Avenue.

When she reached the park, Megan paused to scan for her quarry. As the seconds marched onward, her chances of finding him sank. She was about to give up when a distant scream renewed her hope. She continued the pursuit by heading for the commotion.

"He's got a gun!" a woman shouted.

That's my guy, Megan thought, doubling her efforts. She probably should have stretched properly, but at least her adrenaline system worked efficiently.

To her surprise, she spotted Alex a few hundred feet away. If he'd dumped the gun and kept on running, he might have lost her, but the fool was standing there waving his gun in a hysterical woman's face. Megan joined the small crowd of morbidly curious people, hiding her gun as best she could. She didn't wish to start a stampede.

The situation presented yet another moral dilemma. She could let Alex steal the woman's keys and drive off, which offered a good chance he'd disappear forever. Her other option was to confront him and risk making a hostage of the woman. He had already proven he would shoot anybody who stood in his way.

A few seconds' observation and a new viewing angle revealed why the woman was fighting him so strongly for the keys.

A car seat in the back of the Toyota Camry held a shrieking infant.

Megan immediately discarded the plan to let Alex escape. Putting on her official voice, she shouted, "Everybody back up!"

The crowd flinched in unison, stumbling back instinctively.

"You can do this the easy way or the hard way, Alex," Megan continued, stepping away from the crowd in case he chose to take a shot at her. She suddenly felt like there should be slow Western string music playing in the background. It was high noon after all. "Surrender is the easy way. Running is the hard way, but you are never getting those keys."

Alex shoved the woman at Megan, spun on his heels, and took off like an Olympic sprinter headed down a home stretch.

Hard way. Of course.

Chapter 11:
The Good Son

Lynn Berkley couldn't breathe, and only part of the cause was her daughter's firm embrace. She felt like a prisoner in her own head. An inner voice screeched and shouted orders to get up, go to Kenny, and call for help. But she couldn't move. She was paralyzed. The nicely dressed customer she'd chatted with about loans issued several sharp orders, but Lynn missed them all. When the lady was gone, Lynn's mind started churning again. Thoughts tripped over each other and ended in fragments. Tears blurred her vision. Something squeezed her right shoulder, making her flinch.

"Him you son? Good boy? Good son?"

Lynn couldn't summon the energy to verbally respond to Mrs. Fong's gentle query, but she sniffled and nodded once.

"You go him. Give girl." The old woman motioned for Lynn to give her Katelyn. "She safe with me."

To this point Katelyn had been sobbing quietly, but as Lynn tried to break free, the girl responded by tightening her grip. Lynn grunted with the new pain, but oddly, it snapped her out of the daze. She kissed the top of Katelyn's head.

"Let go, baby."

Katelyn jerked her head back and forth in a flat refusal.

"Please. Just for a minute. We need to help Kenny. I won't be long, but he needs me. Stay with Mrs. Fong." As Lynn's speech sank in, Katelyn's grip loosened. With a surge of strength, Lynn broke free then paused, still holding tightly to both of Katelyn's upper arms. Her hair was sweaty and matted, and tears streamed down her face. "I'll be right back. Promise. But please stay here. And don't turn around." Lynn cupped Katelyn's cheeks between her hands and repeated, "Don't turn around."

Mrs. Fong knelt down next to them.

Steeling her heart against her daughter's tears, Lynn guided Katelyn into Mrs. Fong's open arms before scrambling over to Kenny. He'd fallen back against the left door, pushing it open. Lynn's eyes locked on the bullet hole marring the glass then followed the bloody smear left on the lower half of the door down to the floor where Kenny still lay on his left side.

Lynn rushed to her son, dropped to the floor, tucked her legs under her body, and propped Kenny's head up with her knees.

Help.

She had to get him help. Lynn's eyes darted around the room, taking stock of the people who remained in the bank. Elizabeth stood rooted in place, wringing her hands. Ailani writhed on the floor where she'd fallen, crying, cursing, and clutching at her wounded ankle. Christopher Sims was on the phone. The young couple looked ready to bolt.

She assumed Chris had called the police until she heard him say, "This is a disaster, Harold! You're the lawyer! You tell—"

Lynn's glare halted the flow of words from Chris. Her son could be bleeding to death and his first call had been to the corporate lawyer. Her rage built up so fast, she felt flashes of heat then cold. She wasn't sure words would come until they did.

"Call 911 or you're fired!"

"I've got to go, Harold," Chris mumbled before ending his current call. Not meeting Lynn's gaze, he followed the order.

Once certain Chris would summon help, Lynn gave Kenny her full attention. She blinked rapidly in a valiant attempt to contain her emotions. His life flashed before her eyes. She didn't see a tough guy bank robber. She only saw her firstborn, her son. As she gazed upon his precious face, she pictured him at various stages of life. His perfectly peaceful infant face appeared then disappeared only to be replaced by a red-faced, wailing toddler. The toddler's chubby cheeks thinned as the face changed to that of a beaming Boy Scout with two missing front teeth. The scout was supplanted by a surly teenager. The image jarred her back to the present.

The pale young man before her wasn't the boy she remembered. He had both hands clenched over the chest wound.

Blood seeped slowly from the left corner of his mouth. He made a noise which had little resemblance to a real word, but Lynn understood it.

"Shhhh. I'm here, Kenny. Don't speak, love. I'm here. Help's on the way. Keep fighting. Keep breathing. Keep living. I'm sorry. I love you. Stay with me. For me. For Katelyn. Stay. Please. We need you." Lynn was hardly aware of the words tumbling from her lips. Eventually, they stopped coming, but she kept her eyes locked on his face and wiped the tears as they fell from his eyes.

Strong hands slipped under Lynn's arms and carefully tugged her backward. She tried to twist away, whirl, and slap at the hands touching her.

"No! He's my son! I—"

"Steady, ma'am. We're here to help," said an infinitely patient, deep male voice. "Let us stabilize him. You can come in the ambulance, but we need to help him now."

Lynn almost melted with relief. She scrambled out of the way as best she could, letting the paramedics get to Kenny. She watched like a hawk as they swiftly transferred Kenny to a gurney and wheeled him away. The sight of the blood still marking the door and floor turned her stomach. Slamming her eyes shut, Lynn tried to block it out.

"Ma'am? Are you coming?" The same man who had addressed her before held a large hand down to her. His uniform strained to contain his broad arm muscles. "If you're coming with us, we've got to go now. Come on."

Lynn numbly reached for his hand, suddenly aware of how much blood had soaked the bottom of her skirt.

"What about the rest of us?" Christopher Sims demanded. He looked ready to punch the taller paramedic.

"Stay calm, sir. More units are on the way, but we've got to go in priority order."

"Dave, we can't take her," the other paramedic whispered. He glanced apologetically at Lynn. "Priority order. We've got a GSW to the ankle here." The shorter man had Ailani's left arm draped over his neck while his right arm supported her waist as she hopped along. His name was Joe according to his nametag.

"But she's one of them!" protested the male customer.

Ailani's right foot was one white blob of bandages. Her expression spoke of weariness and pain.

Rage swept over Lynn until a small, thin body slammed into

her and hugged her tightly. The rage flooded out like air from a punctured balloon. As she tucked Katelyn in against her side, she only dimly paid attention to the argument raging above her.

"She's still been shot," Joe argued. "She needs care!"

"She almost got us killed," the male customer retorted.

"The boy was one of them too," reminded the man's wife.

"Then let them both rot!" cried the man.

The vicious response boomed inside Lynn's skull. This man wanted Kenny—her baby boy—to rot. He wanted to delay Kenny getting help. It didn't sit well with her that Ailani should receive help too, but if it saved Kenny, Lynn would make almost any bargain. Reaching up, Lynn gripped the one paramedic's hand and squeezed. She found new strength.

"Take them and go. I'll deal with the people here and stop by the hospital to see my son."

Dave nodded at her gratefully. They had reached an understanding.

Kenny's straw hat had been trampled by Alex and the paramedics. The sight of it tugged at Lynn's heart. Picking up the crumpled hat and forcing herself to stand, Lynn let the paramedics exit and awkwardly maneuvered to block any pursuit. Katelyn had re-pasted her body to Lynn's side.

"Nobody is leaving until the police arrive and take statements." Lynn's voice remained calm, but her eyes promised that anybody who dared to move would regret it.

Nobody spoke right away, but she certainly had their full attention.

"C-can we have our wallets and purses back, please?" The question came from the young female customer holding hands with the angry man.

Lynn considered the request. The police would likely wish to have everything remain untouched, but the people looked restless. She needed to give them something to do. Then again, she also had an obligation to protect the bank's property as best she could.

"The police probably won't want us touching anything," Lynn said. It wasn't her final decision but she wanted time to think.

"What's the point?" the male tourist demanded. "They're gone. *You* let them walk right out of here." He stomped over to the pile that never quite made it into a duffle bag and rooted around until he found his wallet and his wife's purse. Agitation made his movements jerky.

He backhanded the brave woman's purse, yelped, and snatched his hand away. "What's this?" He forgot about his own property and focused on the purse.

Reaching the limit of her patience, Lynn dug deep into her customer service experience and said, "Sir, that purse does not belong to you. Kindly return it to the stack and take only what belongs to you."

Flushing, the man glared at Lynn, shrugged like he didn't care, and dropped the purse like it was a hot potato. It landed squarely on his unprotected big toe with an audible crunch. He didn't cry out but his face turned a deeper shade of red. He leaned forward and took deep breaths until the pain passed.

"Honey, are you all right?" The man's wife squeaked the question. Her hands flew up to her mouth, partly to cover a laugh.

Lynn couldn't conjure much sympathy for him, but her professionalism prevailed.

"Sir, why don't you have a seat right there? Liz, please go to the break room and get the man some ice. Chris, grab a notepad and start inventorying this pile before it gets too disturbed." She entered into a brief staring contest with her Financial Adviser until he heaved a sigh and slipped into his office to grab some paper. Leaning down to her daughter, Lynn added, "Bring me that purse, will you, baby? But be careful with it."

"What's in here, mom?" Katelyn looked surprised at how much heft the purse had. She handed the purse over.

"Answers," Lynn replied.

Though it's generally bad form to search another woman's purse, Lynn needed to set everybody's mind at ease. Unzipping the stylish bag, Lynn peeked in and immediately spotted a gun and an ID case. Plucking out the ID case with two fingers, she flipped it open and read, "Special Agent Megan Luchek, FBI."

Returning with the ice, Elizabeth Mullins had her cellphone clenched in her fist as she listened hard to whoever was on the other end. Throwing the bag of ice at the injured customer, she spun around and ran toward the door marked Employees Only.

"Now what?" the female tourist asked.

As Liz reached the door, it swung open, and she barreled into a very surprised young policeman.

He reacted by catching her left arm and spinning her around into the wall.

"Don't hurt me! Don't hurt me! I didn't do anything wrong! It was a simple job. Nobody got hurt. I swear. I don't know them. It wasn't me. I didn't write the checks. He made me do it!"

"Ma'am, please calm down," the cop pleaded. "Who made you do what?"

Elizabeth broke down sobbing, no doubt spilling her life's story to the unfortunate policeman, but Lynn stopped listening. Quite frankly, she didn't care what the girl had to say. She wanted to find the nearest cop, give her statement, and get to the hospital. She needed to see Kenny.

Chapter 12:
The Hard Way

Although she felt terrible about not being able to stop and explain, Megan pivoted around the hysterical woman and dashed after Alex. As the chase lengthened beyond a few seconds, she started feeling the cumulative effects of her exciting morning. Her body mechanically took in air and complained about the abuse. Athletic discipline set in, and Megan swept aside the discomfort and concentrated on covering as much ground as possible. The beautiful day lent ideal running conditions to both pursuer and pursued. Luckily, Alex couldn't resist glancing back from time to time, which slowed him down. Nevertheless, he sprinted like wild dogs were chasing him.

As Megan began despairing of ever catching Alex, he veered left and started across Ainahau triangle. He halted suddenly, turned around, and raised his arms toward her.

She thought he might surrender.

Tasting victory, Megan's world shrank to running and breathing. Her head filled with the sound of blood rushing between her ears, a kind of runner's nirvana she'd only experienced one other time in her life.

Her vision locked on her quarry.

Nothing else mattered.

His eyes widened at her relentless pursuit. He twisted around and ploughed into a newspaper kiosk, prompting an avalanche of magazines, tabloids, candy, and choice words from the small man running the stand.

The man looked ready to either cry or grab a newspaper roll

and start beating Alex with it.

Seeing Alex's gun fly off to her right, Megan detoured long enough to snap it up.

"FBI. You're under arrest," Megan said, pointing the weapon at the stunned robber.

Her head started to ache as she flipped the suspect over and knelt on his back. That's when she realized she didn't have handcuffs, an ID, or her phone. Her vision darkened, but she knew there was a reason she shouldn't faint right now.

"Freeze!"

"Drop the gun!"

The two orders penetrated the consuming focus, but Megan's headache deepened.

Great. A standoff in a park.

A glance back showed her a pair of uniformed police officers approaching carefully. The kiosk guy hunkered down in his stall. A woman pushing a baby stroller watched open mouthed from about twenty-five feet away. A kid on a skateboard stood next to the mother, looking thrilled.

"Get this crazy—"

Megan thumped her prisoner on the back.

"Quiet, you. Wait for your Miranda rights." Her right knee hurt until she brushed away the pile of candy half-burying Alex. Packets of Skittles were the current cause of the knee distress. Once that was dealt with, she turned to the policemen, and said, "I'm Megan Luchek, FBI. I'll trade you the gun for your handcuffs."

"Put the gun down and lie facedown on the ground," the younger officer ordered. His service weapon pointed squarely in her direction.

Megan glared at the man. He was getting on her nerves, and her left arm felt like the world's largest bee had stung her. She didn't have time for either annoyance. She had worked too hard to let this pup ruin her collar.

"Handcuffs," she said, over enunciating so much that it sounded like two words.

After a long pause while the cops no doubt debated silently, a pair of handcuffs struck the ground next to Megan's right leg. Fair was fair. She dropped the gun exactly where the cuffs had fallen. In a practiced move, she secured Alex's hands behind his back. The task was a little harder than it ought to be because his hands were warm and sticky.

And red.

She stared at her hands curiously. The right one was normal, but the left one was covered in blood. Following the blood back to its source, Megan craned her neck and frowned down at her upper left arm. There was a chunk of flesh missing.

That explains a lot.

Weary, Megan let one of the cops gently guide her from a kneeling position to a seat on the ground. With a firm hand on both shoulders, he then helped her lie down.

He was speaking, but she ignored the words.

Her head felt like a helium balloon tethered by a flimsy piece of string.

I've been shot. But I'm okay.

Blackness sank her mind into a fog, but she fought it back, twisting her head right so she could keep an eye on Alex. She didn't want the snake to slip away into the growing crowd.

The other cop checked the cuffs and helped the suspect stand.

Secure in the knowledge that everything should be smooth sailing now, Megan finally let the creeping darkness claim her mind. She didn't care if there was an audience. After her morning, she definitely deserved a nap.

***

Plans rarely worked out perfectly, but Maxwell Nicholson had never before seen one devolve into complete disaster so quickly. He'd been monitoring the bank job from the security feeds and rushed to do some damage control as soon as Kenny had panicked and left his assigned position. Brian was the loyal sort. He would go to the rendezvous as planned. If he didn't, Max would add him to the cleanup list, but he would go.

As usual, Max had taken his motorcycle because it gave him an excuse to wear a completely concealing helmet. If he didn't do something soon, the cops would take Alex into custody. They were both professionals. Everybody knew the score going into the job, but Max couldn't guarantee Alex wouldn't flip on the client. His window for dealing with the problem was closing swiftly.

He'd already burned through the backup plan when he'd called the Mullins woman and told her to keep her end of the deal. She'd be fine. A good lawyer would have her out on bail in a few hours. She might lose her job, but when he paid her, she wouldn't need a job for many months. Of course, that assumed there would still be a payment. Such arrangements hinged on the plan being successful, which meant that Max would have to salvage this horror show.

Shooting Alex here would be very risky. There were dozens of potential witnesses. He already saw at least three people with their cellphones out recording Alex's arrest. He'd have to use a Spike or risk being the star of a breaking news bulletin. That would be annoying. Spikes cost several hundred dollars and could only be used once. They did the job of a jammer only on a much subtler scale, preventing usable data from being recorded for a short time within a fifty-foot radius of the device. He couldn't believe he was about to launch the backup plan to his backup plan.

He'd worn one of his favorite riding jackets. After today, he'd have to ditch the outfit and hide his bike for a while. Was the payout worth it? He had no choice now. If he did nothing and Alex talked he would never get another job as a Fixer. Nobody would trust him.

Gathering his courage, Max set off the Spike, dismounted, drew the untraceable gun he carried for such emergencies, and jogged a few steps away so he had a better angle.

Alex was being helped up by one of the cops.

"Allahu Akbar!" Max opened his helmet visor to ensure that the words would be heard correctly. He fired into the crowd, making sure Alex was the first to go down.

***

The sound of gunfire blasted through the peaceful oblivion Megan had slipped into. Adrenaline shot through her as she rolled to her feet and assessed the situation.

Shots continued to rip through the air.

She counted thirteen shots in total.

Pandemonium reigned.

People who had gathered to watch the arrest ducked, screamed, and scattered everywhere, often into each other. A few sensible ones dropped to the ground and covered their heads with their hands.

Megan was one of the only brave fools still standing, so she got a good look at the perpetrator, not that it helped her much. Besides the large motorcycle helmet, every inch of him was covered in black riding gear. For one instant, he stood stock still watching her. His helmet dipped in acknowledgement before he tossed the gun a few feet in front and jogged to his motorcycle.

In full fighting form, Megan would have futilely chased the

man on foot, but in seconds, he was simply gone. A bad feeling settled in her gut as she looked for Alex. She found him crumpled in yet more colorful wreckage from the newspaper kiosk.

The young cop who'd been completing the arrest was on the ground moaning and clutching at a wound in his leg. The other cop was assisting the lady with the stroller. A bullet had struck one of the handles and upended the whole thing. The baby girl was in her mother's arms, loudly wailing, which probably meant she'd be fine.

Four bullet holes in the center of Alex's chest told her not to expect much, but Megan knelt down and reached to feel for a pulse in his neck. She found nothing. Normally, she'd try to check the right wrist to be thorough, but his hands were still cuffed behind his back. Standing up, Megan stared down at the robber's body.

"Crazy Muslim," a man muttered bitterly. He got up and brushed dirt from his pants.

"Muslim?" Megan questioned.

"Yeah. The nut job shouted 'Allahu Akbar!' then started blasting everything in sight."

Megan eyed the place where she'd seen the shooter then looked down at the body. She wasn't buying the random shooting idea, with or without a religious motivation. That tight a grouping of shots wasn't consistent with anything random. Somebody purposefully took Alex out, but who would kill an incompetent bank robber? The only semi-logical option was whoever had hired him in the first place, but that explanation left a lot of holes. The distance was maybe fifty feet. Remembering the gun, she sprinted over to where she'd seen it land and scanned the ground.

"Looking for this?" asked the kid with the skateboard.

Megan whipped her head in his direction and swayed on her feet. She staggered left a few steps and leaned back against the tree.

Holding out her good hand, she said, "Put the gun on the ground."

"I found it," said the kid.

"Finder's keeper doesn't apply to mass murder weapons, kid. Now drop it before you destroy any more evidence on it."

The kid's eyes got big as her words sank in. He looked torn between the cool factor of holding a gun and the horror factor of its most recent application. In the end, he dropped the weapon.

Megan slowly made her way over to the gun and carefully picked it up by the trigger guard. She'd clearly seen the man had gloves on, but there had been only thirteen shots. With any luck, the shooter wasn't as smart as he thought. She doubted the gun itself had any fingerprints, but if he'd loaded the magazine himself, the remaining bullets might give her a few usable prints to run. Maybe after she turned in the gun for processing, she would reward herself by passing out again. First, she needed to rustle up a phone to check in with her partner.

Chapter 13:
A New Threat?

Martin Cantrell hated using disposable phones. They made him feel like he was playing a stupid spy game. Reports concerning the operation were not encouraging. His son was in the hospital, his ex-wife—unfortunately—was only there visiting, and his daughter had been thoroughly traumatized. Alex was dead, which would be good news except that it heightened the publicity factor significantly. He shouldn't have let Max talk him into involving Kenny. The scant good news was that the debacle would certainly prompt an investigation. Lynn would have a few days of forced vacation, but Martin wasn't sure if Max could be trusted to enact phase two. The boy was swiftly becoming a liability.

Even the breathtaking beauty of his private beach sanctuary failed to soothe Martin.

Before he placed his next call, he had some major decisions to make and very little time in which to make them. The bank incident was possibly too big. Suspicions would run high and straight to him if anything happened to Lynn in the next few days. Delaying the job would not please Max, but Martin had legitimate reasons to postpone the hit. Katelyn would likely cling to Lynn for a few days. Besides, Kenny wouldn't be able to hang out with her until he recovered. It made no sense to move forward right now, but should he call it off completely? Max would protest, but he had only his own poor planning to blame for the first plan failing so miserably.

If Kenny dies, I'll kill Max.

Martin knew that much was true, but he buried his feelings before calling Max.

"Tell me everything," he ordered.

"You shouldn't call me," Max said.

"I shouldn't be seeing the news stories I'm seeing either, but it looks like we're both going to be disappointed here. What happened?" Martin barely got the question out.

"Your son screwed up," Max snapped. He briefly explained everything he knew about what had happened in the Waikiki branch that morning, emphasizing the part where Kenny ruined the carefully laid plan.

Martin wanted to remind Max that he'd been initially against the idea of involving Kenny, but he *had* approved his son's inclusion on the team. He bore some culpability for letting Max talk him into the bad idea.

"What are you going to do about it? How did you approach Kenny? Does he know anything? What does he know?" Martin's hand hurt from clenching the phone so tightly. He consciously stopped talking so Max could answer the questions.

"I'm taking care of the loose ends. That's all you need to know."

Martin's police contact had already informed him of the shooting in Ainahau Triangle. His fear for Kenny spiked.

"Does that include my son?"

"Kenny doesn't know enough to qualify as a loose end. I made sure of that."

Knees feeling weak with relief, Martin knelt on the sand. To cover for the emotional lapse, he cleared his throat sharply.

"We need to delay the second part of this plan for a few months. I may even call it off completely."

"You can't. You said the insurance policy runs out at the end of the year and you couldn't renew it. I have obligations to meet. Too many parts of the plan are already in motion. There's no such thing as buyer's remorse in this business. You know that." Max let the space of two heartbeats pass so the words would settle. "The best I can do is a short delay."

Outwardly, Martin said, "Fine, short delay it is, but if necessary, I can probably extend the policy on my wife after the bank incident. I'll just have to talk up the concern for my daughter's well-being." Inwardly, he knew that Max was the only major block to calling off the plan.

He can be removed if necessary.

As if hearing the thought, Max said, "In case you're thinking I'm the only one who knows of the plan, think again. I have my own insurance policy of sorts."

Is he bluffing?

"What are you talking about?"

"If you back out of this deal or try to have me killed, six contracts go out on your daughter's life." Max's voice was initially calm and factual before he shifted to a conciliatory tone. "I'm not saying this to upset you, Uncle Martin. We have a good plan. Give me time to execute it, but I agree that we need to delay for now."

In that moment, Martin decided that Max would have to be dealt with soon. The threat against Katelyn was probably a bluff, but even if it wasn't, Martin was willing to bet that men who accepted such contracts could easily be bought.

What if she's not mine?

Hitting pause once again on that thought, Martin said, "Fulfill the contract as soon as it can be safely accomplished." He wouldn't even grace the threat with a direct response. Let Max wonder and worry about what he was really thinking.

"I intend to, but there's also a different matter to discuss." This time, Max sounded hesitant. "The FBI agent."

Martin brought up a mental picture of the agent in question.

"What about her?"

"There's a small chance she'll become a new threat to us." Max sounded almost embarrassed. "I don't think she'll buy the media story about my religious crusader."

"If you knew she was there, why didn't you take care of her then?" Martin shifted to a sitting position on the sand to relieve the pressure on his knees. It would be a shame to waste such looks, but if she didn't buy the story, Max was right, she could make trouble.

"It didn't happen. By the time I made sure the main problem was solved, I needed to leave, but I caught a glimpse of her there. Should I make her a priority?"

"Not yet." Nothing would kick the investigation into a higher gear faster than killing an agent. "But be prepared to move quickly when and if the time comes."

"I want an extra ten thousand dollars, up front, if I'm going to be tangling with the FBI."

"I'm not paying you more until you do something," Martin countered. "We just decided to not deal with the agent problem right now."

"I don't like your tone."

"And I don't like failures. We can salvage this, but you're going to have to work with me and let things settle. I'm going to trust you've taken care of the bank side of things. There are rumors one of the robbers escaped."

"He did, but he's cool. He checked in."

"Really? Did he get any money from the robbery?"

"No, but he's loyal. I used some emergency funds to help him lie low for a while."

"Good to hear. Okay, we're done for now. We shouldn't be seen together, so don't come by. I'll use the other phone to call you when it's time to move forward again."

With nothing else to say, Martin ended the call without waiting for pleasantries to be exchanged. He stared down at the phone and considered smashing it on a palm tree but didn't want to hurt his fingers. Instead, he took a few steps away from the water's edge, wound up, and threw the phone as far as he could out over the incoming waves. It arced up gracefully and plunked down into the cool waters and sank from sight.

It felt like an admission that the last month and a half of his life had been meaningless. The days had gotten shorter and cooler, but he still had a Lynn problem. In fact, that problem may have just grown. Now that she'd shared the bank scare with Kenny, she'd bring up the custody thing again. They'd never formally settled anything on that matter. The agreement had been simply to never make an issue of it, so long as Kenny stayed with him and Katelyn stayed with Lynn.

Kenny would need a great lawyer. Martin had enough friends who would stand up for his son, and he wasn't worried about the trial's outcome. He trusted Max's word that Kenny knew very little about the real plan. He was just the driver. Besides, there were several mitigating circumstances, and in the end, he had defended his mother and sister. Though misguided, Martin admired his son's actions. Kenny came early enough in the marriage that Martin didn't question his paternity.

Katelyn, on the other hand, was a different matter. She was born after a rough patch. Lynn had sworn up and down that her lunch dates with her college sweetheart never went all the way, but Martin's faith in Lynn's word had perished long ago.

As the sun headed toward the horizon, his thoughts moved to the agent. He should check on her. Council members were already clamoring about a formal commendation. While Martin didn't think they would go that far, it was an interesting thought. She'd probably prefer to have a medal ground to powder and added to her wine than let him pin it on her, but the idea of a formal event honoring some local heroes had merit. He would have to set his people to work on something appropriate. He smiled to think that she wasn't even aware of the game they played. One word to Max and the agent would die.

Simple as that.

Martin knew he shouldn't enjoy thoughts like this, but how could he not enjoy the idea of that much power? If he were a younger man, he'd join the army and become a sniper, but since that wasn't an option, he would take his pleasures where he could. The agent was young and capable, but she hadn't been in Oahu long enough to learn every danger.

Stalemate this round, agent. Are you lucky or good at what you do? I'll concede victory and let you live for the part you had in saving my daughter. But next round won't be this easy. That's a promise.

Chapter 14:
Handsome

Megan Luchek rejoined the conscious world reluctantly. Groaning, she squinted up at the harsh hospital lights. Moving slowly, she forced her eyes open and scanned the bare room. There wasn't much to see. She occupied the only bed in the room. To her left was a small wheeled dresser that doubled for a nightstand. A lounge chair took up the corner space by the foot of the bed. Two more hard chairs sat near the line of windows. A small television was mounted from the ceiling directly across from her, but it wasn't currently on. A machine attached to the wall behind Megan loomed over her.

She wanted to get up and check out of this place, but she knew that might be problematic. First, she wore only an open-backed, thin hospital gown. Second, a complicated system of bandages held a needle firmly to her right arm. Third, the dull ache coming from her left arm and the fuzzy feeling that engulfed her head told her she was on some sort of wonderful painkiller.

As she started dozing off, a gentle knock sounded on the room's open door.

"Knock. Knock," announced Dan Cooper. "Permission to approach the wounded?"

"Are you here to get me out?" asked Megan.

"In good time," Dan promised. He raised his right arm which held a black duffle bag. "There are some locals hovering for the chance to take your statements, one for the bank side of the story and one for the chase and arrest. But look, I come bearing gifts." Stopping next to her hospital bed, he dropped the bag to the ground. "It's actually my go-bag since I couldn't find yours on short notice."

"What's wrong with the clothes I came in?"

"They're gonna have a hard time returning that outfit." Dan gave her a significant look.

Megan winced.

"How bad was the damage?"

"Grass-stains, blood, maybe a chocolate stain or two," he reported. "Look on the bright side: they might let you keep it now."

"That's comforting." Megan shook her head cautiously from side to side. "Maddox is going to have my head over this."

"On the contrary, you're a superhero who saved a bank filled with people. Bank of Hawaii suits already dropped by to send their official thank yous." Shifting his voice over to mock-reporter, Dan asked, "How does that news make you feel?"

"Warm and fuzzy," she answered honestly, "but that could be the drugs talking."

"Are you okay to talk to the LEOs right now?"

Megan shrugged noncommittally.

"The girls and I have a surprise for you, but you have to talk to the nice policemen and let me share some good news first."

Since her eyes were about the only thing on her that didn't hurt, Megan executed a fine eye roll at her partner's lame bribery attempt.

"Send them in already. The sooner they're gone, the sooner I get to go home."

Dan Cooper marched back over to the door and waved in the detectives. Megan didn't quite catch their names and didn't feel like asking them. The suits they wore didn't come with convenient nametags to help her out.

Megan answered their questions as best she could and posed some of her own. She learned that the two policemen with her on Alex's arrest were fine. The older one had escaped with only a few scrapes from diving to the ground. The younger one had to have a slug pulled from his left leg. Alex was taken to the hospital where he was pronounced dead on arrival. Both the suspect who first fled from the bank and the one who had gunned down Alex were in the wind. Despite the All Points Bulletins out for their arrest, Megan doubted they would be caught today. Lynn Berkley and her daughter had been treated for shock, given some fluids, and released, but they were both still in the waiting room hoping to hear news from Kenny's doctor. The police officers had no news on the young man's condition, but he'd been in surgery a few hours at this point. The teller who'd been shot in the ankle was three doors down recovering from her brief surgery. She had an armed guard outside her door. Everybody else had their statements taken and were released, except for the other teller.

"What happened to the other teller?" Megan wondered. The way the older detective smirked made her curious.

"Ask your partner, ma'am," suggested the younger detective.

She decided to dub him the hot one. His thick, dark hair was slicked back, and she found herself thinking what it might feel like to touch that luscious hair.

I gotta get some free samples of whatever I'm on right now.

"Thank you for your time, Agent Luchek. That's all the questions we have for you today." The man handed Megan a card. "If you remember anything else or come up with a new question, give me a call. Best of luck with your recovery."

Murmuring thanks, Megan peeked down at the card in her hands.

"Come on, Mateo. Let's roll."

Dan Cooper returned as soon as the detectives exited.

"First, the good news, then the visitors and the gift." He plopped onto the end of her bed. "We're off the case."

"How is that good news?"

"It's great news because we're off the case *and* it's just about closed. They caught one of the forgers today. Once they have a nice sit-down chat with her a lot more of the case should make sense."

"Really? Who?" Megan wanted to be happy that the case was closed, but she felt left out.

"Elizabeth Mullins."

"The teller?"

"The very same," Cooper confirmed. "Turns out she and her brother, Cato, had a very interesting upbringing where they were taught the finer points of check forging. Soon as that business at the bank went down, Ms. Mullins found the nearest cop and confessed everything."

Megan frowned. It sounded far too convenient.

"And Oldwick's buying that? It sounds like a false confession to cover something else."

"Not our problem," Dan said. "Our job was to flush out the bank moles and it looks like whatever went down today did just that. We get to move on."

As harrowing as this case had been, Megan would miss the wardrobe. She hadn't even had a chance to check out all the outfits and accessories she'd bought.

Is it over?

She doubted it, but she couldn't have continued anyway, even if there was more to investigate surreptitiously. Her cover was completely blown. She'd stood in the middle of the bank and screamed her identity to a dozen strangers that morning.

"Are you ready for more company?" Dan's question broke into her thoughts.

Truthfully, Megan wanted to find the nearest hole and disappear for a week, but she calculated that her energy reserves could last a few more minutes. She nodded.

"Come on in!" Dan shouted.

A giggle blasted through the hallway, announcing Megan's new visitors. Released from whatever had held her back, Ashley Ann Cooper came tearing into the room carrying something that looked too big for her.

"Fishie!" The toddler held a large clear plastic bag up as high as she could but it still wasn't high enough to place on the bed.

Inside the sloshing water, a purple-blue betta fish swam from one side of the bag to the other.

Bethany Cooper followed in her daughter's wake. Baby Carolina rode on a ledge created by her mother's arms. She blinked at Megan as if to say: *you see what I have to put up with every day?*

"Careful with the fishie, love," Bethany said. "Hello, Megan. Daniel said you could use some cheering. I would have gotten you flowers except that we were in the pet store when we received the summons. I hope you don't mind."

"Not at all. Thank you. It's a lovely gift."

The bag slipped from Ashley's fingers, but Dan caught the bag before it landed on the floor. Setting a glass bowl next to Megan on the rolling end table, Dan filled the bottom with multicolored rocks and added a few fake plant sprigs. Afterward, he carefully untied the bag and dumped the traumatized fish into its new home.

"Ta-da! One highly agitated fish." Dan bowed slightly as he formally presented the family's gift. "If he survived the trip here, I'm pretty sure he'll live. It's a good thing fish don't get sea sick." Dan lifted the plastic bag he'd taken the rocks out of. "The rest of the pebbles are in here with some fish pellets so you can keep the little guy alive. Directions are on the bottle."

"What will you name him?" Bethany asked.

"I don't know. I'll think of something," said Megan.

"Fishie!" declared Ashley.

"Hush, dear. That's not your fish. That one belongs to Megan. You can name the other fish we got today."

"Fishie!" Ashley argued. She grinned wide and emitted her trademark giggle.

Sighing, Bethany said, "Never negotiate with a toddler. It rarely goes well. I'm pretty sure our fish just officially got named 'Fishie.'"

One name popped into mind, but Megan wasn't sure she should trust her mind in this moment. She gazed at the fish as he executed a dozen laps of his tiny world and then began repeatedly charging the glass, fighting his own reflection. Between charges he would flash his fins to intimidate his foe. If the lovely colors didn't identify him as male, his behavior was a dead giveaway.

"Take your time," Dan said. "Naming your betta fish is a big life step, but first, I have some bad news. Please don't shoot the messenger."

Before Cooper could deliver the verbal blow, a tiny woman zipped into the room carrying a fraction of the energy of a hurricane about with her.

"Ah, Agent Luchek, so nice to see you awake. I trust your afternoon was more peaceful than your morning. I'm Dr. Davy." Her manner of speaking was efficient. "I know this probably isn't what you want to hear, but I'm going to ask that you stay the evening for observation. There wasn't anything to remove from the bullet wound in your arm. I cleaned it up soon after you got here, but there's still a high risk for infection."

Cooper smiled at Megan sympathetically.

"She was about to call your emergency contact. I insisted she wait and ask you in person. Would you like me to call your mother?"

Megan drilled her answer into her partner with such a sharp look he put a hand over his heart.

"I didn't think so."

"You should tell her you're all right," Bethany encouraged.

"Agent Luchek, will you submit to staying overnight?" inquired the doctor.

"She will," Cooper answered for her. Leaning over, he whispered, "Maddox says I can handcuff you to the bed if you refuse to heed the doctor's wishes."

"I need to hear the decision from you," Dr. Davy prompted.

Megan let her gaze bounce from person to person arrayed around her bed. Every eye was upon her, waiting for a decision.

"Fine, but on three conditions," she grumbled. "One, the fish stays. Two, Cooper and Bethany go to my apartment and retrieve some decent clothes for me. And three, nobody—*ever*—breathes a word about today to my mother or my sister. Got that?"

Dan nodded solemnly, but his expression said that the chances of keeping Tara from finding out were slim to none. Megan's older sister seemed to have eyes and ears everywhere.

"Agreed. I'll tell the nurses the fish can stay," said Dr. Davy. "Does the fish have a name I can convey to them?"

"He does." Megan took a moment to recline the bed back and settle further into the mound of pillows. Closing her eyes, she said, "I'm going to call him Handsome."

THE END

Shadow Council Series Book 2:
Revenge Makes it Sweeter

By Julie C. Gilbert

Table of Contents:

Prologue:
Faith, Trust, and Open Season

Today was hands-down the worst day of Lynn Berkley's life. The bank she managed had been robbed and her life had been threatened. The lawyers had explained that she would be on administrative leave until the investigation was finished, so she wasn't sure about her job situation. But none of that mattered when compared to the agony of waiting to hear if Kenny survived his surgery. Her mind ran through the bank incident on loop, torturing her with a thousand *what-if* situations where she could somehow spare her baby boy this hospital fate.

Her arms ached, but she didn't want to move for fear of disturbing her daughter. Katelyn had only just cried herself to sleep in Lynn's arms. Sleep would probably be a good thing, but Lynn's mind wouldn't let her rest. Her head throbbed with each heartbeat, and her breaths came in ragged little gasps as she suppressed sobs.

"How is he?" asked Martin Cantrell.

Her ex-husband's familiar voice immediately put Lynn on the defensive. She'd been hoping and dreading to hear from him all afternoon. She stiffened and pierced him with a glare strong enough to break his stride as he entered the waiting room. Katelyn moaned softly, still sleeping. Anger rose inside Lynn like a flashflood. She made a conscious effort to gently extricate herself from her daughter's grasp and lay the girl across the arm of the comfy chair that they'd been curled up in. Once free, she strode briskly past her ex-husband into the hallway so they could talk without disturbing Katelyn. Lynn leaned on the doorframe, crossed her arms, and waited for Martin to join her.

"How is Kenny?" Martin repeated.

Something in his tone told Lynn that would only be the first of many questions. The worry leeched some of the fiery anger burning in Lynn's chest, but she still flushed with the effort to not scream at him.

"He's still in surgery," Lynn said. She drew a deep breath and let it out in a rush, hoping it would bolster her courage. "How did Kenny end up working with robbers?" Lynn's voice wavered but she held Martin's gaze.

"How should I know?" he asked.

"He lives with you! How could you not know?" Lynn fired back.

"He's an adult now. He can make his own choices," Martin said, using that contemptible, calm, lawyerly tone. "I don't keep him under house arrest. It's not my—"

A short, bitter laugh from Lynn cut him off.

"It's never your fault, is it, Martin?" Lynn felt her anger draining away, taking much of her energy with it. She turned so more of her weight could be supported by the doorframe and sighed. "Look at us. Our son could be dying and we're out here fighting."

"Like old times," Martin commented.

Lynn managed half a smile at that, and they lapsed into an uneasy silence. She watched her daughter. Katelyn's hair was a wreck and tear streaks stained her cheeks, but Lynn thought she'd never looked better. Her fingers twitched to set some order to the girl's hair.

Martin cleared his throat, reminding Lynn they had unfinished business to discuss. She'd sensed as much in his eyes and tone earlier.

"What do you want, Martin?" Lynn asked, deciding to beat him to the punch. She clutched her arms tighter across her stomach as if that would ward off his words. Obviously, he wanted to know how Kenny fared, but he also had another agenda.

His answer still caught her by surprise.

"I want a paternity test for Katelyn."

Lynn blinked up at him, letting the words sink in, trying to absorb the pain of them. Tears stung her eyes. She shut her eyes to keep the tears in check. She'd already spent far too many of them on this callous jerk.

"Why?" She didn't bother hiding the contempt. "We've been over this a dozen times. Just because you couldn't keep the marriage vows, doesn't automatically mean I failed them too."

"This time I want proof," Martin said. He held up a small, clear vial that held a single cotton swab. "And I mean to get it. If I'm going to pay for her, I want to make sure she's mine."

Indignation poured energy into Lynn. She snatched the vial from his hand and side-stepped so that she was in front of her ex-husband, blocking his entry into the waiting room.

"Are you insane?" Lynn demanded. "I'll send you her toothbrush or something, but you will not wake that child over this!" Lynn's eyes flashed with fury. Half of her wanted to let the fool blunder over to Katelyn and ruin any chance at having a meaningful relationship with her. But she knew the damage would be worse for Katelyn.

"Why are—"

"Think about it, Martin! How is it going to make her feel when you waltz in there and tell her you want a DNA sample so you can see if she's really yours?"

He hummed thoughtfully as her point sank home.

"Fine. Send me her toothbrush, but I want it by the end of the week."

In a way, his familiar arrogance and need to stipulate terms was good, for it put Lynn on steadier emotional ground.

"You've waited this long. What's your hurry?" she asked.

"I'd like to get to know her better."

"But only if she's yours," Lynn said bitterly.

"Well, yes, naturally." Martin looked at her like she was a rare species he couldn't understand. "This tragedy with Kenny has got me thinking."

Lynn didn't know whether to be comforted or worried by that notion. Martin could be a very keen thinker. His sharp, scheming mind often thought of angles she'd never imagine. Having that degree of cold calculation leveled at family matters was disconcerting, yet he had money and power. The combination of those two entities could unlock many doors for Katelyn. Grudgingly given child support would only stretch so far. Still, Lynn had firsthand experience in how dirty Martin could fight. His sudden interest in Katelyn could go either way.

Martin's cellphone emitted a happy ding, and he paused to check the text message.

"I've got to go, but call me when you have news about Kenny."

Too weary to be annoyed at the order, Lynn nodded. As soon as Martin left, she sank onto a chair across from her daughter and settled in for the long wait.

***

Cassandra Mirren enjoyed working for the Shadow Council. Their contracts always paid well and offered refreshing challenges. This assignment to spy on one who could soon be a member of the inner circle would be especially intriguing.

"Do you understand your orders, Ms. Mirren?" The man's deep voice rumbled in low, soothing waves.

"I do, Your Honor." She kept her tone even and direct but added his title so he'd understand that she knew who he was just as he knew her true identity. Truth was a rare and deadly thing in the game they played. "Is everything in place?"

"From this end it is. The rest is up to you. But I must warn you. I'm not certain how Maxwell will react to your presence. He has enough contacts to know you for competition. He expects the close ties between his family and the Cantrells to mean he has a full monopoly on such jobs."

"I'll keep that in mind." Cassandra didn't bother pointing out that this was different. Maxwell Nicholson could never gather the sort of information she could, and he was far too close to Martin Cantrell to view the job objectively. "Is there anything else?"

"Yes. Aside from business and case interests, I want you to investigate the rumor that Martin's after his ex-wife." The judge sat back in his throne-like black leather chair, tapping his fingers together in a thoughtful manner.

He didn't say anything more, but Cassandra could fill in the blanks. Putting out a hit on his ex-wife would be a mark against Martin Cantrell's candidacy for the soon-to-open spot on the Shadow Council. The judge probably deemed it simply in poor taste or a waste of good resources.

Or perhaps, he just disapproves of poor results.

Currently, Cassandra knew little more than what the internet news could tell her. An attempted robbery had taken place in the Bank of Hawaii's Keeaumoku branch this morning. The incident would mean little to her if Martin Cantrell's ex-wife wasn't the bank manager and his son wasn't one of the robbers. One coincidence she could accept, but the combination meant trouble and intrigue. If the judge hadn't said anything, she probably would have launched an unofficial investigation anyway. She needed to make everything about Martin Cantrell her business if she was going to be able to make the correct

95

recommendation to the council. It wouldn't surprise her if the nature of her job switched suddenly.

"What would you like me to do if I find out the rumors are true?" Cassandra asked.

The judge thought long and hard before replying.

"Watch and wait. See what happens. I am very interested to see if the old boy can pull it off successfully. If he goes to prison, that will answer our question here, but I'd hate to see that happen. Help him if you can do so subtly, but that is not your primary objective. Understand?"

Cassandra was getting tired of that question, but she swallowed her irritation and smiled faintly.

"Perfectly so. Watch, wait, adapt. See if Mr. Cantrell can handle the rigors of a council position." Cassandra wanted to ask about exactly how much help she was expected to give Martin Cantrell with regards to his dealings with his ex-wife. She refrained for two reasons. One, men like Judge Clarence A. Jackson—the sexist old farts—expected concerned questions from her based on her gender. And two, she didn't want the judge to outright order her to complete the job. A vague request to help could easily be ignored. Cassandra had killed before, but she wasn't keen on taking out random citizens whose only crime was poor taste in men.

Cassandra shifted forward in her seat, ready to rise, but the judge's voice stopped her.

"One more thing, Ms. Mirren. The field of players has become far too crowded of late. The council is of the opinion that the roster could be thinned a bit, but as you know, one does not simply fire a Fixer."

"I will be cautious then. Thank you." Cassandra spoke quickly so she wouldn't have to hear him ask if she understood. "Is this an official Open Season?"

"Not yet, but I expect it may become one soon," the judge answered.

"Do you know the cap?"

"Five or six. We'll make that decision at the next meeting. I will let you know as I learn more."

That surprised Cassandra. She knew council members could warn their favorites, but she didn't think she ranked that highly in the judge's eyes. She'd just been starting out when the last Open Season thinned the crowd of Fixers. Her mentor had shielded her from the ugly but necessary side of the business.

"I appreciate the warning, sir," Cassandra said, standing. "If you'll excuse me, I have some preparations to make."

The judge waved her off dismissively, which suited Cassandra fine. She left as swiftly as propriety would allow. Her heartbeat quickened at the thought of an Open Season. A cap of five or six meant that likely six Fixers would die over the next week. The tradition went as far back as the founding of the Shadow Council and the need for Fixers. When the population of Fixers severely outgrew the amount of contracts, an Open Season was declared wherein the various candidates could vie for promotions.

You kill it, you keep its contracts. The sentiment was a gross oversimplification but essentially the heart of Open Season.

All right, boys, let's see what you've got. May the best Fixer win.

Chapter 1:
Dining with Wolves

Special Agent Megan Luchek felt naked. She wasn't naked, of course, but not carrying a gun was almost as awkward. She was self-conscious about the large adhesive bandage covering the scar forming where she'd been recently wounded. Nothing she owned with sleeves would have been appropriate for an occasion of this sort. She wore a deep purple evening dress with a spread of silver sequins slashing down from the left shoulder, underlining the bust, and sweeping down the left hip, tracing a line to her stunning high-heeled shoes. The dress would not have allowed her to hide a gun. Besides, the guests were required to walk through metal detectors on the way in to this little shindig. If she needed a weapon tonight, she would have to get creative, though admittedly her long, dangly earrings could probably do nicely for stabbing an attacker.

"Stop that," Special Agent Daniel Cooper muttered under his breath.

Megan lifted one freshly waxed eyebrow at her partner.

"You look like you're plotting something," he continued, gently holding her right elbow like an attentive date. "We're off duty at a very nice dinner party partially in your honor. Try to remember that. Think of it as dining with the princes and princesses of our society."

"More like dining with wolves," Megan whispered, even as she turned a high-wattage smile on a passing couple.

A waiter offered them stuffed mushrooms. Megan politely declined, so Dan released her arm and speared two mushrooms on a toothpick. Nodding thanks to the man, he grabbed a napkin before the waiter could walk away to wave his tempting wares beneath other noses.

"Mmm. The mushrooms are delicious. You should try one next time." Dan tossed the toothpick into a strategically placed oversized silver goblet filled with used napkins and more discarded toothpicks. He wiped grease from his fingertips on the tiny napkin. "Perhaps a tad too much butter, but still very nice."

Ignoring him, Megan let her gaze wander the crowd. She spotted Mr. Sims, the bank's Financial Advisor, standing near the bar chatting with an attractive Asian woman wearing a simple black evening gown. Martin Cantrell was talking to a lovely blond woman about half his age who wore an amazing red dress. Megan had debated her mirror image over which evening gown to wear because she didn't want to overdress for the occasion, but she now saw she needn't have worried so much.

One could come out of here with self-esteem problems, Megan thought, continuing to people watch. She didn't recognize many faces, but eventually, she spied Lynn Berkley hiding in a corner with a preteen girl who looked bored out of her skull.

"Let's go talk to Ms. Berkley and her daughter," Megan said, snagging Dan's arm as he reached for something on a passing tray.

"But-but mini-quiche!" he protested.

"There will be more magical trays of food on the far side of the room," Megan assured him.

Taking pity on poor Dan, the waiter quickly wrapped a mini-quiche in a napkin and lobbed it underhanded.

"Thank you much, kind sir!" Dan said. He snatched the swaddled snack out of the air and saluted the waiter before dutifully following Megan as she weaved through the crowd.

The quiche was consumed by the time they got a quarter of the way across the room.

"You'd think you were starving or something," Megan commented, shaking her head at her partner.

"I skipped breakfast and lunch today."

Megan stopped short and whirled on Dan.

"You did what?"

"Hey, it's not every day a poor country boy gets invited to one of these fancy gatherings. I am honor bound to try everything here. That sort of obligation takes some preparation."

Suppressing the urge to roll her eyes, Megan shrugged.

"And here I thought only women got weird about food."

Dan was too busy stuffing a tiny eggroll into his mouth to reply.

"Would you like to try one, ma'am?" asked the young waitress. "They're vegetable eggrolls with a hint of duck sauce."

Megan considered politely declining again but figured Dan shouldn't be the only one trying the decadent goodies floating around them.

"I'd love to try one," she said.

The waitress expertly wrapped the end of an eggroll in a napkin and held it out for Megan.

"Enjoy."

Megan thanked the woman and sampled the eggroll as she herded her distractible partner along in the correct direction. It really was delicious. She had half a mind to abandon Dan in the middle of the food paradise, but she wanted his insights on the coming conversation with Lynn Berkley. Something about the woman intrigued her. The fact that she'd eventually divorced Martin Cantrell was a point in her favor. But what kind of woman married a man like that in the first place? Politicians and lawyers generally weren't Megan's favorite brand of people, but lawyers with political aspirations warranted a special level of wary contempt.

"Good evening, Ms. Berkley. It's so nice to see you again," Megan greeted, specifically choosing a bland opening. "How is your son?" Megan knew Kenny Cantrell had survived the wounds sustained during the robbery, but that was the last she'd heard of the young man.

Lynn smiled hesitantly and looked at Megan with eyes that searched for proper connections.

"Special Agent Megan Luchek, FBI. We met just before the … incident. This is my partner, Special Agent Daniel Cooper."

"It's nice to meet you again, Ms. Berkley," said Dan. He turned to the girl. "And you must be Katelyn. How are you this fine evening, Ms. Cantrell?"

"Fine," Katelyn mumbled.

"I see you have a soda there. Would you mind showing me where you got it? We can freshen that up for you. One could get lost around here." Dan held out his elbow for Katelyn to take. "With your mother's permission, of course." He looked at Ms. Berkley expectantly.

Katelyn and Megan glanced at Lynn to hear the verdict. The woman hesitated before nodding permission.

"Go ahead and walk him to the bar, honey. We'll be right here." Lynn watched Katelyn and Dan meander through the crowd. She waited until they were out of earshot before squaring her shoulders and answering Megan's earlier question. "Kenny's in a lot of trouble, but he's alive and that's what counts. Martin's seen to it that he has a good lawyer. I don't personally like George Fritz, but he's good at what he does."

Megan bobbed her head noncommittally. George Fritz, Esq. was well-loathed in law enforcement circles for constantly keeping the scum of the earth out of prison on technicalities and smooth talk. One of her colleagues had referred to the man as Santa's evil twin, proponent of the guys on the naughty list.

"He has a solid reputation," Megan said. She grabbed a champagne flute from a passing waitress and downed half the contents to keep from having to say anything else. She tapped her fingers absently on the glass, considering the wisdom of asking her next question. Deciding it was worth the risk of stirring up Lynn's emotions, Megan asked, "How is Katelyn handling everything?"

"She's being brave, but I don't think she understands what happened." Lynn followed Megan's lead and snapped up a champagne flute to worry between her hands. As she continued, her words got quicker and angrier. "I can't really explain it to her because I don't know enough. Martin's involved, but I don't know how. Did you know he had the nerve to ask me for a DNA sample from Katelyn?" She mumbled a curse, hiding behind the champagne. "Sorry, I didn't mean to unload that on you." Lynn pasted a strained smile on to her face.

"It's all right. What did he want her DNA for?" Megan prompted. She could guess, but she wanted it in Lynn's words. She quickly scanned the crowd to make sure Katelyn was still out of hearing range.

"Paternity test," Lynn said. Her grim expression spoke her regrets at having said anything.

"I'm sorry. That must be hard." Megan knew she needed to set the woman at ease if she wanted any more useful information. "Did you have her—" Megan stopped speaking abruptly when Lynn stiffened.

"Agent Luchek, I'm glad you could make it." The sound of Martin Cantrell's voice explained much.

Megan turned gracefully and finished the ritual exchange of pleasantries.

"Allow me to present my new assistant, Miss Ashley Reston. She's been heaven sent to help me through the last few weeks." Martin's hand rested on his assistant's shoulder as he spoke.

For her part, the tall blond kept a pleasant expression in place.

Megan stole a glance at Lynn for her reaction. The lady's gaze was decidedly frosty, but she kept her irritation aimed at Mr. Cantrell.

"Ashley, would you mind checking to see if the tables are ready for the guests?"

"Yes, Mr. Cantrell." The young woman ducked her head shyly and slipped away to do as bid.

Shifting position to get a better view, Megan eyed Ms. Berkley and Mr. Cantrell. Both were flushed and breathing heavily.

I wonder if I'll have to break up a fistfight.

Martin fired the first verbal shot.

"I see you have nothing against airing our business in public."

"Well, at least I—" With great effort, Lynn stopped what would have been a fine speech. "No. No. I won't do this with you now, Martin."

"Do what?"

"Fight."

Megan peered at Martin for his rebuttal, secretly hoping he would spark a fight. The further their tempers rose, the less guarded their words would become. He didn't disappoint.

"That's your problem, Lynn," Martin said. "You're never up for a good fight. That's why you never win them."

"Don't lecture me." Lynn's eyes narrowed.

"I wouldn't waste my breath, my dear. Now if you'll excuse me, I need to see if the mayor's comfortable." Martin retreated briskly, head held high.

Megan let out a slow breath she hadn't even realized she'd been holding.

"Is he always this ... confrontational?" she inquired.

"Sorry about that." Lynn stared into the space Martin had recently vacated.

"Don't apologize for his behavior," Megan said. "He seems to want a negative reaction from people."

"He wasn't always like that." The weary note sounded awfully close to defeat. "He was kinder once upon a time."

"What changed him?" Megan wondered.

"Politics. Power. I'm not sure." Lynn finished the champagne and relinquished the empty flute to an attentive waiter. "Probably something to do with his job."

It was a terribly slim lead, and Megan didn't have time to mull it over.

There is no case here. There is no case here.

For some reason, Megan's gut fought that statement. She really wanted Martin to be part of something underhanded so she could bust him. The scary part was she didn't know why the guy rubbed her the wrong way.

"Ladies and gentlemen, we hope you've enjoyed the cocktail hour. Please make your way into the main dining hall and find your nameplates. The waiters and waitresses should be able to help you. You're in for a true treat tonight. We have so many fine people to honor. Come in. Come in!"

Megan almost didn't recognize the cheerful, charming voice as belonging to Martin Cantrell.

Never trust somebody who can change their tune that quickly.

Despite misgivings, Megan allowed herself to be carried along in the current of people. She expected the speeches to be boring, but at least the food would be worth it.

Chapter 2:
Confirmation and Invitation

Tensions with Lynn aside, the dinner party was going exceedingly well. Martin had agreed to make a few announcements instead of delivering an actual speech. He didn't mind public speaking, but he had better things on his mind than stroking egos tonight. This afternoon, he'd received confirmation that Open Season would happen. As much as he didn't want to warn Max, he owed the boy that much. Besides, if he failed to warn him and somebody else did the honors, Max would be upset. The boy had already threatened Katelyn's life should anything happen to him. While Martin was reasonably certain the threat was a nasty bluff, life would be simpler if Max survived the Fixer battle royale to come. Martin's warning would already be on the late side since he wasn't part of the Shadow Council. All of their favorites would have been notified yesterday. Plans could already be in place.

Max will be fine.

"Excuse me, sir, but you wanted to be notified when Zachary Kerrigan called," Ashley said, appearing by Martin's left elbow. "I have him on hold here."

Thanking his assistant, Martin rose, made excuses, and retreated toward the hallway that led to the restrooms. Ashley followed in his wake until he took the phone. Then, she dropped back a few steps to give him some privacy.

"What do you have for me, Zach?" Martin asked, not knowing which way he wanted this to go. On the one hand, if Katelyn wasn't his daughter, he could cut Lynn off from the child support with a clear conscience. On the other hand, he was fond of the girl and would feel bad about leaving her care to Lynn's paltry paychecks. In truth, Lynn probably made decent money, but the mortgage on the house would swallow most of that.

"She's yours!" chirped the lab tech.

"You're sure?"

"Absolutely. I'm staring at the samples you sent me, and they line up beautifully. Would you like the technical details?" The young man sounded very eager to share his knowledge.

"No, thank you. As long as you're positive, send the results to my office. I'll release the final payment for the rush job as soon as it arrives."

He hung up before the lab rat could argue. Since Lynn was here at the party, he could pull her aside and have a serious conversation about Katelyn's future. Martin hadn't spoken with Max since they'd agreed to let things calm down, but the insurance policy had been renewed and things looked to be back on track. As he took out the burner phone and dialed Max's number, Martin saw Ashley standing calmly at the start of the hallway waiting to intercept people before they could interrupt him. He appreciated the view of her backside, but he also liked her initiative. It was a rare trait to find in help these days.

"Ashley, would you please fetch my ex-wife?" Martin didn't want to risk anybody overhearing what he said to Max. Plus, he wanted to speak with Lynn soon. He needed to get to know his daughter if she'd soon be living with him.

"Right away, sir," Ashley said, straightening and heading for the correct table.

Her brisk pace wouldn't give him much time, but he didn't anticipate a long talk with Max.

"What do you want?" Max demanded.

The unsteady tone put a jolt of anger through Martin.

"Are you drunk?"

"Maybe."

"Well put down the bottle and listen carefully," Martin hissed. "We're back on, but an Open Season's been called. That should keep you busy this week. I'll need the time to deal with some things on my end anyway. After that, I want the job completed as soon as possible. The cap's set at five. Keep your head low and let the higher ups bloody each other's noses." Martin hung up before Max could reply. He tucked the phone back in his pocket and checked the weather on his regular phone. The next three days should be nice.

Still on the cool side, but sunny.

Martin opened his calendar to check for a good day to spend with his daughter. The sound of clicking heels brought his head up from the schedule. His breath hitched. He hated to admit it, but Lynn still looked good despite being on the wrong side of forty. The navy blue evening dress had little more than two medium sized straps, a double band of blue satin across the stomach, and a slit down the left leg, but it complemented her complexion nicely. The only thing ruining the overall look was her grim expression.

"Explain why I abandoned our daughter at a table full of strangers to answer your summons," Lynn said.

"Because I just received confirmation that she is indeed *our* daughter," Martin replied.

"Congratulations."

Past the bravado and sarcasm, Martin sensed Lynn's unease. It brought a warm smile to his face. She didn't have the finances to fight him in the legal arena, so she'd have to hear him out. He felt like a spider with a juicy fly freshly caught in the web. Lynn's eyes asked what he wanted, but her lips were set in a tight line to keep them from trembling. He decided to let the moment stretch.

"I want to start seeing Katelyn on a regular basis," Martin announced at last. "Starting this week."

Lynn nodded, folded her arms, and leaned against the wall.

"Something can be arranged." Lynn uncrossed her arms and rubbed her temples as she thought. Letting her arms drop, she asked, "How about Saturday?"

"Tomorrow," Martin said impulsively. He needed to be in court in the morning, and Ashley would have to work a miracle to rearrange his afternoon meetings. But he needed Lynn to know that she couldn't refuse even the smallest detail.

"Tomorrow? But that's a Friday. She has school."

"So? She can play hooky for a day. It won't kill her to relax. You look like you could use some rest yourself." Martin studied her critically, taking in the dark circles under her eyes.

"Thanks, Martin. Just what every woman wants to hear." Lynn heaved a frustrated sigh. "Look, we just got back into a routine. I don't want Katelyn's life interrupted any more than it has to be."

"Do you want to call the school or shall I?" Martin asked, ignoring her last statement. It didn't deserve a response. "I have a court appearance at nine, but I should be free by 11:30. I can have a car pick her up and bring her to my office. See, she won't even miss the whole day. That should please you."

"None of this pleases me." Lynn pushed off the wall and leaned into his personal space. "You ignore her for years then suddenly have a deep-seated need to get to know her. That means you want something from her or me. What is it?"

"I don't know what you're going on about," Martin said, resisting the urge to step back. "But keep your voice down."

"Oh, for once in your life, Martin, be straight with me." Lynn's gaze bore into him. "Promise that your only motive is you want to be a good father."

"What's with the interrogation?"

A man hustled by them on the way to the restroom, looking like he'd rather be elsewhere.

"I don't want to see her hurt any further," Lynn insisted, after waiting for the door to shut behind the man.

"How could she possibly be hurt?"

Your days might be numbered, but I'll protect our daughter.

Lynn's headshake held both sadness and pity.

"You don't even know she goes to see a therapist every week, do you?"

"How should I know a thing like that?" Martin asked, despising the defensive tone. He compensated by firing two more questions. "What does she need a shrink for? How long has this been going on?"

Lynn sidestepped to let the man scoot past again.

"There was a bullying episode two years ago. That was the start of it, but I let her continue because she seemed happier under Dr. Lacey's care."

"Who is this guy?" demanded Martin. "I want to check his credentials."

"This 'guy' is a lady. Dr. Rita Lacey. And her licenses are in order. I got the recommendation from Aaron."

Martin bristled at the mention of the sleazy private investigator Lynn had set on him once.

"Are you still seeing—"

"I was never 'seeing' Aaron," Lynn said. "I hired him to tell me what you were up to during that month you barely came home."

"I had my reasons." Martin cursed his need to have this argument with her again. The month in question had been his initiation into the nameless organization run by the Shadow Council. He'd been forced to spend a lot of time in the company of Pamela. Aaron had taken a bunch of pictures of them together and let Lynn draw her own conclusions. Worse, Martin had to let the accusation stand or risk letting slip his new affiliations. The fact that he had slept with Pamela once or twice was irrelevant. If Lynn had trusted him way back then, none of this would have happened. He wouldn't need to be working so hard to kill her now.

"Yes, I saw some of them. Whatever happened to her?"

"Leave it," Martin growled. He felt the balance of power shift in Lynn's favor.

"You know what? I think I'll do that." Lynn's chin lifted ever so slightly. "I doubt you can answer the question, and I hold a small amount of respect for the man you once were, Martin." She shifted her jaw like it wanted to lock up on her. "Come back to the table and ask Katelyn if she wants to spend time with you tomorrow. I don't approve, but it's her choice. She'll probably say yes just to get out of school, but I won't order it."

Lynn spun away and marched back into the main dining room.

Martin didn't like not having the last word, but at least he would get to see Katelyn on his terms. He'd scored some early points in their verbal clash, but Lynn's closing remarks definitely scored a few hits as well.

Draw, Martin concluded. He followed his ex-wife through the tables until she stepped up behind Katelyn's chair. Leaning down, she whispered something in the girl's ear.

Katelyn whipped her head around and locked eyes with Martin. Her gaze was bold, questioning, and direct. She smiled tentatively, head still cocked as she listened to her mother.

"Hi, daddy," Katelyn greeted. "Mom says you want to ask me something."

Lynn straightened but kept her left hand protectively on the top of Katelyn's chair.

"How would you like to spend the afternoon with me tomorrow? I've been meaning to check out Oahu Sky Adventures. Would you like to go parasailing or take a helicopter ride?"

Katelyn's head swiveled to her mother. Martin couldn't see her pleading eyes, but he heard the excitement.

"Can I go, mom? Please!"

Lynn looked stricken, but she forced a smile.

"You'll have to make up any schoolwork you miss, but yes, you can go with your father."

"Yes!" Katelyn pumped her arms in triumph.

Martin's heart echoed the cry. He would win her over yet.

"Thanks, mom."

That statement stole some of Martin's joy, but he could forgive the child for the mistake. Tomorrow, he would show Katelyn exactly how much he could offer her. He might not even have to let Max kill Lynn. Stealing Katelyn's affections might be revenge enough. He didn't want to go through the hassle of changing the plans yet again, but it was worth some thought.

Chapter 3:
Back in Business

Megan Luchek woke up a few minutes before her alarm and stared up at the ceiling. Something was different about today, but the fog of sleep was taking its sweet time clearing from her head. She slowly stretched both arms out wide, enjoying the lack of pain. She didn't count the brief twinge in her left arm. It was barely noticeable compared to most days during the past three weeks. A few more cautious waves and stretches confirmed the healing progress. She wouldn't want anybody to slap her there for a while yet and arm wrestling was out of the question, but she should have general use of the limb back. Satisfied, Megan snuggled into her pillow just in time for her alarm to shatter the stillness. She flinched, making her arm hurt. She grunted and cast off the cozy covers.

"I'm up," she said to the alarm clock. Too bad the thing wasn't voice de-activated. Matching actions to words, Megan stumbled out of bed and crossed to her dresser where she'd placed the alarm after the last occasion of turning it off and falling asleep again. Her fingers swiftly found the off button.

Now that she was on her feet, she remembered what was different about today.

I am back in business.

Technically, she still had a meeting with Maddox wherein he would officially clear her for full duty, but she had been back in the office for over a week now. One could only spend so many days pushing papers around before even stakeouts started looking exciting.

As she shuffled to the bathroom to start the morning routine,

Megan wondered what sort of case Maddox would throw her way. Judging by the last few, there was absolutely no way to predict the case she would catch. The bank investigation was really Oldwick's case, but she would definitely remember it. Before that had been a straightforward embezzling case and before that a kidnapping case involving a baby and a messy divorce. Megan honestly didn't know what flavor case she wanted to try next. She hadn't had a murder for a while, but those could drag on depressingly long and sometimes go nowhere.

Once showered and dressed, Megan put on the bare essentials of makeup. Then, she raced to the kitchen to grab a piece of bread with strawberry jam. Normally, it would be toast with jam, but the early start had lulled her into taking a luxurious shower.

"And how's my little Handsome this morning?" Megan asked her betta fish. He'd passed the point where she expected to wake up to his tiny corpse floating at the top of the fishbowl. She put off her own breakfast thoughts long enough to toss him a few fish flakes. The fish sampled one, spit it out, and showed his disdain by swimming a few lazy laps around his bowl. "Still not a fan of the flakes, I take it. All right, Mr. Picky Eater. I'll try to get some gourmet fish pellets for you today, but no promises. If I can't make it to the pet store it'll be flakes again tonight, so deal."

He flapped his fins at her and turned away.

"Fine. Be that way. I was even considering buying some freeze dried bloodworms for you."

The fish turned back and practically pressed his face against the glass.

"Glad I have your attention. You be a good boy and maybe I'll even spring for some brine shrimp."

I'm talking to my fish like he understands me. Yikes.

The fish pellets Dan Cooper and family had given Megan with the fish would have lasted three of Handsome's lifetimes, but unfortunately, most of them had been dumped into the sink during a clumsier moment of her early recovery. The fish flakes she'd bought to replace the pellets were obviously not Handsome approved.

"Okay, then. Glad we had that talk. Be good. Don't talk to strangers. And stay in that bowl. I won't be here to put your floppy butt back in if you escape again."

I'm a terrible pet owner.

The disastrous scene of the dreaded first bowl cleaning popped into Megan's mind. Handsome had panicked and managed to wriggle out of the netting when she had laid it down on the counter. Luckily, the container of clean water she had set aside to refill the normal fishbowl stood ready. At first, she'd tried catching him with one hand, but it was like a bizarre game of whack-a-mole. She was afraid that she'd end up squishing Handsome against the counter. When he settled into feeble flopping, she had picked him up by the tail, dropped him into the fresh water, and given him a very long lecture on never doing that to her again.

After wrestling some jam onto a piece of wheat bread, Megan tossed the knife in the general direction of the sink and shoved half her breakfast into her mouth. She glanced at the clock and winced. Her choices were forego stopping for coffee or get to work late.

Crappy coffee vs wrath of Maddox.

She might have risked the wrath of Maddox if she hadn't outright begged for the clearance meeting to be today instead of next Tuesday.

"Maybe Dan will take pity on me," Megan mused.

She proceeded to arm herself with gun and cellphone before grabbing her keys and bolting down the stairs. She swallowed the rest of her breakfast as she speed-dialed Dan Cooper.

"Hi, Dan. It's me—"

"I have a large coffee waiting for you at your desk," Dan said by way of greeting.

"I love you. I love you. I love you."

"I get that a lot from you, usually after buying you coffee with gift cards that keep miraculously appearing on my desk."

"Thanks for being an early riser. I really appreciate it," Megan said. He was too much of a gentleman to ever ask for repayment on the many coffees he picked up for her, but at least he didn't fight her on the random gift cards.

"You're welcome. See you soon."

Megan signed off seconds before reaching her car. Bolstered by the knowledge that coffee awaited her at the office, she started the car with a sense of purpose.

Bring on the day.

Only two traffic laws were bent slightly as Megan made her way to the Prince Kuhio Federal Building. The security check dragged on long, but eventually, Megan made it to her cubicle and found the treasure. She took a delicate sip to make sure it was a decent temperature then gulped down a third of it, being careful not to spill any on her white blouse. She tried to avoid wearing white on the job, but working a desk for the past few days had made her complacent about such things.

"Easy there. You're likely to drown yourself that way," Dan said from the threshold.

"I have a whole minute until I'm expected in Maddox's office, and I intend to make the most of it," Megan declared. She spoke quickly, so she'd have more time to drink coffee.

"Far be it from me to stand between a lady and her morning coffee, but stop by later. Maddox kicked me the Ainahau Triangle shooting, so I want to hear your insights again."

Megan almost groaned at that announcement. She'd talked through every angle of that case with half a dozen agents she couldn't even remember. The case was like a hot potato nobody wanted. Nevertheless, she owed Dan for a lot more than keeping her supplied with coffee.

"Will do. I'll try to stop by after my meeting." Megan reluctantly set the large cup back on her desk and straightened her suit jacket. "Wish me luck."

"Good luck."

A brisk walk brought her to Special Agent in Charge Bryan Maddox's office. The administrative assistant had a phone pressed to her left ear but maintained enough awareness to wave Megan to a seat and hold up a finger. Megan nodded and followed the directive.

Less than five minutes later, Megan stood as the assistant waved to her.

"Mr. Maddox will see you now, Agent Luchek," she whispered, holding a hand over the phone receiver.

"Thank you, Ms. Walker."

A flurry of butterflies took flight within Megan's stomach as she approached her boss's door.

Moment of truth.

She knocked politely.

"Enter," called Maddox.

Megan wasn't sure what caused the nerves this morning. She had asked for this meeting. Drawing a bracing breath, she entered and paused until Maddox indicated she should be seated.

"So, you think you're ready for the field again," he said without preamble.

"Yes, sir," Megan answered crisply.

"Why?" The question exploded in the office like a firecracker. Maddox picked up the file in front of him and scanned a few lines. "The last time you were in the field you got shot in a crowded park and let your suspect get gunned down before your eyes." He pierced her with an intent look. "That's a rough patch for any agent. Like being kicked by a horse. Are you sure you're ready to ride again?"

Megan had expected some pointed questions, but she was hoping he'd be a little less confrontational. Her prepared speech refused to come out, so she spoke from her heart.

"Yes, sir. I am ready. This is the only job I've wanted for most of my life. My arm is almost a hundred percent, and I started my physical training again last week."

"Have you been to the range?"

"Not yet," Megan admitted. For an insane moment, she considered lying about that, but he could blow her bluff to smithereens with a simple phone call.

Maddox nodded and gazed steadily at her.

"All right. I believe you," he said, after a painfully long pause. "I'll put you back on full active duty as of this moment, but I'm not assigning you to a case until you get cleared by Agent Tayheur down at the range. Make an appointment as soon as possible."

"I'll do that, sir. Thank you." Megan sat straighter in the chair in anticipation of being dismissed.

Instead of letting her leave, Maddox looked at her sympathetically and spoke softly.

"Agent?"

"Sir?" Megan responded. She'd never seen such an odd expression on her boss's face before.

"I've been where you are right now. The range is going to hurt like the devil no matter how you try to compensate." Maddox rose to indicate that this was a closing speech. "Nobody will fault you if you need more time, but for what it's worth, welcome back to the field. As soon as I hear Tayheur's cleared you, I'll have a case waiting for you."

Megan thanked her boss one more time and left the office. Her head buzzed with the news of Maddox having been wounded. She rushed to ask Dan about it. Finding him tapping a pencil against his desk, she figured she wasn't interrupting anything too important.

"Do you know anything about Maddox getting shot in the arm?" Megan asked.

Used to her random questions, Dan picked up the conversation effortlessly. He lifted his left shoulder in a lazy shrug.

"Everybody knows that. It happened well before our time though. Nobody talks about it much."

"Why not?"

"Don't think they ever caught the guy who winged Maddox," Dan said. "It's kind of a sore subject with him, but it's so far in the past it doesn't affect much." He tapped his pencil on his desk a few more times. "I imagine this case could go that way, but before we talk about that, how did it go in there?"

"I'm good to go for taking cases, but he won't actually give me one until Agent Tayheur gives his blessing," Megan reported.

"Ah. I see. Do you think your arm's ready for the range?"

"It feels pretty good today, but Maddox said it's going to hurt like the devil. He's not exactly the type to exaggerate."

"Only one way to find out," Dan said. "Go ahead and make an appointment before you lose the nerve."

Finding no fault with the advice, Megan stepped over to her office and made an appointment at the gun range. She glanced down at her arm.

How much trouble are you going to give me over this?

Chapter 4:
Mental Games

Katelyn Cantrell could barely sit still in most of her morning classes. The early dismissal note burned in her pocket and looked ragged by the time she actually got to spring it on her history teacher. Mr. Taira looked relieved as he wrote out a pass to the main office.

As a relatively good student Katelyn rarely got sent to the office. She had wanted to come to school to take a science quiz so she wouldn't have to study over the weekend, but by the time her ride showed up, Washington Middle School felt like a prison.

She recognized the woman who had been following her father around during the party last night but didn't jump up to meet her. For some reason, the beautiful woman made her nervous. She was too cheerful.

"Hi. I'm Ashley Reston, Mr. Cantrell's personal assistant." The woman's voice was crisp and cool but pleasant enough. Her shoulder length blond hair curled over her right shoulder. "I'm here to pick up Katelyn Cantrell for her father. I have a note from him saying as much, and I was assured the girl's mother would call this morning to confirm it."

"Yes, Ms. Reston. Ms. Berkley called as you say. Katelyn's waiting right over there. I can release her into your care as soon as I see the note and proof of your identity."

The note was skimmed, and the woman's license was checked. The school's secretary returned both documents and waved Katelyn over.

116

"Have a good time, dear. Enjoy the sunshine."

"Yes, Mrs. Hayworth, I will," said Katelyn.

They walked to the car in mutual silence, but as they reached the shiny black Lexus, the woman stopped and turned to Katelyn, blocking the back door with her body.

"We haven't formally met, but I'm guessing you know my name from the introduction I gave the secretary back there. Just call me Ashley. If you need anything, don't hesitate to ask. Now, how would you like to be addressed?"

"Katelyn's fine."

"All righty then, Katelyn. Let's get you to your father." Ashley opened the car's back door and ushered Katelyn inside. "Careful, the leather seats are going to be hot at first until I get the AC cranking."

Katelyn started changing her opinion about Ashley. She couldn't help it. The woman's cheerfulness was genuine and infectious.

A few minutes later they were in front of the courthouse. Katelyn had been gearing up for another long wait, but instead, she saw that her father was waiting outside. She scooted over so he could climb into the back seat with her. A new sense of unease gripped Katelyn as she hugged her dad awkwardly.

"You ready to have some fun today, princess?"

"What's the plan?" Katelyn narrowly avoided rolling her eyes at being called *princess*. That had been cute and made her feel special when she was five. "Parasailing or helicopter ride?"

Her father gave her a sly smile.

"I never was very good at making such decisions." He leaned over conspiratorially and lowered his voice. "What would you say to doing both?"

"Let's do it!" Katelyn felt her heart soar. She'd always wanted to see what Oahu looked like from the sky. Parasailing looked like so much fun. Helicopters scared her, but she'd embrace the fear with the thrill.

"There's only one catch," her father said.

Katelyn's feelings took a sharp downward turn.

"Your mother expressed some concerns over parasailing, so I told her we'd go to the aquarium today then take a helicopter ride." He winked at her. "Can you keep a secret?"

She nodded but her stomach twisted.

He wants me to lie to her.

The thought didn't sit well with Katelyn.

"M-Maybe we should go to the aquarium then," said Katelyn.

"Is that what you want?"

Her father's gaze felt like a two-ton brick landing square on her head.

"No, but—"

"Then, we're going parasailing. That's all there is to it." Her father must have sensed her continued hesitation. "You can tell your mom what you like about the day. She can't take it back after it's done. You concentrate on having fun. Let me worry about your mother."

Less than an hour later, Katelyn was on a boat strapped to a man who wore an intimidating amount of gear.

This is a mistake. The thought was violently sucked out of her head along with her breath as the parasailing chute caught the wind and carried her skyward. She drew in a fresh batch of salty air and screamed. It started out as a frightened scream and changed mid-way through to one of delight.

Katelyn's head swiveled in every direction, trying to absorb the gorgeous sights. The turquoise waters of the Pacific Ocean stretched out beneath her, inviting her to dive into the cool, clear waves. The perfect, white beach sand promised warmth and rest. The people lounging on blankets and hiding under umbrellas looked like toys in a sandbox. Fluffy white clouds stretched to her right, hovering over the land beyond the Waikiki buildings.

She saw her father standing in the boat with his arms crossed, watching her. Katelyn waved before returning her attention to the freedom of flight. Her parents' problems and mental games couldn't touch her up here. The empty noise of the passing wind soothed her.

All too soon, the wonderful ride ended. Her father tried to turn down his ride, but Katelyn insisted he go through with it.

The helicopter tour was also nice, but the noise and constant vibrations made it less peaceful than the parasailing had been. Katelyn remembered being on a plane when they'd flown to the mainland to attend her great-grandmother's funeral, but this was different. The co-pilot who doubled as the tour guide, kept up a steady stream of comments on the sights they were seeing. A quarter into the ride, Katelyn tuned him out. She knew the local geography well enough to name most of the places, and she wanted to concentrate on enjoying the beauty.

Their helicopter ride finished as the sun set across the ocean. Her father wanted to rush off to their dinner reservation at Chart

House Waikiki, but Katelyn made him watch the end of the day with her. They stood side by side as the sun went down in a blaze of glory. Katelyn imagined that half the water was lit on fire. Around the brilliant yellow and oranges the clouds and water took on deep purple and blue colors that only made the light colors brighter.

"I love sunsets." Katelyn kept her voice soft because it seemed appropriate.

Her father looked up from his phone, hummed agreement, and dashed off a text message.

"Do you like sunsets?" Katelyn asked, suddenly finding the conversation difficult.

"They're nice."

Her father's matter-of-fact tone demoted sunsets to a mundane fact of life instead of the magical light shows that brought her joy.

Dinner chat stayed on the same surface-level for most of the evening. As soon as they ordered, her father sent her to the restroom to wash up. The nagging made her smile because it was exactly something her mom would do. Katelyn's father peppered her with questions about school and half-listened to her answers about teachers, classes, and friends. Truthfully, she didn't have many close friends, and she was okay with that.

"Why don't you have any friends?" her father asked, offended on her behalf.

Katelyn shrugged.

Why don't you get along with mom?

She barely kept that question in, wondering what had formed it in the first place. It had nothing to do with their discussion about her lack of friends.

"I have some friends," Katelyn said. "We're just not that close outside of school."

Her father made a disapproving noise but didn't comment.

The food arrived, so Katelyn concentrated on cutting her steak. The filet mignon was excellent, but she could barely eat half of it. She automatically compared the meal to last night's dinner. The sides here were very good, but she had enjoyed the variety of appetizers at the party. Still, if she had to pick a favorite dish, the current garlic mashed potatoes would probably win.

As the evening wore on, Katelyn picked at her food and thought about her mother. She didn't want to compare her parents, but she couldn't help it.

Mom would never take me to a place like this. After considering the thought, Katelyn revised it to: *Mom would take me to a place like this for a special occasion then worry for a few weeks afterward.*

"Is something wrong with your food?" her father demanded.

"No, but I'm full," Katelyn replied.

It had been a long day. The fresh air and sunshine had been wonderful but draining.

"Can we go home soon?" asked Katelyn.

"What's the matter? Don't you like the company, princess?" Her father smiled to indicate he was joking, but his voice had an edge to it.

Katelyn shook her head.

"It's not that at all. I enjoyed everything. Thank you … for everything. I'm just tired. That's all." Katelyn wondered why thinking was suddenly twenty times harder than normal.

"Drink some more water," her father suggested. "Maybe it'll wake you up." He put the cup to her lips and helped her drink some of the ice water.

It helped for a few seconds, but then, she felt even more tired.

"Let me get the check, and I'll take you home."

Katelyn didn't know if he said anything else because she slumped in the large booth and fell asleep.

***

Lynn Berkley's heart nearly stopped when she answered the doorbell and found her ex-husband cradling their daughter in his arms.

"What happened? Is she all right?" Lynn leaned heavily on the doorframe so she wouldn't knock them over if she fainted.

Martin unleashed a charming smile.

"She's asleep. Too much excitement and fine food for her own good." He shifted his grip on Katelyn. "May I come in?"

"Of course. Better put her up in her room." Lynn stepped back and held the door open for Martin. As soon as she shut the door, she led the way up the stairs to Katelyn's room. "Careful. The floor's a mess." She flipped the light switch on so they could at least see the hazards.

Martin carefully laid his burden on the cheerful, flower-filled quilt adorning the bed. He took a small step back and stepped on a shirt.

Lynn quickly removed Katelyn's shoes and tossed them into a corner. She next stripped off the girl's socks and considered how much effort it would be to wrestle her into a nightgown.

It would be easier to wake her.

As she reached over to shake Katelyn's shoulder, Martin's hand brushed her arm.

"Let her sleep," he said, quickly removing his hand. "She's had a long day."

"How was the aquarium?" Lynn tried not to think about the surprising longing that brief touch sparked.

"We didn't go to the aquarium." Martin's gaze was defiant. "She wanted to go parasailing, so I took her." He shrugged like the change in plan was no big deal.

Anger flared up in Lynn, but she forced herself to spend five seconds breathing deeply.

"This is why I can't trust you, Martin."

"You can't protect the girl from life forever."

Lynn knew this was destined to become an argument.

"Let's not do this here." Lynn marched out of Katelyn's room. "Come with me to the kitchen. We can discuss things there."

"You're overreacting, as usual," said Martin.

And you're not listening, as usual.

To keep from responding, Lynn clenched her teeth until her head hurt. Upon reaching the kitchen, she rummaged around the refrigerator until she found two bottles of water. She had some wine she could offer, but she wanted this conversation over ten minutes ago. Her mind cast about for words that would sink through the thick walls of Martin's skull. Plunking the water bottle down in the no man's land in the center of the kitchen table, she glanced up at the light fixture and remembered words could carry through it up to the second floor.

"Keep your voice down so the sound doesn't reach Katelyn," Lynn instructed. She sat down heavily and motioned for her ex-husband to take a seat on the far side.

"I don't think that will be a problem," Martin assured with a small, irritating smile. "You're going to have to get used to plans changing if this is going to work. Not everything in life can be planned out to the letter."

They'd started the verbal duel minutes ago and Lynn already felt like surrendering simply to get rid of him.

"It's not about the change so much as it's about the lies." Lynn opened her bottle of water but then left it untouched. If she held it in her hands now, she'd spill water all over the place when the flimsy bottle met her stressed grip. Her voice wavered with controlled anger. "You probably decided you were going parasailing hours before picking Katelyn up, probably even the minute I told you I didn't want her trying that yet. Why didn't you tell me?"

"I wanted to avoid an argument," Martin said. He waved as if her anger proved his point.

Clenching her fists and tapping them on the table, Lynn worked her jaw to keep from crying.

"I would have yelled. Sure. But then it would have been over. I couldn't really stop you anyway, could I?"

"No, you couldn't. And you can't." Martin took a long drink of the water.

"Please. Try to work with me." Lynn folded her hands and stared down at them. "Are you even capable of telling the whole truth and nothing but the truth?"

Martin's laugh was short, sharp, and unpleasant.

"This isn't a courtroom, my dear." He rose, finished the water in a few large gulps and smashed the bottle against the table until it was a small, twisted wreck of plastic. "This is the real world where money and power make the rules. Since I have way more of both than you, you're going to abide by my rules. In all fairness, let me be clear with you. I'm going to see my daughter whenever I want, and you're going to let that happen because if you fight me on this, I will take her."

Lynn didn't even watch him go, but as soon as the front door slammed, she let the tears come.

Chapter 5:
Fallen Fixer's Revenge

Cassandra Mirren checked two of the three bars she knew Max liked to hang out in and found him sitting in a lonely corner of The Hideaway Bar. She struck up a conversation but didn't learn much. Even with liquor-loosened lips, Max kept to a basic cover story. He wouldn't even admit to knowing Martin Cantrell. Cassandra hadn't expected him to give her a signed confession on every job he'd done for the man, but a few hints would have been nice. Though frustrated, she kept up her subtle interrogation until well after one in the morning.

When they finally parted ways, Cassandra decided to follow Max home. She liked to be thorough. Besides, knowing as many of his bolt holes and residences as possible would certainly help if she needed to flip him against Martin someday. That possibility was remote at best, but she counted most information as good knowledge.

As Max reached the building's main door, she made a mental note of the location and prepared to pull away. Her window was down to take advantage of the cool night air. She had always found sounds to be great clues about a neighborhood. The number of dogs barking and the level of nocturnal human activity could be very telling. Fortunately, this neighborhood was dead quiet.

The unmistakable muffled pop-hiss of a silenced gunshot hit her ears a split-second before Max arched his back and fell into the door.

Cassandra froze.

Every sense suddenly snapped to attention. Swift footfalls moved away from her down the street in the opposite direction from which her car faced. She could check on Max or chase the assassin. If Max was dead or dying, he could hardly tell her much, and she really wanted to meet this new player. She hadn't sensed anybody following her as she tailed Max. That was disturbing. He could just have easily snuck up on her and placed a bullet in her head.

Annoyed both at herself and the assassin, Cassandra put her car in drive, thankful she'd already killed the running lights for the quiet pursuit of Max. At least she'd thought to bring the untraceable car stolen several years ago. One never knew when a car's time would run out. She had a feeling tonight might be her last night in this car.

She worried that the assassin had a motorcycle waiting, but two blocks down he hopped into a beat-up old Chevrolet Malibu. A motorcycle would have made the chase much more interesting. Since it wasn't exactly a high-speed chase yet, Cassandra pulled her gun out of the glove compartment. It already had a suppressor attached because she preferred shooting with less recoil.

Before the assassin could get the car going faster than fifteen miles per hour, Cassandra hit the gas pedal and struck his car from behind. She'd considered pulling around in front, but he was armed. She wanted every advantage she could get if the move sparked a shootout.

Taking a calculated risk that he hadn't bothered with a seat belt, Cassandra swiftly exited her car, raced to the driver's door, and shot out the driver's window. Reaching in, she pressed the gun to the dazed man's head.

"Get out," she ordered.

His invective-laced response told her he was unlikely to cooperate, so she slugged him with the pistol. Her reluctance to knock him out was trumped by the fact that she really didn't want to conduct an interrogation in the middle of the street. Glad she had kept up with her workouts, Cassandra hauled the slender man out of the car and relieved him of his gun. Next, she checked his pulse, bought a few more minutes by clocking him again, and retrieved her car. Wrestling a hundred and eighty something pounds of unconscious man into the back seat of her car wasn't an enjoyable task but it needed doing. After he was bound in seat belts in the back, she took a moment to quickly search his car. Oddly, she felt better when the search revealed nothing. That was a point in the man's favor for professionalism.

A half-hour later, Cassandra pulled into an abandoned warehouse she'd recently added to her list of lairs. Deciding against a second round of back strain, Cassandra released the temporary seat belt bonds and did a more thorough job with duct tape. Then, she put on a ski mask, grabbed a high-powered flashlight, and woke the unfortunate assassin with a few light slaps.

"Who are you?" Cassandra asked her prisoner.

She kept him blinded by the light. He might have glimpsed her before, but she doubted he would remember much beyond the sight of her pistol near his left eye. She might get an order to kill him later, but if the judge wanted him to live, she wanted to be able to comply.

He answered with few mumbled curses.

"You're not very good at this," Cassandra noted sympathetically. "Here's how it works. I'm a professional. You're a professional. I have a few simple questions before I contact my superiors for an answer on what to do with you. I would like to put in a good word on your behalf."

The man didn't respond, but he stopped cursing and listened.

"Better, but not much of an improvement. Are you ready to answer some questions?"

The man clenched his eyes against the bright light and nodded miserably.

"Excellent. Let's start simple again: who are you? Trade name or real will suffice. If I think you're lying or you refuse to answer, I'll start shooting. There are a lot of places I can put a bullet that won't be fatal. Don't make me wait long for my answers. I'm not a patient person."

"Kyle Paterson."

"Do you know who you shot tonight?"

"Maxwell Nicholson. And before you ask, I don't know my client. It was a double-blind job set up by The Broker. If you think—"

"Hush. Wait here."

The mention of The Broker changed the dynamics. He—or she for that matter—occasionally arranged such jobs for Shadow Council members, but The Broker's sphere of influence mainly lay in the Wang family's business.

A moment later Cassandra had the judge on the line. He wasn't happy about the night call, but he forgave her once she explained the situation.

"What should I do with him?" she asked, uncertain of which way she wanted this to go. Dealing with a body would consume the last few hours of night. If she let him go, she might manage to catch some sleep before reporting for work later today. On the other hand, if he figured out her identity, she'd have to add him to the list of potential future problems.

"Dump him wherever you'd like, alive, preferably. I doubt he's attending to Council business, and it's probably not an Open Season hit. Maxwell wasn't high enough on the food chain to warrant it. If your prisoner is working for The Broker on behalf of the Nightmares or a different gang trying to get a foothold here, they can deal with him as they see fit."

"Very good, sir." Cassandra felt like a butler.

"Do it quickly too. You're needed at the hospital."

"For what, sir?"

"Maxwell survived. And he's preparing to spill his guts to an FBI agent. Finish him before he speaks."

"Won't that risk my cover as Martin's assistant?" Cassandra sadly bid the idea of sleep farewell.

"This is more important. Maxwell might only be able to implicate Martin, but it opens a can of worms we don't want opened."

Cassandra confirmed receipt of the new orders and shook off her fatigue. Long nights were a job hazard she'd embraced long ago.

***

Megan Luchek glared murderously at her phone as it sang out the cheerful notes of an incoming call. The clock read 2:38. Groaning at the injustice, Megan picked up her phone and checked the caller ID.

What does the Honolulu Police Department want at this unholy hour?

Sitting up, she cleared her throat and tried to think happy thoughts as she accepted the call.

"Agent Luchek speaking. How may I help you?"

"Hello, Agent Luchek. This is Detective Liam Callahan, HPD. We met a few weeks ago at the Queens Medical Center."

"Yes, of course. What can I do for you, detective?" Megan asked, hoping she sounded like she remembered him.

"I have a GSW victim here who won't speak to anybody but you. He won't even give me his name, just yours. Figured I should call you tonight. The bullet did a lot of damage, and I doubt he'll last long. I've taken the liberty of sending a police car for you. It should be there soon."

His words blasted the sleepiness out of Megan.

"I'll be there."

She hung up and hopped into the first presentable outfit she could pull from the closet. A blue suit and white blouse wasn't anything special, but it would suffice. Grabbing a brush, she beat out some of the tangles a few hours of sleep had put in her hair. Cellphone, gun, backup gun, purse, and keys rounded out the necessities of life.

Megan arrived outside her apartment as an officer climbed out of his unit to fetch her.

"I'm here," she called, sprinting to the car. She entered the cop car, aware the officer would have to let her out when they reached the hospital.

It crossed her mind that this could be an elaborate plot to kidnap her, but she chalked the paranoia up to sleep deprivation.

The ride to the Queens Medical Center went swiftly because most normal people were tucked into their beds. Contrary to paranoid fantasies, the young officer pulled right up to the front and promptly let Megan out of the car.

"Detective Callahan should—"

"Agent Luchek! This way. Hurry!"

Megan recognized the man waving to her as the older detective who'd questioned her after the Ainahau Triangle incident where she'd been shot. She stepped briskly in the direction indicated, slightly disappointed not to be met by the young, hot detective. She couldn't remember much about him besides those impressions.

"The doctor's about to strangle somebody. Stay out of her way if you can," warned Detective Callahan. He led the way toward the trauma and emergency services area of the hospital. "The man won't submit to surgery until he speaks with you."

Megan was about to ask which doctor when she saw Dr. Davy popping in and out of one doorway like a gofer. Spotting them, she charged their way. Megan had to concentrate on walking to keep her legs moving in the right direction.

"You have five minutes to talk to him before I have my people prep him for surgery." Dr. Davy spun on her heel and stalked off.

Megan glanced at the detective who shrugged.

"Clock's ticking, agent." He waved her ahead.

Squaring her shoulders, Megan stepped into the room and found herself staring at a stranger. That set her off balance a moment, but she didn't have much time to waste. Taking out her badge and a digital recorder, she held them up so the man could see both.

"I'm Special Agent Megan Luchek, FBI. You asked to see me. May I record the conversation?"

"Yes." The man's croaked response was barely audible. Blood-soaked bandages covered his chest.

Permission granted, Megan engaged the recorder and stowed her ID badge in her purse.

"We don't have much time, so tell me what you can. Start with who you are and why you asked to see me. Do I know you?"

"No."

The recorder had decent pickup, but Megan wanted to help it every way she could. She held the recorder as close to his lips as she dared.

"My name is Max Nicholson. I'm a Fixer." He paused like he expected her to ask about that. Or maybe he just needed to take a few labored breaths.

"Go on." Megan really wanted to know what a Fixer did, but that would have to wait. She guessed he had more important things to tell her than definitions.

"Fixers take care of rich people's problems." Max's dark eyes grew stony with pain and anger. His next words almost made Megan drop the recorder on him. "I was hired by Martin Cantrell to kill his wife."

"Why are you telling me this?" Megan whispered the question like speaking too loudly would break a spell.

"I'm dying." Max groaned weakly. "Taking ... him ... with me."

"I see. Do you have any proof?" Megan leaned even closer, eager for an answer. His recorded testimony would go far, but it was not binding evidence, especially if it could not be corroborated with sworn testimony.

Max nodded but his eyes grew unfocused.

"Storage locker. Kuhio Beach Park. Key ... in my truck."

"Okay, Max. I'll get them. Do I have your permission to enter your truck and storage locker?"

"Yes."

"Time's up, agent," barked Dr. Davy.

Megan moved to turn off the recorder but a sharp look from Max stopped her.

"Agent, if I die, save the girl."

"What girl?" Megan demanded.

Her question went unanswered. Max's energy was completely spent, and Dr. Davy looked ready to perform surgery or commit murder if she was delayed much longer.

"I'll be in the waiting room until I review my notes. I'll leave my cell number with the front desk. And here's my card." Megan placed her card on the end table next to Max's head. "Call me if anything changes."

She didn't want to say "if he dies" but she had a bad feeling about Max's chances of survival.

Chapter 6:
The Long Night

Before one of the nurses could kick Megan out of the room, she searched through Max's personal effects until she found his keys and his wallet. Taking out her phone, she snapped several pictures of the various cards in Max's wallet, especially his driver's license and truck registration. She wanted to leave the wallet in case the worst should happen, and the doctors needed to learn more about him.

Thoughts of sleep burned up in the mental activity sparked by the short conversation with Max. Questions about Fixers, assassins, and danger to a nameless girl danced around the delicious promise of evidence that would cast Martin Cantrell into the deepest prison pit she could find.

Should I call Dan or Maddox?

Dan Cooper would probably tell her to call Special Agent in Charge Maddox. Megan didn't want to do that because there was a fifty-fifty chance the boss would tell her to stand down. She had gotten in a nice round of shooting practice during the previous afternoon, but her appointment with Special Agent Tayheur wasn't until three thirty today. Technically, she shouldn't be investigating anything, but the case wouldn't exactly wait for her to get the official seal of approval.

Looks like I'm calling Dan anyway.

Getting a warrant to search the locker would be tricky. Judges were a tad grumpy at three in the morning. Megan could press the time-sensitive nature of the case, but the question about why she wanted to get into the locker would present a stumbling block. The justice system had made great strides toward gender equality in the recent decades, but sometimes, the upper echelons still functioned as a Good Old Boys' club. Her previous investigation of Martin Cantrell had not gone well, and opening a second case would make it look like she had a vendetta against the man. The testimony of a random gunshot wound victim was shaky ground during the best of circumstances.

As she stepped through the doorway, Megan nearly bumped into Detective Callahan.

"What did he say?" the detective demanded.

Megan sucked in a sharp breath. She'd forgotten about him. After a long hesitation, she primed the recorder and hit play.

I am in the market for help, and he's a cop. And he's my ride since I don't have my car.

Detective Callahan whistled low.

"What girl is he talking about?"

"I have no idea," Megan answered. "But we don't have to worry about that as long as he's alive. I need to get into that storage locker. Any ideas on getting a warrant at this hour?"

"Well, he did give you permission to check the truck and locker. That will go a long way." Despite the words, the detective's expression said he understood her pain. "Tell you what. It's still an HPD case. Let me handle the warrant thing while you find the key and locate the locker. Officer Natter can take you there or to your car, whichever you prefer. Go easy on him. He's new."

"It's as good a plan as any," Megan said, nodding agreement. "This is turning into an all hands on deck situation. I'll get things rolling from my end as well."

Callahan looked like he wanted to argue, but he simply summoned the same young officer who had driven her to the hospital.

"Take Agent Luchek wherever she instructs and provide her with backup until I can get there."

"Yes, sir." Officer Natter smiled at Megan. "Where to, ma'am?"

As much as she enjoyed being driven around, Megan liked controlling her fate more.

"Please take me back to my apartment, so I can pick up my car. Then, we're going to the victim's place to check his truck." Megan talked as she walked toward the exit. "Your car's this way, right?"

"That's correct, ma'am."

"Name's Megan." She absently corrected the young officer on

his form of address as she dialed her partner.

"Sure. I'm Andrew. You can call me that or Officer Natter."

Megan mumbled something she hoped would acknowledge without encouraging the young man to speak. She needed to call Dan. The line was picked up almost immediately. Unfortunately, the voice that answered was female.

"Do you know what time it is, Agent Luchek?" Bethany Cooper asked.

"I'm sorry about the hour," Megan said sincerely. She glanced at the dashboard clock in the police car, read the time, and winced. "I need to speak with Dan." She swallowed a *please* and *it's important* plea. No amount of niceties could make this better.

A disgruntled sniff answered her, but in short order, Dan took over the phone sounding way too chipper for 3:04 in the morning.

"Good morning. To what do I owe the pleasure of hearing your voice at this fine hour?"

Megan explained the situation as quickly and thoroughly as possible.

"I thought somebody ought to know in case this goes sideways," she finished.

"Call Maddox," Dan advised without any of the previous levity.

"I will later."

As soon as it's too late for him to stop me.

"I'm serious, Megan. This could blow up in your face big time."

"I know, but I have to do this. I told Max I would."

Dan growled at her stubbornness.

"Call me every half-hour or I take the whole story to Maddox." His tone said it was not an idle threat. "In the meantime, I'll coordinate with the detective on the warrant and try to contact the security people at the locker complex."

Thanking him profusely, Megan ended the call. She stared at the phone and thought about calling Maddox now but stuck with the notion of delaying that unpleasantness. He already knew she fought occasional loose-cannon tendencies. The sooner she saw what kind of evidence Max had for her, the sooner she could take down Martin Cantrell. There was also that disturbing business about a girl being in danger. Hopefully, the locker would hold answers to that mystery as well. She couldn't afford a bureaucratic delay of even a nanosecond.

Megan spent the remaining minutes of the ride finding the address on Max's truck registration, pulling up a GPS map on her phone, and studying the route. When they arrived at her apartment building, the young officer released her from the back seat. After an especially nice breath of fresh air, she thanked him and dashed to her car.

As she sped down the road, Megan belatedly hoped the young cop would inform nearby units to let her through.

Approaching the correct street, she started mashing the unlock button until she spotted the truck responding to the signal. Barely taking the time to put her car in park, she leapt out. Her paranoid mind flashed an image of the truck exploding as she ripped open the door, but that only made her hesitate half a second. What she found was much more mundane.

The truck cab was relatively clear of debris. One cup holder held an old soda cup from Kristen's Café. Megan scrambled into the driver's seat and started a systematic check of the usual places people would store keys. She found a key in the center console but checked the glove compartment and sun visor as well to be thorough. It was attached to a simple piece of string and bore only faded numbers. The first number was 2 and the second was 3 but the last number had been scratched off.

Key. Check. Now to find the right locker.

A wave of fatigue hit Megan as she slammed the truck door and returned to her car. She knew how to reach the Kuhio Surfboard Lockers on Kalakaua Ave, so she didn't need the GPS this time.

A security guard met Megan and Officer Natter and escorted them to the bank of lockers. He waved in the general direction as if to say good luck and walked away. Part of Megan wanted to call the man back and ask if he had a master key.

That would make this process go a little faster.

She frowned at the long rows of storage lockers.

"Where do you want to start?" asked Officer Natter.

"Locker 230," Megan replied. "I can't read the last number, but it has to be something that starts with two three."

Before trying the key in locker 230, Megan called her partner.

"Any word on the warrant?" she asked when he picked up.

"The judge wasn't happy, but he promised to get it within the hour."

"We don't have an hour," Megan said grimly.

"What's your hurry?" Dan wondered. "Max isn't going anywhere."

"This is much bigger than Max. I can feel it, and no, I can't back that feeling up with anything that would stand up in a court of law."

"Go back to your car and take a nap while the cop stands guard. I'll call you the second the warrant comes through."

"You don't know how tempting that is," Megan said.

"You're dead on your feet. I can hear it in your voice. You know I'm right," said Dan.

"You're right, but I'm still standing next to these lockers until you call me. Don't keep me waiting." She disconnected before he could protest further.

Long minutes slowly passed. Megan finally sat in a chair to rest with Officer Natter standing watch. Her phone startled her awake. She sat bolt upright.

"Dan?"

"Agent Luchek? This is Dr. Davy. Are you there?"

Megan knew the news wouldn't be good from the doctor's weary yet urgent tone.

"I'm here." The words came out hard as she braced for the only bad news the doctor would bother delivering.

"For legal reasons I cannot tell you much. I shouldn't even be calling you, but he kept whispering 'save her.' If that means anything to you, then use it."

"Thank you, Dr. Davy. I'll do what I can." Megan could do precious little while waiting for the warrant, but extenuating circumstances demanded she act soon.

If Max had died, the power of his testimony diminished greatly, making the locker evidence more crucial. But the longer she waited, the more danger somebody faced. If the locker held the slightest shred of hope for that person, she owed it to them to check as soon as possible.

"What is it?" asked the alert young officer.

Ignoring him, Megan held up a finger and placed yet another call to Dan. If she was going to throw her career on a sword here, she wanted to make sure she didn't take Dan with her.

"Still waiting," Dan said.

"Call Maddox and explain everything," Megan instructed. "Tell him you tried to stop me."

Her partner groaned.

"What am I trying to stop you from doing?"

"I'm pretty sure Max is dead. According to him, that puts some girl's life in danger. I'm opening the locker right now. I can't wait for a warrant."

"Megan, we don't even know if that guy was telling the truth," Dan reminded her. "Are you willing to bet your case against Cantrell and your career on some stranger's word?"

"Are you willing to bet some girl's life on the hope he was lying?"

His silence told her the words had struck home.

"I'm sorry, I—"

"No," Dan said hoarsely. "You're right, but I hope you're wrong. And I hate myself for it."

She knew exactly what he meant. Being right meant the danger to an unknown girl was real and opening the locker could lead to the clues that could save her. Being wrong meant needlessly endangering the evidence against Martin Cantrell. A mistake that large would have some serious fallout.

"Does this mean I have your blessing?" Megan asked, trying to infuse her voice with some mirth.

"Get the evidence and go to the office. I'll meet you there."

Once committed, Megan fell into an easy rhythm: lift lock, insert key, and move on to the next one. Officer Natter stayed out of the way, but she could feel his intent stare.

At locker 236 Megan felt the lock click. She lifted it clear and whipped the door open. A black backpack lay inside. A quick check confirmed that it held a set of papers with Max's face and the name of Brenton Little. A few thousand dollars in cash, a thin file, and a digital recorder completed the contents.

"I'll take those files, agent," Officer Natter said. "Nice and slow now."

Megan froze with her hands still deep in the guts of the backpack. She palmed the thin digital recorder and slipped it up her left sleeve. She didn't have to look to know Natter's service weapon was pointed at her back. Gripping the files, Megan slowly drew them out with her right hand and turned around.

"Mr. Cantrell sends his regards," said the officer.

Two muffled gunshots rang out.

Megan instinctively dropped to the ground and waited to feel the pain.

To her surprise, she found Natter's lifeless body inches from her face.

Chapter 7:
Damage Control

Cassandra Mirren dumped her trussed up prisoner in a random alley then headed toward the hospital. As she pulled into the lot, her direct line to the judge rang. She suspected that meant she was too late, but she knew better than to ignore the call.

"You're no longer needed at the hospital, but I do need you to do some damage control." The judge's voice was as deep and methodical as ever. "My source tells me that Maxwell may have left some evidence against Martin in a public locker near the beach. Go to the Kuhio storage lockers on Kalakaua Ave and wait. An FBI agent should be there eventually with a key. Let her get the files and then take them from her."

"Should I kill her?"

"Not unless you have to. They become a royal pain when one of their precious agents dies. There might be a police officer with her though. He's one of Martin's men, and he's expendable. I want that evidence brought to me."

"Shouldn't I destroy it?" Cassandra inquired.

"Martin is quickly becoming a liability, but he is an old friend. Seek him out and see if you can help him. His application to the Shadow Council is suspended for now. You can tell him that. There's too much intrigue surrounding him at the moment. When that's sorted, he can reapply."

"What should I do if I can't help him?"

"Protect the Council," the judge said without hesitation. *Kill Martin or kill his wife.*

Cassandra wanted time to give that some thought, but she didn't have much time. To the judge, the choice would be simple, remove the stumbling block from Martin's life. However, her primary objective must always be to protect the Council. In the long run, it might be more beneficial to remove Martin. Most of the Council members had learned to trust her judgment, but as a matter of self-preservation, she needed to make the decision the majority would support.

"As you wish. Are you certain you want the police officer killed? That may raise as many questions as the death of an FBI agent."

"It's the lesser of two evils. I want the police focused on their fallen brother and the FBI questioning their agent's actions. Divide and conquer."

Cassandra assured the judge she would do her job and made her way over to the storage lockers. She had time to think as she watched the agent pace in front of a particular bank of lockers. Martin Cantrell wasn't a very likable man, but he was powerful. If Cassandra decided to remove him, the kill would have to be squeaky clean. She had only briefly met Lynn Berkley. Aside from the dirty looks the woman cast her way, Cassandra sensed something likable about her. Personal preference supported killing Martin, not Lynn, but professional courtesy demanded she at least hear him out.

Gambling that the wait would be at least a few minutes longer, Cassandra placed a call to Martin Cantrell from her normal cellphone.

"Ashley? Why are you calling me at this hour?"

"Good morning, Mr. Cantrell. My name is Cassandra. The judge wanted me to convey a few messages to you and offer my services as a Fixer. Are you free to speak now?"

Martin sounded far more alert when he responded.

"Go on."

"Your application to the Shadow Council is suspended until this plays out," Cassandra said. "Maxwell Nicholson was killed this morning. I'm told he had some evidence against you, and I'm on the verge of recovering it now. If you have anything to add to that, let me know."

Martin was silent a few heartbeats.

"You probably have orders to keep the evidence to use against me, but I'll pay triple rate if you bring it to me."

"That's not possible," Cassandra said, surprised he'd even make such an offer.

"At least take a look at the evidence before you do anything with it. If it mentions my daughter, Katelyn, I want to know right away."

"Why would it mention your daughter?" Cassandra wasn't often surprised in these types of exchanges.

"Max feared I might have him killed. He said he had an insurance policy that boiled down to if he dies, Katelyn dies."

"I'll look into it." Cassandra paused because she was about to transition to a very important point. "What did you hire Max for?"

Martin didn't answer.

"I think I know, but if I'm to take over his contract, I need to know for sure," Cassandra continued.

"That doesn't matter right now. Find out about my daughter first. Once I know she's safe, we can talk about Max's original contract." Martin hung up before Cassandra could acknowledge the order.

He might have a few decent bones in him after all.

A flurry of movement pulled Cassandra's thoughts away from her evaluation of Martin Cantrell. The FBI agent had opened one locker and was leaning inside. Cassandra exited her car and jogged to a better position. Suddenly, the police officer pulled his gun out and leveled it at the agent.

Though surprised, Cassandra didn't hesitate. She shot the cop twice and sprinted toward the agent. As the woman came to her knees, reaching for a weapon, Cassandra brought her forearm down hard across the back of the agent's head. She'd come to with a headache in a few minutes.

The agent had dropped a file. Cassandra recovered the file and peeked into the locker to see if there was anything else of interest in there. Finding a backpack, she picked up the whole thing and took two steps back toward her car. That's when inspiration struck. She used her shirt to clean the prints off the gun she'd killed the cop with. Then, she pressed the gun into the agent's right hand. Cassandra didn't enjoy being weaponless, but she could make it to one of her stashes in ten minutes. The inconvenience would be well-worth it, if it kept the agent out of the way.

***

The sound of police sirens woke Special Agent Megan Luchek from the forced nap. Her fingers curled reflexively around the gun in her right hand and the digital recorder in her left hand. Funny, she didn't remember drawing her gun. She remembered reaching for the weapon but never making it. As more of her brain cells woke up, she realized her gun was still in its holster. She struggled to stand up and stared down at the gun in her hand.

Definitely not mine.

Her eyes flicked between the gun and the body now lying at her feet.

The police sirens shrieked even closer now.

Her mind raced. Getting caught holding the weapon that had likely killed a cop would wrap her in so much red tape she'd be lucky to get untangled by next month. She stuffed the recorder in a pocket and used her blouse to wipe down the handgun as well as she could before dropping it next to Natter's body. Then, she sprinted to her car. The police knew she was there and would want to question her, but they'd have to catch her first.

"Hey!" called the security guard. "Come back!" He probably would have said more but his next statement ended in a cry of alarm that hit some impressive high notes.

Must have seen the body. Probably his first.

Megan made it to her car and dove inside. She forced herself to take a few deep breaths before starting the car and pulling out. If she drove like a maniac, she'd have cops all over her in a hot second. Despite riding an adrenaline rush, she knew she'd crash soon enough. Then, she would need to take a dozen painkillers and get some sleep, but her apartment would be the first place officers would check. The sight of Max's keys lying on her passenger seat gave her a crazy idea.

This is a very bad idea.

Officers would eventually be sent to search Max's place, but Megan bet they wouldn't show up until a decent hour. If the guy was dead, they had no reason to rush. She could probably crash in his apartment for a few hours.

She remembered the way back to Max's apartment. As she pulled up, her heart sank. A cop car sat right out front.

How did they know?

A bored-looking officer stood near the front step. Dim light shone down from above the officer's head, revealing a dark red stain on the stoop.

"Max must have been shot here," Megan mused aloud. "That means the guard's watching the scene, not looking for me. I can work with that."

After considering several approaches, Megan settled on the most direct one. She didn't have to pretend to be weary, but she worked hard not to appear drunk. As the only person out here, she had the officer's full attention, but all he saw was a tired woman trudging up toward the building he was watching.

"Hi," Megan mumbled.

"Sorry, ma'am. This entrance is off limits. You'll have to use the back door. Manager said she unlocked it."

"Oh. What happened?"

"There's been a disturbance," the officer hedged.

"You don't have to tell me. It's probably none of my business anyway. Good night." Megan shrugged and veered off the path to circle the building.

"Good night, ma'am."

On the way to the back, Megan searched her phone images until she found the registration and prayed it listed an apartment number. She was in luck. Max lived in apartment 3C. The elevator and the stairwell were right next to each other. As much as Megan dreaded the thought of three flights of stairs, one glance at the elevator convinced her taking the stairs would be safer and swifter.

As she stumbled into the correct apartment, her phone buzzed in her pocket. Reaching for it reminded her she should listen to the digital recorder as well.

"Yes, Dan," Megan answered. She located the bathroom and started riffling through the medicine cabinet.

"Where are you?"

"Safe," Megan replied. Her voice slurred slightly with fatigue.

"Megan, I have a very angry HPD detective crying for your head on a platter. What happened?"

"I don't know," she admitted. "Hang on a second." Her hand closed on a container of Advil, so she put her phone down and turned on the sink. Megan wrestled the container open and shook three pills out into her palm. Then, she caught as much water as she could and used it to swallow the pills. Having cold water at her disposal, Megan cupped both hands, took a long drink, and splashed water on her face. Finding no hand towel, she wiped her face on her suit jacket sleeves and her hands on her pants. Finally, she picked up her phone. "Sorry, I needed to take something for the headache I got when somebody clocked me after they killed that cop."

"The security guard said he saw a woman running away. He

identified you as the one who'd come to open the locker."

"Unfortunate but inevitable," she answered.

"What did you find in the locker anyway?" Dan asked.

"A backpack with a file, some cash, a set of fake IDs, and a digital recorder. I took the folder but had it stolen from me, and I haven't had a chance to listen to the recorder yet. Let me put the phone on speaker and we'll hear what Max thought important enough to lock up."

Megan made her way to the living room and collapsed onto the couch. Once settled, she hit play. The recorder documented several intriguing monologues and conversations between Max and a man who sounded awfully like Martin Cantrell. The FBI tech people would need to confirm it to be sure, but Megan breathed a little easier knowing tonight's efforts were at least well-spent. The recorder hissed to empty air after several minutes of conversation.

"So, Max was the shooter. I guess that closes my Ainahau Triangle case," Dan commented. "Guard that recorder with your life. It might be the only thing that can save your career."

"Agreed. I need to sleep for—"

The recorder made a clicking noise like it had been turned off and on again. Max's voice filled the air.

"I don't trust Martin. He's the sort to kill his own mother if it suits him. He's getting cold feet and will likely cancel the job. And he knows I won't let him. If something happens to me, you know what to do. Brayden is receiving the same instructions, so try not to kill each other. Just get the girl."

Megan's tired brain locked on the truth even as Max's voice rattled off an address.

Martin. Girl. Katelyn!

"Dan—"

"I'm on the paperwork side. Get to that address. Do you have Lynn's number?"

"No."

"Forget it then. Go! I'll be there as soon as I can."

Chapter 8:
Guardian Angels

Cassandra's admiration for Max increased as she read through his notes. Trust was a rare commodity in her line of work. Most Fixers kept records of their contracts so they could hold the clients accountable, but she didn't often see such thorough work. The notes identified Brayden and Harker as the men who would receive instructions and payment to kill Katelyn Cantrell whenever word of Max's demise spread. They wouldn't have been her first choices, but they were honest enough to carry out an insurance job where many others would simply take the money and do nothing. The nature of an insurance job meant that the work was done after the client's death.

Since she was near one of her apartments, Cassandra ducked in, took a quick shower, changed clothes, rearmed, and ate a sandwich.

Do I have enough time to sleep?

Harker liked to work at night, but he probably didn't even know Max was dead yet. Brayden, ever the ambitious one, was probably stalking somebody for Open Season. The network would inform them both of Max's fate eventually, but such things took time. Still, there was a small chance they would be told tonight. To be safe, she should probably secure the girl as soon as possible, but the lack of rest ran the risk of making her sloppy.

Coming to a decision that satisfied both her caution and her exhaustion, Cassandra set her alarm for one hour, crawled onto her bed, and fell asleep instantly.

***

I probably look like walking death.

Megan Luchek ran her fingers through her long brown hair and vainly wished for a hair tie and a handful of bobby pins. She double and triple checked the address before ringing the doorbell and pounding on the front door as hard as she could. She repeated the bell and knocking cycle until a light clicked on and she heard stirring from within.

"Who is it?" asked a young, sleepy voice.

"Go back to bed, Katelyn. I'll handle this," said a woman.

A moment later, several locks disengaged, and the door opened cautiously.

"Yes?" Lynn's voice was hesitant this time.

Megan held her badge out so Lynn could clearly see it.

"I'm sorry to disturb you, Ms. Berkley. It's me. Megan Luchek. I work for the FBI, and I need to talk to you. May I come in?"

The door swung open wider. Megan stood still as Lynn Berkley's gaze took in the entirety of her disheveled appearance.

"You look like it's been a long night. Come on in. I'll start some coffee." Lynn stepped back and waved for Megan to enter. After shutting the door, she tightened the strings on her bathrobe and led the way to the kitchen. "Would you like something to eat?"

"Please." Megan was too tired to hide the traces of desperation.

"Hi, Agent Luchek. Are you okay?" Katelyn Cantrell stood in the threshold like she expected her mother would exile her upstairs soon.

"Katelyn, I told—"

"It's just Megan, Katelyn. I need to talk to your mom alone for a few minutes. Then, we'll call you, and I need to talk to you as well."

"Why can't I stay the whole time?" The girl's voice held a trace of a whine.

"Go," Lynn said firmly. She didn't even look up from her coffee preparations.

"But stay away from windows and don't turn on any lights," Megan added.

Katelyn half-smiled like she thought Megan was joking. She'd probably stop mid-way up the steps and eavesdrop, but Megan had other things to worry about, like making sense as she explained things.

Lynn's eyes widened but she refrained from interrogating Megan until Katelyn had retreated.

"Out with it," Lynn demanded. "What brings you here in the middle of the night?" She had the grace not to say: *looking like a refugee,* but her eyes held similar concerns. She plopped a packet of chocolate chip cookies and a bag of pretzels in the center of the kitchen table. "It's going to take a few minutes to prepare a proper breakfast, and you look half-starved so have some snacks. Is scrambled eggs and toast okay?"

"That sounds wonderful, thank you," Megan said. She plucked out a few pretzels and ate them as she continued organizing her thoughts. She wanted to be tactful and delicate, but she didn't have the time or energy for either consideration. "I have reason to believe somebody may try to kill your daughter soon."

"What? Why?" Lynn nearly dropped the egg she was about to crack open over a bowl. Without waiting for an answer, she put the eggs down, went over to the sink, and splashed water on her face. After patting her face with a towel, she took several deep breaths and resumed the food preparation. Lynn cracked three eggs and scrambled them. Next, she put two slices of white bread into the toaster oven.

Megan was always fascinated by how people reacted to news of danger. Lynn barely paused, but her grim expression said the news was echoing around in her skull.

The elephant is officially loose in the room.

Partly to distract the woman and partly to get her to focus, Megan asked, "Do you know a man named Maxwell Nicholson?"

"Sure. His family was close to Martin's family. I think he's Martin's godson or something." Lynn poured a large cup of coffee for Megan and put milk and sugar on the table for her to fix it the way she liked. Clearing her throat, she said, "Can we get back to the 'somebody might try to kill my daughter' thing?" Her tightly controlled voice reflected her tension.

"They're one and the same," Megan explained gently. "I believe Martin hired Max to do something, but then they had a falling out. And I believe as a result Max hired people to kill Katelyn to punish your husband."

"Ex-husband," Lynn corrected. "Very ex." She plated the eggs and served them to Megan.

The toaster oven dinged, and Lynn raced to rescue the bread before it burned. The toast soon joined the eggs on Megan's plate.

"How would that punish Martin? He's hardly seen Katelyn in the past three years." Lynn added butter, salt, pepper, and ketchup to the items on the table.

Megan used eating as an excuse to delay answering, but Lynn's sharp stare could only be ignored for so long.

"Lousy human being or not, Martin probably still cares for Katelyn," Megan said cautiously. "But I honestly can't answer questions about motivation. It's a long story, but the short version is that I found a recorder from Max explaining what he'd done."

"He really hired somebody to kill my baby?" Lynn lowered herself unsteadily onto a kitchen chair.

Ah, the news sinks past the iron emotional wall.

"Yes. Two people, in fact." Realizing that might not be comforting information, Megan took a quick sip of coffee to wash down bits of egg and toast. Clearing her throat, she hastened to explain further. "My partner's working on the paperwork to get you and Katelyn into protective custody as soon as possible. I'm going to stay with you until he gets here."

"You're like a guardian angel sent to protect us," Katelyn piped up from the doorway. "Can I see your gun?"

"Been called many things, but that's a new one," Megan said. "And no, you can't see my gun." She was glad the girl wasn't freaking out, but she also wasn't sure the danger was sinking in. She didn't feel very angelic either. If she'd had a sword, she'd find Martin Cantrell and smack him with the flat side for setting these events in motion. Megan didn't know exactly *how* he fit in, but she vowed to get answers today.

Looking like she was fighting tears, Lynn waved her daughter over. Katelyn flew across the room and wrapped Lynn in a fierce hug.

Megan took advantage of the moment to finish her breakfast. As she drained the last of the coffee, she felt her brain functioning at a slightly higher level than it had ten minutes ago.

"What can we do?" Lynn asked softly.

"Stay with me until my partner arrives," Megan answered. "Agent Cooper will take you to a safe house."

"You're sure this threat singles out Katelyn?" Lynn wondered, still holding her daughter tightly.

The girl's back was to Megan, but her ears were wide open.

I think your husband started this mess by hiring Max to kill you.

Megan gave Lynn a significant look that conveyed some of that message. She now had enough brain functionality to attempt delicate wording.

"There may be more to the story, but I'd rather not discuss it this second." Megan was pretty certain her hunch would pan out, but she didn't want to voice her suspicions in front of Katelyn. The accusation alone would be terrible for the girl to hear. Having it turn out to be true would be infinitely worse.

Lynn bobbed her head in understanding.

"How long will we need to wait?" she asked, running a hand down Katelyn's hair.

"An hour, maybe two," Megan guessed.

"Can I have something to eat?" Katelyn asked, pulling out of her mother's arms.

"If you can get it yourself," Lynn answered, attempting a smile. "Careful, the stove and egg pan are probably still hot. If you're doing scrambled eggs, throw an extra one in for me, please."

While Katelyn bustled about the kitchen preparing a new round of breakfast food, Megan allowed Lynn to pull her aside.

"Tell me the truth. What do you think Martin hired Max to do?" There was a steely glint in Lynn's blue eyes. She kept her voice low so as not to let Katelyn overhear.

"You know what I think," Megan replied.

"Would he really dare? I mean, I know we have our differences but—"

"It's just speculation at this point, but I want to arrange a long talk with him," said Megan.

"So do I," Lynn said darkly.

"Let us deal with him." Megan placed a calming hand on Lynn's arm. "I know it's going to be hard to wait, but please, stay with Katelyn. Let my partner take you both to a safe place."

Lynn grudgingly agreed to the arrangement.

The two women stood in silence until Katelyn announced the eggs were ready.

The girl stood by the counter, shoveling eggs into her mouth.

"Katelyn, sit at the table," Lynn instructed.

Shrugging, the girl obeyed.

"Help yourself to more coffee," Lynn said waving at the pot sitting on the counter. She dropped onto the same seat she had occupied before and started picking at the eggs Katelyn had prepared.

"Thanks." Megan retrieved her cup and moved toward the large, inviting pot.

She never made it.

The sound of breaking glass at the back of the house shocked her into action.

"Stay here!" she shouted to Katelyn and Lynn. Megan put the

mug on the counter, drew her gun, and cautiously stepped toward the noise.

Katelyn yelped and sprang toward Lynn who instinctively grabbed her arm and pulled her into a secluded corner of the kitchen.

Megan found a large rock in the middle of the family room. Even as she came to a stop, Megan sensed a trap. She spun and raced back to her charges.

"Do you have a room without windows?" she asked, directing the question to Lynn.

The woman stared at her with fear-glazed eyes but nodded.

"Bathroom," she mumbled.

"Go there and wait for me." Megan hauled first mother then daughter to a standing position.

Lynn grabbed Katelyn's arm and hustled her to the tiny bathroom next to the kitchen.

Megan considered turning off the kitchen lights, but she left them on to cut down on the angles the attacker would have to approach. A large bookcase stood to the left of the bathroom. Megan pressed her back against it, brought her gun up to a ready position, and shut her eyes briefly. The situation was far from ideal, but at least she probably wouldn't have to wait long for something to happen.

The sound of a single gunshot confused her.

Megan waited two excruciating minutes, but when she heard nothing more, she knew she had to investigate.

"I'll be right back. I need to check something."

"Don't leave us!" called Katelyn.

"Hurry," said Lynn.

It took Megan a few seconds to trip over the dead guy in the center of Lynn's family room. He'd been shot in the back of the head. The dark clothes and silenced gun lying next to him spoke of evil intentions.

I'm not the only guardian angel you have. Interesting.

Megan gripped her gun harder and returned to her post outside the bathroom.

"Hang tight. I'm going to call my partner and see if I can light a fire under him." Megan kept her voice steady, but inside, she was shaken. Fresh bodies weren't really a routine thing for her. The fact that somebody kept killing off bad guys was only marginally comforting.

Who are you? And what do you want with them?

Chapter 9:
Obtaining the Bait

After taking care of Brayden, Cassandra Mirren pondered her next move. She was glad she'd limited her nap to an hour. She had barely begun her vigil over Martin's wife and daughter when Brayden threw a rock through one of the back windows. The move was crude, but few lay people could resist investigating such an occurrence.

Through her night vision scope, Cassandra had watched Brayden slip into the family room and wait. She realized he too must have some sort of night vision because he didn't shoot the first figure to approach the room. As he crossed the room to begin a proper search, Cassandra took the shot. She would register it as an Open Season kill to avoid tipping off Harker or anybody else. If they knew she was hunting them because of taking Max's insurance contract, they would be much harder to deal with.

The FBI agent stood in the doorway between the kitchen and the family room. The shot would be easy to take, but Cassandra moved her finger off the trigger. The agent's presence actually solved a dilemma for Cassandra. The expression on the woman's face said any would-be assassin would have to go through her first. The added layer of protection would allow Cassandra to pursue Martin. She wasn't quite sure when she'd decided to kill him instead of solving his problem. It probably had something to do with him not trusting her enough to tell her about what he'd hired Max for. The answer was glaringly obvious, but he could have had the decency to share the information with her.

Showing up at Martin's house and killing him there would be

the simplest option, but the Council frowned upon hits in people's homes. The idea came from a bygone era when honor codes existed among the elite. They wouldn't hesitate to order you dead if you failed in some way, but you could at least be sure your home was a sanctuary.

If Cassandra tried to call Martin for a meeting, he'd see right through the ploy and stay holed up in his house.

I wonder if his ex-wife would help me.

Her brief interactions with Lynn Berkley told Cassandra she wouldn't help if she thought Martin might get hurt, but the lady didn't have to know everything. Questions were probably burning a hole in her. Getting her to want to meet Martin wouldn't be a problem. The trick would be to get her to arrange the meeting at a place where Cassandra could quietly handle the messy business without disturbing any neighbors.

Feeling like a morbid matchmaker, Cassandra retreated to her car to think. The timing would have to be perfect or the FBI agent would get in the way. If that happened, she'd just have to go, but professional pride dictated that Cassandra attempt to obey the order not to kill her.

If I had Martin's kid, he'd go anywhere I wanted.

Cassandra held the idea in her head for only a short time before discarding it for a number of reasons. One, she firmly believed if she couldn't do her job without stooping to that level she was in the wrong business. Two, Martin probably had enough contacts to know whether she was bluffing. He had asked her to retrieve Katelyn, but the kid was probably safest buried up to her ears in FBI agents. Three, Cassandra didn't want to traumatize the girl by killing another person in close proximity to her. Years of therapy awaited Katelyn already, she just didn't know it yet.

Sorry I can't move Brayden's body for you.

Dismissing the idea of using Katelyn to manipulate Martin brought Cassandra back to getting Lynn to help. To start, Cassandra put a tracking unit under the back bumper of Lynn's car. Next, she looked up the lady's cellphone number in Martin's contacts, which she could access from her phone.

Now, how should I approach Lynn Berkley?

It didn't take long to decide on a modified version of the truth.

***

Megan flinched when Lynn's cellphone rang from inside a brown purse that had been tossed onto one of the kitchen chairs.

149

The door cracked open, and Megan met Lynn's curious gaze.

"Should I answer that?" Lynn asked.

Megan couldn't see any harm in it, but even those few feet of empty space looked like a kill-zone.

"Let me get it for you," Megan said. Before she could think about it too much, she closed the bathroom door, dashed to the purse, and snatched up the whole bundle. She grunted at the sudden weight of it.

Is she carrying a cannon ball in there?

The phone stopped ringing for a few seconds then started up again.

After lugging the purse back to her post, Megan knocked gently.

The door opened and Lynn reached out with both arms to accept the purse.

"Thank you."

Nodding, Megan shut the door again. Part of her wanted to listen to the conversation to make sure Lynn didn't get into any trouble, but she respected the woman's privacy, what little of it there could be had in a 6 ft. x 6 ft. space one shared with a preteen.

Deciding she could risk dividing her attention, Megan called Dan.

"Is she safe?" Dan demanded.

"For now, but something's going on. I've got them holed up in the bathroom right beside me, but I don't think they're safe here."

"What makes you say that?"

"I think there's a dead guy in the family room," Megan answered.

"You think? Shouldn't it be obvious one way or the other?"

"I heard a gunshot and tripped on a body that looked like it had been shot in the head, but I didn't check for a pulse."

"Megan! Somebody could be bleeding to death while we speak. Don't you think you ought to check on that?"

"Fine. I'll check, but you need to get here and get these two away like an hour ago. If I'm right, I'm not the only one watching over them, and the other person has a very active trigger finger."

"You're not making much sense. Did you get any sleep?"

"No, but I'll be doing the Long Sleep if this maniac popping bad guys has a change of heart." Megan tried not to sound too annoyed, but lack of sleep wasn't helping her temper.

150

"Uh-huh," Dan said, clearly not understanding what Megan was trying to say.

"The cop—the one who tried to steal the files from me—he got shot tonight," Megan explained. "Somebody knocked me out and stole the files. If the notes held the same message as the recorder, that person would have the same information we do."

"But why would he help?"

"I don't know," Megan said, biting back a sarcastic response.

I'll ask him if I get the chance to chat with him at the next tea party, assuming he doesn't shoot me first.

"Just get here as soon as you can. Please." Megan dashed away some tears brought on by fatigue.

"I'll be there in ten minutes," Dan said. "But Maddox wants a word first."

Megan cringed, but before she could protest, her boss's voice boomed from the phone.

"Luchek! What the blazes is going on out there? I've got reports of a cop getting killed and one of *my* agents fleeing the scene! Cooper has been hounding people for protection papers. And I'm hearing rumors of big evidence against one of Honolulu's most prominent citizens! Have I missed anything?"

"No, sir. That about sums it up," said Megan.

"If you're wrong on this, I'm throwing you to HPD. They have a long list of questions for you. Meantime, see it through. Get the recorder into the hands of lab techs here then stand down."

"Yes, sir." Megan wanted to argue the *stand down* part. The longer they waited, the more time Martin would have to slip away. Fatigue made her bold. "I'd really like to start the warrant for Martin Cantrell's home and office."

"Don't push it, Luchek," growled Maddox. "Evidence, analysis, and then warrant. That's the order. When Cooper gets there, he'll take over the protection detail. That's when you make a beeline here."

Megan reluctantly agreed to the plan.

I hope the delay doesn't let Martin slither away.

***

When the purse landed in her outstretched hands, Lynn Berkley dove for the phone. She had to move the mini-iPad out of the way to get to her phone, so she plucked that out too and tossed it to Katelyn who was perched on the toilet. The girl beamed and fell on it like a starving man given a steak.

The caller ID said: UNKNOWN.

"Hello?" Lynn asked, breathless.

"Hello, Ms. Berkley. You know me as Ashley, but that's not my real name, nor am I going to give you that information." The female voice was brisk yet efficient. "Please listen to my proposal. It might be the best chance you and Katelyn have of surviving the day."

"What do you want?" Lynn turned her back to Katelyn so at least her expressions couldn't alarm her daughter.

"I need to meet with Martin in a neutral, remote location."

"Aren't you his assistant?" Lynn asked. "Why are you involving me?"

"He wants me to bring Katelyn to him," the lady explained. "Since I doubt that's in line with your wishes, I figured you could meet him and explain that she's safe with the agents. Your word will go a lot further than mine in that regard."

I wouldn't bet on that.

Lynn chuckled.

"Martin hasn't listened to me for a very long time. How do you even know we're in danger?"

"Did you hear a gunshot a few minutes ago?"

"Yes."

"That was me killing an assassin sent to your home. If you don't believe me, ask the agent with you to confirm it."

Lynn didn't know how to respond. Suddenly, the air seemed ten times thicker than before. Her breaths grew short and quick.

"Please don't faint, Ms. Berkley. Your family has attracted several unsavory characters. I am doing the best I can to protect you, but I need your help in getting Mr. Cantrell to do the right thing."

"Who are you?" Lynn whispered the question, leaning hard on the wall so she wouldn't fall over. She pictured the friendly blonde in her mind. The image didn't fit the voice coming through the phone.

"I'm here to help. That's all you need to know."

"Why are people after my daughter?" Lynn spoke the question as low as she could while still being heard. She didn't have the energy to face the wall again to hide the worry.

Katelyn looked up from the iPad. Her expression hungered to know more.

"Your ex-husband has some powerful enemies, but if he does his part right today, I think we can make this go away."

Lynn's heart latched onto the words and held them tight. She drew a deep breath.

"I'm on board. What should I do?"

"Leave your daughter with the FBI agent and get to your car. Then, call Mr. Cantrell and have him meet you at Tantalus Lookout. It should be quiet enough for our purposes."

What exactly are 'our' purposes?

"She's not going to like that," Lynn pointed out. She didn't have the courage to ask the other question.

"Who?"

"The agent."

"Agreed, but it has to be this way. If you leave, I can almost guarantee, she'll stay with your daughter."

"Almost?" Lynn's voice cracked with the strain.

"Relax, Ms. Berkley. The agent with you seems competent. Trust her to do the right thing."

The call disconnected.

Lynn blinked at her phone, willing it to re-establish the connection and force answers from the mysterious woman.

"Katelyn."

Her daughter looked at her expectantly, not even pretending to play anymore.

"No matter what happens. Stay with the agent. She'll protect you."

"Where are you going?" Katelyn asked.

"To end this." Lynn hoped it was the truth. She paused to splash some water on her face then picked up her purse and reached for the door handle.

Chapter 10:
Remote Rendezvous

Megan was tense. Her left arm ached from holding the gun two-handed. Any moment, she expected a boogeyman to leap out of the shadows and attack her. She did not expect movement to come from the direction of the bathroom.

The door opened and Lynn Berkley breezed out, power walking toward the front door.

"Wait!" Megan shouted. She took two steps toward Lynn before realizing the bathroom still held Katelyn. "Where are you going?"

"I need to leave. Stay with my daughter." Lynn tossed the statements over her shoulder as she reached the front door. In another moment, she was gone.

This is not happening!

Megan nearly pulled a leg muscle as she forced herself to not pursue Lynn. Whirling, she holstered her gun, charged into the bathroom, and knelt before Katelyn who was seated on the porcelain throne looking scared. Picking up the girl's hands, Megan squeezed them firmly.

"Do you know where your mother is going?"

"I-I wasn't supposed to be listening." Katelyn's warm brown eyes flickered with uncertainty.

"I know you want to be loyal to your mother, but this is important. Did you hear where she's going?" Megan gave Katelyn the hardest stare she could muster.

The girl broke the eye contact.

"She was talking to a lady who told her to meet my father at Tantalus Lookout." Katelyn looked stricken by the confession.

"Megan?" Dan Cooper's voice floated to her from near the front door.

"We're in here," Megan called.

A short time later, Dan arrived at the bathroom door flanked by two young agents.

"Was that Lynn Berkley who almost ran us over out there?" he demanded. "Why did you let her leave?"

"I didn't 'let' her leave," Megan said fiercely. Releasing the girl's hands, Megan gave the kid a tight smile and stood to face her partner. "She barreled past me, but I know where she's going thanks to Katelyn. I'm going after her."

"Maddox said to send you back to the office," Dan insisted.

"He didn't know Lynn would run off." Megan moved to squeeze past the agents crowding the doorway.

A pair of clammy hands stopped her.

"Mom said to stay with you." Katelyn's voice was small, but her grip was solid.

Megan figured talking the girl down would be easier than wrestling her arm free.

"Katelyn, you've already met Agent Dan. He'll take good care of you. With him are Special Agents Thomas and Zeller. They're not so bad either."

"Why can't I go with you?" Katelyn begged.

Megan stopped to think her answer through before speaking. Telling the girl her mom was insane and probably headed into a world of trouble would hardly help her mental state. She didn't want to tell her she'd only be in the way either.

As she turned to face Katelyn fully, the digital recorder in her pocket thumped against her side. Pulling the recorder out, Megan cradled it in her palms.

"This is a very important piece of evidence in my case. See, I'm giving it to Agent Dan for safe keeping, but I need you to go with him and make sure he gets it to the lab people at my office. Don't let him get sidetracked." Megan handed the recorder over to Dan who glared. Turning back to Katelyn, Megan said, "Excuse me. I need a word with Agent Dan."

She extricated her arm from Katelyn's grip and prodded Dan well into the kitchen.

"You want me to take her to the office? Are you out of your mind?" Dan hissed.

"Where else is she going to be safer?" Megan challenged. "The evidence needs to get to the techs pronto, and I can't take it there right now. You can move her to the safe house when the errand's done."

"What am I supposed to tell Maddox when he discovers you're not personally delivering the evidence?"

"Tell him I'm pursuing a lead and that I need backup," Megan suggested.

"At least take Thomas and Zeller with you," Dan said, sounding desperate to make Megan heed sense.

"You know they have to stay with Katelyn. Lynn's going to meet Martin at Tantalus Lookout. I'm headed there to make sure she doesn't get herself killed. That is the last place on earth Katelyn should be right now."

"Are you armed?" Dan's expression was still not pleased.

"Yes, sir. I have a gun and a backup piece strapped to my ankle."

"Are you okay to shoot?" Dan pressed. Some of the glare left in favor of concern.

"I'd like to avoid it, but I'm ready if necessary." Megan didn't want to spend the time soothing Dan's ruffled feathers, but she owed him that much.

After a few more cautions, Dan finally let Megan take up the pursuit.

***

On the way to Tantalus Lookout, Lynn Berkley called Martin and demanded he meet her there as soon as possible to discuss Katelyn. He tried to play the *I'm-a-very-busy-man* card, but the news that there might be a body in her house changed his mind. Next, she called the police, gave them her address, and informed the officer somebody might have gotten killed there. She didn't bother telling the officer her name, though he probably already had the information from caller ID. They would have a lot of questions for her later, but hopefully, she'd have some answers after speaking with Martin. As she reached her destination, Lynn began compiling a list of pointed questions to bring up with her ex-husband.

Since the weather was nice and clear, Lynn parked, got dressed in some old clothes she'd stuffed in her car, dealt with her bedhead, put on some makeup, and walked up to the lookout. She'd always loved the view from up here, but she rarely took the time to visit. For one thing, it had been a special place for her and Martin during their dating years. For another, life as a single mother did not afford one much leisure time.

Leaning on the railing, Lynn took in the majestic view. Somehow the distance turned the buildings of Honolulu into something beautiful and serene. The rich forest green colors of the plants in Manoa Valley further soothed her.

She recalled the first time they'd brought Kenny and Katelyn here. They'd had a lovely picnic in a secluded shady spot then watched the children roll around in the grass. She and Kenny had played tag since Katelyn was too small at the time. Martin had even joined in briefly.

The early morning sun felt good on her skin, yet enough of the night chill remained that she shivered. She had escaped the house in her bathrobe, but luckily, Lynn kept a bag in her car in hopes of one day making it to a gym. The clothes in the bag were wrinkled and far from stylish, but the T-shirt and shorts at least let her feel less self-conscious.

Facing the sun, Lynn closed her eyes and listened to the birds greeting the day. A breeze rustled her T-shirt and played with her hair. She'd left her purse in the car and didn't feel like returning to retrieve a hair tie. She kept her eyes closed until her ringing phone reminded her why she had come.

"I'm here at the lookout," she answered without looking at her phone. Only two, maybe three, people would be bothering to call her at this hour: the FBI agent, the mysterious woman, or Martin.

"Thank you for coming, Ms. Berkley," said the same female voice that had urged Lynn to set up this meeting. "Mr. Cantrell should be arriving shortly. You will then have a few minutes to get the answers you need from him. When I call again, please get in your car and go to the FBI. They will know where your daughter has been taken for safe keeping."

"What are you going to do to him?" Lynn's throat held no moisture.

"What he hired people to do to you," the woman answered.

"What are you talking about?"

"Please don't be naïve, Ms. Berkley. I have some very interesting notes in my possession. They speak of a deal between Maxwell Nicholson and Martin Cantrell. The bank robbery a few weeks ago was meant to set things in motion so Maxwell would have an opportunity to kill you."

"I don't believe you." Despite the protest, Lynn believed every word. She was just having a difficult time processing them. She knew Martin could be ruthless, but she couldn't picture him actually hiring a killer to come after her.

"Yes, you do," the woman argued. "I've given you no reason to doubt me and even told you some hard truths. I'm on your side. Please stand still and let Mr. Cantrell come to you."

"And if I don't?" Lynn asked, feeling lightheaded. She leaned heavily against the railing, scanning for locations that could hide the woman.

"Don't bother looking for me." The woman sounded almost bored. "The situation has the potential to end right here and now. If you warn Mr. Cantrell and he escapes, it could go on for weeks, months, or even years. Ask yourself if you want to do that to your daughter. Do you want her to be an orphan?"

"So much for being on my side," Lynn muttered. She was too tired and angry for the fear to truly grip her.

"Try to understand. You are a means to an end. Best case scenario: you let me do my job. Worst case scenario: you interfere, and I shoot you. You are not my target and killing you would be unfortunate. I would count it as a personal failing."

Well that's … something.

"I don't know if I can do this." The phone trembled in Lynn's hand.

"You're doing fine," the woman encouraged. "It's almost over. Here he comes. Stay as you are until he approaches and keep this call open so I can hear your conversation."

Lynn longed to end the call, but simply keeping the line open meant she didn't have the lady's voice in her ears.

What do I do?

Her mind raced. She could follow the instructions and say nothing, letting the woman kill her ex-husband. That would actually solve a lot of her headaches, but it would also be wrong. The option of warning him and likely dying for him wasn't a great alternative.

You or me, Martin. How did it come to this?

***

Megan Luchek feared she'd be too late, but as she reached Tantalus Lookout, she saw Lynn Berkley and Martin Cantrell standing by the far

158

railing having an intense discussion. She started jogging toward them, hoping her presence might help keep things civil.

Lynn's posture would have impressed military commanders. Her expression was fierce. Martin had his back to Megan, so she couldn't read his face.

"Do you even know who she is?" Lynn's question struck Megan as odd.

"I don't have time for your petty jealousies, Lynn." Martin threw up his hands to emphasize his disgust.

Megan unconsciously halted her approach to assess the situation.

Lynn looked stunned, then furious.

"You self-centered, self-righteous—" she cut herself off, clenched her jaw, and squeezed her eyes shut, probably counting to five to keep from ranting. She stared down intently at her phone and then stabbed it with a finger like she was ending a call. When she next looked at Martin, her gaze held both contempt and pity. "You have no idea she wants to kill you, do you?"

"Why would Ashley want to kill me? She's nobody. She answers my phone and sets up appointments."

"Martin, I don't even want to know what you did to make this mess." Lynn swallowed hard. Her eyes were glossy with tears. Her voice wavered. "But I want it to go away now. Whether you believe me or not, the woman you call Ashley is here, and she is more than ready to kill you. I don't even know if you'd make it if you ran, but you should try."

The note of defeat and surrender in Lynn's voice slapped Megan.

The air around the lookout crackled with danger.

Megan drew her gun and sprinted toward the trouble.

If I get shot protecting Martin Cantrell, I'm gonna be ticked. I don't even like the guy.

"Lynn drop!" Megan barked.

The lady followed the command.

A pair of silenced gunshots split the air.

Martin fell over.

Thus far, Megan and the assassin seemed to have similar goals, but that time was over.

Chapter 11:
Throwdown

Eyes shut, Lynn Berkley huddled against the railing, head tucked into her chest and arms wrapped around both knees. After ending the call with the assassin, she clutched the phone so hard her hand ached. Waiting to feel a bullet pierce her back put her lungs in a state that made breathing difficult.

The world was falling apart around her. Martin lay dead or dying. The assassin had promised to kill Lynn if she warned Martin, which she'd foolishly done. The FBI agent could get shot any second. Thinking of Agent Luchek snapped Lynn's eyes open. She locked eyes with the agent and shook her head frantically. She had to keep her away.

The agent halted momentarily but cocked her head in thought.

The phone in Lynn's hands rang. She stared at it listlessly. Lynn couldn't ignore the call, but she also couldn't bring herself to greet the woman who'd just shot her ex-husband. So, she simply accepted the call and cradled the phone to her right ear.

"Give the phone to the agent," said the lady.

"Why?"

"Because I want to speak with her." The assassin's voice was slow with strained patience. "You're not doing great with following instructions, and I'm still trying not to kill you. Now, give her the phone."

Lynn knew her life depended on following that instruction, but she couldn't remember how to stand. Fight or flight instincts had collided, leaving her physically and mentally exhausted. She managed to raise her eyes to meet the agent's again. She didn't know what kind of messages her eyes were conveying, but in another few seconds, she would lose what little composure she had left. Praying the case would earn its keep, Lynn flung her phone like a Frisbee toward Agent Luchek.

***

Megan was still trying to interpret Lynn's cryptic looks when the lady's phone hurtled her way. She instinctively caught the missile in both hands and tucked it in toward her stomach like a football receiver protecting a successful catch. Her hands stung. For a banker, Lynn had a decent throwing arm.

Miraculously, the phone line was still open. The urge to drop the phone and step on it battled common sense and curiosity.

"Agent Luchek, FBI. With whom am I speaking?" Megan asked, letting her training handle the introductions.

"You've met me as Mr. Cantrell's personal assistant. Call me Ashley."

"Right. Not your real name. Got it." Megan drew in a deep breath and released it slowly, trying to kick her brain into gear. She pulled up a mental image of the blonde she'd seen shadowing Cantrell at the party. Nothing about the woman stuck out. "I take it you're the one dropping bodies all over Honolulu last night and this morning. You gave me a headache too."

"I apologize for that, but the alternative was to kill you."

Megan grunted but silently agreed the alternative was worse.

"Why did you kill Mr. Cantrell?"

"No answers right now, agent. We have more urgent business. Your backup's probably well on the way, so you're going to help me escape."

"I'm going to what now?"

"You're going to help me get away," the woman repeated. "And I hope for your sake you're better at following instructions than Ms. Berkley."

Mention of Lynn made Megan check on the woman. She still sat huddled by the railing at the end of the lookout, rocking and appearing like she wanted off the ride now. She also appeared to be muttering, but Megan couldn't make out any words from this distance.

"What did you tell her to do?"

"Focus, agent. First, unload your gun and take off any holdout pieces you have on your person. Leave them on the walkway. Then, go

161

to Ms. Berkley and help her stand. I'll be there shortly to give you further instructions. Before you ask, refusal or disobedience will get her shot."

"Her? Not me?" Megan was genuinely surprised. "Not that I want it to be me, but what did she do to you to deserve that?"

"Ask stupid questions," the woman said flatly. "And not follow instructions."

"Points taken." Megan reluctantly followed the instructions and jogged over to Lynn Berkley. On the way, she switched the phone to her left hand, so she could use her stronger arm to haul Lynn up as necessary. She wanted to keep her backup pistol but decided not to risk it. The holes in Martin Cantrell were enough proof that the woman would carry out the threat. Megan cast her mind about for an escape plan. All the training classes in the world couldn't predict every situation. The FBI had tried valiantly to prepare her, but field work had a life of its own, complicated by a nasty sense of humor.

"I'll … think about it," Lynn whispered as Megan helped her to a standing position. Her gaze was fixed on Martin.

Megan was ready to believe sanity had fled Lynn until she heard labored breathing and saw Martin Cantrell's chest rise and fall. Leaning Lynn on the railing, Megan knelt beside Martin and checked his wounds. One bullet hole probably blasted through his sternum. The other was slightly lower and left of the center wound. As Megan reached to put pressure on the bullet wounds, a voice stopped her.

"Don't bother. He'll bleed out in another minute or two. Help's at least fifteen minutes away."

Megan could see that much was true, but she felt obligated to try to save the man anyway.

"Let me rephrase. Step away from him. Now." The speaker came up beside Lynn and pointed a gun at the woman. "Quickly, agent. If I hear sirens, she's dead, and you're my hostage."

If Megan was in Lynn's position, she might have had a chance of fighting the assassin for the gun. Since she was a few feet away and kneeling next to Martin, that option didn't exist.

"Let me take her place," Megan volunteered. Her training instructors had always accused her of being borderline reckless, but they admitted the unconventional approaches often resulted in favorable outcomes. She had zero hero aspirations here, but she needed to change the dynamic or Lynn would suffer Martin's fate. "Having a hostage that might faint any second won't do you any good."

"Not going to happen. Stand up and take a step away from Martin. Place your cellphone and car keys on the ground by your feet. Keep this phone with you. Are you carrying handcuffs?"

"No." Again, Megan obeyed, determined to be compliant until she could get the drop on this crazy lady. As she stooped to place her keys and cellphone on the ground, her eyes sought Lynn's.

The lady's panic level seemed to have dropped slightly.

"Then, we'll just have to use mine." The assassin tossed a pair of handcuffs at Megan's feet.

Of course, the assassin never leaves home without her handcuffs.

"Cuff your right wrist then sit down and stick your hands through the railing bars before closing the—"

With an ear-assaulting scream, Lynn leapt for the assassin's gun. The other woman pulled the weapon back and whipped it forward into the side of Lynn's head. The bank manager went down with a moan.

As the assassin shifted the gun to shoot Lynn, Megan entered the fight. She'd dropped Lynn's phone before scooping up the car keys and handcuffs. The keys she threw at the woman's face, causing enough distraction to allow Megan's fist to land on her target's left ear. In a second, Megan was up and over the railing. Her left arm protested the strain.

The assassin backpedaled to get enough space to raise the gun and fire.

Megan's dirty slide tackle swept the woman clear off her feet.

The gun flew away and landed somewhere in the grass. Megan would have preferred control over the weapon, but having it far away from the trigger-happy assassin was satisfying.

From there the fight proceeded like a barroom brawl, only the combatants had very sharp fingernails. The women traded a few punches before resorting to scratches. The assassin's right hand clamped around Megan's left forearm and drew blood. Fighting back the pain, Megan slapped one half of the handcuffs around the offender's right wrist and yanked upward. Using the momentum to swing her body under the assassin's right arm, Megan gripped the arm like an axe handle. Driving her shoulder up into the woman's armpit, Megan flipped the assassin onto her back, gave the arm a painful twist, turned the lady onto her stomach, and finally finished handcuffing her. A quick search of the prisoner resulted in a handcuff key, a switchblade, a miniature pair of binoculars, and two cellphones.

I need a backpack to carry all this stuff.

After relieving the prisoner of the tools of the trade, Megan used her remaining adrenaline rush to roll the cursing assassin over to the lookout and handcuff her bound arms to the railing.

"By the way, I lied about carrying cuffs," Megan confessed, leaning over her prisoner. She'd ache everywhere later, but for now, she felt really good about the fight.

"P-please move," said Lynn Berkley.

Megan's heart sank. She didn't need to look to tell that Lynn had recovered the gun.

Why am I always surrounded by crazy people with guns?

"Lynn—" Megan began.

"She killed Martin." Lynn's voice was distraught.

"Release me or—"

Megan drove her right knee into the assassin's face to shut her up. It was crude, but she only possessed the mental capacity to talk down one nutcase at a time. She'd also met her threat quota for the month.

"She's been captured, Lynn. I'll make sure she goes down for shooting Martin. Let me make some phone calls. Maybe we can still save him."

The gun in Lynn's hand changed course to point toward Martin.

"Whoa!" Megan sidestepped into the line of fire. "Listen to me, that woman bound to the railing may have just done the world a favor by putting a few bullets into your ex-husband, but if you pull that trigger, I'll have to arrest you. Don't make me do that." As she gave her reasonable speech, Megan took tiny steps toward Lynn.

When she was in range, Megan snatched the gun away from Lynn who merely hung her head and let tears fall.

"It's all right. Sit down and have a good cry," said Megan. "Just stay away from the prisoner."

Megan wasted no time recovering her gun and the two cellphones from the middle of the walkway. As she bent down to pick them up, she saw a young family striding with purpose toward the lookout.

"Sorry folks, you'll have to come back later. There's been an incident."

"What kind of incident?" The question came from the mother

pushing a stroller holding a slumbering toddler.

"Look, daddy. That man's sleeping." A child of about four-years pointed to Martin's body.

The parents exchanged dazed looks.

"He's not sleeping, and you should go." Megan gave them a small smile and gently crowded their space until they retreated. "Come back in a few days. The view will be much better."

After sending the family packing, Megan checked Martin's vital signs and called Dan.

"What's wrong now?" he grumbled.

"Actually, I think things are starting to work out."

"Is that so?"

"Martin Cantrell's dead. I didn't shoot him, and I kept Lynn from doing the deed too. The lady who did the shooting is taking a nap tied to a railing and missing out on a spectacular view." Megan went on to describe the recent events. She ended by saying, "There's just one small problem."

"What's that?" Dan asked cautiously.

"I threw my keys at the assailant before we had our little throwdown. They're somewhere up here on Tantalus Lookout. You'll have to help me find them."

"I think I can handle that." Dan sounded relieved.

"Anything exciting happen on your end?"

"We arrested a man trying to access the locker you emptied earlier," Dan reported. "I think he's the second hitman hired to kill Katelyn Cantrell. We're still waiting for an ID on the body in Lynn's house. You're keeping forensics busy today."

"This is hardly my fault," Megan protested.

"Maddox is setting up an inquisition, so be prepared," said Dan.

"Thanks for the warning." Megan truly appreciated how often Dan stuck his neck out for her. "What's your ETA?"

"Five minutes. Try not to have any more crises without me."

"No promises."

Chapter 12:
Tough Choices

Lynn Berkley wanted to restart the day. She finished crying and used the gym T-shirt to wipe her face. Then, like a recurring nightmare a cold female voice spoke to her.

"Step this way, Ms. Berkley."

Lynn's mind fired off a dozen denials. The woman had been unconscious and handcuffed to the green railing less than a minute ago. The glint of discarded cuffs showed she hadn't dreamed up that part. Yet, now the woman stood in the far right corner. A small gun pointed toward Lynn but the lady diverted some of her attention to watching Agent Luchek. Wearily, Lynn stood up, almost wishing for a swift end to this terror.

"Drop the gun!" The order came from Agent Luchek to the assassin.

"I have two bullets, and she's not that far away. You fire, she's dead." The woman's voice was casual. "You have a choice, agent. Pursue me, or save her."

With that, the woman fired.

***

Megan watched Lynn collapse.

"One bullet left, agent," said the assassin. Her gun now pointed at Megan. "We can trade shots or you can stop her from bleeding out, and I disappear."

Katelyn's face came to mind.

It wasn't much of a choice, and it could potentially be fatal if the assassin was a good shot and inclined to kill her. On the other

166

hand, her boss would have her head if she let somebody that dangerous walk off.

"All right." Using the Simon-says principle, Megan slowly pointed her gun up.

When the assassin relaxed for a fraction of a second, Megan fired.

By some miracle, the bullet caught the other gun and sent it flying out of the assassin's hands. Megan had been aiming center mass, but her shaky left arm wasn't as supportive as usual.

The woman fled, bringing Megan back to the same tough decision. She could chase the woman on foot or check Lynn.

Shoving her gun back into its holster, Megan sprinted to the railing and vaulted it for the second time that morning.

The bullet had caught Lynn in the left shoulder. The placement was such that it shouldn't be fatal, but it certainly needed treatment.

Megan scanned the area for the assassin, but she was already gone.

Great, I'm not going to sleep for a month.

A quick check showed no exit wound. Lynn moaned when Megan placed her hands over the bullet wound. Each frantic heartbeat pumped blood toward the wound. Megan needed to calm her down. Sitting on the ground with her legs crossed, Megan pulled Lynn half onto her lap, keeping the wounded side elevated. Each move earned a fresh round of small cries. Tucking her right arm under Lynn's neck, Megan embraced the victim. She covered the wound with her right hand and used her left to hold the right in position. From afar, it might look like she was trying to strangle Lynn.

"I know you're scared, but try to relax," Megan instructed. "The faster your heart beats, the more blood you'll lose. Katelyn needs you. My partner said they made a second arrest, so she should be safe. Keep thinking about that."

"It hurts," Lynn said.

Probably an understatement.

"I know. Don't think about it. Concentrate on breathing."

Lynn followed the instruction for a short time, before asking, "What should I do?"

"Try to distract yourself," Megan replied.

"I mean about Martin. He … wants me to keep his secret … from the children."

"What secret?"

"His ... part in all of this."

"What exactly was his part?" Megan felt bad about questioning a woman with a bullet hole in her shoulder, but if it distracted her, perhaps it was a kindness.

"He tried to kill me. He doesn't ... want them to know."

Megan had to bite her bottom lip to keep from saying Martin's wishes no longer mattered.

"That's not easy, but you don't have to make a decision right now." Megan wished she had something profound to offer the woman.

"Yes, I do. I could die here."

"I know it feels like that, but it's not a fatal wound."

Lynn moaned again.

"Would you kill me if I asked you to? Maybe it'll stop hurting."

Megan chuckled.

"Shhhh. Don't talk like that."

"I'm rich, you know," Lynn said listlessly. "That's a ... sweet revenge by itself."

Megan considered checking the woman for a fever. She was starting to sound delirious.

"Really. Martin explained before he died."

"What?"

"He wanted to kill me ... and get richer. To safely renew the insurance policy on me he ... kept up payments on a plan for himself. He also ... made me a beneficiary with the children."

"Wow. Congratulations." Megan was happy for Lynn. She deserved to have something go right after a morning like the one they'd just shared.

"Know any good lawyers? I'm going to need one."

"None come to mind, but I'm sure one of Martin's friends will help you."

The blessed sound of car doors slamming and footsteps running reached Megan. Several voices called her name.

"Over here!" she shouted. "Past the end of the lookout."

And the body.

She kept that part in out of deference to Lynn. It couldn't be easy to have the man you'd loved once upon a time gunned down a few feet away.

Three agents, including Dan Cooper, reached the body and the railing.

"Call an ambulance," Megan said. "And get an APB out on

Martin's assistant, Ashley something or other. That's not her real name but it should give us a starting point."

Dan pocketed his phone.

"An ambulance was already on the way to pick up the body. I told them to step on it. Maybe I should call a chopper."

Megan shrugged. Now that help had arrived, she wanted to quit thinking.

"I'm on it, sir," said Agent Thomas.

"What's he doing here?" Megan blurted. "Where's Katelyn?"

"Maddox has her locked down tight at the office," Dan assured her with a calming gesture. "Last I saw, she had four agents asking if she wanted something from the vending machine. Agent Zeller's practically handcuffed to the kid."

"Can I see her?" Lynn asked.

"You're going to the hospital." Megan had almost forgotten about Lynn. "But we'll bring her by as soon as we clear it with the doctors."

"Don't worry, ma'am. She's got plenty of company for the day," Dan said.

"Call my mother," Lynn suggested. She sounded sleepy.

"We'll do that," Megan promised. She felt the woman's body relax. "Lynn, keep talking to me. I know I told you to relax, but you have to stay awake too."

"Why?" Lynn's voice slipped into a dreamy tone.

"Because it's good for you, and you'll want to see the helicopter coming for you." Megan knew her logic was weak. "Think happy thoughts."

"Can't. She escaped." Lynn's head rested more heavily on Megan's arm.

Won't be forgetting that anytime soon.

"I don't think she wants you dead," Megan said, knowing that was small comfort compared to the current pain.

"Will she go after Katelyn?" Lynn wondered.

"There's no way to tell for sure, but I don't think so. Most of her actions today seemed about protecting you and Katelyn." Megan shot her partner a *say-something-reassuring* look.

"We'll find her," Dan said.

The answer seemed to satisfy Lynn, which was good enough for Megan, but she knew the part that Dan didn't voice. It could take months or years before the FBI caught up with the assassin.

The distant, droning thump of an approaching helicopter made Megan's heart leap with joy and relief.

The next few minutes were controlled chaos as the medivac crew strapped Lynn to a stretcher and loaded her into the helicopter. One of the rescue workers did a quick check of Megan. Upon finding nothing wrong besides a few scratches, he handed her several sanitary wipes and a white towel to clean up with.

Although she would have preferred to nap right there on the lookout, Megan allowed Dan to herd her to his truck. Agent Thomas had instructions to find her keys and drive her Honda Accord back to the office.

Megan caught a brief catnap on the way, but it wasn't nearly enough to prepare her for the rest of the day.

Dan dutifully escorted her in a back entrance so she wouldn't scare anybody in the lobby. Then, he led her to a restroom where a young agent met them with her go-bag. Once she had changed into suitable clothes, Dan abandoned her in Maddox's office where the boss grilled her on recent events.

"What am I going to do with you, Luchek?" Maddox asked, after getting most of his specific questions and rants out of the way. "This makes two incidents in less than two months. Why does trouble seem to find you?"

"I don't know, sir. I guess I'm just lucky like that," Megan said, aiming for a contrite tone. She glanced down at the deep fingernail marks marring her left arm.

Maddox made a noise that combined snort, grunt, and growl.

"You are lucky," he muttered.

"Sir?"

"Dr. Davy called on behalf of Lynn Berkley before you stepped into my office. She said the woman raised a fuss until she got assurance you'd be all right." Maddox hated politics messing with how he ran his office, but this time, he looked amused.

Megan gave him a puzzled look.

Me? She's the one who got shot this time.

"I'm not happy that this Ashley woman escaped, but I'm not inclined to damage your career over it either. Get some rest then eat. You're scheduled to take Katelyn Cantrell to her mother later this afternoon."

Thus dismissed, Megan thanked Maddox, rose, and left his office. The rest and eating part of the plan were wonderful. She found an abandoned break room with a quiet couch to have a proper nap on then ate a deli sandwich Dan had ordered for her. Finally, she tracked down Agent Zeller to take Katelyn off his hands.

"Are you ready to visit your mother in the hospital?" asked Megan.

"How'd she get hurt?" Katelyn asked, instead of answering the question.

"It's a long story, and I'm going to wait and see how much of it she wants told right now."

"I already know my father's dead," Katelyn said quietly. She tried to maintain a brave face, but tears pooled in her eyes. "I overheard the agents talking about it."

Megan glared at Zeller who reddened.

"Sorry, ma'am," he murmured.

"I'm sorry you had to hear the news that way," said Megan to Katelyn. She gave Zeller a brief nod to acknowledge his apology then returned her attention to the girl. She didn't want to see the kid cry, but she feared offering sympathy would open the floodgates further. "Do you want to talk about it?"

Katelyn shook her head fiercely.

"Luchek! A word," Maddox called.

Megan excused herself and jogged to her boss's office.

"Change of plan," said her boss. "The doctor says you can't see Ms. Berkley until tomorrow morning."

"What's wrong?" Megan asked, alarmed.

"She didn't say, but she mentioned the surgery went fine," Maddox said. "Go home. Take the rest of the day off to make up for the early hours."

"Shouldn't I stay with Katelyn, sir?" Megan cast a glance back at the girl who was watching her closely.

Maddox raised an eyebrow at her like she was missing a point. The ghost of a smile crossed his face.

"Take the girl with you, Luchek. The mother gave verbal permission for the arrangement. Take her to the hospital tomorrow at ten." Maddox didn't wait for a reply before ducking back into his office.

What do I do with her between now and then?

Before Megan's mind could work itself into a panicked state, Dan appeared at her side.

"You look like you're facing a firing squad. What'd he say?"

171

When Megan explained, her partner burst into laughter.

"What's so funny?" Megan narrowed her eyes at Dan.

"You're more comfortable chasing assassins than taking care of a girl."

"What do I do with her?" Megan made sure her back was to Katelyn, so the kid couldn't read her lips.

"Feed and water regularly," Dan replied. "It's only slightly more complicated than taking care of a fish."

Megan's hand flew to her forehead at the mention of fish.

"I've got to get to a pet store. I knew I forgot something the other day."

"Like what?"

"Fish food," Megan answered. "Handsome's decided he doesn't like fish flakes, so I'm going to try pellets again." Well, she did have the rest of the day off. Patting her pockets to make sure she had her car keys, Megan stepped toward her office to collect her purse, which Agent Thomas had kindly dropped off.

Dan cleared his throat until he had Megan's attention. Without a word, he pointed at Katelyn.

"Oh, right. Thanks." Megan beckoned Katelyn over.

Only slightly harder than taking care of a fish ... nothing to fear.

Epilogue:
Fixer's Reflection

Cassandra Mirren studied her new look. She had enjoyed being a blond, but the FBI had effectively ruined that look for the foreseeable future. Her whole head felt strangely lighter without the few inches of hair she'd removed. Dark brown suited her. She would need to lay low for a while, but the judge had authorized a bonus based on the Open Season kill of Brayden. She could afford a lengthy time off.

The judge regretted the loss of Martin Cantrell, but after Cassandra explained the reasons for her actions, he'd agreed it was for the best. Mr. Cantrell had been foolish to hire a known contact like Maxwell Nicholson for a hit on his wife. His obsession with playing mental games with his ex-wife also showed a weakness. He was also a certified scumbag, but Cassandra had kept that reasoning to herself. The judge only cared about reasons that affected the Council.

In reflecting on her performance, Cassandra identified several areas for improvement, but she still gave herself pretty high marks. She hadn't needed to kill Lynn Berkley or the kid. She'd successfully protected them from Brayden, and she'd fought the agent to a draw.

The fingers on her right hand hurt, but she'd been lucky not to lose a finger when Martin's small gun got shot out of her hands that morning.

Our paths may cross again, Agent Luchek. Until then, sleep tight. You're now on the Shadow Council's radar. Pray you stay a low priority.

THE END

Shadow Council Series Book 3:
Christmas Makes it Chaos

By Julie C. Gilbert

Table of Contents:

Prologue:
Terrorism Makes Strange Bedfellows

It took a lot to shock Cassandra Mirren, but Judge Clarence A. Jackson was well on his way to doing so twice in one conversation. His first surprise was that the job would take her from the warm embrace of Hawaii to the cold continental United States, likely to somewhere in the Northeast: New York, New Jersey, or Pennsylvania. The second shocker was his plan to pair her with FBI Special Agent Megan Luchek. The man was either a genius or genuinely insane. It had only been a couple of weeks since that messy business with Martin Cantrell trying to take out his ex-wife. Cassandra had thought her down time would last much longer, especially since the Shadow Council was undergoing some serious restructuring.

The Council had no official name, but Cassandra had taken to thinking of it as the *Shadow Council* because the small group of men and women ruled pieces of the world from the shadows. Several contenders had risen to fill the sudden vacuum, but the judge quickly emerged as the clear victor and undisputed leader. Perhaps the power infusion was frying his brain cells. She would have to keep an eye on him in the future. Part of his easy victory had to do with the fact that one major contender was mentally unfit for the pressure, and the other lacked the judge's long experience.

"Why her?" Cassandra blurted, wrenching her thoughts back on track. She cringed inwardly. She hadn't meant to ask that, but it was better than waiting for the judge to ask if she understood his orders. She waved the thin file he'd given her in an attempt to gain some focus. It had only been open long enough for her to read one sentence of

Agent Luchek's psychological profile, a footnote about a childhood fascination with Catwoman.

The judge leveled a weighty look at Cassandra, deciding if explaining would be worth his time.

"Do you doubt her abilities?" He intoned the question in a deep, unhurried manner that somehow put more power behind the words.

"Not at all," Cassandra replied. "But what makes her right for a job like this? And what makes you think she'll even consider working for the Council?"

"There is no need for her to know who she is really working for." The judge's Southern accent turned the statement into a rolling, soothing thing. "You can read the full file later, but I can give you the highlights. What would you like to know?"

"Why am I making contact with her?" Cassandra wondered. "Our last encounter was ... contentious." As a general rule, Cassandra tried to avoid stuffy words, but being in the judge's presence put her in the mood to use them.

The judge chuckled deeply.

"Yes, I do recall the pair of you exchanged blows."

And bullets.

"But I firmly believe y'all are capable of putting aside your differences for the greater good," the judge continued. "Special Agent Luchek may have some loose cannon tendencies, but I believe the lady's a patriot." Stroking his chin thoughtfully, he added, "We might even need those tendencies unleashed if the reports are true."

"I work better alone," Cassandra pointed out as a last-ditch effort to get him to be reasonable about this assignment.

"Do you read and speak Farsi or Arabic? Are you familiar with the Northeast?"

Cassandra shook her head and internally conceded the points.

If she's so perfect, why do you need me?

The flash of self-pity made her flush.

"No, sir." Cassandra could think of a dozen arguments, but she didn't want to voice them for fear of making him doubt her commitment.

Judge Jackson sat back, perched his elbows on the armrests, and folded his hands.

"I know I'm asking a lot of you, Ms. Mirren, but this is a delicate situation. Quite frankly, I don't believe anybody knows exactly what you can expect to face out there. This is not exactly in our comfort zone, but the Council has always existed to protect order."

Stifling an exasperated sigh, Cassandra settled back in her large chair to wait out the lecture she'd inadvertently prompted.

"At best, the rumors turn out to be unfounded, and I'll have sent you into the cold for nothing." The judge's gaze hardened. "But if there is some truth to this, do what you have to do to preserve order, save lives, and protect this Council. Do you understand my meaning?"

"I do, and I accept the job," Cassandra said, hoping to bury her frustration behind formality.

"Excellent. Payment will be made via the usual channels, and I am willing to add ten percent from my discretionary fund for use as you see fit. Maybe you can bribe the agent or hire local help as necessary."

By the time he finished speaking, Cassandra was shaking her head vigorously. "Bribing her would be exactly the wrong move, sir. I think she'll respond best to proof that it's the right thing to do."

The judge raised a hand and nodded.

"I'll leave those details to your judgment, Ms. Mirren. Just get it done. I do not want to be reading about another 9/11 incident in New York City." Judge Jackson's stare drilled the responsibility into her.

"You won't, sir," Cassandra vowed. Rising gracefully from the chair, she held the folder delicately between her hands. "Will that be all?"

"Be careful, Ms. Mirren." The judge hesitated, like he wanted to stop himself from uttering the rest of the warning. "There is a small chance this is merely misinformation meant to draw you out into the open."

"Me?" Cassandra was a ghost. Nobody should know she existed let alone care what jobs she took.

"Well not you specifically, but I've made no secret of hiring you in the past. My enemies are unfortunately your enemies at this point."

"I see." Cassandra gave a thoughtful nod. "I will be cautious then." She waited for the judge's official dismissal then strode out of the room with thoughts already swirling furiously.

Eager to begin, Cassandra went to the small law library located in the basement. She could have read the file in the judge's office, but she preferred to form her first impressions in solitude. The case could be an elaborate hoax or the worst thing to happen on US soil in decades. As she pored over the notes, summaries, and commentary crafted by the judge and his minions, Cassandra couldn't help but be grimly amused by the turn of events. The judge's rise in stature had the potential to bring her a whole new level of cases. She'd become one of the Shadow Council's elite Fixers—part-time diplomat, part-time assassin, and full-time problem solver—because it was exciting, challenging, and a way to take back control of her life. Now, here she was being groomed as a silent savior. Maybe Sister Pamela had been right, God had an interesting sense of humor.

Cassandra hoped Agent Luchek also had a sense of humor or at least a bone-deep sense of patriotism. Finding her would be easy. The judge had provided a detailed itinerary. As fate—or pulled strings—would have it, the agent had been assigned to attend an antiterrorism conference in Philadelphia next week. Convincing her to help would be the first major hurdle for Cassandra. For one thing, the FBI agent would not be easy to get alone, and for another, getting her to talk without sparking a replay of the Tantalus Lookout showdown would take a combination of luck and ingenuity.

The thought conjured a mental image of the agent. The brown haired woman might be medium in height and weight, but she was quite the scrapper. Her punches packed hours of gym experience, and she wasn't afraid to fight dirty. On the one side, it would make more sense for the Council to simply notify the proper authorities and let them deal with the possible terrorists in their own, heavy-handed way. Then again, such a plot would most likely be drowned out by the hundred and two false alarms received each day. Letting other entities handle their business simply didn't fit with the Shadow Council's style. At its heart, this was a scouting mission. The FBI agent could probably call down a solid SWAT hammer if necessary, but the subtle approach let relevant higher ups cling to their precious plausible deniability.

That brought Cassandra back full circle to needing Megan Luchek.

Traditional methods wouldn't work in this instance. Instinct told Cassandra that Luchek would be offended by a bribe, and she didn't have a child to threaten. Her pet was a betta fish, and her closest relatives were her parents, her sister, and an ailing great-aunt. Of those, the sister would normally be the logical target, but Judge Tara Olivia Sidell was not the sort of person who could be quietly disappeared for a few days. Besides, as a method, coercion had its flaws. A coerced person could accomplish much, but they never really embraced the cause. If the threat outlined in the brief was real, Cassandra might end up trusting the agent with her life. For that to happen without tragic results, the agent would need to be one hundred and fifty percent sold on the mission.

In order to get the agent to listen to the entire proposal, Cassandra would need to gain her complete attention. Drawing her into a trap would be delicate business. Live bait tended to work well for these sorts of schemes, but that was out of the question since the job required full cooperation, not merely grudging compliance. Perhaps sending a peace offering would work. What kind of message or gift would be received as nonthreatening? A few minutes of thought led Cassandra to conclude that a simple note would work best. At least it would prime the pump for the discussion to come. Unfortunately, sending a note would also kill the element of surprise, which would make the job of arranging a physical encounter—that didn't turn deadly—much harder to accomplish.

Terrorism really did make strange bedfellows.

In truth, the idea of doing her job for a good cause held a lot of appeal. Being a Fixer often involved putting one's personal feelings aside, but one would have to quit the human race to not feel some pull toward the idea of preventing chaos from rocking a lot of innocent people's worlds during the holiday season.

Well, Agent Luchek, you wouldn't be my first choice for an ally, but I'm just a cog in this machine. We either make this work or die trying.

Chapter 1:
A Warm Surprise

"Brace yourself," Megan Luchek warned her partner.

Special Agent Daniel Cooper blundered through the thick glass doors separating the temperature controlled climate of Philadelphia International Airport from the brutally cold natural air outside. The tall Texan's whole body stiffened as icy wind sliced through his thin jacket. He muttered something that might have been a quiet curse aimed at their boss. Squaring his shoulders, he stepped outside and spun to hold the door for her. His jaw clenched to keep his chin from trembling.

Megan would have laughed at him if the cold wind didn't immediately remind her how spoiled she'd become living in Hawaii. Her phone had informed her that the outside temperature was actually 27°F, but it felt like 2°F to her.

You've gotten soft.

She nodded thanks for the door assist and pulled her giant suitcase across the threshold.

They hustled to the line of waiting taxis, loaded their luggage, and dove inside. Megan rattled off the hotel's address and put her hands near the heating vent where a feeble stream of warm air was doing little to help the situation.

"Can you turn up the heat please?" she inquired.

"Is up all the way," replied the driver. He motioned toward the controls where the dial was indeed well into the red zone. Despite the man's thick accent, his message was clear. "I have blanket in back. You want me to get it?"

"No, thank you," Megan said, knowing he would have to open

the door and dig through the trunk to get at the blanket buried beneath their luggage. "We'll be fine."

She cast a sideways glance at her partner. His expression was set to neutral, but his expressive eyes spoke volumes about the miserable cold.

"Next time SAC Maddox asks for a favor, turn him down," Cooper advised.

"Sorry," Megan said, shrugging. "But you could have backed out."

"And left you to have this winter wonderland all to yourself?" he asked, gesturing out the window where fluffy white flakes drifted down from the heavens. The snowflakes weren't adding much to the road slush, but there were significant snowbanks lining the sidewalks and roadways from a previous storm. "I think not."

"The conference is only one day," Megan encouraged, partly addressing the pep talk to herself. "You'll be back in Hawaii in time for Christmas."

"And you won't?" Dan's right eyebrow reinforced the question. "Since when?"

"Since my mother found out I'd be within a hundred miles of home," she answered.

"I forgot you had family in the area. That should be nice."

"Nice, yes, but stressful," Megan said. "Tara's in the middle of a big case, but I think my mother's on a mission to convince me to drive down and see her."

"At least you'll eat well while with family," Dan pointed out. "Your mom could open up her own restaurant. I still can't believe she shipped lasagna from New Jersey, but it was amazing."

Megan chuckled, recalling the mailman straining against the bulky package. She'd invited Dan and his family over to help her since the lasagna in question had been designed for fifteen people.

"My mom's always been afraid I'll starve fending for myself." Megan reached up and twisted her hair into a haphazard updo. The original hairstyle had died sometime during the insanely long trip from Hawaii to California to Pennsylvania. "That and dying single are her two greatest fears for me."

Dan patted her knee sympathetically.

"She loves ya."

"I know, and I'm lucky to have the parents I do." Megan shrugged, trying to find the right words to express her frustration

184

without coming across as whiny, pathetic, or both. "I just wish we could hold a conversation without an inquisition about my love life, or lack thereof. They don't get that I'm too busy for a social life."

Her partner twisted so he could face her more directly.

"Megan, you make time in life for the things you really want." Dan raised a hand to indicate that he wasn't finished. "I'm not saying your ma's right, but don't use the job as an excuse. If you want to find somebody, start looking. That's all I'm saying."

She nodded and let his speech linger in the cold air because she didn't want to spark an argument. He meant well, even if he did side with her mother on the love issue. Megan knew how hard Dan strived to make his marriage work. That's why she'd gone behind his back to arrange a surprise for him.

"What's that smile for?" he asked, sounding worried.

"You'll see soon," Megan promised, letting the smile widen.

Their taxi pulled up in front of the hotel.

"Go grab the bags," Megan instructed. "I'll deal with the fare." She reached into her purse and scrounged up enough cash to cover the cab ride plus a moderate tip. Generally, she liked to tip large, but moderate seemed fair since the ride had been uncomfortably cool. A small, internal voice told her not to be stingy, lousy heating situation or not, so she dug up an extra ten dollar bill and added it to the stack ready to be handed over. The inner voice congratulated her on doing a good deed, and she banished it to the back of her mind since she wasn't entirely pleased with it at the moment.

After squaring the bill and thanking the driver, Megan climbed out of the cab in time to see a short, pink blur zip by her.

"Daddy! Daddy! Daddy! Look! We're here!" The pink blur giggled and launched itself at a stunned Dan Cooper.

Dropping the luggage, he instinctively caught his daughter. The furred hood fell back, revealing a mop of messy blond hair.

"Do you like my new coat, daddy?" asked the child.

"I do," he said, letting his Southern accent lengthen the answer. "That is a mighty fine coat you've got there, missy."

"Santa gave it to me," the child declared.

"He did?" Dan's inflection made it a question which he aimed at his wife who was approaching with a squirming bundle swathed in bright purple. "How did he manage that?"

"Mommy said Aunt Maggie said Santa said it was okay to give us presents early because we wouldn't be near our chimney at

Christmas." Ashley Ann Cooper spoke with all the authority of a three-year-old.

Dan shot Megan a questioning look.

She'd known the prospect of spending the holiday season away from his family had been hard, and she appreciated his willingness to accept the assignment. In big ways and small, Dan often sacrificed much for her, and Megan was glad to finally be able to do something nice for him.

"Surprise," Megan said, grinning at her partner. "Looks like you'll have a white Christmas after all." She stepped forward and greeted Bethany Cooper with a warm hug. "You made it, Beth. Welcome to the Northeast. You'll get used to the mind-numbing cold." She noticed that the other woman was shivering. When she disengaged, Megan took Beth's sleepy, yet restless, charge with her.

Curious about the motion, the baby opened her eyes long enough to peer at Megan. Yawning, she snuggled closer to Megan and closed her eyes to take a nap.

"I don't know how people can live like this," Beth remarked. Turning to her husband, she stood on tiptoes and planted a kiss on his frigid cheek. "Hi, honey. Are you surprised?"

"Absolutely," he answered, leaning down for a better kiss.

"Yucky!" shouted Ashley.

"Kisses aren't yucky," Dan countered. He proved it by peppering her face with tiny kisses until she started giggling again.

"Kisses are wonderful," said Bethany, placing a kiss on her daughter's cheek then putting an arm around her husband.

"Giggles, can you come here a minute?" Megan called, figuring Beth and Dan needed a moment. "Santa wanted me to deliver a few more things."

Leaping out of Dan's arms, Ashley raced over to Megan.

"What is it? What is it?" If the kid were a puppy, her tail would have been wagging nine hundred times a minute. As is, her tiny body vibrated with energy and excitement.

"I don't know," Megan answered. "But we can find out. Go open the front pocket on my suitcase. It's the blue one over there next to your father's suitcase."

The one that makes his suitcase look like a kid's toy.

The child conquered the zipper in no time and emptied the pocket of four neatly wrapped packages.

"Open?" Ashley asked. Her eyes begged for permission.

"The green package is yours," Megan confirmed. "Go ahead and open it."

The girl ripped open the paper, flinging fragments everywhere. Megan did her best to unobtrusively collect the pieces so there wouldn't be too much littering going on. She'd considered suggesting they move the reunion inside but left well enough alone. Ashley was making enough noise to cause a disturbance, but the bitter cold had already driven most other parties indoors. Once the girl had the pair of bright green mittens in hand, she stared down at them.

"What is it?" Ashley looked first to Megan then to her parents for an explanation.

"They're mittens," Megan answered. "You put them on your hands to keep them warm."

Trying to help Ashley took some serious coordination since one arm was already occupied by the baby, Carolina Michelle Cooper. By the time both of Ashley's hands were ensconced in the mittens, Megan's arms ached.

How does Beth do this all day?

She had a newfound respect for the petite mother of two.

"Whatcha got there, Giggles?" asked Dan.

"Mittens!" Ashley announced. She waved her hands just in case her father missed them.

"Look. There are more packages. Would you like to deliver them?" Megan stuffed the paper fragments in her pocket before picking up the other three packages. Holding up the larger two gifts, Megan waved them at Ashley. "Here. Give this one to your mommy and this one to your daddy."

Ashley accepted the packages as if they were firewood, curling her arms up to her chest to trap them. Then, she rushed over to give them to her parents who thanked her and feigned surprise as they each discovered a thick pair of winter gloves.

"They're lovely. Thank you," said Bethany.

"Santa's been extra generous this year," Dan commented with a smile of thanks aimed at Megan. His eyes held a question.

"I had some frequent flier and hotel points to burn from my jet-setting days." Megan ended her explanation with a shrug. That much was true, though even then she'd been working, flying here and there in the Middle East perfecting her language skills. The program had been a CIA recruitment ploy, but in the end, she'd nicely told them her heart belonged to the FBI. Though disappointed, the recruiter had introduced her to the right people and helped her obtain an age waiver due to her language skills.

"Who's this?" Ashley waved the last package back and forth frantically.

"You mean 'What's this?'" Beth corrected.

"No! Who's this?" Ashley shook the package hard.

"That one's for Sweet Pea," said Megan, solving the child riddle first. "But I don't think she'd mind if you opened it for her." Megan glanced down at the drowsy child in her arms. With her tiny body and easy disposition, Carolina Cooper was aptly nicknamed.

Giggles ripped into the new package and pulled out a pair of fuzzy purple mittens.

Dan came over, knelt, and balanced Sweet Pea on his left knee so Megan could guide the baby's hands into the mittens. Then, he returned her to Megan who wandered over to stand by Beth while Dan engaged Giggles in a snowball fight.

"Where did you find mittens in Hawaii?" asked Beth.

"The internet," Megan answered. "It's amazing the stuff you can find on there."

"This is nice, but we could never repay you." Beth looked uncomfortable.

"It's my pleasure," Megan assured. "Just enjoy yourself. Dan and I have some work to do, but I'll make sure he takes some time off to spend with you and the girls. I'll even throw in a free babysitting gig if you'd like to check out one of the fancier joints in the city."

"I think you might be my new best friend," said Bethany. She watched her husband and daughter play in the semi-dirty snow.

"Go on," Megan urged. "You haven't lived until you've gotten into at least one grand snowball fight. Sweet Pea and I can watch from the safe zone by the door. Just make sure to use your new gloves or your hands will freeze right off."

Bethany Cooper pulled the gloves on with purpose and marched over to a snowbank to prepare for battle.

***

Cassandra Mirren watched the pair of FBI agents meet with the male agent's family. Their presence opened up new possibilities and complications. She had expected Megan's partner to also attend the antiterrorism conference and factored that into her plans. The wife and kids changed the dynamics. This might work out in Cassandra's favor, leaving her more time to chat with Agent Luchek alone.

Chapter 2:
Close Encounter of the Hostile Kind

Megan cheered on all sides of the Cooper family sidewalk snowball fight. Dan and Beth took turns helping their daughter tag each other until everybody was soaked through and exhausted from laughing. Afterward, she accompanied them into the hotel's restaurant for a round of hot chocolate and a plate of Christmas cookies.

By the time she made it up to her room, Megan wanted to roll into bed and take a nice long nap. However, since Hawaii's time was five hours behind Eastern Standard Time, her biggest challenge might be falling asleep tonight, so she crossed napping off the list of possibilities. She could read over the conference paperwork or reread some of her personal cold case files. She liked to keep the details fresh just in case she ever had the opportunity to return to those cases. Reading held little appeal though, so Megan decided to exercise. The long day's travel weighed her down. She needed some fresh energy.

Changing into a gray FBI T-shirt and some workout shorts took only a few minutes. Finding the gym took another couple of minutes, but then, Megan lost herself in the comforting rhythms of running and cycling. They didn't have a punching bag, but they had a pull-up bar. She personally despised pull-ups, but knew they helped build upper body strength. Much of her job could be tedious, but the exciting moments could get physically demanding in a heartbeat. Running in a gym couldn't match the real deal of street running, but she didn't feel like hurtling through Philadelphia in the dark. Instead, she added an extra, high-resistance treadmill session to the end of her workout.

A check of her phone said she'd killed an hour and twenty

minutes. She had just enough time to shower and change before meeting Dan and his family for dinner in the hotel's restaurant. Megan had tried to gracefully bow out, but Beth insisted they treat her to dinner at least once after everything she'd done for them in arranging the trip.

The quick, hot, glorious shower left Megan's mind and body in a nicely relaxed state until she set foot back into the main room.

A premonition made her pause. Something wasn't right. Every light in the room had been turned on, and her clothes had been moved from the bed where she'd laid them out. A cloud of steam followed her out of the bathroom, cutting down on visibility, but movement from her left caught her attention.

She tensed and turned in time to catch the bundle of clothes hurled at her chest. She caught them instinctively, realizing her hands were now both occupied.

"Agent," greeted a voice she recognized.

"Assassin," Megan returned, preparing to toss the clothes back and launch herself at the taller woman.

She noticed the woman's hair was now a rich brown color instead of blond. Although tied back, the hair appeared shorter than it had upon their last meeting. The assassin's youthful looks combined with jeans and a Drexel sweatshirt to give the impression of a harmless co-ed, but her piercing blue eyes countered the image.

Contacts?

"Get dressed," the assassin ordered. "We need to talk, and I'd rather not have to shoot you. You'll feel better with clothes on."

Megan considered her options. She could go with Plan A and throw the clothes before trying to tackle the woman, but the silenced handgun aimed her way discouraged such a move. She could follow the directive and get dressed, though that would put her at a further disadvantage. She could also try to keep the woman talking and hope she made a mistake that gave Megan the upper hand. The only difference between the waiting plan and the following directions plan was whether Megan had more than a towel on, so she opted for Plan B: comply for now.

Dropping the clothes, Megan quickly donned each item then kicked the towel back into the bathroom. The assassin had been right. She felt better once fully clothed, but she still had the wrong end of a gun pointed at her. She knew that ought to make her nervous but for some reason she believed the assassin's claim about wanting to talk. It was really the only thing that made sense. Like it or not, the assassin had caught her completely off guard. Talking could still be a precursor to a hail of bullets, but something about the other woman's wary expression said there was more to the story.

"Good. Now please sit on the bed with your hands underneath your legs. I know you don't trust me, but I'm not here to hurt you. I need your help with a job."

Megan's eyes widened, but she followed the instruction, acutely aware of the gun tracking her movements.

"You have a heck of a way of asking for help," Megan commented.

"We didn't exactly part on good terms, but trust runs both ways. If you agree to hear me out, I'll lower the gun. What do you say?"

"I'm all ears," Megan said.

As promised, the assassin lowered the gun. It didn't actually improve Megan's situation, but it did make her feel marginally better.

The assassin took a steadying breath and bit her bottom lip as if reconsidering this madness. Deciding to take the plunge, she launched into a well-rehearsed speech.

"My name is Cassandra, but you'll never find it in a database, even the FBI's. I'd prefer to keep it that way. I work for an organization few know about and fewer still understand. You've only seen part of my role, but you've already met another like me."

"Max," Megan murmured. Her brief meeting with him had sent her on an adventure she wasn't likely to forget. Connections slammed together in Megan's head. "Are you a Fixer too?"

"Yes, and being one encompasses much more than carrying out hits and spying on powerful people. The organization is really about order." Cassandra held up a hand to wave off a protest. "I'm not here for your approval. I'm here to save lives." She winced at the statement. "There's a file behind you that will explain in more detail. Slowly reach back with your right hand to grab it."

Now more curious than frightened, Megan patted the section of bedding behind her until she found a folder. Pulling it around front, she opened the file and started skimming. The more she read, the more her confusion grew.

"Why are you bringing this to me instead of Homeland Security or dropping it off at the FBI office?" Megan quit reading long enough to fire a long look at the assassin. She wasn't fishing for validation. She genuinely wanted to know what made Cassandra trust her over the official channels.

"Please. You know better than most people how ponderous those organizations can be."

"Not when it comes to stuff like this," Megan argued, wagging the file in her hands.

"They get hundreds of crackpot plans dumped in their lap every day. There's a small chance this is just one more, but I'm not willing to bet thousands of lives on that possibility. Are you?"

Cassandra's question hit Megan squarely in the chest.

"No. Of course not," Megan said, clearing her throat. "But I'm also not sure what you think I can do that you can't."

"Come with me to investigate this, or check out the site on your own. If we find enough evidence that this is real, you call in the eight-hundred pound gorillas."

Megan's phone rang from where she'd placed it on the end table next to the bed.

"That would be Dan. I'm supposed to be meeting him downstairs for dinner," Megan said. She didn't want to let the assassin know about Dan's family if she didn't already have that information. "What do you want me to do?"

"Answer it," Cassandra instructed. "Tell him you're going to be late, but do not tell him anything about me or this assignment."

"He could help," Megan offered. Receiving no comment, she slowly crossed over to where the phone lay and picked it up.

The gun was loosely pointed in her direction again, emphasizing the fact that she shouldn't say anything stupid.

"Hey," she greeted. "I just got back from the gym. I'll be a few more minutes. Go ahead and start without me."

"All right, but don't be surprised if you get a frowny face from Giggles when you get here," Dan warned.

Megan had to smile at that mental image. The mirth died almost as quickly as it came when she thought about the file she'd left at the foot of her bed. If the plot was real, ruined Christmas plans would be the least of everybody's problems.

"I'll try to hurry," Megan said, aware that her voice suddenly sounded hoarse.

"You feeling all right?" Dan inquired.

"Yeah. Jet-lagged and starving," Megan reported. "Let me go so I can clean up and get down there."

"You got it," Dan said, ending the call.

Megan listened to the empty air for a few seconds before lowering the phone.

"He really can help," she said, trying one more time to get Cassandra to let her read Dan in.

"He also might try to stop you or insist on coming," Cassandra countered. "It will be hard enough to sneak around with the two of us. You need to be there in case I need your language skills, and I need to be there in case you need protection. Leave him a note if you must or call him from the road. It'll take us a few hours to get there anyway."

"We're leaving tonight?" Megan asked.

Cassandra nodded.

"Yes, but late. Go to dinner, get some rest, and then we can head out." The gun lowered as Cassandra gave the situation some more thought. "Then again, it might be better for us to travel separately."

"Why?"

"Greater chance for success," Cassandra answered. "That place could be crawling with moving targets. If I leave now, I can do some scouting before you get there."

"What happened to being my 'protection'?" Megan quirked an eyebrow at her unofficial new partner.

"You won't need protection if I can deal with them first," Cassandra pointed out.

"And what happens if you get into trouble?" Megan marveled at the strange direction this was taking. She tried not to be concerned for the woman who'd used a gun to initiate the conversation. She expected a brave response and received a surprise instead.

"Then I'd better hope you can kick those gorillas into gear quickly." Cassandra tossed a couple of small things at her.

Megan caught them reflexively.

"What are these?"

"Tracking devices," Cassandra responded. "The place where we're headed is pretty remote. We'll need to take snowmobiles part of the way. Do you know how to handle one of those?"

Megan nodded. She'd only driven one once, but she had plenty of experience with jet skis and motorcycles. The machines were similar enough at their core.

"Good. My people should have left a pair of them for us to find," Cassandra said. "Wear one tracker and leave one on the snowmobile in case something happens to the one you're wearing. There are three readers. I'll have one, you'll have one, and you can leave the third for your partner to find. He'll be our backup plan, but tell him nothing until you're well on your way."

"Are you sure you don't want me to run that file through official channels?" Megan asked. "I can probably get it through a few rings of red tape."

"The gorillas aren't subtle. No government agency ever is," Cassandra explained. "If we tip our hand, these guys will scatter and parts of the plan may still take place."

Although she hated to admit it, Megan agreed with the woman's assessment.

The gun finally disappeared, presumably into a holster secured to the assassin's back.

"As I said, go eat something," said the assassin. "I need an hour to arrange to get you a car anyway. With any luck we'll have you back in time to attend the afternoon sessions of your conference tomorrow. I'll text you the location of the snowmobiles and the compound in question. If I'm not at the meeting spot, wait a half-hour then come find me."

Cassandra held up a third tracker and tossed the corresponding reader onto Megan's bed. She started for the door, but as she reached it, she turned back to say one more thing.

"Don't forget your gun."

Chapter 3:
A Strange Note

Dinner stretched longer than anticipated, but since they had started early, Giggles still brimmed with energy. The kid would hopefully crash when it came time for bed, but according to Beth, the girl had slept most of the long flights. Daniel Cooper suggested a few rounds of Candyland to occupy the evening hours. He had noticed you could rent various board games from the front desk for ten bucks an hour. At that price one could practically buy the whole game, but that and movies offered the only stay-in entertainment that might satisfy a small child. Giggles cheered, Beth shrugged, and Megan begged off, claiming to have a headache.

After almost three hours of being trounced at Candyland by his wife and daughter, Dan knocked on Megan's door. His purpose was twofold. He wanted to check on her headache battle, and he wanted to bum an Advil from her to fight one of his own. He loved Giggles to death, but the kid had one heck of an ear-splitting screech. Getting no answer, he knocked again, a little more firmly this time.

"Megan? Hello? Anybody home?" he called softly. Still getting no response, he figured she was sound asleep.

Shrugging, Dan checked that he had his wallet and made his way down to the front desk. Google maps could tell him where to find a convenience store, but he wasn't dressed to take on the freshly falling snow. The same evil pamphlet that had alerted him to the board game rentals also mentioned reasonably priced, single-serve over-the-counter drugs. He nearly turned back when he saw what the hotel deemed "reasonably priced," but the ache in his head had sharpened enough to make him complete the transaction.

"Hey, babe, what took you so long?" Beth inquired, when Dan returned to their hotel suite. "How's Megan?"

"I don't know," Dan answered. He headed for the bathroom and filled a cup with water to wash down the headache medicine. For good measure, he tossed water onto his face and used a hand towel to pat off the excess liquid. He met his wife's gaze in the mirror as she stood in the doorway. "She didn't answer when I knocked twice, and I didn't try a third time. I didn't want to wake her if she'd already turned in for the night."

"I hope she's okay," Beth commented. "I thought she was using a headache as an excuse to escape us."

"So did I," Dan said, shrugging. He sipped at the water, put the pills in his mouth, and swallowed them with the rest of the water. "Since I couldn't rouse Megan, I headed to the front desk for some meds and came back. What happened while I was gone? It's so quiet."

Stepping into the restroom, Beth kicked the door then leaned back and applied pressure until the latch caught. Going to tip-toes, she wrapped her arms around her husband's neck and leaned her head on his shoulder. He slouched to make it easier for her to reach.

"You were gone quite a while," Beth reminded him. "I had enough time to wrestle both girls into nighties, brush their teeth, say prayers, tuck them in, and give good night kisses."

"Speaking of good night kisses," Dan said. "Do I get one?"

Pulling back slightly, Beth grinned up at him.

"Are you sure you only want one?"

"I want as many as you'll give," Dan responded. He leaned into a nice, long kiss. Seeing as they were alone, hopefully, it would be the first of many. He was tired, but sleep could wait a little longer.

***

Next morning, Dan groaned when his alarm rang at 6:30. The conference didn't start until eight, but they still had to grab breakfast, get to the Pennsylvania Convention Center, and find the right room. Beth stirred, stole more of the covers, and rolled over. Now bereft of both her warmth and the covers, Dan got up. He called Megan but wasn't surprised when she didn't answer. She may not have remembered to set her alarm, especially if she turned in earlier than expected. Dan rushed through his morning routine so he could provide an adequate wakeup call for his partner. She was very good at many things. Rising on time happened to not be one of them. He called her again as he approached her door. When her recorded voice started telling him to leave a message, he ended the call and knocked firmly.

"Megan, this is getting old," Dan said to the closed door. "Wake up."

He placed a third call and strained to hear if he could detect the ringing from inside. Even if she forgot the alarm, she shouldn't have the phone on silent. Inspiration struck him, so he scrolled through his list of contacts until he found Hotel Front Desk and hit the call button. After explaining the situation to the young woman working the desk, Dan asked her to call Megan's room through the landline. She made him repeat the request and the reasoning twice before reluctantly agreeing.

A moment later, the ringing phone could clearly be heard from inside Megan's room. It rang ten times. Dan counted. Then, his cellphone rang.

"I'm sorry, sir," said Kayla from the front desk. "No one answered the courtesy call."

"I know. I was listening to it ring," Dan said, trying not to sound too grim. "Is there any chance I can get someone up here to let me in to check on her?"

"I'm sorry, sir, but I don't—"

"May I speak with a manager, please?" Dan asked. His mind went to several awful scenarios. By all accounts, this should be a quiet assignment, but Megan had a knack for finding trouble wherever she went.

"Hold, please." Kayla's professional tone couldn't mask her relief at being able to turn Dan over to her boss.

"Victoria Blake speaking. I'm the General Manager on duty. How may I help you?" The voice was cool, brisk, and efficient.

"Good morning, Ms. Blake. I'm FBI Special Agent Daniel Cooper. My family and I are staying in suite 406, but I'm standing in front of room 610 trying to wake my partner. We have a conference to get to in an hour. I've called her cellphone a few times, and I've had the woman at the front desk call the room directly. I heard the phone ring. Nobody would be able to sleep through that. Would you be able to send somebody with a key card to let me check on her?"

Silence ruled the connection for a few uncomfortable moments.

"Is it possible she left early?" Victoria Blake inquired.

"Not without telling me," Dan answered. "I know it's an

unusual request and it's probably against your policies, but I really need to know where my partner is. If she's in the room, I'd like to know why she can't hear the phone, and if she's not in the room, then I've got an investigation to launch." He had about a dozen more points to raise, but he held them back to let the manager answer.

Another long silence ensued before the manager came to a decision.

"I'll be up with a master key card in a few minutes, but I want to see your credentials before I let you in that room." Victoria Blake did not sound pleased.

Dan thanked her and returned his cellphone to the belt clip. He wanted to call Bethany but didn't want to worry her. He considered calling Megan yet again, but knew it would be futile. Above all, he tried not to wonder why his partner was out of touch, which let him think of nothing else. To his knowledge, she didn't have any hot cases; neither did he for that matter. Their last joint operation had been another embezzlement case against a mid-level manager of an investment firm. They had closed that case in record time because their informant—the man's disgruntled secretary—had practically gift-wrapped the evidence and mailed it to them.

"Agent Cooper?" asked a woman approaching cautiously, flanked by two large men whose name badges identified them as security.

"That's me," Dan confirmed. He slowly reached into the breast pocket and extracted his badge. "Here's your proof."

Victoria Blake was a tall, mid-forties woman wearing a tan skirt suit and a *let's-fix-this* expression on her dark features.

"Thank you," she said, after reading every word on the badge.

At a nod from Ms. Blake, the security guys relaxed, but they remained in a position to help her at a second's notice.

"I'll open the door, but I want to be the first one in there," said Ms. Blake.

"No," said Dan.

"Absolutely not," said the older security guard at the same time as Dan spoke.

"We don't know what we're going to find in there," Dan explained.

"B-but she's a guest. I don't want her frightened by a bunch of men barreling in like linebackers," argued Ms. Blake.

Dan admitted her point was valid, but he still wasn't about to let her enter an unknown situation.

"She's also my partner," Dan said patiently. "Let me go in and clear the room. If it's safe, I'll call you right in. She might be upset when she sees me, but at least I'm a familiar face."

The argument won Ms. Blake over once both security men agreed with Dan's logic. She slipped the master key card into the lock, twisted the handle, and pushed the door open an inch. Drawing his gun, Dan cautiously entered Megan's room. It took him about five seconds to clear the room and determine that neither the main room nor the bathroom held anybody.

"It's safe," he called, returning his gun to its shoulder holster.

"What did you find?" Victoria took in the empty room as she asked her question.

"Exactly what you see," Dan answered, gesturing to the empty room. Even as he said it, he spotted a folded piece of paper on the end table. The paper sat next to a small black box about the size of a deck of cards. Dan picked up the paper.

Scrawled in Megan's messy handwriting, he found these words:

Gone to investigate a possible terrorist cell. Crazy, I know. Cover for me. I'll call sometime today. If I don't call, follow with the tracking device. Bring lots of backup if it comes to that. ~Megan

"What's this?" Victoria picked up a file from near the end of the bed.

"Nothing," Dan said, snatching the file before the woman could open it. He cleared his throat. "I'm sure it's just paperwork my partner left lying around. I'm sorry to have disturbed you."

"Where is she?" demanded the younger security guard.

"Not here." Dan stated the obvious in what he hoped was a conversation-ending tone, but his three-person audience looked highly dissatisfied. He met Victoria's hard gaze. "You were right, ma'am. She stepped out without telling me. Again, I apologize for the inconvenience. I won't take up any more of your time." He nodded suggestively toward the door.

"Are you sure she's safe?" Victoria asked, ignoring the hint.

Oh, I'm sure she's doing her level best to find trouble.

"No, but I am certain she's very capable," Dan answered.

"Then why do you look so worried?" challenged the older security guard.

"She's … extremely impulsive. That's always cause for worry."

Dan shooed the trio out the door and sat down on Megan's bed to re-read the note and find out what the file had to say. He read every word twice then started again. A glance at the clock told him he was going to be late for the conference. He'd have some serious explaining to do if he couldn't report back to Special Agent in Charge Bryan Maddox about the conference. On the other hand, he would have some serious explaining to do for Bethany if she ever found out he let Megan undertake such craziness alone.

Rock, meet hard place. What should I do?

Maddox could probably be persuaded of the necessity of skipping the conference if he understood what Megan was trying to accomplish, but telling him would be exactly the opposite of covering for her. Banking on the principle that forgiveness was easier to seek than permission, Dan headed downstairs to grab an early breakfast and ponder the situation. He'd give Megan time to get in touch, but if he didn't hear from her soon, he would launch an appropriate rescue.

Chapter 4:
Long Wait, Short Chase

Megan Luchek despised waiting. The distaste was magnified by the terrible hour and the fact that she couldn't define why she trusted Cassandra enough to follow her out here to a lonely stretch of Pennsylvania in the middle of a snowstorm. Megan longed for her old winter parka lined with Gortex. Unfortunately, that was stored at her parents' place as it had been since she moved to Hawaii. As an early Christmas gift to herself, she'd bought a stylish gray winter outfit complete with a matching faux fur hat, but the coat wasn't made for roughing it outdoors for long periods of time.

At least the gloves are warm.

She smiled at the memory of Ashley Cooper ripping open the packages. Arranging for Dan's family to arrive in Philadelphia and get to the hotel before them had taken some serious coordination and communication skills. The look on Dan's face had been priceless.

Thoughts of her current mission intruded on the pleasant memory. She'd come to this cold state to discuss terrorism as a subject and an idea, but battling some of the madmen had not been on the itinerary. She'd worked hard to get Dan's family here, and the possibility of inadvertently bringing them into harm's way hurt. The odds of something bad happening to people she knew were low, but if something bad did happen it would involve people precious to somebody. Random acts of violence ticked her off, which was good in that it warmed her with fiery indignation.

I wish Kai were here.

Megan searched her feelings. She'd been nervous about leaving her best friend in charge of her betta fish, Handsome, but when it came to facing a task of this magnitude, she trusted nobody more than the spitfire detective. She knew Kai was slowly warming to the idea of joining the FBI, but Megan hadn't convinced her yet. It amused Megan that trusting Kai with her pet was harder than trusting the woman with her life. Maybe it was the way Ailani, Kai's Golden Retriever, had eyed Handsome as Megan delivered him. She dismissed the idea, concluding that her nervousness stemmed from the fact that the detective's personal life could often best be described as a hot mess.

That's part of her charm.

While indulging in fantasy thoughts, such as Kai teleporting from Hawaii, Megan wished Dan would wake up, find her note, and rush to stand with her during this frozen vigil. As the minutes dragged on, she added Kristen Sato to her terrorist-fighting dream team. As much as the tenacious reporter annoyed Megan, she had an admirable way about getting to the bottom of a story. If she wanted to turn detective, she'd be one heck of a private investigator.

Kai would have your head for such a thought.

If Megan locked those two in a room together she could make a bundle selling tickets to the fight. She didn't doubt that her friend would be victorious, but the reporter wouldn't go down quietly. Maybe Megan should rope both of them into the MMA fight club she'd been meaning to join. That could be fun and productive. They could work out their differences in a straightforward manner. If more people settled scores by beating each other inside an official ring, perhaps there would be less of this angry-guy-goes-postal thing on top of the terrorists-running-amok thing.

There. I've solved the problem of world peace. Can I go home now?

A gust of icy wind cut through her winter jacket like it wasn't there. She hunched her shoulders, endured the blast, and considered getting back into her car, but she wanted to be ready to go the moment Cassandra showed up. Never mind that the woman's signal hadn't moved significantly in the last twenty minutes. Besides, Megan hadn't had time to disable the car's interior light. If she opened the door the thing would light up like a beacon. If nobody knew of her presence, she preferred to keep it that way.

Fighting off the impulse to check the time, Megan blew on her hands, crossed her arms, and leaned against the sleek, blue snowmobile sitting exactly where Cassandra's instructions had said it would be. According to her estimated timeline, Cassandra should have been waiting for Megan, not the other way around, even building in an extra hour for surveillance and investigating.

Should I go after her? How will I find her?

The GPS tracker could get her to the correct vicinity, but if there were several buildings together, it would be difficult to obtain a true position lock. While the tracker stayed on her mind, Megan turned and studied the snowmobile, trying to determine a good hiding spot to stash the device. Putting it close to the engine probably wasn't a great idea, and the storage compartment would probably get checked first if anybody found the machine. The tracker had an adhesive side to help with mounting, but that failed to solve the placement problem. Noticing the windshield and front dash were completely black, Megan tucked the flat disc directly onto the tiny flat zone between the handle bars and the windshield.

Jamming her hands back into the gloves, Megan fingered the remaining tracking device. Carrying it in her pocket had worked so far, but she had been traveling safely by car, not bouncing around on a snowmobile. That she hadn't lost it already surprised her. The prospect of sticking the thing to any part of her body held no appeal. After considering the options, she tucked it under the laces where the tongue merged with the boot. She had to remove the gloves again to get it situated, and by the time she'd finished, her fingers were stiff with cold.

Her mental clock, which was typically accurate, told her a half-hour was almost up if not already expired. Checking her watch would require moving her sleeve enough to see it.

It's been long enough. Quit stalling and get moving.

Reluctantly, Megan donned the helmet, climbed onto the snowmobile, and started the engine. A wave of warm air rushed over her hands and slammed into her face. Her boots felt distinctly warmer too. Reaching for the controls, Megan wondered why she'd waited so long anyway. The snowfall had picked up over the last few hours, but she could still see which direction Cassandra's snowmobile had gone. To be on the safe side, she rechecked with the reader and found no significant movement.

Pointing her machine in the correct direction, Megan started forward, aware that she was headed into unknown territory. The rumble of the powerful machine filled her with a sense of anticipation and adventure. With her left arm fully recovered from the bullet wound, it was about time she did something brave or reckless. She guessed this qualified as both. Her mother would have heart failure if she knew half of Megan's adventures from the last year or so.

With luck, she'll never ever know.

As she traveled, the heat slowly thawed Megan's hands and feet, making them tingle. The falling snow looked gorgeous in the headlight beams as they whizzed past like miniature shooting stars. She'd considered riding without headlights, but her level of snowmobile expertise wasn't up to driving blind. A mere thirty-six hours ago she'd been wearing a T-shirt and shorts while she packed for this trip. Now, she was skimming across a sheet of snow and ice half a world away. As she started to relax and enjoy the ride, she spotted an abandoned snowmobile ahead.

Megan slowed instinctively as she approached the vehicle. Cassandra's signal was still beyond the abandoned machine, but something wasn't right. The uneasy feeling exploded into full-blown alarm when four sets of headlights came on in quick succession. Accompanying engines roared to life. Executing a sharp turn, Megan headed back the way she'd come.

I can't be caught with the tracker reader.

There would be time to consider what went wrong later, but right now, Megan needed to lose her pursuers. Before the snowmobile could hit its top speed, she reached into her pocket, grabbed the reader, and flung it as far away as she could before gripping both handles again.

The sound of two possible gunshots reached her, but she couldn't be sure over the growl of her engine. Resisting the urge to look back took a lot of willpower. Megan gunned her engine. She kept going in a straight line for another few seconds until something thudded into the back of her snowmobile, prompting her to weave randomly. More willpower battled the instinct to dig out her gun and return fire. The unexpected jolts from patches of uneven ground were hard enough to handle without steering one-handed.

Suddenly, another snowmobile loomed near Megan's right side. Either she wasn't getting enough speed from her machine or the pursuers owned better vehicles. For a terrifying second, Megan feared she'd crash into the other snowmobile, but she managed to steer left without completely surrendering to the panic building in her chest.

She heard four more gunshots.

Megan hunched down, trying to present the smallest target possible.

Yet another gunshot blasted through the winter air. This time, it was followed by a thud and a crack as plastic yielded to the projectile. The snowmobile's engine sputtered, and the steering became unresponsive. Megan crushed the handle brakes with little effect. A tree that had been far away suddenly appeared uncomfortably close and right in her way. The options were hold on for dear life as she crashed into a tree or jump off before the impact.

The tree would kill her.

The fall might kill her.

Megan wrenched the reluctant steering mechanism to the left to cause a skid and threw her body left, trying to distance herself from the doomed machine. She landed hard on the snow and tucked her arms tight to avoid breaking them. The impact stole her breath, but by some miracle that seemed to be the worst of the damage. In a way, she was lucky the bullet had killed the engine as quickly as it did or the crash might have happened sooner and with more speed.

As it was, Megan felt like each of her limbs had been bent at a wrong angle, but at least she could feel them. Her head struck the ground a few times while she rolled, but the helmet did its job, leaving her brains feeling only partially scrambled. After rolling for an eternity, Megan finally landed flat on her back.

A timeless moment passed while her body struggled to remember how to breathe. The area around her was unusually well-lit for the middle of nowhere. Her ears rang and her skull felt like it had been used to repeatedly strike the sides of a brass bell, but she was alive.

Hands fell on her arms and legs almost simultaneously. The helmet was lifted away. For a moment, Megan mistook the hands as being helpful. Some of the hands held her down while others executed a quick, efficient search. Words reached her, but none made sense. Slowly, the ability to breathe returned, but Megan couldn't speak yet. She felt the hands relieve her of the reassuring weight of her gun and saw her car keys and a few bits of wrapping paper being pulled from her coat pockets.

By this time, enough senses returned to allow her to take stock of the situation. One man held her arms and another put pressure on her legs. A third man knelt over her, and a fourth man stood a short distance away speaking into a radio.

She couldn't hear exact words, but she recognized the cadence of the speech. The man was speaking Arabic.

She never got the chance to listen closely because the man

turned and barked out an order. A booted foot glanced off the side of her head, and she blacked out.

Chapter 5:
Clear Evidence of a Confusing Case

Cassandra Mirren picked the door lock with the ease of a cat burglar. Catwoman—and Megan—would be proud. It amused her that the comic book heroine had fascinated both her younger self and the FBI agent. Knowing that innocuous fact provided an important reminder that nothing one said in an official interview was truly sacred. Megan had mentioned the admiration for Catwoman during a battery of psychological tests designed to get at the heart of what made her mind tick before the Bureau extended an invitation to join its coveted ranks. The information had been included in the file the judge's people had prepared concerning the FBI agent in preparation of this mission.

A time check told her Megan would be arriving soon since getting this far had taken Cassandra two hours longer than anticipated. She thought about texting the agent a message that she needed more time, but having her here to sort the paperwork mess would be helpful.

Getting to this point had taken much longer than anticipated because there were a lot more bad guys roaming this place than she had factored into her calculations. Most of the men stuck around two cabins being used as barracks, but patrols walked the perimeter and grounds at seemingly random intervals. Sneaking in had stretched Cassandra's patience very thin. Knocking out a pair of guards would have been satisfying, but also suicidal, as the patrols checked in with their controller fairly often. Whoever coordinated them had some skill at running a tight ship. The frequency had forced her to stay put until she'd discovered the pattern in the patrol schedule. Once she realized they were coming through spaced at five, then ten, then fifteen minute intervals, Cassandra simply waited for the fifteen minute window and made her move.

Unfortunately, it then took her searching two wrong buildings before finding the one that housed the head honcho's office.

Slipping inside, Cassandra snapped on a powerful penlight and took in the room.

Lair.

The word fit the space perfectly. Conspiracy theorists would sell part of their soul to get a glimpse of this guy's office. Cassandra had no clue to the man's identity, but according to the décor, it definitely belonged to a man. Magazines focused on guns, weapons, and terrorists organizations like ISIS lined the walls in stacks. One wall held a map of the tristate area, including lower New York, Eastern Pennsylvania, and all of New Jersey. Pushpins of various colors marked a wide variety of locations. Sticky notes peppered the map, filled with deep, dark marks in a language she couldn't read. Cassandra snapped several photos of the wall, taking the time to note only three of the locations, two bridges separating New York from New Jersey and a small town in Pennsylvania.

She tried to angle her body so the flash would be directed into the wall and hoped nobody wandering the hallway would notice any light leaking out the bottom of the door. After two pictures, Cassandra put some of the magazines to good use. Grabbing a handful, she angled them to cover the small gap between the floor and the door. One of the magazines slipped off the stack and landed open on the floor. Cassandra was surprised to find the article written in English. A check of two more magazines also revealed them to be written in English.

Unsure of what that meant, Cassandra took a picture of one of the articles to add to her evidence. Then, she added the magazines to the light shield and turned back to the wall to get some better snapshots. This time she noted that the bridge pushpins were green along with one down off the map marked with another unreadable sticky note. Next, she focused on the desk. She took a picture as a whole then zeroed in on the paperwork, taking dozens of photos. Showing Megan the lair would be better, but if that didn't work out then at least Cassandra would have something to show her when they finally got to compare notes.

Finding a laptop tucked into the top right drawer, Cassandra pulled it out and turned it on, hoping it wasn't password protected.

When the box popped up asking for a password, she frowned and considered how much longer she could afford to stay here. Deciding to risk it, Cassandra reached into a cargo pocket and pulled out one of the few high-tech toys she'd brought on this excursion.

It looked and felt like a simple flash drive, but it held a sophisticated program that would slip around the password protection, dig deep into the computer's guts, and copy each of the drives. Her only hesitation in using the special flash drive was the time it took to work its magic. The time depended on how much information it had to sort through, and disconnecting the flash drive early would net her nothing.

While waiting for the light on the side to switch from red to green, Cassandra searched more of the office. She found the usual pens, pencils, stapler, pads of sticky notes, and other stuff one expected to find on and in a desk. However, in addition to these typical things, she also found an English-Arabic dictionary with three short notes written in perfect English. That was the second item—the first being the English magazines—that didn't fit the scenario of the man being a foreign terrorist. In the top center drawer, she found a pack of cigarettes, a lighter, and a book of matches.

Flashing her light around the room, Cassandra searched for a prayer rug and riffled through the desk drawers in search of a Koran. Finding neither, her suspicions deepened.

Could this guy be an American?

Footsteps pounding down the hallway made her stiffen. She snapped off the light and closed the laptop lid most of the way to cut down on the light leaking out from the screen. Her special flash drive still shone a steady red color. Muffled shouts reached her, but she couldn't make out individual words. Even the language eluded her at first then just confused her as she realized it was a mixture of English and something she couldn't identify. The footsteps rushed right past the door, but Cassandra held her breath for another thirty seconds beyond the blissful silence.

She needed to get out.

Having nothing to do while waiting for the flash drive to finish, Cassandra opened her phone and started emailing the picture files to several accounts, including a personal one set up for this job. The pictures wouldn't all fit in one email, so she resorted to a series of emails. Deciding to summon backup, she also composed a message for Special Agent Daniel Cooper. She'd memorized his contact information as part of her mission preparation. After the mission, she would have to trash the phone, but that was an acceptable loss. She went through more phones than anybody she knew, but it was a standard job hazard.

Peeling off the tracking device she'd stuck to her left arm, Cassandra placed it on the underside of one of the desk drawers.

By the time she finished, the flash drive indicator had flipped to green. Ripping the thing free, Cassandra dug out a specialized adapter cord that would allow her to hook the flash drive to her phone. If the tech genius she'd hired set up the program correctly, the drive would do the work for her. She opened the appropriate app and added Agent Cooper and Agent Luchek as approved contacts to receive the massive files being prepared. The program would parse the information into appropriately labeled zip files and email them in packets of varying sizes. Hopefully, at least some of the packets would slip through the spam filters. She had set up four email accounts so the program could spoof several sending emails to ensure that something would make it. After attaching the small drive and checking that everything worked, Cassandra wrapped the cord around her phone and tucked it into a secure pocket.

With her mission more than half accomplished, Cassandra had only to escape, meet up with Agent Luchek, and wait for the FBI agents to finish the job.

More heavy footsteps rushed past the door. That could be a problem, but she'd noticed that most of the men wore outfits like hers. Some out on patrol even wore black ski masks. If she could get outside and avoid talking to anybody, she could wander the campus with some degree of freedom. Winter clothes were good at hiding one's gender. Slipping her mask on, Cassandra put the magazines back where she'd found them and stared into the penlight enough to get her eyes used to brighter amounts of light. She listened closely at the door as she tucked the light away. Hearing nothing, Cassandra quickly exited and ran down the hall, making as much racket as the men who'd dashed this way before.

As she exited the main lodge, a man grabbed her arm, said something unintelligible, and tugged for her to follow him. He too wore a ski mask, but he sounded young enough to be a teenager. Grunting, she knocked his arm away and waved for him to lead on, not really having a choice about following.

Excited shouts rang out from several directions. Some of them were in English.

"What's going on?"

"I can't see."

"Stop pushing!"

"Where did they find her?"

Cassandra had trouble picking out the speakers in the crush of about two dozen men crowded around a group of four snowmobiles lined up with their headlights lighting up the night. She couldn't decide if she should press forward to see what was happening or try to slip away. She did take advantage of the crowd to lose the boy who'd led her here.

Suddenly, the men fell quiet. Cassandra felt the figures on her right side jostle her left, so she stepped that way as far as the pressing crowd would allow. The snow had stopped, but the bite to the winter air made ski masks common. About three quarters of the men had donned protective head gear.

Score one for small favors.

The sea of men parted to allow one figure to enter the semicircle formed around the snowmobiles. As the semicircle closed again, Cassandra moved forward enough to see the source of the excitement.

Her heart sank.

Megan!

"We couldn't find the partner, but there's another snowmobile out there, sir," one of the drivers reported.

English and what Cassandra guessed were Arabic curses came from the man who'd parted the semicircle.

"I told you what to look for, where to find it, and when to look," he grumbled. "Do I have to do everything for you?" Looking hard at the crowd around him, he raised his voice. "There should be another woman around here somewhere. Find her!"

Nobody moved.

"What do we do with this one?" asked the head of the snowmobile crew.

The leader whipped his head back around to regard the man then swung his gaze down to Megan who'd been dropped facedown onto the snow. Cassandra wanted to check on her but didn't dare. Like the men around her, she could only watch and wait. The large leader's body was backlit by the snowmobile headlights, casting his features in deep shadows, but something about his profile looked familiar. The man's English was flawless, and his skin, despite the tan, was definitely pale.

"Bring her inside to my office and secure her to a chair," he ordered, gazing at Megan. "We have some things to discuss."

"And how do you want the search conducted, sir?" inquired the speaker for the snowmobile guys.

The continued use of *sir* had a vaguely military ring to it.

"Wake every man. We need to find the other woman quickly. I'll be in my office adjusting the plan and questioning our friend here. Let me know when you find her partner. Otherwise, don't disturb me." When the words failed to prompt action, the leader whirled and cuffed the nearest man. "Go! Now!"

Cassandra and the rest of the crowd finally took the hint and scattered.

Chapter 6:
A Cold Challenge

A hand gently slapping Megan's cheeks brought her back to consciousness. Even before she opened her eyes, she registered blessed warmth, but the peace didn't last. The hand tapped her left cheek once more and then moved higher, brushing the side of her head until it found a tender spot. She jerked her head away. The sudden movement caused a stabbing sensation to lance through her brain and brought her fully awake.

"Salam, mahbubeh," greeted a smooth male voice in Farsi.

Hello, sweetheart. Megan's muddled brain translated the words as she opened her eyes to a familiar, ruggedly handsome face.

"Megan Luchek. I didn't think you'd come," said Keith Danielson, switching to English. His eyes swept her from head to toe. "You look good."

"Keith." Megan's head crowded with too many questions to do much more than acknowledge the man's name. She tried to sit up straighter but her arms wouldn't move. They were bound behind her back with something broad, flat, and strong.

Duct tape. Keith's favorite.

Back when he was trying to recruit her to the CIA, Keith had pointed out the many uses of duct tape.

Her legs wouldn't move either. She leaned forward until she could peer down at her left leg and see that it was secured to the chair with more duct tape. Her winter coat lay in a heap next to her. Wanting to avoid eye contact, Megan took in the room as a whole. It looked like the cave of a madman, which she supposed was true. Keith had always

213

struck her as a feral human. A giant map took up much of one wall. Stacks of magazines lined the other two walls she could see. The chair she sat in faced the door. She finally returned her attention to Keith who waited patiently for her to absorb the situation.

Conclusion: not good.

"You remember me." Keith's green eyes sparkled when he smiled. "I'm flattered."

"Why am I here?" Megan aimed for a demanding tone, but her body delivered only weary curiosity.

"Funny. I was about to ask you the same thing."

"From your first statement, I gather you tried to get me here. So, again, the question becomes why? Why me? Why here? Why now? And why all that?" Megan tilted her head toward the wall holding the map. "Is that real?"

Keith knelt so their eye levels were even. His light brown hair was shaggy. He would have looked like a caveman if his beard and mustache weren't so neatly trimmed. His eyes were bright with a crazy gleam.

"Ah, Megan, so logical, so predictable. You're like her you know, from what I can tell. I don't actually know her very well."

"Who are you talking about?" Megan wasn't thrilled about indulging Keith's delusions, but the longer he talked, the longer she lived.

"The other woman—Cassandra—if that is her real name. One can never tell with these Fixers. At least I'm assuming that's her running around out there. I did try to get her here. Would you set my mind at ease about that if I asked nicely?"

What do you know about Fixers?

Megan blinked at him, daring him to make sense.

"Don't you want to know why I'm after Cassandra too?" Keith whispered the question.

"I'm sure you'll tell me anyway, but if it helps, I'll ask. Why are you after Cassandra?"

"Simple. She's the favorite of a rival of mine. The end." His knees cracked as he stood up. "Would you like a cigarette?"

Megan shook her head.

Keith walked past Megan. When she twisted her head right as far as it would go, she glimpsed a large, wooden desk. The sound of opening and closing drawers was followed by a match being struck. Soon after, Keith sighed contentedly, and a cloud of smoke drifted through the room.

"When did you take up smoking?" Megan asked. The Keith Danielson she knew had been a complete health and exercise nut.

"A lot can change when the years aren't kind to you," he commented, coming around to stand in front of her again. "Are you comfortable?"

"Not particularly." Despite not having the winter coat on, the rest of the cold weather clothing combined with the room's heat to make her uncomfortably warm.

"I'm sorry about that, and I'm sorry things couldn't be different for us." Keith shook his head sadly and took a few contemplative drags on the cigarette. "You had so much potential. You could have prevented all of this if you'd joined me when you had the chance."

"Joined you?" Megan asked, confused. "You mean work for the CIA? Do *you* even work for the CIA these days?"

He shrugged noncommittally then grinned again.

"You'll never know. Doesn't that drive you crazy?"

"Either you do or you don't." Megan tried to keep her voice even. "This is either a very elaborate, highly illegal, operation to trap some terrorists or you've gone rogue. None of which explains why you wanted me here."

"Dooset daram," he said, declaring that he loved her in Farsi.

"Dorogh gu," she replied, calling him a liar in the same language.

Keith laughed, finished his cigarette, and walked to the trash can to dispose of the butt.

"I've always loved you, but you were too wounded by that business with your ex-boyfriend for anything to come of it," he said upon his return. "That's why it broke my heart when you chose the feds over defending your country against those who would harm her."

Why is it I attract psychopaths?

"Keith, the only threat I see is you." Megan cast her eyes in the direction of the wall map. She refused to waste any thoughts on Travis right now. "What's with the map?"

He looked at her with a serious expression.

"Did you know that terrorists are going to destroy multiple soft targets this holiday season?" asked Keith.

The many map pins suddenly had new meaning. Megan squinted at the map, trying to read the names of doomed places. Even though she couldn't read the names, the position told her a few of the targets.

"They might even murder a hotshot young FBI agent and post the video for the whole world to see," he whispered.

The threat to her life rolled over and off her as Megan considered the magnitude of what she was seeing on the map.

He's marked the bridges and the tunnels. It'll be chaos.

"You should feel honored, Maggie. Does your mother still call you that? You're going to help me one way or another. Either work with me or become a martyr for the only cause that matters. Peace."

Megan's head started throbbing as she tried to follow his twisted thought patterns.

"How will attacking bridges and tunnels help bring peace?" she demanded. Megan moved her shoulders to loosen them.

Keith shook his head, feigning disappointment.

"We're not going to really attack the bridges or the tunnels, just the malls, restaurants, and schools. Don't you see the difference in red and green?"

Now that he mentioned it, Megan did notice that the bridges and tunnels to New York City were marked with green pushpins.

"Decoys. Diversions, so you can get at the soft targets."

"Precisely. Now you're catching on," he praised. "Think of the things I could have done with that sharp mind of yours, not to mention that body." He enhanced his creeper status by raising his eyebrows at her. "Have you pinned down my motives yet?"

She hadn't, but as his mocking gaze bore down on her, at least some of the pieces clicked into place.

"You're fighting the war on terror from the PR front," Megan ventured. "Painting the terrorists to be worse monsters than everybody already believes them to be."

"Go on. What are my motives?" he repeated.

"Either you own stock in a weapons company, you're punishing people for not listening to you, or you have a distasteful proposal that you're hoping will gather momentum after these events."

"Bravo. Two of three correct, but now that you mention it, I think I'll go buy some stocks when we finish up here. I believe we've finished with the opening phase. Now, on to the proposal."

Keith suddenly lashed out with both palms, tipping the chair backwards. Megan yelped in surprise. She didn't fall far though because something, presumably the desk, caught the chair. She slid back and down, crushing her hands. For a moment, Megan stared directly at the ceiling, but then she lifted her head. Keith loomed over her. Gently, he ran his fingers down her face.

"There comes a time in life, Megan, where we find out what defines us, what shapes us, what tells us who we are deep inside. Are we heroes, villains, or simply people willing to make the tough choices for the good of the world?" Keith let the question linger between them. "I know what I am, and I'm eager to discover what you're made of too. Will you hear me out?"

"I can't exactly stop listening," she pointed out.

"But you could close your mind and your heart. I need you to open both to me."

Megan bit the inside of her cheek to keep from calling him crazy. She'd faced evil before, but not quite from this angle. She didn't know the how or even really the why, but somehow Keith had targeted her through Cassandra's organization. That meant he must be connected to the Shadow Council, but she had no idea in what capacity.

Her neck was getting sore, so she rested her head on the desk, preferring the sight of the ceiling to Keith's face.

"You can tell me your proposal, but I'm not helping you kill innocent people," Megan said. She tired of this game. If he was going to kill her, she couldn't really stop him, but she could deny him the answers he wanted.

"Don't be so hasty." Keith lit another cigarette. "I admit my plan involves sacrificing a few people, but I refuse to call them innocents. Nobody is innocent in this cursed world."

Get to the point. Get to the point. Megan's mind chanted.

"What do you want from me?" she asked.

"I want you to alert your bosses to the terrorist threat against the bridges and tunnels. Mobilize Homeland Security and the FBI. Move them to where I want them."

Megan shook her head.

"There's got to be more. An anonymous tip from anybody, even you, would accomplish that if you gave them enough proof of a credible threat. Why make me your messenger?"

"You underestimate yourself, and you said it yourself, I need a credible threat. You can lend the necessary credibility." Keith continued to puff away at the second cigarette.

Megan tried not to choke on the smoke.

"As for the 'why you' part, I think I've already answered that.

Of all the recruits, you were always special to me. I'm going to immortalize you."

"So even if I help you, I die," Megan noted. "That's not great motivation to help you."

"What about pain, friends, and family?" Keith tilted his head like a curious puppy. "Are they better motivators?" He reached down and fingered the top of her shirt, pulling down enough to expose the skin on the upper part of her sternum. Without warning, he briefly touched the lit end of the cigarette to her skin.

Ouch! Hot. Hot. Hot.

She flinched and glared up at him.

He responded with a smile.

"Just something to think about for later, but now I need your help."

This was about the point for her to tell him to go to the hot place, but she got distracted by the sound of the door opening.

"No. No. Don't speak. We can talk later. My men are having trouble locating dear Cassandra." He tapped his left ear and turned slightly so she could see the subtle earwig. "Now we can test your charisma. Will she come for you?"

"You realize we were in a shootout with each other in one of the only other times I've met her, right?"

"That only makes this more interesting." Plucking a roll of duct tape off of the desk, Keith ripped off a small section and pasted it over Megan's mouth.

Two men reached down, righted the chair, and used medical scissors to cut through the duct tape around Megan's wrists and ankles. Though relieved to be free of the chair, she knew her situation hadn't improved. She considered fighting them, but didn't have the energy. They wrestled her into her winter coat and zipped it up. Megan winced when the cloth brushed the fresh burn on her chest.

"Put her gloves on too," Keith ordered.

The men obeyed.

"Perfect. Just one more thing."

Two more men entered lugging a large basin filled with water. Their intention struck Megan as one of the two guys holding her arms kicked her behind the right knee, buckling it. She tried to fight them, but it was far too late to resist. Pressure from above forced her to kneel. Her right arm was twisted up behind her back until all thoughts fled. She held her breath as a hand drove her face into the water. They let her up but the damage was done. Her entire head dripped with water.

Two of Keith's goons hustled Megan out to the center flagpole. One man pressed her back against the flagpole while the other grabbed her hands and handcuffed them behind her back. A portable spotlight had been rigged to shine on her face. Keith's intention became clear, but in case anybody missed the point, he announced it over the loudspeaker.

"Good morning, Ms. Mirren. I know you've eluded my men so far, but I really want to talk to you. If you surrender, no harm will come to you or Agent Luchek. You have an hour to decide. Come to my office. I'll be waiting for you. Please note that she's already soaking wet. More water will be poured over her head every fifteen minutes. If you refuse to surrender, I'll have her coat stripped off. Without that coat, she'll freeze to death."

Chapter 7:
Kicking the Eight-Hundred Pound Gorillas into Gear

"Howdy, stranger. Fancy meeting you here."

Daniel Cooper froze with his coffee cup halfway to his mouth and saw his wife sauntering up with the baby propped on a hip and one hand gripping Ashley's shoulder.

"Whoa. What's that brooding look mean?" Bethany released Ashley, and the girl raced forward to throw her arms around Dan's waist.

He quickly placed his coffee on the table so he wouldn't spill it on his daughter. Since she was going to climb into his lap anyway, he helped her along by picking her up and settling her in place. Then, he reached for his wife's hand.

"Hi, daddy!" Giggles whispered in her booming inside voice.

Dan looked down at the girl fondly.

"Hey, baby."

"Not baby!" Giggles protested. "That baby!" She stabbed a finger in her sister's direction.

"Dan?" Bethany questioned, looking worried.

"We need to talk, but let's get some food for the girls first," said Dan. "We can take it up to the room."

Seeing his family had made the decision easy. There was no way Dan would waste his time at a conference while his partner battled terrorists. They would face their boss together after the crisis. Additionally, the list of possjible targets included some places his wife had expressed an interest in seeing over the next few days.

While Bethany ordered breakfast for herself and the girls, Dan searched for the right arguments, suggestions, and pleas. Outright ordering her to stay in the hotel room would go over about as well as a hydrogen filled balloon. It would work fine until it exploded in his face. Besides, hotels were on the possible hit list too. The file gave no specifics, and there were dozens if not hundreds of hotels in Philadelphia. Still, he wanted his family out of the city, which wouldn't be easy by public transportation alone. Renting a car was an option, but where could he send them?

Megan's parents.

It could get awkward for all parties concerned, but Dan would take awkward over dead any day.

What if they're targets too?

Dan dismissed the thought as paranoia. Thinking Megan's parents were in danger required admitting that his partner was a primary target. Nothing in the file suggested that either. The case could be an elaborate hoax or a legitimate threat much wider than one woman. Megan's involvement seemed to be random.

The woman's a certified trouble magnet.

A tiny hand slammed into his chest.

"Look here!" Giggles demanded, giving him a grumpy face. The expression morphed into sugar and sweetness. She giggled upon realizing she had his attention.

"Ashley, that's no way to talk to daddy," Beth scolded.

"I see you," Dan assured his older daughter. He tightened his hold on her and affected his mock-villain voice. "And I've got you! You'll never escape me!" He planted baby kisses on her cheeks and tickled her tummy, earning some high-pitched squeals from Giggles and some dirty looks from the few other early morning risers.

The food arrived in to-go containers along with the bill. Dan left enough cash to cover the bill and a tip.

"You want the live cargo or the yummy cargo?" he asked his wife.

"Half and half," she answered, glancing down at their slumbering younger daughter.

Kid sure can sleep, Dan thought, mildly envious.

He shrugged and rose.

"All right, monkey, we're gonna have to do this travel style," Dan told Ashley.

"Yay!" The girl clambered down then hopped up onto the chair and leapt onto Dan's back.

This left his hands free to pick up the breakfast containers. Bethany took the container holding two large coffees and a carton of milk. They made it back to the room, and Dan fished the key card out of his pocket.

"Me do," Giggles said, dropping off of his back with a thud. She snatched the key card while it was still on the way to the door and expertly guided it home even though the slot was well above her head. When the light turned green and the lock deactivated, she yanked the handle down.

Dan looked to his wife.

"When did she learn to do that?"

"I've stopped asking that question," Bethany said, entering their room ahead of him. She wasted no time in putting the drinks down, settling the baby in a carrier, relieving her husband of the food sack, and laying out the goods.

After arranging everything so Ashley could eat, Dan pulled Beth to the far side of the room.

"Where go?" Ashley asked, shifting to get down and join them.

"Mommy and daddy need a time out."

Beth's statement earned quite a look.

"Mommy and daddy bad?" Ashley wondered.

"No, love, just boring adult stuff," Beth answered patiently. "Have a tea party with some imaginary friends. You can tell me about it later."

Giggles regarded them like odd creatures but then decided pancakes were much more interesting.

"You're a genius," Dan complimented in a low voice.

Turning so their nosy daughter couldn't see her expression, Beth Cooper speared Dan with a look that demanded answers.

"What's going on?" She checked her watch. "You're either going to be very late for your conference or you're skipping it. And with that look the reason's got nothing to do with wanting to spend more time with us. So give."

Once again, Dan silently ran through the options. Finally, he settled on a version that held mostly truth with a few little white lies of omission.

"My partner picked up a case, and I need to be here to run some paperwork up the proper channels for her." He hesitated then forged on. "I can't say much, but it's got to do with possible terrorist attacks on public locations."

Beth's eyes widened.

"Until we get it sorted, I'd feel much better if you and the girls stayed out of public places."

"Daniel, *this* is a public place!" Beth hissed. "Where exactly are we going to go?"

He held up his hands like that could stem the rising tide of anger.

"I've given that some thought, and I think you should go visit with Megan's folks for the day. They live in central New Jersey. I don't know where exactly, but I can find out."

"If you're staying here, then we're staying here," Beth declared.

Dan started to shake his head but stopped when her hands gripped his.

"You have to stay to do your job. I understand that, but we're not going away." She spoke in a fierce whisper. "I will not let my life be dictated by the possibility of an attack, and I am *not* raising those girls without you, mister. So, like it or not, we're staying right here."

He pulled her into an embrace and kissed the top of her head.

"Will you at least stay in for the day? I'll feel better if I know where to find you."

She nodded against his chest.

He breathed an inward sigh of relief and enjoyed the moment of peace.

"Mommy, come eat!" called Ashley.

The girl's shout woke her sister who started fussing. Dan released Beth and started toward the baby carrier, but his wife stopped him.

"I've got this. Go save Megan from herself."

As if prompted by her words, Dan's phone chimed to let him know he had an email. Then, it chimed again and again. Ripping it off of his belt, he punched in his code and stared at the machine curiously. One by one, his email box flooded with new messages. Picking one at random, he started reading.

To Special Agent Daniel Cooper, FBI:

I'm sure Agent Luchek has already briefed you or left you the file I prepared for her. This is some of the evidence I've gathered, but I still don't know enough to say whether the threat is real. Have your analysts take a look. Outwardly, it appears genuine, but several pieces don't fit. I will work with Agent Luchek to find out more.

Should the analysts say the threat's real, I trust you can awaken the 800-pound gorillas. We're going to need them.

~C.

Dan opened two more emails and found the same message with different photo attachments. Every few seconds, his phone would chime again as a new email hit the inbox. He considered forwarding them to the tech people at his home office, but it was about two thirty in the morning over there. At best, he could hope a skeleton crew would be manning the stations. The better bet would be to wrangle an official introduction to the locals from his boss. He groaned, dreading waking Maddox.

Slipping into the restroom for privacy, Dan turned on the light and fan before locking the door. As he searched his contact list for Special Agent in Charge Bryan Maddox, Dan ran over opening lines, not liking any of them. The phone rang three times before his boss answered.

"Maddox," came the gruff voice.

"It's Agent Cooper, sir. I'm sorry to disturb you at this hour."

"Get to the point, Cooper. What's she done now?" Maddox sounded fully awake.

"I don't know, sir," Dan answered honestly.

"The pair of you are supposed to be tucked up safe in an antiterrorism conference in the City of Brotherly Love. The fact that you're calling me at this hour tells me that's not happening. Why isn't that happening?" Maddox's last question was practically a growl.

Dan launched into the shortest explanation he could manage, which still ran at least a minute in length.

"Do you know anybody in the Philadelphia office, sir? I need access to their computer analysts and a translator as soon as possible," Dan finished.

A beat of silence passed.

"Where is Agent Luchek?" Maddox inquired, sounding like he knew exactly where she'd be.

"She's investigating more directly, sir," Dan answered. He decided not to lie to Maddox. If Megan was in danger, she could be mad at him after they rescued her. "She's supposed to call to check in sometime today. I have a tracking device that should let me follow her if necessary."

Maddox breathed heavily into the phone.

"I'll make some phone calls and get back to you. Meanwhile, get over to the Bureau office on Arch Street. Ask for Assistant SAC Linda Felding or SAC Louis Hatcher. Either of them should be able to help you."

"Thank you, sir."

"Don't thank me yet, Cooper. I'll also be calling the DHS boys. They don't like us, but this is their ballgame too."

"If it's real, I'll take all the help I can get, and I'm sure Agent Luchek would say the same," Dan assured their boss.

"Speaking of Luchek, have her call me when she checks in. If she doesn't check in on time, and I mean if she's so much as three seconds overdue, you gather a team, you go get her, and you haul her to safety by the ears if you have to. Clear?"

"Clear, sir," Dan answered. Normally, he tried to mollify their boss, but this time the crackling tension fit the grim situation.

"I've half a mind to lock that one in the basement and lose the key," Maddox grumbled.

Dan agreed with the sentiment if not the solution.

"Yes, sir."

"Get moving, Cooper. You've got a lot of work to do," Maddox prompted. "I want the chance to bawl her out when she gets home."

Dan took the statement as Maddox's version of concern for Megan.

"I'll make sure you get that chance, sir," he promised.

But I get first crack at her for making me worry, again.

Chapter 8:
Challenge Accepted

Cassandra Mirren didn't like that the man issuing the challenge knew her name. Not even Agent Luchek had known her full name, which meant the man already had the information. That was a disturbing thought, but she didn't have time to mull it over.

What else does he know?

Pushing the question aside, she weighed her options. Escape was a high priority, but she wasn't eager to abandon Agent Luchek. The mission needed completing, and she also needed to deal with the idiot shouting her name through loudspeakers. With everybody running about like headless chickens, escaping alone would be relatively simple, but that wouldn't solve her other two problems.

First things first, Megan had to be set free. If they were going to complete the mission, the two of them would stand a much better chance together than either of them had alone. A half-dozen plans were formed and discarded before something with at least a quarter chance of succeeding crossed her mind.

Enough men were still rushing past the spot where Agent Luchek had been left leaning against the flagpole. The bright spotlight might have helped keep the agent warm if it was closer, but it had been rigged about six feet away. Cassandra couldn't hope to get close to Agent Luchek with that light blazing away. The quality of light and the angle from which it glowed created a bizarre image like the agent was a witch being burned at the stake.

The light needs to go.

Cassandra made several passes across the courtyard pretending to be on one urgent errand or another. Most of the men were doing the same, rushing about looking for her, and rousing their companions to help conduct the search. In another few minutes enough order would be restored and her chances of a successful rescue would drop to nothing. If she was going to make a move it had to be now.

"There! Over there!" Cassandra shouted, deepening her voice as much as possible.

She pointed directly past the spotlight and sprinted straight for it like she was headed for the woods beyond. As she approached the light, she adjusted her gait enough so that her right boot collided with the light, kicking it several feet away. Several men had started to run where she'd indicated, but they froze when the light emitted a wounded electrical noise and blinked off. Cassandra threw herself to the ground and cried out in pain like she'd twisted an ankle.

One man came forward to help her stand. Cassandra batted his hand away.

"I've got this. Go! We've got to find her now!" Cassandra's man voice wasn't perfect but it worked.

The boy sprinted away, waving and shouting for the others to follow him. A few hesitated but the men at least jogged toward the area she'd pointed out.

Knowing the window of opportunity would slam shut in a matter of seconds, Cassandra leapt up and raced to Megan. Digging deep into her left pocket, she came up with the handcuff key she always carried. Most handcuff models worked with a universal key. She fervently hoped that would be true for these. As she pressed the key into Megan's gloved hands, movement from her right side caught her attention.

Rolling left, Cassandra pulled a knife from her right boot and stayed crouched in the snow, ready to receive the attack. Uttering a challenging cry, a man charged her, arms wide to wrap her in a crushing embrace. Getting hit by him would not be a pleasant experience. Cassandra waited until the last possible moment then dropped to the ground, tucking her arms close to her chest, and propelling her body through two revolutions to the right. As her arms faced the ground for the second time, Cassandra pushed upward and brought her legs underneath her body. Whirling, she saw the big man was ten feet beyond her, skidding to a stop. She didn't have time to let him turn and try again. The other men would return soon. For a timeless moment, she thought the man would shout for help, but instead, he turned toward her for a renewed charge.

The mistake cost him dearly as Cassandra ended his life with one deft flick of the knife. She relieved him of a handgun and two magazines, tucking them into a cargo pocket. Megan would need them later, but right now, the agent needed to be warmed up quickly.

It made her nervous that more guards weren't watching over Megan.

Where'd the leader go? Shouldn't he be keeping watch over his trap?

Cassandra shook off the disturbing questions and turned back to the flagpole to find the agent free but barely managing to keep on her feet.

"Don't quit on me yet," she muttered, as she caught the agent's arm and draped it over her shoulders to lend support. She paused, trying to determine the best place to go.

Megan's teeth were chattering too much to let her answer.

"We've got to get you inside right now," said Cassandra.

A working knowledge of which buildings housed the men was one benefit of her earlier surveillance. Knowing that most of the men had emptied out of the barracks, Cassandra headed there, dragging the frozen FBI agent. If anybody got in her way, they'd just have to die.

Upon reaching the welcoming warmth, Cassandra dumped her charge onto the nearest bed. Next, she locked the door and moved a small end table in front of it. Fortunately, since it was still early, the blinds were already drawn. She listened to the sound of snowmobiles firing up and receding as the men took the search for her into the woods. They wouldn't stay gone forever. Snapping herself back into motion, Cassandra pawed through drawers and closets until she found a few towels, a hair dryer, and some clean clothes that would sort of fit Megan.

After toweling off the worst of the water, Cassandra dragged Megan over to a place within reach of a plug, sat her down, and turned the hair dryer on full blast. When the agent thawed enough to handle the hair dryer, Cassandra retrieved a fresh towel and continued attacking the woman's wavy, brown hair until they'd driven off most of the water. The droning noise from the dryer made Cassandra nervous, but the need for quick warmth outweighed the preference for quiet.

A couple of minutes later the agent stopped resembling a human ice sculpture.

"Thank you."

"We're not done yet," said Cassandra. She gathered up the

bundle of clothes and brought them to the agent. "Tell me truthfully. Can you change on your own or do you need help?"

"I think I can manage."

"Good. Then strip. I need your bra."

The agent arched an eyebrow at Cassandra, who flushed because the room was too darn hot.

"Look, we're not going to find a replacement here." She waved to the ample evidence around them that this was a male dormitory. "I can dry it with the hair dryer and have it back to you in a few minutes."

Nodding, the agent slipped off her wet shirt and pulled on one of the two long-sleeved black T-shirts Cassandra had pilfered from a drawer. Then, she wriggled out of the bra and tossed it to Cassandra who turned the dryer's might against it.

Reaching into the pocket where she'd stashed the spare gun, Cassandra handed it to Megan along with the extra magazines. Since the dryer was making a racket, she pointed to her eye then to the door. Catching the message, the agent checked that the gun's magazine was fully loaded and turned her attention to the door.

Two tense minutes later, Cassandra returned the bra and started rummaging again.

"What are you looking for?" Megan wondered, as she fixed her clothing situation.

"Food," Cassandra replied.

"Good idea." Megan started to stand.

"Rest. I'll find something."

"I have to use the facilities anyway," Megan said.

By the time the agent returned from the bathroom, Cassandra had quite the array of junk food spread out on one of the beds. Considering power bars as the least of the evils displayed, Cassandra picked up two and tossed them to the agent. Then, she picked up two more and devoured them on the way to the bathroom. She needed to rinse her face. The long night was getting to her. When she returned, Megan wordlessly handed her an energy drink. She frowned at it, but accepted the inevitable. She would need the energy.

"What the—" the sleepy voice cut itself off and ended with a curse when two guns swung his way. The skinny young man raised his hands and retreated a step. His dark hair stuck up in odd patches, giving him the look of a freshly roused teenager.

"Stop," Megan ordered.

Cassandra traded her gun for her knife. She might need every bullet later.

She raced forward and had the point of her knife up under the man's chin before he could do more than blink stupidly at her.

"Don't kill him!" cried Megan.

Grunting with disgust, Cassandra reversed the knife's direction and slammed the hilt into the man's temple to buy them some time to debate the issue. This is why she preferred working alone. Straight-laced people like Agent Luchek always got mushy when it came to killing with knives.

"We can question him," the agent argued.

"About what?" Cassandra returned.

The young man moaned and slowly shook his head.

"How many men we might face."

"A lot," Cassandra supplied.

"Where we can find more weapons," said the agent, undeterred.

Cassandra was about to shut her down again, but the wisdom of finding more weapons made her pause. She pressed her lips together, pride not wanting to let her surrender the point.

"Fine." She traded the knife for her silenced handgun again and stepped back to a safe range. Steadying up the shot, she said, "If you want to live, start talking. Where can we find more weapons? How many men work here? What's going on? Who is the leader and where can we find him? If I think you're lying, you die. Start with the first question."

Cassandra had to repeat the first question for the young man, but he soon told her of three separate weapons caches. One with only assault rifles, handguns, and some ammunition was located in a back closet in this building. Cassandra sent the FBI agent to check. Megan returned a few minutes later and confirmed that the man had spoken the truth.

"Good start," Cassandra commented. "How many men are there?"

"I don't know." The young man looked nervous about that answer. "Two dozen, maybe three. It varies. People come and go."

"Who is your leader?" asked Megan.

From her tone, Cassandra could tell she already knew the answer.

"I don't know his name."

Megan looked frustrated and gave the barest shake of her head.

"Wrong answer." Cassandra fired a bullet into the wall an inch from the man's head. "And last warning."

He yelped and hunched his shoulders, holding his hands out in surrender.

"Okay. Okay. His name is Keith, but that's all I know, I swear!"

Cassandra's eyes flicked to the agent who nodded confirmation. She'd have to question Megan privately later.

"Good. Do you have a phone?" Cassandra inquired.

The man nodded.

"Back pocket."

"Slowly reach back and retrieve the phone then toss it to my partner."

The man followed Cassandra's instruction perfectly.

"What am I supposed to do with this?" Megan asked, catching the phone.

"Call for help when the time comes," Cassandra replied. Turning back to the man, she said, "Last important question. What's going on here?"

He slumped against the wall and put his head in his hands.

"I don't know. I was hired to drive an empty white van across the George Washington Bridge. That's it." He looked up with tears glistening in his eyes. "I knew it was too good to be true." The young man sniffled.

Cassandra looked to Megan for a verdict.

"Is he telling the truth?"

"Probably," Megan answered.

"What's your name?" Cassandra inquired.

"Frank Baum."

"Congratulations, Frank. You get to live. Lie facedown on the floor until my colleague secures your hands and feet."

The young man followed the instruction, but he had to wait a moment for Megan to tie him because she first needed to use Cassandra's knife to butcher a few pillowcases.

For good measure, Cassandra clobbered Frank with the butt of her gun. They couldn't afford to have him escape. They also couldn't stay here much longer. Already, she heard the sounds of angry men milling about.

"Show me the arsenal," Cassandra ordered.

"It's not much of an arsenal," Megan warned.

Nevertheless, she led Cassandra to the back room where the

men had stashed a supply of guns and ammunition.

"Take a few more clips," Cassandra suggested. "You might need them."

"I hope not," Megan said. "Two dozen men are going to be hard to hold off with a pair of handguns, even if you are a great shot. I'm not liking our odds of surviving a shootout."

Chapter 9:
Comparing Notes

When they returned to the main room, Megan started to move their captive, intending to put him on one of the beds, but once she figured out how heavy the slender young man was, she gave up the notion. Instead, she picked up his legs and lugged them over to the right so they lay parallel to the wall. It helped that his feet were bound together. This new position left his body looking uncomfortably twisted, so Megan pushed him onto his right side, scooched him out a little, and pressed on his left shoulder until he rolled onto his back. Finally, she snatched a pillow off one of the beds and tucked it under his head. She felt bad that Cassandra had knocked him out but knew it had to be done. Trying to make his unconscious form more comfortable was merely to salve her conscience. As a finishing touch, Megan arranged his bound hands so that they folded across his stomach.

"He looks dead, but better than before," Cassandra commented.

Megan plodded over to one of the beds and sat down heavily.

"Can I take a nap?" she asked, only partially joking.

"Only if you want it to be permanent," Cassandra said, checking her gun for damage caused by colliding with Frank's head. "We need to move out soon, but first, I want you to look at some pictures. Tell me what you see, then tell me everything you know about that man." She reached into one of her many pockets, drew out her phone, fiddled with it, and tossed it to Megan.

Opening up the photo app, Megan flipped through the recent pictures. It didn't take her long to recognize the office. She tensed at the memories the sight triggered and absently tugged the shirt away from the burn on her chest.

"What's wrong?" Cassandra asked, crossing to where Megan was sitting.

"It's nothing," Megan murmured.

"Show me."

"I'm fine," Megan insisted. Nevertheless, she hooked the top of the shirt with a finger and tugged the cloth down enough to show the other woman the tiny burn. "It's just a cigarette burn, a souvenir from my chat with Keith. The cold was good for it."

That's about the only thing it was good for. She shivered, dreading the thought that in another few minutes, she'd have to step out into that cold again.

Cassandra released a hybrid noise that was part grunt and part snort before disappearing into the back room and returning with a first aid kit.

"Hold your shirt aside while I get some burn cream onto that," Cassandra instructed. "And start talking. I want to hear everything you know about this Keith guy." After spreading a generous amount of burn cream onto a bandage, the woman carefully centered the barrier over the burn.

"His name is Keith Danielson," Megan began. "He's either CIA or ex-CIA. I'm not sure which."

"He could be current CIA?" Cassandra's tone was sharp.

Megan nodded slowly.

"I'm hoping he's gone rogue because I'd prefer that over the thought that somebody working on behalf of the United States government could conceive of this plan." Megan held up the phone which displayed a picture of the map in Keith's office.

"Do you know the plan? What is it?" asked Cassandra.

"I don't know everything," Megan admitted with a slight shrug. "From what he told me, I'm guessing there are at least two parts to the plan. There are actual attacks on random places like airports, schools, and restaurants and fake attacks against larger targets. In theory, I suppose the fake attacks will tie up the potential help, then the real attacks will take place. Keith indicated that the green pushpins marked fake attacks and red ones marked real ones, but he could have been lying."

"There are some photos of notes that were in or around his desk. See if you can read them. Maybe that will help." Cassandra took the phone from Megan and scrolled over to the notes before handing it back. "What do they say?"

Megan squinted down at the tiny, messy symbols. Her written Farsi was rustier than her speaking skills, but slowly, the gears in her head moved enough to interpret part of the notes.

"It's mostly religious ranting and outcry about taking down the West," she reported. "But it feels ... off somehow."

"What do you mean?" Cassandra prompted.

"I think we were meant to find it," Megan said, voicing her gut instinct. "It sounds like Keith, but it also sounds cobbled together from other texts. If that's true, then it's a plant."

"To what end?"

"I don't know yet. He seemed very eager for my help, but I can't tell you why." Something that had been nagging Megan popped into her mind. "Is your last name really Mirren, and if so, how did Keith know? He said you were a favorite of a rival of his, does that mean anything to you?"

Cassandra's expression turned guarded, and she didn't respond right away.

"It means he's connected to the Council," she said at last. "Deeply connected. If he's after you that would explain why I was directed to seek you out, but the order came from a different source. If Keith has the ability to manipulate Council information like that, then he's very high up."

"Does this situation sound like something they'd put together?" Megan wondered. "Could they be backing Keith's play here?"

Once again, the assassin let a few beats pass before answering.

"I'm not sure." The woman's jaw tightened. "The Council wouldn't hesitate to go to great lengths to ensure order, but I've never experienced anything involving this amount of deception and potential destruction. It's not their style." She absently reassembled the first aid kit then met Megan's gaze. "We won't be able to sort out the motives right now and maybe not ever, but I for one am not letting this happen." Her eyes conveyed a question.

"I'm with you," Megan assured her. She was surprised at the conviction she read in the assassin's expression. This wasn't really her fight. "What do you want to do?"

Declaring that they would stop the plans in motion was a far cry from derailing Keith's work. Provoking a shootout would get them both killed, and Megan hadn't explored enough to know where and how to best sabotage the plans.

A slow smile spread across Cassandra's face.

"They have most of their vans stashed in the large barn, and Frank told us where to find some of their weapons. I think I know where they keep the explosives too. I say we set their party off early."

"You want to blow up the barn?" Megan asked, not quite believing her ears. "How are we going to do that without killing ourselves?"

"They didn't teach you that at the Academy?" Cassandra asked, feigning surprise.

"Not really," Megan said. "They were more interested that we know how to recognize explosives so we could call in the experts."

The traces of amusement vanished from Cassandra's face.

"Today we are the experts and the only thing standing between death and life for a lot of people. I doubt Keith's going to wait around much longer, especially with us on the loose. He has two choices: cancel or move up the timetable. He doesn't strike me as the sort of man to cancel his plans."

"We should split up," Megan suggested. "You handle the explosives. I'll distract them."

Cassandra shook her head.

"We're on borrowed time here, but setting off explosives isn't difficult. It's doing it safely that's the hard part. I might need your help. Besides, if we split up we might end up doing Keith a favor by accidentally killing each other. That would really ruin my day. I barely know this man, and I want to kill him."

"What if we did kill him?" Megan could hardly believe she was asking that question. "Would the plan collapse without him?"

"We can't take the risk that they'll quit just because their leader falls. We don't even know if he's the true leader or a puppet. We need to go after their ability to enact the plan in the first place. That means the explosives, the weapons, and the vehicles, everything must go."

Megan blew out a breath.

"That's not going to be easy," she commented.

"Never said it was," Cassandra said. "We need to pick an approach. We can go after the explosives first and use them to take out the other weapons and the vehicles. Or we could go for the weapons and use them to attack the vehicles and explosives from afar. The third option is to go directly for the vehicles and quietly sabotage them. That would be a delaying tactic, but it's also the quietest."

Megan weighed the options.

"Vehicles, weapons, and then explosives. That's my vote. You?"

"Agreed on the vehicles, but I'd hit the explosives next," said Cassandra. "Once they go, everybody's attention will be there, and I think they're stored near the vehicles. They could already be loaded into vehicles for all we know. Our first priority on that front should be the vans, then the trucks, then the snowmobiles. We should leave a few of those intact for an escape. Only the vans and trucks are large enough to carry significant amounts of explosives, but I'd rather not be chased by thugs with guns."

"Yes, let's avoid that. I already crashed a snowmobile today thanks to thugs with guns." Megan's back ached at the thought, but the energy drink had finally kicked in. She got off the bed and reached for her jacket.

"There's one more thing. The barn's probably guarded."

Megan nodded that it was a reasonable assumption.

"We've chosen the quiet plan," Cassandra continued. "That means any men we meet will need to be dealt with silently. Your borrowed gun doesn't have a silencer, I didn't see any in the mini-arsenal, and I take it you're not an expert with knives." She took out her handgun and held it by the barrel as she offered it to Megan. "So, here. Use my gun."

"Okay," Megan said reluctantly. She held the borrowed handgun out to trade for Cassandra's.

The woman waved her off.

"I'll grab another from the back. You might need both." Cassandra reached into a pocket and took out two spare magazines.

"I've got no place to put those." Megan's pockets were already bulging with magazines for the gun from the back. "If it takes more bullets than I've got in here, we're in serious trouble. And when it's out, you can have it back. What's your plan for getting out of here?"

"Ski masks and luck," Cassandra replied.

"Should we take one of the larger guns?" Megan inquired.

"No. If we're hitting the vehicles first, we're going for subtle. Assault rifles aren't subtle." Cassandra rubbed her temple like she didn't really like the plan. "I'll leave first because I know where to find the barn. It's light out now, but once we get inside, we need to head to a certain area. You should change your jacket too. That one will definitely stand out. We also need to get you a knife so you can help slash tires and fuel hoses."

As Megan acknowledged the wisdom of changing her jacket, she spotted a man's bulky black jacket lying in a heap near one of the beds. It didn't smell too pretty, but she put it on anyway.

"Maybe there's a knife in the back. I'll go check." Megan had been about to protest the knife part until she heard the reason Cassandra wanted her to have one. Sure enough, she found a very nice selection of box cutters and tactical knives beneath a box of ammunition for the assault rifles. She chose one of each, then picked up a utility belt that didn't look too large. "They do have everything here," she noted, strapping on the belt. It held a flashlight, a small holster for the tactical knife, separate slots for holding gun magazines, and even a gun holster. Megan considered asking for the extra clips for the assassin's gun but decided to switch back to the Glock-19 she'd picked up earlier.

"Are you done shopping?" Cassandra called. "I'm about to leave. Toss me one of those guns and three clips."

"I'm ready," Megan said, turning to face her co-conspirator and aspiring saboteur. She threw Cassandra the requested items and added a gear belt to the mix. Even with endless pockets, the belt would allow Cassandra to keep more ammunition in a spot that was easily accessible.

Attempts to think of something lighthearted were choked off by fear. Megan's stomach executed a few flips in anticipation. She was fed, watered, and fueled on artificial energy. They had a tentative plan. If nothing went wrong and luck favored them very heavily, they might even survive the mission.

"For what it's worth, I'm glad we're on the same side this time, agent."

"Likewise, assassin." Megan managed the hint of a nervous smile as she mentally braced for stepping out into the cold.

Let's go save Christmas.

Chapter 10:
Nobody Messes with Christmas

By midmorning, Bethany Cooper needed to get out of the hotel. Her husband and Megan Luchek were off saving the world again, and she was trapped with two small children in a room that seemed to shrink every minute. Megan had gone out of her way to make this time special for their family. It would be a shame to let fear remove some of that joy.

Nobody messes with Christmas.

"Girls, we're going out," Beth declared.

"Where?" Ashley asked. She paused in feeding her baby doll its bottle, dropping the unfortunate doll onto its head in her haste to rise.

"I'm not sure. Let's ask Sami."

Cheering with delight, Ashley leapt up and raced over to Beth's purse. Watching her pick up the heavy bag amused Beth, but she went over to help her daughter. Ashley wasn't allowed to go rooting through the purse, except on these rare occasions when Beth was there to supervise. The child located the iPhone almost immediately and waved it in Beth's face.

"Unlock, mommy," she ordered.

"Hold your hair-piece there, little lady," said Beth, earning one of Ashley's famous giggles. "I'm right here." Accepting the phone, she tapped out her unlock code and held down the home key to bring up Sami, the phone's helpful persona.

A question popped up on her screen followed by a statement when she didn't ask a question in the first two seconds.

What can I help you with? Go ahead, I'm listening.

"Hi, Sami," Ashley chirped, tugging at Beth's hand so she could lean toward the audio intake.

"Hi, there," answered Sami's slightly mechanical yet cheery female voice.

"How are you?" asked Ashley.

"Very well, thank you."

My daughter's exchanging pleasantries with a machine. That is either very cool or incredibly sad.

"Where can we find a card store?" Beth asked.

"Okay, here's what I found," Sami declared.

A map materialized with a dozen red pins marking various store locations.

"Thank you!" Ashley shouted.

"You're welcome," Sami replied.

Trying not to roll her eyes, Beth scrolled through some of the pins then zoomed in on a few. There were three possibilities in a two-block radius of their hotel.

Stroller or no stroller?

The stroller would be a big pain to drag around, but Beth wasn't sure of the exact distance. If it was only a block, she could carry the baby while holding Ashley's hand, but any more than that and she'd be in trouble. Beth opted to take the stroller. At least she would be able to pack properly for the outing. By the time she made sure Ashley visited the restroom, gathered the diaper bag and her purse, and wrestled both children into winter gear, Beth was tired but more determined than ever to get some fresh air.

Less than ten minutes later, Beth spotted the perfect diversion: a dollar store. She and Ashley adored dollar stores. Ashley enjoyed looking at the bright aisles filled with endless amounts of stuff, and Beth loved how exploring could entertain her daughter for many minutes. Having a few dollars stretch to several toys was also a nice bonus.

As they wandered up and down the aisles stuffed with holiday decorations and craft supplies, Beth felt the urge to do something creative. Secretly planning for this trip with Megan had consumed much of her mental bandwidth over the past few weeks, so she hadn't gotten Dan a gift from the girls yet. He didn't expect anything, but Giggles was getting to the age where giving something sentimental would be sweet.

"Ashley, we should make something nice for daddy. Would you

like to do that?"

"No!"

Beth gathered the necessary supplies anyway. The kid would come around eventually.

"Maybe Aunt Maggie would like something pretty too," Beth said.

"Okay!" Ashley shouted. She pointed to one item high on a shelf above her. "Glitter!"

Well, that was a quick turnaround.

Beth hesitated, not sure if she wanted to go down the glitter road. Spotting the school glue and construction paper sitting next to the glitter, Beth gathered her courage and swept the three items into the basket.

Live daringly. Go glitter.

***

Megan Luchek donned a ski mask and followed Cassandra Mirren out into the cold. Wearing mostly borrowed clothes felt strange. She'd kept her own pants because nothing else would fit and they hadn't really gotten wet. The assassin kept to a pace that conveyed urgency but not panic. Some of the men had started to mill about and a few leaders were trying to get them into order to intensify the building-to-building search. It looked like most of the snowmobiles had returned. The trip to the barn holding the vehicles and explosives rattled every one of Megan's nerves, but they made it safely.

To her pleasant surprise, only one man guarded the entrance to the vehicle depot. He surrendered immediately when Megan pointed the silenced handgun at him, and Cassandra quickly knocked him out by putting him in a chokehold that deprived his brain of oxygen and then clobbering him with the handle of her knife.

"Start with the van and truck tires," Cassandra ordered, as she eased the unconscious man to the ground. "I'll check on the explosives." She pulled a thin piece of metal from a compartment in her unobtrusive belt.

"You seriously carry one of those around with you?" Megan asked, incredulous.

"You'd be surprised how many times I've had to break into a car for a job," Cassandra said.

Shaking her head, Megan unstrapped the tactical knife and knelt by the right rear tire. Before she could stab it, Cassandra's voice reached out from inside the van.

"Stab the sides; the rubber's a little weaker there. Just make two to three punctures and move on. And try not to look at it directly. You don't want to get anything in your eyes."

The instructions irritated Megan, but she obeyed anyway. She wanted to believe she was competent enough to slash a tire on her own, but the task didn't consist of just one tire. Dozens of tires needed to be punctured. Taking a deep breath, she knelt and braced her body with her left hand while her right drove the knife hard into the side of the tire. She expected a pop or an explosion, but instead, experienced a quiet gush of air.

Watching the air exit the first tire was kind of exciting, but the glamor quickly wore off. By the eighth tire, Megan's knees hurt and her hand ached. Who could have guessed stabbing tires would be so much work? Sweat beaded on her forehead and her breaths grew labored by the time she'd finished with the fifth van and begun attacking the truck tires.

"You can stop slashing tires now and move on to fuel hoses," Cassandra called.

Relieved, Megan put the knife away, climbed to her feet, and flexed her fingers.

"Is that safe?" Megan wondered.

"Of course not," Cassandra said, looking amused. "We're going to flood the place with fuel then light it on fire so it blows up the explosives. I couldn't find enough safe triggers on short notice, so I rigged the gas tanks with gasoline-soaked rags."

"That's the craziest plan I've ever heard," Megan declared.

"It's better than standing here and lighting a match," Cassandra pointed out.

"True, but how are we going to set a fire and get away in time? Do you even know the blast radius of those explosives?"

"I do know the blast radius of those explosives, and *we* don't set a fire. *I* do," said Cassandra. "You cut the hose lines and then get out."

"I'm not leaving—" Megan began.

"You have to," Cassandra said firmly. "Get out and call for help. Try to distract them on the way, but don't get caught. Keith's not going to be pleased with our accomplishments."

Megan wanted to argue, but a man's surprised shout reminded her there wasn't time for disagreement. Cassandra whirled, drew her gun, and fired by the time Megan located the source of the shout. The bullet caught the man in the head and stopped his forward progress cold. He dropped to the ground as the gunshot's echo died.

"We're going to have company soon. Better get moving, agent. You get the fuel hoses on this side, and I'll deal with the tanker truck on the other side."

"At least take your gun," Megan insisted, holding the weapon out like a peace offering.

"Keep it. We're beyond silencers at this point in here, but you might still need it out there. If we both survive, I'll come collect it someday." The assassin sprinted toward the far end of the warehouse.

Since standing there dumbfounded wasn't improving the situation, Megan stumbled over to the fuel station and turned on each of the two pumps. She used a rag to keep the handles compressed and tried to direct the flow of gasoline toward the collection of vans and trucks. The fumes started to make her lightheaded, prompting her to retreat. She hoped Cassandra had a lighter or a match because she had neither. This wouldn't work well without something to light the fuel.

Having done her part, Megan took one last look at her handiwork and fled.

"Fire! Move! Move! Move!" Megan shouted as she sprinted away from the barn.

She passed three men who seemed torn between chasing her and rushing into the barn. Megan couldn't decide which course of action she preferred they take. Hopefully, the shock would keep them in place for a few seconds, not rushing to their deaths or snapping at her heels. She raced back to where she remembered seeing a collection of snowmobiles by the flagpole and hopped onto one. Confirming that it had fuel, she moved the snowmobile a short distance away, drew Cassandra's gun, and paused. She wanted to leave one machine intact for Cassandra, but there was no way to guarantee the assassin would be the one to find the working machine first.

Deciding to play it safe, Megan dismounted, aimed for the fuel tanks, and fired several shots into each. Unlike in the movies, the tanks didn't explode, but they leaked fuel everywhere, rendering the machines useless. The silenced shots emitted muffled sounds closer to a whine than a bark, but the impacts with the tanks resulted in satisfying crunching noises.

A gunshot rang out behind Megan, making her duck instinctively and throwing off her last shot. She scrambled for the snowmobile, fighting off the urge to dive to the snow. Hunkering down would get her killed. Her only hope was a fast exit. Keeping as low as possible, she climbed onto the snowmobile and fired it up, turning away from the gunfire.

More shots and shouts split the morning air, but miraculously, nothing struck Megan as she pointed her machine in the direction of the open fields leading to a dark forest in the distance.

As she reached the tree line, Megan stopped the snowmobile and looked back. She didn't want to duck into the woods unless necessary, so she needed to see what, if anything, pursued her. She spotted a pickup truck headed her way and grunted annoyance at not having time to properly disable every tire.

Before she could turn away and continue her mad dash, movement caught her eye. The distance gave Megan a nice, panoramic view of the scene. In slow motion, a black clad figure in the bottom right corner of her vision leaned over, then turned and sprinted behind the nearest building. A wall of flames erupted behind the figure and raced back toward the barn.

Megan couldn't tear her gaze from the barn. She watched men scurry back and forth, waving their arms frantically.

Everybody knew what would happen, but some of them just stood and stared.

The wait was endless.

Finally, the barn exploded with a bright flash and an impressive boom that flattened the onlookers.

At this point, pursuit seemed unlikely. Megan climbed off the snowmobile and watched the flames consume the barn. She was practically home free. All she had to do was reach into her pocket and use Frank's phone to call in the cavalry.

She couldn't do it.

Cassandra was about to enter a firefight with a few dozen angry men. Sitting on the sidelines never suited Megan. It would take the men a few minutes to recover from the shock, but they would recover and seek revenge. Once again, Megan turned the snowmobile around and headed back toward the fray.

Assassin, I think some of your crazy is catching. Don't you dare die on me.

Chapter 11:
Cavalry and Cleanup

Daniel Cooper pressed his right foot to the floor, hoping to will the car to a faster speed. Grateful as he was to Agent Cameron McAlister for the ride, for once, Dan wished Megan was driving. He couldn't take his eyes off the tracking device reader, which displayed a steady blinking light where presumably he'd find his wayward partner.

"Don't worry, sir, we're almost there," said McAlister. The agent's messy dark hair, pale blue eyes, and five o'clock shadow made him appear young and inexperienced, but his neatly pressed suit jacket and perfectly knotted blue tie argued against the point.

"How do you know?" Dan demanded. His worry made him peevish.

"The only thing up this way's an old, abandoned winter sports resort and a few run-down farms," replied the agent. "If your partner's up this way—"

He never finished his thought because a muffled boom caught their attention and the sky ahead filled with smoke.

"Step on it," Dan ordered. He felt a cold calm settle over his body.

"I-I'm sure Agent Luchek's not—"

"Oh, she's there all right," Dan muttered. "She's probably responsible for that." He gestured to the ever-thickening cloud of smoke.

"I've gotta meet this woman!" Agent McAlister said with awe.

"How far behind are the SWAT teams?" Dan asked. "Tell them to mark this location and report." He gave the agent the coordinates.

245

Agent McAlister picked up a radio set, conveyed the information, and asked for a status update from the two Special Weapons and Tactics teams following them. The local guys were fifteen minutes out and the FBI boys estimated twenty minutes to target location.

Twenty minutes!

Dan didn't think they could wait that long. Twenty minutes in any sort of armed conflict was an eternity.

They crested a ridge and looked across an open space toward a group of about a dozen buildings. His eyes immediately went to the largest building which was engulfed in flames.

The car stopped moving.

It took Dan a few seconds to register that they weren't drawing any nearer to the target area.

"What are you waiting for?" Dan pierced the young agent with an icy glare. "We need to get down there."

"We should wait for the teams to get here," said Agent McAlister. "Anything could be going on over there."

"Exactly." Dan stabbed a finger at the window control letting the glass slide down a few inches and admitting a blast of cold air into the car. The crisp cracks of gunfire met their ears. "My partner is down there, probably getting shot at. She needs us now, not in fifteen minutes. Agent Felding said you were to help me, so get this car moving."

The pale young agent looked torn. He glanced at the wreck of a barn then at Dan and back again several times.

Realization struck Dan.

"You've never been in a firefight before, have you?"

McAlister shook his head.

"No, sir."

"Then this'll be good for you," Dan encouraged.

"What are the rules of engagement in a situation like this?" asked Agent McAlister.

"If they fire at us, fire back," Dan replied. He hoped Megan would have enough sense not to fire on them.

Sighing, the agent popped the trunk, climbed out, and came back with two bulletproof vests.

"Fine. We go in, but we're wearing these." McAlister handed one vest off to Dan.

Hating the delay but acknowledging the necessity, Dan

strapped the Kevlar vest over his borrowed FBI jacket and took out his handgun.

As they approached the compound, Dan tried to figure out the warring factions. It seemed like a one-sided fight with about two dozen men hunkered down behind woodpiles, snowdrifts, snowmobiles, and anything else handy, firing on a lonely cabin at the end of a long chain of similar buildings. He directed Agent McAlister to stop the car, let him out, pull the car left, and park so they could use it as a barrier against the men they were flanking.

"And tell the SWAT guys to move it," he ordered.

Their presence changed the game. The gunfire barrage into the cabin stopped while the men scrambled left or right to get out of the pending crossfire.

Several men leapt onto snowmobiles and sped away or fled on foot.

"Should we chase them?" asked McAlister.

"No, stay put," said Dan. He wanted to climb back in the car and run the men to the ground, but he couldn't leave now. He couldn't even send McAlister after the snowmobiles because that would take away his only protection. "Let's see what happens."

His cellphone rang. Dan crouched behind the car's trunk and cautiously picked up his phone.

"Cooper."

"Dan! Is that you out there?" called Megan.

"Yes, ma'am, your help has arrived," Dan replied. "It's just me and Agent McAlister for the moment, but SWAT teams are on the way. What's your status?"

"We're alive, but we're also running out of ammunition," Megan reported. "We have to end this soon. If they coordinate, they can overrun both positions in minutes."

"I'm on it," Dan said. "Try not to shoot me or McAlister."

A plan started to take shape. The young agent looked suitably obsessed with the protocols. He'd probably be more useful speaking than shooting.

After checking to see that nobody significant had moved, Dan inched closer to McAlister.

"Do you have a loudspeaker?"

"It's in the back seat," said the agent.

"Good. Let's switch positions. Get the loudspeaker and order them to surrender," Dan instructed.

"Yes, sir," replied the wide-eyed agent. He maneuvered to the right position and fumbled with the door handle. Soon, he had a white loudspeaker clutched in his left hand. "Attention. This is the FBI. Put down your weapons and put your hands on your head."

One man tucked behind a large woodpile took a potshot at McAlister. The young agent dropped the loudspeaker and returned fire. His shot pinged off a chunk of wood inches from the man's head.

"Nice shot," Dan complimented. "That should help drive home your point. Repeat the order to surrender."

The success bolstered McAlister's courage. Picking up the loudspeaker, he again ordered the men to surrender.

"I repeat. This is the FBI. Throw your weapons out of reach and put your hands on your head. You won't be harmed if—"

"I ain't going to jail!" declared the man by the woodpile. He fired another shot into the side of McAlister's car.

"That's it. Keep them talking," Dan coached.

***

"I think it's time we part ways again, agent." The assassin knelt next to the window she'd been shooting from only a minute ago. "Thanks for coming back. I'm not sure I could have held out this long by myself."

"Where will you go?" Megan thought perhaps she should stop the woman, but she'd had quite enough fighting for one lifetime. It wasn't her place to bring the woman to justice right now, even if she could. Their last physical fight had ended in a draw.

"I'm pretty sure Keith was on one of the fleeing snowmobiles. I'm going after him." Cassandra's expression dared Megan to protest. "If he escapes, he'll only try again."

"Be safe," Megan said. She knew she ought to say something to prevent Cassandra from attempting to kill Keith, but she agreed with the woman.

The assassin nodded, smiled, and headed toward the back of the cabin.

"Take care of Frank for me."

Megan sniffed. They'd instinctively ducked into the cabin they'd sought shelter in before. Frank had awakened when the shooting started, but he was still trussed up and stretched out along the right wall as one entered the cabin.

The next ten minutes passed tensely as the young agent with Dan tried to convince the men to surrender. The stalling tactic worked. The arrival of two vans of SWAT guys ended the fight almost before it

248

began. Most of the men threw down their weapons and raised their hands. The man by the woodpile gave a defiant shout and opened fire with an assault rifle. He was shot several times by one of the responding agents, but not before putting a few bullets in the first man in line.

Once they'd dealt with the fourteen prisoners outside, the agents started searching each building. Megan heard Dan inform them where to find her.

The incident with the woodpile guy made the agents jumpy, which in turn made Megan nervous. She didn't bother trying to shout her identity to them. Instead, she waited patiently on the floor under the window she'd been defending, hands held out so they could see she didn't have a gun. Nevertheless, they held her at gunpoint, cuffed her, and searched for weapons. The treatment irked her, but she knew they had good reason to be cautious.

Two agents took Frank into custody while another two escorted Megan out of the cabin. The midday sun shone off the snow, making her blink.

"Is this her?" called the SWAT team leader.

Dan's head swiveled in their direction, and he jogged over.

"That's her," he confirmed. "You can take off the cuffs now."

"Sorry about that, ma'am," said the leader as he unlocked the handcuffs.

Megan nodded to let him know she'd heard the apology, but she couldn't think of anything to say. Understanding their actions didn't mean she was ready to let them off the guilt hook right away.

Dan surprised her by wrapping her in a warm hug.

"You really had me worried this time," he admitted.

Speaking of guilt trips ...

"Sorry," Megan murmured, returning the embrace. "Bad habit."

Fire engines could be heard in the distance. Upon releasing her, Dan kept one arm draped around her left shoulder and angled their bodies so they could watch the burning barn.

"Do you ever do quiet and peaceful?" Dan inquired.

"I try," Megan said. "It doesn't always work out the way I envision."

"You ran off at the behest of an assassin chasing possible terrorists. What did you expect?" Dan let her go but kept a stern gaze upon her.

"Fair point," Megan conceded as Dan led her to a bullet-ridden government sedan. "But this part's over and—"

Several cries of alarm and barked orders cut her off.

Whirling toward the disturbance, she saw that one of the men had looped his handcuffed hands around a dark-haired young agent's neck. Instinctively, Megan reached for her gun, but the SWAT guys had confiscated her weapons.

Dan raised his gun.

"Let him go," he ordered calmly.

"No! He's my ticket out of here!" shouted the wild-eyed man. Because he was shorter than the agent, he stayed pretty well shielded by his prisoner. His bushy beard and stringy brown hair made him look like a misplaced confederate soldier.

Megan started side-stepping to draw the man's attention to her.

"You're surrounded and outnumbered," Megan pointed out. "Giving up's your safest option."

"I'm not—"

The man's protest stopped when Dan slammed the handle of his gun down on the guy's skull. The young agent slipped out of the chokehold as the man collapsed.

Dan and Megan each started to help, but the young agent waved them off.

"I've got this." His grim tone conveyed a simmering anger.

"As I was saying, the dangerous part's over," Megan said dryly. She retreated a few steps so they could have a little privacy.

Dan chuckled as he followed her and returned his gun to its holster.

"The dangerous part may be over, but the tedious part hasn't even begun. ASAC Felding's gonna have you pushing papers for a week before she lets you out for fresh air again, and then, you get to go home and explain this mess to Maddox."

"Thanks for that horrible reminder," Megan said with a grimace.

"I need to know what happened here too. These guys look like a collection of mountain men and Middle East refugees." Dan held up a hand to forestall a response. "I'll let ya explain when we get back to the Philly office. We're supposed to head back right away."

"I need to gather my things from Keith's office," Megan stated, shaking her head at the idea of leaving right away.

"Who?" Dan queried.

"Keith Danielson. He was—or still is—a CIA agent I knew from a few years back."

Alarm shot through Dan's features and body like lightning. He pushed Megan back into the cabin.

"You *know* the bad guy?" he demanded. "When were you gonna tell me that?"

"I just did," Megan returned, annoyed at being manhandled after her lousy night.

"Megan, he could be out there with a sniper rifle getting a bead on your thick skull right now." He snapped his phone off his belt and stepped away from her.

"Who are you calling?" Megan asked, fearing the answer.

"Felding. We need to get you into protective custody."

"No," she said flatly. "Get the manhunt for Keith started. Look, I'll go to the Philadelphia office with you and give a full report. I'll even lie low for a day or two while the manhunt continues, but I won't have resources wasted babysitting me when they could be helping to catch him."

Megan won the staring contest. Dan grunted, looking like he wanted to plow his head into the nearest wall.

"Do you have somewhere safe to go?" The tone of his question added that she'd better have a satisfactory answer or all bets were off.

"I've been meaning to visit my great-aunt for a while anyway. She lives about an hour outside of Philadelphia. I can go there for the rest of tonight or go there early tomorrow and then head to my parents' place in New Jersey on Christmas."

The answer partially mollified her partner, but she could tell he still wasn't convinced.

"Don't worry. I—"

"I really hate when you say that," Dan interjected. "It never bodes well."

"I just wanted to say thank you and assure you that I've got nothing but a quiet Christmas Eve planned. You don't have to worry about me, or follow me to my great-aunt's place. Go back to the hotel and enjoy some time with your family."

Dan's semi-guilty look confirmed that she'd correctly guessed his reaction.

"Are you sure?"

"Positive." Megan took a deep breath. "Now take me to Philly so I can start on the paperwork. I want to finish by the New Year."

Chapter 12:
A Quiet Christmas Eve

The day before Christmas opened to an overcast sky. Exhausted from the many debriefing interviews and nearly endless report forms, Megan slept in until 8:30, then ate breakfast and made arrangements to rent a car. After the madness of the last two days, she was looking forward to some down time catching up with Great Aunt Celia.

As usual when thinking about the dear old lady, Megan felt guilty for not keeping in better touch. At ninety-one, the woman had already lived a wonderfully long life, but according to Megan's mother, her health was finally fading. Her hearing had gone before Megan was out of diapers, but recently, thick cataracts had rendered her nearly blind and a bout with pneumonia had weakened her lungs.

Pulling into a parking spot in front of her great-aunt's tiny apartment, Megan reflected that she probably should have called and cleared a visit first. She had always been welcomed at Aunt Celia's place, but most of the times she'd taken up the offer had been years ago when the woman's health was vibrant.

After ringing the doorbell, Megan checked her watch, which said a quarter to two. For traveling on Christmas Eve, she'd made great time, but a brief stop for lunch and a longer delay to get a gift for her aunt tacked on almost an hour. Her late start could be blamed on Dan's wife who'd needed quite a few assurances that Megan was healthy, sane, and not about to do something highly irrational.

She was about to ring again when she heard slow footsteps approaching.

The door swung open, and a tiny, frail woman practically leapt into Megan's arms.

"Megan! Mia bella bambina! Come va?"

My beautiful baby! How it goes?

Megan chuckled at the same greeting she'd been getting for decades.

"Sto bene, grazie," she replied, enjoying the rolling cadence of the Italian words as she told her great-aunt she was fine and thanked her for the concern. As her mother's family had deep roots in Italy, Megan had always liked speaking Italian. As a child, she'd loved languages so much she studied them in spare moments, watching endless movies in foreign languages.

After the pleasantries were exchanged, her great-aunt continued to chatter away in Italian.

"I'm so glad you came. I was starting to worry. We've been waiting almost an hour. Come in! Come in!"

"We?" Megan stiffened.

"Your friend," Aunt Celia said, smiling up at Megan and switching to English. "Such a pleasant young man. Your mother will be pleased."

Keith Danielson materialized in the shadows behind Aunt Celia. Megan started to reach for her gun, but he slipped around the older woman, gave Megan a big hug, and kissed her on the lips. She tried to twist away but his grip never wavered, pinning her arms to her sides. With his head still bent toward her ear, he spoke.

"Play along or I'll kill her."

The look she gave him was murderous until worry for Aunt Celia's fragile health siphoned some of the anger away. Megan forced a tight smile and jerked her arms.

"Let go," she whispered.

"Come in from the cold," said Aunt Celia. "I will make some tea."

"That would be great." Keith pivoted but kept a heavy arm draped across Megan's shoulders. "Take your time. I just need a few moments to speak with Maggie alone." He guided her across the threshold and into the foyer as the old woman slowly tottered away.

"What are you doing here?" Megan hissed. She placed the small gift box on the shelf above the coat rack to free up her hands, but as she thought to check for her gun again, he closed the space between them. She backed into the side wall as his hands plucked the gun from its holster.

"I'll hold that for safe keeping," he said, waving the gun past her face, then lowering it to gut level.

The position of their bodies concealed the gun from anybody approaching from the kitchen.

"I feel bad about how our last conversation ended," Keith said.

"The one where you dunked me in water and left me outside in a snowstorm. That conversation?" Megan's voice crackled with anger but she kept the volume low so Aunt Celia wouldn't hear them.

"You weren't cooperating." Keith sounded sad, and the gun jabbed Megan in the side until she winced. "I hope you're more compliant this time around."

"Would you like milk and sugar?" called Aunt Celia.

"Both, please," Keith answered loudly. Lowering his voice, he added, "We might want to continue this discussion in a more secure location. You should invite me up to the guest room. That would be the polite thing to do."

"What do you want?" The last place Megan wanted to be was locked in a bedroom with this unhinged guy.

"You ruined my plans. I deserve some compensation." He leaned forward like he had a secret to share and whispered even though there was no hope of Aunt Celia overhearing even with her hearing aids. "I'm going to kill you. Slowly. Right here in dear Aunt Celia's apartment, and if you give me any trouble, the old lady joins in the fun. I bought a fresh pack of cigarettes to share. You remember how much fun they were, right?" His fingers flitted over the burn mark on Megan's heart.

Megan's fight or flight reflexes launched into overdrive. She needed to distance herself from the madman to safely disarm him, but the gun dug harder into her lower left ribs.

"Move. Up the stairs. Quickly and quietly, and if you make me shoot you—"

"I get it," Megan said tightly.

She turned and headed for the stairs, plotting the best place to make a move.

"Aunt Celia, we're going upstairs for a few minutes. Megan's not feeling well," Keith called.

"Oh, what's the matter, dear?" Aunt Celia inquired.

"I just need to rest a minute," Megan said, trying to sound convincing.

"Stay down here. The tea will be ready shortly. Tea is good for resting, you know," Aunt Celia insisted.

Megan looked to Keith for permission, which he granted with an imperious nod.

"I guess there's enough time for tea," he whispered. "But I'm keeping your gun and it'll be pointed at you the whole time, so mind your manners."

"Wouldn't dream of forgetting," Megan murmured.

At Keith's subtle direction, Megan settled onto the far left couch cushion. He sat on the middle cushion and used a pillow to shield the gun from view. Her mind still raced for a solution to the current crisis. Maybe she could jump him while he was distracted with the tea. She'd throw the scalding liquid in his face if it helped, but whatever move she made had to completely incapacitate him quickly or Aunt Celia might reap some of the consequences.

They waited in tense silence until Aunt Celia slowly entered bearing a heavy tray filled with cookies, tiny cups on saucers, and an ornate teapot. Normally, Megan would have leapt up to help with the tray, but the gun pointed at her ribs discouraged sudden movement. Serving tea took longer than it might have in past years, but Megan knew it was a point of pride for Aunt Celia to play hostess.

Megan received her tea last.

"Here, dear. This one's for you. I made it special to help you relax," said Aunt Celia as she handed Megan a cup that had already been prepared. "It's chamomile with two lumps of sugar, just the way you like it."

"Thank you," Megan said, graciously accepting the cup. She plastered a grateful smile onto her face, but her curiosity was thoroughly piqued. Chamomile was about the one thing on Earth she had a severe allergy to ingesting. For a moment she worried Keith might know that, but a subtle glance his direction gave no indication either way.

"You might want to wait a while, it's very hot right now," Aunt Celia warned.

Since Keith's dark plans would commence after teatime, Megan was more than happy to let it stretch out forever. She absently engaged in small talk with Aunt Celia, longing to speak Italian, but sticking to English for Keith's sake. He knew six different languages, but last she'd heard, Italian wasn't one of them.

When the cup stopped steaming, Megan pretended to sip at the tea. Meanwhile, Keith finished his tea and reached for the teapot with his free hand, intending to refill his cup.

"Please, allow me to serve you," Aunt Celia said, placing a delicate finger on his wrist.

"Why, thank you. That would be appreciated." Keith leaned back, and his posture relaxed. He practically slumped into the couch.

Leaning over, Aunt Celia carefully filled Keith's cup to the brim and rose smoothly, still holding the teapot. She turned as if to say something to Keith and ended up pouring hot tea into his lap. He yelped and started to stand, but the old woman brought the heavy, pointed top of the teapot up under his chin before ramming the bulk of the pot into his chest.

As soon as Keith dropped her gun, Megan snapped it up and turned it on him, pressing it against his skull, but his head lolled to the side and he started to snore softly.

"You drugged him," Megan said in disbelief. She kept her eyes on Keith to make sure he was really out.

"All those white powders, so confusing!" Aunt Celia exclaimed, speaking in rapid-fire Italian. "These old eyes aren't what they were once upon a time." She grinned widely at Megan. "He won't be giving you trouble today, bambina."

"How did you know something was wrong?" Megan asked, still stunned.

"I told her to expect trouble," answered Cassandra Mirren, entering the sitting room from the kitchen.

A tall, broad-shouldered man with dark hair followed a step behind the assassin.

Megan kept her gun focused on Keith's unconscious form, but her emotions were going haywire. Anger and relief tussled in her stomach, making her queasy.

"You used me as bait," Megan said.

"No, I *let* you be bait," Cassandra corrected.

"You let him in here with Aunt Celia." Megan's irritation started to burn into anger again.

"They asked for my help, love, and I was happy to do it," declared Aunt Celia. "Put the gun down. Let them do their job."

Megan lowered the gun but still kept it pointed in Keith's direction. She wasn't sure if she'd need to use it on Cassandra soon.

"I knew Keith would want swift revenge against you, so I staked out this place and had others watch over different places you might be found in the next few days," Cassandra explained. "When he came here, I called for backup. This is a Council matter now."

"What are you going to do with him?" Megan dreaded the answer because she might have to defend the creep.

"Nothing for now. We have orders to bring him in to face a trial," Cassandra said. "You and your great-aunt should go for a late lunch. When you return, we will be gone."

Megan wrestled with her conscience for a few seconds. She knew perfectly well that Keith would never see the inside of a prison cell. Either he'd have enough friends in high places to help him escape, or the Council's Fixers would permanently deal with him. Thinking about what he'd threatened to do to Aunt Celia helped straighten her morals. Finally, she tucked her gun back into its holster and stood up.

"Of course, we could just shoot him here and report it as an intruder," offered the man with Cassandra.

The assassin quirked an eyebrow at Megan and shrugged.

"It's your choice," she said. "My colleague's suggestion is doable."

"No, I think we'll go for lunch," Megan said, crossing to where Aunt Celia stood and taking the older woman's arm.

I really, really don't want to know the details.

"Good choice," said Cassandra. The assassin bowed slightly, stepped forward, and placed a black card with a number scrawled on the back onto the coffee table. "I'll leave this with you in case you need to reach me with questions or concerns." She straightened and waved for her colleague to start gathering up their charge. "Farewell, Agent Luchek."

Chapter 13:
Peace is Priceless

Megan's leisurely lunch with her great-aunt managed to take her mind off the craziness of the last two days. She thought about reporting the incident in Aunt Celia's apartment but decided not to do so. A report would leave a paper trail and raise a lot of uncomfortable questions. Common sense told her that revealing what little she knew about Cassandra, Fixers, and the Council would be dangerous. Besides, doing so would seem like a betrayal. No illusion of friendship clouded Megan's thinking, but for some reason, she trusted the assassin. Part of that could be attributed to having recently fought side by side with her, but it went deeper. Instinct told Megan not to push the Fixer away.

She'd spent Christmas Eve with Aunt Celia, catching up properly. The elderly lady even convinced Megan to call her mother. They made arrangements for Megan to drive Aunt Celia to her parents' place on Christmas day, a feat that hadn't been accomplished for five years. Normally, Megan would have regretted the long hours in a car, but no amount of inconvenience ought to keep family apart this time of year.

Before she left to be with family, Dan summoned her to his hotel room to celebrate Christmas morning with his family. She almost declined because she didn't have any more gifts for them, but he sensed her hesitation and the reason behind it.

"Come on down and join us anyway. I think Santa misfiled a few gifts here that were meant for you." Dan waited two beats, but when she didn't immediately reply, he continued, "If you turn me down, I'll turn Giggles loose on you. She's in a tickling mood today."

258

"I'll be right down," Megan promised.

Strapped for gift ideas, Megan relied on the Italian half of her heritage and deeply ingrained instincts.

When in doubt, feed them.

Grabbing her purse, she slung it over her shoulder, exited her room, and raced for the elevator. She'd noticed the hotel's restaurant had a pretty decent bakery, so she ordered a few odds and ends to be delivered on a coffee cart in about twenty minutes.

The door to Dan's room swung open and a tiny blond head peeked out.

"Aunt Maggie!" Giggles flung the door open so hard it smacked the wall. Heedless of the noise, she bounded out of the room and threw her entire body at Megan.

Expecting such an attack, Megan caught the pink human missile and pulled her into a tight hug. Miraculously, once situated, Ashley Cooper went uncharacteristically still, laying her head on Megan's right shoulder.

"We missed you," Giggles declared. She leaned back in Megan's arms and cupped her cheeks with both hands. "Mommy said you were saving the world with daddy. Is ... is it better now?"

Megan smiled at the child's question.

"Yeah. It's a little better," she answered.

"Giggles, no hogging the guest," Dan said. "Let her come in."

Dutifully, Ashley squirmed down, seized one of Megan's hands, and pulled her into the room.

"Surprise!"

The shout slammed into Megan from every corner of the small room. She froze as her gaze swept over the grinning faces surrounding her. Great Aunt Celia, Mom, Dad, Tara, Cousin Vinny, Cousin Jack, Aunt Clara, and Uncle Georgie crowded close for proper greetings. Susanne Falco Luchek—Mom—elbowed Cousin Vinny aside at the last second to reach Megan first. After a long hug and a few hasty kisses, she pulled back and launched into a speech punctuated by flailing arms.

"Maggie! My baby! Are you hurt?" She placed a hand to her forehead in case Megan missed her distress. "Why do you keep such a dangerous job? You should be chasing babies, not men with guns!"

"Come on, Sue, leave the girl alone," said Dad impatiently. He waited until her mother finally relinquished her death grip on Megan then moved in for a proper hug. Planting a kiss on her forehead, he spoke in Italian. "We worry because we love you, but you're a big girl. Make us proud." He always spoke Italian when he wanted to be sentimental. He'd learned the language so he could date Megan's mother once upon a time.

As Megan embraced her father, she found Dan and glared at him.

He held up both hands to ward off the look.

"It wasn't me," he said. "I think there was a news crew stalking Agent McAlister though. Kid spilled some of the beans before I could rescue him."

Wonderful. Hopefully, it was just local news.

"Don't you keep up with the national news?" asked Cousin Vinny. "You're famous."

So much for that. Maddox is gonna be thrilled.

"Don't hate him too much. I think ASAC Felding and SAC Hatcher already reamed him for loose lips," Dan continued.

Megan decided to shrug it off. The damage was already done.

After making the rounds greeting her family, Megan stepped back to gain some personal space. Her family members divided into groups of two and three and filled the room with a lively mix of Italian and English. The selection of pastries, cakes, and other goodies arrived, giving them more to fuss over

Bethany Cooper subtly directed Megan to a wooden chair. Ashley immediately raced over carrying a heavy looking card. Each step the child took shook glitter from the card. Megan watched in dismay as Giggles plopped the card onto her lap, resulting in an explosion of glitter. It was like a snow globe bursting over her black pants. As the glitter dust settled around her, Megan rolled her eyes and laughed.

The card showed crude stick figure drawings of a man, a woman, and a baby. The latter figure was confined to an awkward little box. The caption read: *Baby Jesus's family.* When Megan opened the card more glitter dusted her pants. The inside picture featured a man, two women, a girl, and a baby. This caption read: *My family.* Each stick figure was labeled. The one marked Aunt Maggie was filled in with glitter. Initially, Megan thought that must be the source of the glitter storm, but when she turned the card over, she found one more picture. The entire back was filled with glitter hearts, and a tiny caption was squeezed into the bottom: *We love you.*

Megan wasn't usually much for sentiment, but she found the homemade mess very touching. Placing the card on the table, Megan pulled the card maker onto her lap and held her close, absorbing the innocent joy that surrounded the child. Suddenly everything she'd gone through made sense. Her mother might not understand, but Dan, Dad, and Tara would. Moments like this were exactly why she worked for the FBI. Anybody who threatened people like this deserved to be battled at every turn.

Peace is priceless.

Epilogue:
More Questions

"Is Mr. Danielson secure?" asked the judge.

"Ariel assures me they'll take care of the final details," Cassandra confirmed. She couldn't keep the disapproval out of her tone.

"This is good for the Council," the judge assured. "Mossad owes us. Danielson can provide valuable information to help them defend their country."

Cassandra understood that Judge Clarence A. Jackson was doubly pleased with the outcome because it removed Keith Danielson as a potential threat to his control over the Shadow Council.

"I've read your report and find no fault with it except that you say little about the FBI agent's performance," said the judge. "How did she do? Would she be willing to accept future assignments?"

Cassandra had anticipated the question, but she considered her words before speaking anyway. Over the years, the judge had developed a talent for finding new people with Fixer potential. Megan Luchek had most of the right ingredients to become a formidable Fixer, but she lacked the ruthlessness. Cassandra needed to convey that message without painting the agent as a threat if she didn't want to be reading about a mysterious murder in the next few weeks, or worse, being tasked to take the woman out personally. Somehow Cassandra's reluctance to partner with the FBI agent had turned into a strange sort of respect. They wouldn't be exchanging birthday cards, but if another crisis arose, Cassandra figured she could do far worse for a temporary partner.

"Her instincts and investigative skills are more than adequate, and I think she would work with us again. That said, the type of task assigned to her would have to be similar to this: a high-stakes but righteous cause. She's a fighter but not an assassin."

"I see. Thank you for your honesty, Ms. Mirren. I've cleared the remaining funds for you. They should be in the usual account by tomorrow morning. Do you have anything else you wish to discuss with me?"

He knew very well that she had at least one issue to raise with him.

"Did you know, sir?" Cassandra kept her anger in check, but the tone still sounded tense.

"About Keith? Oh, I suspected, but I didn't want to taint your impressions of the case," said the judge. "Regardless of who was behind the plot, it needed stopping. I didn't want you to think it involved a personal vendetta."

Not knowing almost got me killed.

"Next time, tell me, sir," Cassandra stated. "I need all the facts every single time. It might have saved us some trouble. Was he still working for the CIA?"

"As far as I can tell, Danielson was not authorized to attempt a mission like that, but I have some people asking more questions," said the judge. "If he was under orders, that is a cause for concern."

Massive understatement.

One more question nagged at Cassandra.

"Did you know of Danielson's connection to the agent?"

"That I did not know," intoned the judge. "Small world we live in, and it's getting smaller all the time." He sighed. "Take the win, Ms. Mirren. I will call upon you again as necessary. The Council thanks you for your continued service. Good day." He disconnected the call without waiting for her to reply.

Cassandra would have liked more of an apology for the oversight, but she settled for the small thanks. With the assignment officially completed, she had the rest of Christmas to relax. As it was five o'clock, the sun had already set. Needing some fresh air, she stepped out onto the hotel's roof. Sometime while she was finishing her report for the judge, the storm clouds had disappeared. Cassandra gazed up at the stars. Only the brightest ones could outshine the city streets, lit up in red, white, and green.

Beautiful.

The cold air filled her lungs and stung her cheeks, reminding her she was alive.

Peace on Earth is a lie, but it's an attractive one.

Her thoughts turned to Megan Luchek.

Enjoy the respite, agent, you've earned it, but we may need you again. Evil never rests easy.

THE END

Shadow Council Series Book 4: Treachery Makes it Tense

By Julie C. Gilbert

Table of Contents:

Prologue:
The World Gone Mad

The second she crossed the threshold into Judge Clarence A. Jackson's large office, Cassandra Mirren knew this meeting would be life-altering. Her senses jumped from *aware* to *hyper alert* in an instant, and her gun appeared in her right hand. She evened out her weight and drew a bead on the back of a man's head. She saw movement to her right in her peripheral vision but didn't break her focus. If she was going to die, she would take down the man in front of her anyway.

"I'd prefer if you didn't shoot my *guest*, Ms. Mirren," drawled the judge from behind his imposing desk.

Quick analysis of the way the judge said *guest* told her he wasn't entirely pleased with the man either. The figure with light brown hair stood equidistant between her and the judge's desk. Even though he had his back to her, she knew him.

"You're supposed to be in prison," Cassandra said grimly, ignoring the judge.

Keith Danielson pivoted toward her and beamed a smile perfect for advertising toothpaste. He kept his hands away from his body in a non-threatening manner.

"It didn't suit me," he commented.

Cassandra's gaze flicked over to the judge for an explanation.

"I told you not to bring a gun," the judge scolded. "I knew you would react violently."

"Why is he here, and why shouldn't I shoot him?" Cassandra asked.

"He's here so we can clear up these misunderstandings, and

you shouldn't shoot him because he outranks you," Judge Jackson explained patiently. "Besides, his associate would kill you a second later, and I've grown rather fond of working with you."

Cold realization settled in the pit of Cassandra's stomach, but the gun didn't waver. A dozen Fixers had more experience than she did, but this man was no Fixer. Her people tended to have higher standards than the creep in front of her.

"So you're the new Council member," she muttered. Cassandra shifted a half-step left and turned enough to keep an eye on the Danielson's associate.

A young, eager, dark-haired kid in a suit had a Glock 17 pointed at her.

"At your service," Danielson said with a mock, sweeping bow.

Cassandra now regretted that the Council's open slot didn't go to Martin Cantrell. She'd take *fool* over *psychopath* any day. As she pushed the useless thought aside, something Judge Jackson had said gave her a sour taste in her mouth.

"Misunderstanding?" Cassandra shot her boss an incredulous look. "He tried to kill a couple of thousand people a few weeks ago."

"He had good reasons, even if his methods were misguided," said the judge.

Danielson's green eyes were wide, full of innocence and false remorse.

Grunting, Cassandra put her gun away and straightened out of her shooter's stance. She couldn't imagine what sort of sweet talking Danielson must have done to worm his way out of the last mess he'd created. Her body remained ready to spring at a moment's notice. If necessary, she'd take this guy down with her bare hands. Junior over there in the corner probably couldn't hit a whale from ten feet away.

"The Council held a vote and decided that Mr. Danielson's vision merited a pardon … and a reprimand," said Judge Jackson. "But you have nothing to worry about. He's on probation, and we'll monitor his movements closely for the next several months. His CIA contacts could prove invaluable."

Somehow, the words failed to comfort Cassandra. If Danielson launched another crazy scheme, there were very few people qualified to stop him.

"A slap on the wrist and a promotion," she summed up. Her expression declared disgust, and she began to doubt the Shadow Council would ever live up to the ideals that once governed it. "What is wrong with the world?" She muttered the question under her breath, but Keith answered anyway.

"Everything. That's why the Council needs men like me." He looked at her sympathetically, like a dull student who simply couldn't grasp an easy concept.

Cassandra bit back the words she wanted to fling at the delusional ex-CIA agent. While escorting Danielson to what she thought would be justice, Cassandra had learned from her good friend—Owen Ramsey—that even the spooks thought he was too nuts to keep around. She pierced her boss with a frustrated gaze.

"Why am I here?"

Once again, Keith Danielson ignored the fact that he wasn't being addressed.

"I have a plan, and I'd like your help with it. Otherwise, I believe you'll interfere if you can," he said. Danielson moved to the front of the judge's desk and perched on the edge, bracing himself with his arms. He looked cool, calm, and completely in control. With a casual wave, Danielson got his lackey to stand down. Then, he stared at her expectantly, waiting for her to voice the obvious question.

"What plan?" Cassandra spat the question through clenched teeth.

"I believe you've lost perspective, Miss Mirren," Danielson noted gently.

"About what?" she snapped, longing to reach out and shake the plan loose.

"The fact that you don't know only proves my point," Danielson said. Smugness dripped from his words.

The judge cleared his throat.

"He believes Agent Luchek may become a threat to us. Do you agree?"

"I gave you my report on Agent Luchek" Cassandra said. She kept her voice even, but her mind raced. She sensed them baiting a trap, though she couldn't predict where it would lead. "She'll help us again, but only if she believes in the cause, like stopping terrorist threats from within."

"What would you say if your new orders were to kill Agent Luchek?" asked Danielson.

"I'd say you're being delusional and stupid," Cassandra said without hesitation. She glared at Danielson then shifted the hard gaze to the judge. "She's one of the few idealistic sorts who has the brains—and the guts—to do her job well."

"Then it's a good thing I'm not saying that," Danielson said with a predatory smile. He cleared his throat. "I agree with your assessment, but as I was telling His Honor earlier, it's only a matter of time before Luchek becomes a threat to us." Keith Danielson pushed himself to a standing position again and nodded slowly. "She bears a grudge against me from long ago." This last statement didn't seem to have a target.

"Long ago? Did you forget trying to kill us around Christmas?" Cassandra wondered. "If I were you, I'd be more worried about the grudge *I* bear."

"Please, Ms. Mirren, listen to his proposal," said the judge. "It's quite elegant."

Setting her jaw, Cassandra glared at Danielson while he explained.

"My plan will solve three problems," he began. "One, the rampant flow of designer drugs hitting the city streets; two, Agent Luchek; and three, the question of your loyalty."

"I didn't know my loyalty was in question," Cassandra said, feeling her temple throb with anger.

"I saw how hard you fought to save the FBI agent's life in Pennsylvania," Danielson said. "I believe you feel a sense of loyalty to her, and that concerns the Council."

"She was my partner at the time," Cassandra argued. "Of course, I fought to protect her. That was the job the Council sent me on: work with the agent to discover the threat. And that threat turned out to be you. So why is my loyalty in question?" She slid her eyes back to the judge to drive home the question. Before he could answer, she looked to Danielson and fired another question. "And how do you expect to use Agent Luchek to derail the drug problem?"

On par with nobody answering their assigned questions, the judge fielded the drug query.

"Most of the drug lords keep their operations modest and have the decency to inform the Council of their movements so we can control the flow, but there's a troublesome newcomer who will need to be removed."

That kind of straightforward plan sounded more to Cassandra's liking.

"Great. I'll take the job," she said, preparing to march out and do just that once they gave her a name.

"It's not that simple," said the judge. His tone implied that he wished it could be that simple. "Mr. Danielson made a good point before you arrived. He noted that there are a half-dozen others poised to follow suit. This can't go down as a simple, clean assassination."

"Why not? Dead is dead. The rest will get the point." Cassandra could hardly believe they were arguing the finer points of assassination.

"It must be ... messier," said Danielson.

Cassandra fought down her distaste and opened her mouth to say she could handle whatever job specifications they laid out, but the judge waved away the offer before it was born.

"If the death is memorable, they might heed the warning," the judge explained.

"What does this have to do with Megan?" Cassandra regretted using the agent's first name as soon as it left her lips, but she buried the feeling before it could show up on her face.

The slip brought a flash of triumph to Danielson's eyes.

"She's going to take the fall for the murder."

"Agent Luchek has a vested interest in the case against Donean Gavriel, so when the case fails tomorrow, she'll have a motive," Judge Jackson elaborated.

Cassandra stopped herself from asking how he knew the case would fail. The obvious answer came to her: he was probably the presiding judge. Even if he wasn't, he'd find some way to get the case dismissed. The Shadow Council owned people at every level of state and local government, including court officials and law enforcement personnel. It's what made them so effective, powerful, and dangerous.

"Not her style," Cassandra muttered. "Besides, framing Agent Luchek for a brutal murder isn't going to send the sort of message that will warn other drug lords to heed the Council."

"It does if we provide evidence she works for the Council," Danielson countered.

"That's where your reports come in," said the judge. "You're going to rewrite them so that it appears she was working for us the whole time. These new files will be circulated to the appropriate parties."

Cassandra shook her head before he finished.

"I'm not altering my reports. You want them changed, make somebody else do it." She turned to leave.

"You are not dismissed yet," growled the judge. He waited for her to turn her head enough to make eye contact before saying more. "Your reticence is making the accusations against your loyalties more valid by the second." His features softened slightly. "But I can sympathize with the awkwardness of the position we've placed you in, so if you don't want to participate, I understand. If you won't help, your new orders are to lay low for the next few weeks. Can you do that?"

"It probably goes without saying, but don't contact the agent," said Danielson. "You'll only make things worse if you warn her."

Something in his tone told Cassandra that he wanted her to disobey. She didn't know if he was going for reverse psychology or not. Part of her believed he genuinely wanted her to defy the Shadow Council. She nodded tightly to the judge in response to his last question and backed up a step, intending to leave but unwilling to turn her back on Danielson.

"Report back tomorrow afternoon after the trial," said the judge. "I'll send you a text when it's over. By then, I should have an assignment that will take you away from here for the relevant time frame. I'm serious. I won't force you to go against your conscience in these matters."

A glance at Danielson revealed nothing new, but Cassandra understood that she wouldn't receive a similar promise from him. She backed toward the door and exited the room with all possible speed. With Danielson involved and scheming again, she had plans to put into place and some major soul-searching to do.

Chapter 1:
Watch Your Backs

Megan Luchek's insides roiled. The judge's gavel pounded the final nail into the coffin of the case she and her partner had poured their hearts and souls into for several months. Setting her jaw, she headed for the door. She wanted out before she had to see that smug piece of crap give her one more suggestive smile.

"Hey, agents!" Donean Gavriel called out. His voice held delight and triumph. The buoyant attitude came from watching a possible fifteen-year prison sentence disintegrate in a matter of minutes.

Megan paused involuntarily. Her Italian-Irish-German blood rose from a simmer to a boil in a flash.

"Keep moving," her partner whispered. FBI Special Agent Daniel Cooper pressed a hand into the small of her back and ushered her forward.

"This is my town now, so watch your backs!" Gavriel taunted.

Flushing deeper, Megan turned to respond, but her partner gently shoved her out the door with a few quiet pleas to ignore the fool.

"Why aren't you more upset?" Megan hissed, once the door clicked shut behind them.

"I am upset, but there's nothing we can do about it," Dan said tightly. His Texas accent thickened as he added, "Let's get some air." He slipped around her and headed for the door leading to the steps outside. His cowboy boots clicked on the polished floors almost as loudly as Megan's black suede pumps.

They'd be expected back at the office in a half-hour or so, but Megan didn't feel like facing her cubicle walls any time soon. She needed to process the gross miscarriage of justice. Losing a case wasn't new to her, but losing a case because some tech lost half the key evidence was new.

"How does someone lose six kilos of designer drugs?" Megan demanded as they shoved through the door leading out of the building.

"They don't," Dan replied, still facing away from her. He pivoted enough to look at her. "They were probably paid to tamper with the evidence."

Hope sprang into Megan.

"If we can prove—"

"Forget it," Dan interrupted. "The case was dismissed. No judge will ever look at it again." He ran a hand through his short, dark blond hair and let his arm flop to his side. His fingers twitched like he wanted to strangle a cowboy hat.

Megan heaved a sigh.

"We're really back at square one," she lamented.

"*We're* nowhere," Dan corrected. "Gavriel knows us. Maddox won't let us touch the next case involving him."

"If only we could have gotten closer, maybe Gavriel would have taken a swing at one of us," Megan said wistfully. "Then, we'd at least have him on that."

Dan snorted.

"The odds are better that you'd be the first to swing."

"Fair point," Megan admitted, shrugging. She forced a smile. "It might be expensive, but it definitely would have been satisfying. I would have made it count."

"Let it go," Dan advised. "It stinks but dwelling on it is only going to let it eat at your insides like a rampant fungus."

"Thanks for the visual," Megan said, quirking an eyebrow at her partner. "Where did that come from?"

"Sorry, Beth and I were cleaning this past weekend. We found some interesting things when we moved some of the family room cabinets."

Megan noted that her partner's blue eyes softened when he spoke of his wife. She found it cute, but decided not to point out her observation.

"Now that the house is presentable, you should come over for dinner again. Giggles misses you. Are you free tonight?"

Shaking her head, Megan called up an image of little Ashley Ann Cooper. Dan claimed the golden haired toddler could be a tyrant, and Megan believed him, having witnessed a tantrum.

"I booked a dinner date with Kai tonight," she explained. "Besides, you should give your wife more than a few hours of notice before springing guests on her."

"After the Christmas trip you arranged for us, you're practically family," Dan protested. "I still don't know how to thank you for that."

"I had fun," Megan said, waving off the thanks.

When I wasn't being shot at. She pushed the thought away before it could get her thinking about Keith Danielson. That would bring back her foul mood in a hurry.

Dan gave her an odd look, like he didn't know whether to laugh or contradict her.

"You can't even do a working vacation without coming across a crisis," he commented.

"Your life would be dull without me," Megan said.

"Duller anyway," he replied.

After a few companionable beats of silence, a concerned look came into Dan's eyes.

"Are you calmer now?" he asked tentatively.

To Megan's surprise, her blood pressure felt like it was approaching normal. Once the fiery sparks of anger stopped exploding in her head, she pondered the dead case again.

"Yes," she murmured absently.

"Uh-oh, I know that look," said Dan.

Megan stopped staring into nothing long enough to shoot Dan a questioning glance.

"It means: 'something doesn't add up here.'" Dan folded his arms and leaned against one of the metal railings. His face assumed the neutral expression Megan thought of as his *therapist* look. "What's on your mind?"

She considered pacing the stairs, but in her distracted state—and the heels—she figured she might end up tumbling down them. After bullying her thoughts into some semblance of order, Megan presented her misgivings.

"It takes a lot of effort to make evidence disappear like that," she began. "That brings up the question of motive."

"To get Donean Gavriel off the hook," Dan supplied.

"Right, but he's a medium-size, shiny new fish in a big pond with some old players," Megan noted. "He probably doesn't have the contacts to pull off something like that."

Dan bobbed his head thoughtfully to show he was following her logic.

"If Gavriel doesn't have friends in high places, then who would bother springing him?" Dan asked. "Anonymous benefactors don't just crop up in the circles he runs in. Everybody wants something."

"Exactly." Something else that had nagged at Megan surfaced in her mind. "And Judge Jackson dismissed the case too quickly. The bricks of Dragon's Fire weren't our only evidence, just the most conclusive." She rolled her eyes at the drug's street name.

The chemical name was one she couldn't pronounce, but Dragon's Fire made it sound like a spicy barbeque sauce. Her anger started rising when she thought about Gavriel being set loose to sell the highly addictive drug to desperate people. At least two kids had died from consuming the stuff during the course of their investigation.

"I agree, but what's done is done," Dan said philosophically. "He's on our radar now, and he'll slip up again. Maybe Gianna will catch the case. You know how she feels about drug dealers."

The thought of setting Agent Gianna Krantz on Gavriel's case comforted Megan a little.

"I know, but the control freak in me is complaining about passing the case off to another agent," said Megan. She grunted in frustration, longing to hit something. Maybe she could squeeze in a quick trip to the gym before meeting Detective Kailani Lang for dinner. "We had him dead to rights!" As the exclamation left her lips, her mind latched on to a slightly different question than motive. "Forget the why, who has that kind of influence? Do you think the judge was bought too?"

"Good questions, but we may not want to kick that particular hornets' nest," said Dan.

"Why do you say that?" Megan tilted her head curiously. "I thought we always wanted answers."

"Because organizations with that kind of power come with deep pockets, long memories, and few scruples," Dan explained. He raised a hand to forestall her retort. "Don't get me wrong now, I'd love to make that sort of bust, but it's a long, long shot. We've got plenty of work to occupy our time. Speaking of which, the last few cases we've caught have been downright gifts. We should go see what Maddox has assigned us this time around."

As they made their way up to the FBI offices, Megan mulled over her partner's statement about organizations with tremendous power. She could think of a half-dozen gangs who wished they had that sort of power, but even if they had the ability, none of them would have the inclination to get a rival like Gavriel back on the streets. The only entity she knew about with the appropriate level of influence always had questionable motives.

Unconsciously, her hand slipped into the suit jacket pocket where she'd tucked Cassandra Mirren's black business card containing emergency contact information. Making a few inquiries couldn't hurt anything, and it would satisfy her curiosity. Maybe once that happened, she could follow Dan's advice and drop the Gavriel case.

Does the Shadow Council have the right contacts to destroy our case? Do they have a reason to do so? Gavriel's small potatoes, but he's poised to become a much bigger problem. According to Cassandra's background file, the Shadow Council stands for ultimate order in governments. If that's true, they'd sooner destroy a guy like Gavriel than set him free.

With that many enemies, Megan was almost tempted to pity the guy. Then, the memory of one of the dead teenagers who had overdosed on Dragon's Fire came to her and blew the sympathy away. With considerable effort, Megan forced thoughts of Gavriel aside and sat down at her desk to open the plain manila case briefing.

All right, what's next?

Chapter 2:
Hostile Takeover

As expected, Judge Jackson's text message came through shortly after eleven the following morning. Cassandra had spent the last half-hour killing time in a coffee joint a block away. She wanted to be in his office as soon as possible before the afternoon demands stole his attention. There was a slim chance she could talk some sense into him. She would have tried yesterday if she could have gotten a moment alone with him, but Keith Danielson's presence poisoned the air.

The security guard nodded and waved her through the metal detector. She removed her laptop and placed it in a bin before tossing the satchel onto the conveyor belt and stepping through the metal detector. Cassandra tapped her foot impatiently while the guard waved a wand over her body. Satisfied, he restored her laptop and its satchel to her.

"Don't they have electronic versions of that book, Ms. Parker?" asked the guard, catching a glimpse of the giant law book stuffed into her laptop satchel.

"There's nothing like the real thing, Harold," she replied easily, shouldering the bag. She'd had variations of this same conversation several times over the past few months with the various guards.

"Just seems a shame to have to lug that thing around everywhere," he commented.

"Always best to be prepared," Cassandra said, patting the bag.

"I guess," the guard agreed. "Well, you have a nice day."

Cassandra returned the wish and made her way up to the judge's office. As she walked, she amused herself by wondering what Harold

Whitman would say if he ever opened that book he'd been eyeing. He wore a gun on his belt, but she doubted the man had ever fired a shot outside a range.

The Prince Kuhio Federal Building might seem to have tight security, but they were no match for the level of toys Cassandra could access. To slip a gun through, she could go with a small ceramic weapon, but she didn't bother. Instead, she tucked the gun in a special box that looked like a thick legal tome entitled, *Modern Case Law*. She didn't understand exactly how the box worked, but she understood the general principle of utilizing nanotechnology to spoof the density reading on the x-ray machine. If anybody bothered studying the screen while the bag went through, they might wonder why the book registered such a high density. However, most security checkpoint guards were trained to look at density differences to ascertain the shape of threatening objects. They naturally concluded that if it looked like a normal book shape, it must be a book.

Plenty of people walked in and out of the building with guns, but they possessed higher clearances than her bogus paralegal's photo ID. Besides, the people with proper clearance for toting a gun in the building used the other entrance.

Cassandra wondered how Keith Danielson managed to smuggle his weapon in before concluding the less she thought about that man, the better. As she stepped beneath the security camera, Cassandra removed the gun from its hiding place and tucked it behind her back. The practiced moved barely caused her to break stride. She abandoned the bag by the big, ugly planters flanking Judge Jackson's office door. She didn't always attend meetings with the judge armed, but the unpleasant addition of Danielson to yesterday's meeting convinced her to take the risk.

Knocking politely, Cassandra waited for an invitation to enter. She got one but it sounded unusually tense.

"Enter!" The judge sounded like he was chewing gravel or about to rip into a paralegal who'd made a terrible mistake.

Cassandra slipped inside and absorbed the familiar scene in an instant. Judge Jackson sat in his throne-like leather chair, sweating profusely. Keith Danielson stood behind the judge's desk, just out of Jackson's touching range. Danielson's suited lackey stood in his corner pointing a gun at Cassandra.

A moment later her gun leapt to hand and honed in again on Danielson.

Trap. Lovely.

"Couldn't we have finished this yesterday?" she wondered as the door clicked softly shut behind her.

"Gavriel's trial needed to fail first," Danielson explained. He didn't seem worried about the possibility of dying.

"This is an outrage!" blustered the judge. His dark features hid a flush, but his bulging eyes drilled holes into Danielson. "You can't kill me. The Council won't stand for this—this abominable behavior! They'll hunt you down with every resource available."

"No," Danielson drawled. "They'll hunt her down." He jerked his head sideways to indicate Cassandra.

The statement provided just enough warning. Cassandra dropped to her knees and rolled toward the suit-wearing minion occupying the corner to her right. The tranquilizer dart pinged off a framed diploma on the far wall just as Cassandra's elbow slammed into the side of junior's head.

He crumpled.

She would have hit him with her good hand, but she needed that to reestablish her aim at Danielson's head.

"What's my motive for killing my employer?" Cassandra inquired. She wanted to shoot Danielson and be done with it, but if there was a small chance to talk him down and save the judge, she needed to seize the opportunity.

"You're upset with his severe lack of judgment and leadership," Danielson said.

"Granted, but unlike you, I don't kill people because I disagree with them."

There would be a lot more dead people if that were the case.

"You're a saint," Danielson mocked.

"Never made that claim," said Cassandra. "I know what I am, but what I'm not sure about is what's become of the Council."

The lackey stirred, so Cassandra kicked his head to keep him from complicating her life. She didn't dare look, so it was only a glancing blow. Hopefully, it would keep him out long enough. This would be resolved inside a few minutes anyway.

"They're fine. I can control them." Danielson's voice held a sickening amount of confidence. "He's the last obstacle in my way." He addressed Cassandra, but his attention stayed fixed on the judge.

Cassandra didn't bother correcting Danielson's errant assumption. He thought she was referring to the whereabouts for the remaining Shadow Council members, but she really meant that the Council she worked for and the one he was trying to create were mutually exclusive.

"What is it you want?" asked Judge Jackson. "I'm willing to consider your proposals, but we've got to go about this the right way."

Danielson's laughter filled the office.

"Loyalty purchased by a gun is fickle. You, sir, need to die." He took a small step back so the blood spatter wouldn't hit him.

"Do something!" the judge demanded of Cassandra.

Like what?

Her mind raced for an acceptable solution. Each passing second sealed the judge's fate tighter. If she shot Danielson first, he'd squeeze the trigger reflexively and the judge would die. If he shot first, she'd get to kill him, but the judge would still die. The longer they stayed in their shooting stances, the less accurate their shots would be, but Danielson was far closer to his target.

"You have a choice, Ms. Mirren." Danielson's voice was even and conversational. "Try your luck at shooting me, or escape. I'll give you a thirty-second head start before I put the judge out of his misery and call the Council to report your unjust slaying of our fearless leader."

"You know what your problem is, Danielson?" Cassandra asked.

"Do tell."

"You think too much, and one of these days, you're going to outthink yourself."

You're far too fond of head games.

"Funny. I was just thinking, I thought just enough. It's called good planning." Danielson slowly reached into his left pocket and withdrew a cellphone. "See, with the touch of a button, I can summon extra help. Who do you have coming? You now have twenty seconds to start running."

Cassandra didn't have anybody coming to back her up, but she didn't let it bother her. Distraction could get her killed.

"It's called paranoia, and you should really forget the judge and turn your gun on me because if I walk out of here, I will kill you someday."

"Challenge accepted," said Danielson. "Dale, please get the door for the lady. She was just leaving."

"Dale, stay put." Cassandra shifted her aim to emphasize her order. The last place she wanted the lackey was behind her. "I can get the door myself." She took a half-step backward.

"You're going to leave me here?" The judge's normally low voice reverberated with outrage.

Actually, her shaky plan was to distract Danielson long enough to give the judge a chance to save himself.

It worked.

However, instead of reaching for something substantial that could do some damage, Judge Jackson grasped a letter opener.

For the next two seconds, Cassandra saw everything in slow motion. Danielson started to grin in triumph, but the expression quickly morphed through grimace, scowl, and look of pure hatred and pain. Danielson's gun spat a delicate stream of fire as it released a bullet. The thin blade of a letter opener shaped like a sword had sliced a six-inch cut down the length of his right forearm. The first shot missed the judge's face by millimeters. An animalistic growl escaped Danielson as he viciously clubbed the judge with his left fist and fired six more times.

At that range, nobody could miss.

Cassandra fired twice, but then the minion tackled her. She managed to hang on to her gun, but she could already hear shouts, screams, and footsteps pounding down the hallway, some toward her and some away. She needed to get out now. If the judge wasn't dead already, he would be soon. Cassandra coiled her body left, then let it spring back, driving her right elbow toward the minion's face. He ducked in time to catch the blow on the top of his head causing her elbow to go completely numb. She dropped the gun into her other hand and shot her hand forward, driving the weapon into the same spot her elbow had just softened. The kid dropped like a stone, but she couldn't spare a moment to admire her handiwork.

Rolling up and over Danielson's lackey, Cassandra sprang to her feet and opened the door. The hallways were chaos with people streaming back and forth shouting orders and generally getting in each other's way. A quick glance in both directions showed her two security men rushing from the left and one from the right. Choosing the path of least resistance, Cassandra tucked her gun away, grabbed her bag, and disappeared into the crowd.

She needed to warn the FBI agent and escape the building.

Chapter 3:
Midday Murder

Excitement ripped through the office like a shockwave. Agents popped their heads out of their cubicles like gophers checking out a new danger. Security men were walking with purpose toward Special Agent in Charge Bryan Maddox's office.

Variations of "What's going on?" rang out up and down the hallways. Almost as quickly, professionalism asserted itself, and the agents disappeared into their offices to hunker down, expecting an official lockdown to be announced soon.

Daniel Cooper appeared before Megan looking grim. He gestured for her to back up into her cubicle.

The lockdown announcement came as Megan reached her chair and sat down.

"What's up?"

The serious expression Dan wore didn't bode well. He moved in as far as he could without invading her personal space.

"There's been a shooting a few floors up," he reported.

"How do you know already?" Megan demanded. She doubted even Maddox knew anything concrete.

"This." Dan took out his phone and flipped to a text message exchange with a D. Sims.

She took his phone to read the message.

Shooting in JJ's office. KUP

"What's 'KUP'? Who are JJ and D. Sims? And how does D. Sims know this information before everybody else?" Megan knew if she thought about it, she could come up with the answers, but firing questions at Dan seemed easier.

"KUP is Keep You Posted in texting speech," Dan reported. "Sims is one of the new tech guys I've been working with to upgrade the gadgetry around here."

"Since when?" Megan inquired.

"Since yesterday," Dan replied. "That's the case I caught a few days ago while you were in all those Gavriel briefing sessions. Just met the Sims kid yesterday. He seems nice enough."

Megan wasn't sure if she wanted to be jealous or relieved not to have been assigned that case. It sounded interesting with the potential to go deadly boring in a few days.

"You met him yesterday, and you're texting buddies already?" Megan let her expression emphasize the question.

Dan rolled his eyes.

"He's a modern kid. I think he'd have two phones in hand to text separate people if he had the chance." Dan's amusement vanished. "You know who JJ is," he said quietly.

As soon as he said it, Megan's mind conjured the answer.

"Judge Jackson," she whispered, stunned.

"I don't know how Sims got the information, but I wouldn't put it past him to have some sort of prototype surveillance equipment in place."

"Wouldn't that be highly illegal?" Megan asked.

A small shrug was the only response she got. Dan didn't have time to give a verbal answer.

SAC Maddox suddenly filled the entry to Megan's cubicle.

"Luchek! Cooper! Drop your cases and get up to Judge Jackson's office pronto! I want a report on my desk in two hours!" Maddox roared the order then disappeared in the direction of his office, followed by a collection of security men and assistants.

Megan strapped on her gun, plucked her ID from her pocket, and headed for the nearest stairwell. The elevators would be locked down, and guards would be posted at each entrance and exit. They'd have to badge their way through the checkpoints.

A shooting inside a federal building fell under the FBI jurisdiction, but Megan was surprised Maddox would give them the assignment. She guessed it might have something to do with convenience, seeing as both their current cases were brand new and therefore easy to set aside. She and Dan weren't huge fans of Jackson, but curiosity alone made this a coveted case. The fact that they'd dealt with him recently gave them a slight edge in the investigation, assuming they had to deal with him as a perpetrator or victim.

The government alphabet soup occupying this building would make it big news. Megan wasn't looking forward to dodging reporters, but catching a case like this sure beat analyzing incidence reports concerning drug-related crimes.

As they climbed the stairs, Megan realized she shouldn't be making assumptions before seeing the scene. A shooting didn't automatically mean a murder had taken place, and the location didn't equate to Judge Jackson being an integral part of the disturbance.

When they finally made it into Jackson's office, Megan saw that, despite their mad rush, they were still tardy. Normally, she would have liked to inch her way in, taking the time to absorb the scene, but the plush carpet clearly showed signs of high traffic. A clutch of people over by the massive desk on the far side told Megan where the action must have taken place. Four guards were huddled on the right side of the desk. A fifth guard questioned a hysterical woman clutching a wad of tissues.

Dan's long strides allowed him to reach the desk a second before Megan. He didn't say anything, but a subtle stiffening of his shoulders alerted Megan before the sight struck her. Judge Jackson's bulky body lay curled on its side facing them. It might have looked like he'd chosen to take a nap if there wasn't a pool of blood soaking the light gray carpet. Megan sucked in a breath and grimaced. She'd seen bodies before, even brutally murdered bodies, but this reached a new level of savagery.

"His head's gone!" the woman screamed.

They'd have to question her later, but Megan wanted to move her to a more comfortable setting before talking to her. The judge's head wasn't so much gone as pulverized by several close range shots. Counting actual holes would be difficult before the body received care from the medical examiner, but one bullet wouldn't have done this much damage. The judge's left hand was frozen around a sword-shaped letter opener. Megan didn't see it until she knelt next to the body. The treasure would surely thrill the forensic techs.

As politely as possible, Dan ordered the security guards to tell him their names and vacate the office. Megan could tell from his tone he wanted to bawl them out for trampling the scene. He instructed the one comforting the woman to wait with her outside. Four of the men complied immediately, looking relieved. The other man gave the agents hard looks, but then, he too exited with brisk steps.

Megan jotted some notes about her impressions of the scene and put in an order for a forensics team to give the office the deluxe treatment. She considered taking some pictures with her phone, but she didn't want to deal with legal issues if her phone ever got lost or stolen. The past few weeks hadn't exactly been quiet and peaceful. Nothing truly noteworthy had happened, but she felt on edge. Her gym bag had been riffled through, a rock had been thrown at her car, and she'd gotten two hang-up calls from a blocked number. Now that she thought about it, perhaps the series of annoying incidences meant more. She'd have to ponder the possibility later. The scene deserved her undivided attention.

Having worked other crime scenes together, Megan and Dan fell into their usual pattern. They each spent about five minutes writing down every question and observation that occurred to them as they studied the room from different angles. How much they moved depended on the state of the scene. Since this one had already hosted a herd of security guards, they felt free to move around more than usual.

When Megan was satisfied with her first round observations, she looked to see if Dan had finished as well. Finding him still busy writing, Megan retreated to a corner and pulled out her phone to call Kai. The dinner date was officially off. She'd be pushing papers or tracking down leads for this case long into the night. Upon reaching the corner, Megan noticed the carpet fibers had been disturbed because some of them had shifted colors where someone's shoes had rested. The impressions weren't adequate for determining the type of shoe, but Megan guessed they'd been made by a man from the size. This time, she did take a picture with her phone. That photo wouldn't be controversial if it fell into the wrong hands.

To Megan's surprise, Kai picked up on the second ring.

"Let me guess, you want to cancel our dinner plans," said Kai. "Does this have anything to do with the excitement in the federal building?"

"I'm so sorry, Kai. I know this is like the third time I've cancelled on you, but I'll make it up to you. I promise."

"Why don't I bring dinner to you?" Kai offered. "I know you can't talk about an active investigation, but if you're on the case I think you're on, you'll need the breather tonight. Think you can smuggle me into the building?"

"We might have to promise your firstborn child to security, but sure," Megan said. She'd had every intention of turning her friend down, but she needed a good dose of Kai-time. "Dan might want to crash our party, but if you bring him a large coffee, it might pacify him. What were you thinking of ordering for dinner? Anything but cafeteria food is okay by me."

"They're open in the wee hours?" Kai's inflection made it a question.

"No, but even if they were, I've spent most of this week eating there," Megan responded. "Time for a change."

"I was thinking of grabbing something from Romano's Macaroni Grill," Kai said.

A call came in from a blocked number, but Megan ignored it. Normally, she would click over for curiosity's sake, but one could only take so many hang-ups in a week.

After only a slight pause, Megan spoke.

"Great. I'll have the Caprese salad. Dan will probably want the Rosemary Ribeye. You can get whatever you want. Since you're handling pickup, I'll pay for everything when you get here."

Kai tried to protest, but Megan reminded her that besides being her turn to pay she had canceled on Kai the last two times.

"Why do you know their menu?" Kai asked, once the issue of who would pay had been settled.

"My mother would probably disown me if she knew I liked the Italian chain, but sometimes, time is short and it's better than going hungry."

"I can pick a different restaurant," Kai offered.

Megan chuckled.

"Between you and me, I like Romano's." Shortly after this confession, Megan wound the conversation to a close.

When she finished the call, Megan found Dan ready to compare notes. She took a moment to switch her mind back to case mode.

"Did you notice the marks on the carpet over here?" Megan asked.

"Yes. It could be nothing, but that's an unusual spot to stand in," Dan commented. "We don't know if the marks were made today, yesterday, or even this week, but they're worth considering. I only saw one clear set of marks right next to the corner. Did you notice how they're spaced?"

Megan hadn't even registered the set Dan was referring to, but when she looked, she immediately saw what he meant.

"They're shoulder width apart," she said softly. "Shooter's stance." The implication slammed into her. "Was there a second shooter?"

"It's possible," Dan admitted. He didn't sound pleased with the notion. "What do you think? Was this the result of passion or a plan?"

Megan considered the scant information they had on hand. Two shooters on scene would change the dynamics and possible motives drastically. One shooter meant they should focus on grudges from cases that went poorly for certain parties and scenarios involving passion and impulse. In terms of ease, that would be ideal for their investigation. Impulse meant mistakes that could be exploited. Two shooters meant a wider conspiracy and scenarios involving planning and cold calculations.

"It's too early to tell, but I'm getting mixed signals," said Megan. "Multiple shots is a vote for passion, but the body's position tells a different story. Either he was knocked down or he was kneeling. The former says crime of passion and the latter says execution."

Chapter 4:
Soft Targets

The second she heard the breaking news of a shooting inside the federal building, Bethany Cooper pulled her blue minivan to the side of the road and called her husband. He answered on the first ring.

"Hey, honey," Dan greeted. "Sorry I didn't call, but it's been a little hectic around here."

"It's fine," Beth said, willing her heart to slow down. She savored the warm richness of her husband's voice.

"I know from your tone it's not fine," Dan noted. "I assume you heard the news. Can't talk about it, but it wasn't our part of the building. We're all alive and well." He waited a beat in case she wanted to say something. "Listen, I'll—"

"Be late coming home," she finished for him.

"I'm sorry," he said again.

"Me too," Beth replied. She wanted to say so much more. She also wanted to scream, cry, or fling a few curses, but she didn't want to spark an argument now. She could berate him about finding a safer career later, but the more he could concentrate, the sooner he'd finish for the day and come home to her and the girls. "Be safe."

"Love you."

"Love you," Beth echoed.

When the call disconnected, she listened to the dead air for a short while, composing what she should have said to him. She wanted to be the supportive, understanding wife, but he could have made it easier by pursuing a job that didn't involve bad guys and guns. As a proud Texan, Beth didn't mind guns—she even shot them from time to time—but she couldn't abide the thought of losing Dan. She'd mistakenly thought the short army stint would satisfy his need for action and adventure.

Battling the urge to curl into a useless ball of worry, Beth pulled onto the road and headed back to work from her extended lunch break. The temptation to have her assistant, Anuhea, cancel her afternoon appointments almost consumed her, but she pushed the feeling aside. She wanted to swing by the daycare and pick up her girls, but it wouldn't be fair to her patients or her colleagues. The afternoon appointments were a fairly recent addition to her schedule as she eased back in after taking time off to bring her daughter, Carolina Michelle, through the first year of life and see the family through the transition to Hawaii.

Like it or not, people counted on her. Physical therapists didn't have the luxury of ducking out without affecting anybody. If she took the rest of the day off, one of her colleagues would have to cover for her.

Beth assumed the work would help pass some of the afternoon hours, and she was right. Walking her patients through the repetitive exercises to deal with their various problems and talking them through pain management techniques kept her too busy to worry. She loved the variety she could expect in a day. One of her favorite aspects of the job involved designing exercise programs specifically tailored to each person's health needs.

Her last appointment for the day cancelled suddenly, so she got in a quick run before she picked up the girls.

Despite running around at the daycare, Ashley had some extra energy, so Beth stopped by the Honolulu Sheridan Community Park to let her play for a while. Thankfully, Carolina contentedly watched the world from Beth's arms. The comfort of holding the baby restored some much-needed peace to Beth. Ashley ran around with abandon pretending to be a plane, making new friends, and releasing ear-piercing squeals often.

When her stomach started rumbling, Beth lured Ashley to the minivan with the promise of food and packed both children inside. As soon as the engine started, Carolina fell asleep. Ashley chattered incessantly, mostly to herself.

The trip home went smoothly, as did dinner preparations. Beth had planned to make steamed snapper with mushrooms, but since Dan wouldn't be home to enjoy it, she joined the girls in homemade macaroni and cheese with a side of cinnamon applesauce. Ashley had a grand time feeding gooey noodles to her little sister. Laughter filled the kitchen. Beth considered using her phone to video the feeding but was too tired to get up and retrieve the phone from her purse. When it looked like the food might start flying purposefully instead of accidentally, Beth intervened.

"Dinner's over. Time for baths," she announced.

"No!" Ashley declared.

"You love baths," Beth reminded the toddler. "Don't you want to play with Mr. Bubbles?"

"Bubbles!" Ashley's face lit up at the mention of the rubber ducky that soaked in water through small holes in its side and spit the water out through its mouth when squeezed. "Wanna play Bubbles!"

Beth snatched up a washcloth and rinsed it with warm water for the pre-bath cleaning. Carolina fussed, but Ashley endured the wipe down with only small signs of impatience. If Beth didn't clean them up slightly before letting them down from the high chairs, her house would be messier than ever. As soon as Ashley's feet hit the floor, she tried to sprint away. Anticipating the move, Beth held tight to her arm.

"Hold up there, cowgirl. Let me get your sister out."

The doorbell rang just as Beth got the straps loosened and began easing Carolina free of the high chair.

"Mine!" Ashley declared, racing for the door.

"Wait!" Beth cried. She didn't think Ashley would break the rule about opening the door, but she wasn't willing to risk it. Yanking the baby clear, she hustled to the front door.

Ashley's tiny hand reached for the handle.

"Ashley Ann Cooper, you *will* wait for me," Beth declared. The combination of all three names plus her serious tone froze the toddler in place for a crucial second.

The bell rang again.

Ashley cast desperate eyes on Beth and hopped in place impatiently.

"Now, mommy?" she asked, when Beth arrived.

"Let me see who it is first," said Beth. She leaned over her daughter to peer out the peephole.

A chill charged through her when she saw a young man wearing a dark suit. He wore sunglasses, despite the fact that the sun had already set. His black hair was neatly trimmed yet still wavy.

Heart in her throat, Beth reached for the door handle.

"No, me!" shouted Ashley, reminding her of their unspoken deal.

Beth looked down startled. She'd momentarily forgotten the girl was there. Nodding tightly, she let Ashley reach up for the handle and haul back with all her might. Catching the door when it was partially open, Beth maneuvered her body to block Ashley from making an escape.

"Can I help you?" Beth inquired cautiously.

The young man responded with a question.

"Are you Mrs. Cooper?" He flashed an FBI badge.

"Yes." Beth hardly dared to breathe. Her mind immediately jumped to a hundred horrible scenarios, yet she clung to the hope that the FBI wouldn't send an inexperienced agent to deliver bad news. If anything, they'd probably send someone close to her husband, like Agent Luchek.

Ashley's arms wrapped around Beth's left leg, and she tried to squeeze her head into the small gap to see the stranger.

"I work with your husband," said the young man.

"Is he all right?" asked Beth.

The question startled the young agent.

"Of course." He grinned nervously as he put his badge away. "Oh, I'm sorry, I didn't mean to scare you, ma'am. He's fine. He sent me over to show you something. May I come in?"

Relief and suspicion tussled within Beth, freezing her with indecision. The situation was beyond bizarre, and in her heart, she knew Dan would text or call if he was sending someone in his stead. As she reached a conclusion and started to close the door, the young agent drove his shoulder into the door, knocking Beth and Ashley back a step. The toddler fell and started crying. The door banged shut. Beth tripped over Ashley but managed to hang onto the baby.

Before she could right her balance though, the young man grabbed her right arm and yanked forward violently. As she stumbled into him, he pivoted and slammed her against the door. She instinctively turned to catch the blow on her shoulder. She clutched the baby tighter, muffling the infant's sobs against her chest. Beth hunched her shoulders and twisted sideways to put more of her body between the assailant and her baby. Adrenaline flooded her, but before she could move a terrified squeak drained all resistance from her.

The attacker knelt behind Ashley. His left arm looped around the toddler's waist and his right hand clamped firmly over her mouth. He didn't bother with his weapon because he didn't need it. Enough pressure from his hands would still kill Ashley.

The sight broke something in Beth. Tears blurred her vision as she pleaded for her daughter's life.

"Let her go. Let her go. Please! You're hurting her! Just tell me—"

"Calm down," growled the man.

Ashley started to slump in the man's arms, so he shifted his grip to allow the child to breathe. The compromise allowed Beth to regain marginal control over her emotions. She adjusted her grip on Carolina and patted the baby's back to calm her. She couldn't take her eyes off the man, but she didn't dare move away from the door.

He waited while she composed herself.

Slowly, her ragged breaths evened out. She wanted to fire a thousand questions, but at the same time, she wanted to stretch the moment until Dan got home. He'd know what to do. Whatever this man wanted from her, it couldn't be good.

"Grab a bag for the kids. We're going to get in your minivan, and you're going to drive where I tell you to. I'm going to wait here with this one. If you try to run, I'll kill her, and then, I'll find you and kill—"

"I get it. No running."

"No running," the man repeated solemnly. "And no stalling either. You've got two minutes to get what you need for our road trip. If you try anything, I'll—"

"I won't," Beth promised.

She didn't need to hear further threats. Arms trembling, she raced to the baby's room and stuffed extra diapers into the go-bag. Then, she stopped by Ashley's room and haphazardly jammed a few changes of clothes, diapers, and some toys into another shoulder bag. For once, she regretted making Daniel lock the guns in the safe by the front door. Then again, she didn't think she'd be able to stop shaking enough to aim a gun properly. Resigned to obeying, Beth returned to the front entry.

Her phone rang from the kitchen where she'd left it. Beth longed to answer it, but she knew the man would never let that happen.

Two steps from the bottom of the stairs, Beth stopped and stared.

The man had used the time to wrap duct tape around Ashley's

arms and ankles. A third piece covered the child's mouth.

"Take the tape off!" Beth demanded. The outrage overcame some of her fear. "You could suffocate her."

"It'll make her easier to control," the young man explained, looking slightly embarrassed. He wiped the expression away and glared defiantly. "If you follow my instructions, I'll free her when we get to our destination."

"At least remove the tape from her mouth," Beth pressed.

"She might scream," the man argued. "I can't take that risk."

"I can keep her quiet," Beth promised.

"You'll be driving."

"What difference does it make?"

The young man considered the question carefully.

"I guess that's okay," he said. "But I'm going to have to tape your ankles and put handcuffs on you."

The hesitation convinced Beth somebody else must be in charge. This kid was definitely following a game plan he didn't design.

While he seemed agreeable, Beth decided to press her luck.

"Let me leave the girls here. There's no reason to take them. Once we're away, I can have a neighbor check on them."

The kid's head shook swiftly.

"Nope. I've got orders to follow." He lifted Ashley with one arm and drew his gun. "Let's go to your van."

Beth followed the command in a daze. Dread made her footsteps heavy, but she managed to make her way to the garage, pausing only to grab the keys and hand her phone over to the scary guy. The van usually represented safety and the comforts of home, but now, it seemed like an angry metal beast waiting to devour them.

Chapter 5:
Exit Strategy

Getting out of the federal building proved ridiculously easy, but contacting the FBI agent balanced that by being impossible. Either Megan Luchek wasn't taking blocked numbers, or she was too busy to answer right now. Deciding not to leave a message, Cassandra Mirren disposed of the burner phone and planted a tracking device on the agent's car. Next, she ran through the list of safe houses she maintained in Honolulu. The closest one was located on Date Street about ten minutes away if she drove, and she had a nicer place on Kahala Avenue five minutes beyond that. Assuming nothing had happened with the automatic payments, she had three more options scattered around the city and another three on other islands. She never stayed in one place more than a few weeks in a row.

The Shadow Council also kept safe houses Fixers could access in a pinch, but Cassandra wasn't about to put her life in those hands until she sorted friend from foe. Keith Danielson could still be a lone rogue, or he could have twisted the entire Council by feeding them any number of lies.

After retrieving her car, Cassandra made her way to the closest apartment. Odds were good that Danielson would target the agent at some point, so keeping tabs on Megan would eventually lead Cassandra to her quarry. Nobody was paying her to take Danielson out, but he'd made it personal by trying to frame her for Judge Jackson's murder. She didn't need to know the extent of the history between the agent and the psychopath to know the man couldn't resist trying to ruin Megan's life. Even if the agent wasn't lucky enough to draw the judge's case, she would stick close to the action. The woman attracted trouble without even trying.

Reaching the apartment, Cassandra picked the lock and headed to the bathroom to throw water on her face. She'd seen people gunned down before, but not like this. Though far from perfect, Judge Jackson had been a clever leader with realistic goals and modest ambitions. His vision for the Shadow Council kept the machine running smoothly. She wasn't naïve enough to label the Council's actions as *good*, but they did contribute to the overall order that existed within the city of Honolulu and other major cities around the world.

The quick rinse with cold water refreshed Cassandra. She stared into her reflection in the bathroom mirror, weighing the worth of changing appearances. A check of the cabinets revealed scissors, a bucket, hair dye, an extensive battery of makeup, and a collection of subtle prosthetics to change the shape of her face. There wasn't much she could do about the hair length unless she wanted to go extremely short. The dark-brown hair color could easily be shifted to black or bleached back to blond, but she didn't see the point of changing now. When this battle of wits and wills ended, she'd either be dead or in serious need of a new identity. The question of black hair vs blond hair could be determined later.

Rummaging through the kitchen yielded a bottle of water and some cheese crackers. Switching safe houses often meant foregoing fresh food. Cassandra needed a nap, a plan, and a proper meal. She delayed the hunger issue with the crackers and water. Then, she retrieved the large, locked case from beneath the spare bed. It wasn't a unique hiding spot, but the case's size and heavy-duty combination lock would discourage the average burglar.

Inside, as expected, she found passports under several names from a variety of countries. These she put in a neater pile but set aside, hoping she'd get the chance to use one of them. She didn't doubt her skills, but Danielson attracted gun-toting flunkies in alarming numbers. Despite the collection of other handguns within the case, Cassandra simply retrieved two spare magazines that would fit her current weapon choice, a Glock 22.

She set her phone timer for one hour, gripped her handgun, and settled in an armchair for a nap. The couch in the living room or a bed would have been more comfortable, but this was a working-mode nap. Sacrificing comfort for the ability to come awake a fraction of a second faster had saved her life on more than one occasion.

Two minutes before the timer would expire, Cassandra snapped awake and pointed her gun at an approaching figure.

"I come in peace," said a deep male voice. He held his arms up and away from his body to be less threatening. "Do you always sleep with a gun?"

"Don't you?" Cassandra returned, lowering the weapon.

"Yes, but I spend most of my time in foreign cities where the locals hate everything I stand for. It's a little out of place in a luxury apartment." He started to lower his arms. "Permission to approach?"

Cassandra tucked the gun away and stood to greet her friend. Public displays of affection—even in private—weren't really her thing, but she always made an exception for Owen Ramsey. The tall, muscular man looked more like a marine than a Central Intelligence Agency operative. His dark hair looked freshly buzzed. Since his arms were still slightly elevated, stepping under them wasn't an issue. After giving him a big hug, she leaned up to kiss his right cheek. At the last moment, he turned into the kiss, catching her lips. The move surprised her in a good way and flooded her with an odd mixture of emotions. She rode the wave of relief and longing for several seconds before pulling away.

"Owen. We talked about this," Cassandra said. Her tone pleaded with her friend to see reason. She had to crane her neck back to meet his brown eyes.

He gripped her shoulders hard.

"No, Cassie. You talked, just before you walked away." His eyes bore into hers. He tried to keep his voice steady but flecks of pain and frustration bled through. "Yet here we are again."

"I'm sorry," she said, "I know it's not fair." Though it went against her instincts, Cassandra forced herself to stay still. "And I wouldn't blame you for leaving and not looking back. You don't have to help me."

"Is Danielson involved?" Owen's tone could have blasted a hole through a foot of concrete.

"Most definitely." Cassandra relived the judge's last moments in her head.

Owen flashed a feral grin.

"Then I have to be here."

"This is *your* assignment?" Cassandra didn't know why that surprised her. Owen's involvement in the Pennsylvania affair had been as a personal favor to her, but it sort of made sense that the international spooks would want a piece of Danielson. Technically, the CIA wasn't supposed to operate on US soil, but in reality, that translated to *don't get caught*.

"The man's an embarrassment and a liability," Owen said, releasing his grip on her shoulders.

Cassandra took a half-step backward, as if the extra six inches would help clear her head.

"If you're working officially, perhaps—"

Owen's warm, rich laughter cut her off.

"Nothing I do is ever official."

His levity irritated her.

"This isn't a game. I'm going to kill Danielson, or die trying."

Sobering, Owen ran a palm wearily down his face.

"For once, the higher powers agree with you." He sighed. "You should let me help you. The agency resources are vast and could help level the playing field. Face it, you need somebody." He closed the distance between them and leaned forward, lowering his voice. "Job aside, I want to help you. Always have. You know how I feel about you."

The words prompted an ache deep within her chest. She could barely meet his eyes.

"I'm no good for you, Owen," she whispered. "You know what I am."

"I know what you could be," he countered. "The offer we discussed before still stands."

"Really?" Cassandra's tone conveyed her doubt. "How would they justify that?"

After they'd transferred Danielson over to the team that should have delivered the man to justice, Owen told Cassandra that the CIA wanted to recruit her.

He lifted his shoulder in a partial shrug.

"Desperate times and such." Owen's expression turned thoughtful and his gaze became unfocused. "I don't think it'd be much different than accepting Shadow Council contracts, only different masters, more toys ... and me."

She raised an eyebrow to request an explanation.

"I'd be your handler," he said. A smile said his mind was wandering elsewhere with that statement.

Cassandra blew out a breath.

"It's an interesting proposition, but we're getting ahead of ourselves. Danielson's still on the loose with a need to be disruptive. If I live to the end of the week, I'll think about it."

"Promise?" he pressed.

"Well, I will need a new job," she said. "I'm not quite ready to retire, but if the Council's dumb enough to let a guy like Danielson take over, I'm done with them."

"Great, let's go hunting." Owen grinned like a schoolboy before a long break. "Do you have a plan?"

"It's not so much a plan as a strategy," Cassandra said. "Danielson's attempt to frame me for Judge Jackson's murder was pretty clumsy, but he's no fool. He's got something else planned, and I'm not the only target."

Owen nodded slowly. Cassandra's brief request for aid this morning had included those first facts.

"You think he'll go after the FBI agent."

"He's after her and a drug dealer," Cassandra explained. "Since I don't know where to begin searching for the drug dealer, the agent's the best bet. If we follow her, we'll eventually find Danielson. I'm already tracking her car, but we're going to have to keep a close watch on her. He probably wants something from her, but when he tires of his game, he'll kill her. I can't let that happen."

"You haven't known her that long, and from what I understand, you started out at odds," Owen pointed out. "Why do you care what happens to her?" He held up a hand before she could respond. "What I mean is, it took me five years to break through your defensive screen. What is it about this FBI agent that accomplishes the same in a matter of weeks?"

"Maybe I'm getting sentimental in my old age." Cassandra knew the answer wouldn't satisfy him, so she paused to sort the fragments of reason swirling in her brain. "Truth is, Megan has an innocence worth protecting."

Owen's expression contained questions.

"It's not about toughness or competence," Cassandra continued, struggling to articulate her thoughts. "It's about idealism. She still believes justice is worth fighting for though legal means." Cassandra couldn't help but smile, especially when she saw Owen shake his head in disbelief. "It's naïve, but charming. Anyway, it also makes her a clear target."

"Sounds like protecting her could be a fulltime job," Owen commented.

"It will be for me tonight—and you, if you're serious about helping. But I don't think Danielson will make us wait long."

"Do you think he'll make a move soon, like within the hour?" asked Owen.

Cassandra considered the possibility then shook her head.

"Assuming he spoke the truth about framing Agent Luchek for the drug dealer's murder, he'll need to track the man down, set the trap, and arrange for the agent to be drawn into the trap. That's going to take time. I think we have until late tonight before he makes a move we can deal with."

"Good. Then, I'm ordering food," said Owen.

Chapter 6:
Gift-Wrapped Bad Guy

Megan Luchek didn't leave the federal building until a quarter to midnight. She might have stayed and caught a nap on a cot like Dan was planning to do if Kai hadn't reminded her reporters might be hunting for her tomorrow. Men could pull off the I-just-slept-on-a-couch thing and still look distinguished. Megan didn't have that gift.

On the way to her car, she thought about Judge Jackson's fate. The medical examiner's office wouldn't have a report until late tomorrow at the earliest, but the harried tech had told her unofficially that there was damage from at least five bullets. Professionals didn't tend to waste that much lead on a guy. Either the perpetrator had been an amateur or he—or she—wanted to be taken as one.

As she neared her car, Megan sensed a presence a second before she saw him. He was tall and large and standing near the back passenger door.

"Good evening, Agent Luchek."

She didn't recognize the voice, but being addressed by name in the middle of the night made her jumpy. Her hand automatically flew to her gun. If she dove forward, the bulk of the car would shield her.

"I wouldn't do that." The man didn't appear to have a gun pointed at her, but he did hold something small in his right hand. Turning the object around, the man placed it on top of her car and slid it toward her.

Keeping one hand near her weapon, Megan caught the phone and saw a picture of a blond woman holding a baby and hugging a small child. The woman and child looked back at her with haunted eyes. Duct tape covered the woman's mouth.

"What's this about?" Megan asked. She spoke carefully, but her heart pounded hard enough to give her a headache.

"The code for that phone is 1-1-1-1-1-1. In the text messages you'll find an address. Go there, and you'll get some answers. In case you didn't recognize them, that's—"

"It's Dan's family. I know," Megan interrupted. "What I don't get is why there's a picture of them on this phone."

"Check the time and date stamp if you need to."

Megan did so and saw that the picture had been taken a few hours earlier.

"The navigation system is already programmed to guide you to the correct address. If you deviate from the course, we'll know. If you call Agent Cooper, we'll know. If we suspect anything but complete compliance, you can explain their deaths to your partner." The man took a step backward. "Same goes if you try to stop me. You've got ten minutes to reach your destination, agent. I suggest you get started."

A quick tour of the phone confirmed everything the man had said. The photos section contained three additional pictures of Bethany Cooper and the girls. Megan checked to see if the pictures were tagged with a location and found that the feature had been disabled. She stuck the key into the ignition but didn't start the car. Instead, she closed her eyes and reviewed every protocol on handling threats. The training seminar hadn't covered a scenario like this. If the threat rested on her, she would have risked notifying somebody, but she didn't feel confident enough to gamble with Dan's entire family.

The clock on her dashboard changed, reminding her time marched onward.

Her phone rang as she pulled out of the parking space. The number came up blocked again, so she ignored it. She doubted the kidnappers would call so soon. She wasn't even sure why she'd been allowed to keep her gun and phone. Megan contemplated texting Kai for help, but she had to consider that her car bore some kind of surveillance device. The man's threat of knowing whether or not she obeyed the instructions might be empty, but Megan doubted it. Somebody crazy enough to concoct a situation like this wouldn't simply forget a detail like her gun.

The deadline loomed large in her mind. The real-time ETA consistently stayed a minute too late. The traffic at this hour was light, so she drove a bit over the speed limit. Fear of being pulled over kept her from slamming the accelerator to the floor. Thoughts of sleep and rest burned up. Megan spent the drive time planning various courses of action. She needed to find Dan's family and warn him without getting them killed or winding up dead. Maintaining the appearance of obedience would be important.

Aware she'd crossed over into one of the rougher neighborhoods, Megan slowed to a stop as the navigational assistant cheerfully informed her she'd arrived at her destination. A beep from her phone reminded her she had a message, but she didn't have time to check it. Tucking her phone away, Megan picked up the other phone and stepped out of her car, expecting an ambush. The place was strangely quiet. Normally, one could find a few drug-related transactions happening along this street.

Killing her didn't seem to be a priority for these people, but that was cold comfort given the elaborate nature of their scheme. Drawing her gun made Megan feel a little better.

After rechecking the address, Megan carefully made her way into the abandoned storefront. The front room was clear, so she crept back to the door marked: Employees Only. As she cleared the doorway, a floodlight blinded her. Even after slamming her eyes shut, a large white spot floated in her vision. Instinctively, Megan crouched to present a smaller target.

Nothing happened.

Somewhat amazed to be alive, Megan blinked furiously and raised a hand to fend off the brilliant beam of light.

A dark shape appeared in front of her. Eventually, the blur assumed the shape of a man sitting in a hard-backed chair. When Megan's vision adjusted enough, she eased forward a few steps until she recognized the man bound to the chair.

"Do you like your gift, Maggie?"

Megan spun and pointed her gun dead-center of a man's chest, but this time, he wasn't the speaker. He held another phone out to her like a peace offering. The voice came from the phone which had been set to speaker mode. Only massive willpower kept her from blasting the phone into tiny shards. Questions crowded her head. She recognized the speaker, but everything in her complained about the impossibility.

"What's he doing here?" she asked.

The bound man groaned.

Holding her gun on the man with the phone, Megan slipped

over to Donean Gavriel and checked for a pulse. He moaned again at her touch. A once over revealed a deep gash over his right eye and several bruises on his cheeks. The jerky way he breathed, told her the beating hadn't been confined to his face. The zip ties holding his wrists to the chair were so tight his hands were almost purple.

"You're going to kill him," Keith Danielson announced.

Megan didn't respond. Her gun still loosely pointed at the man with the phone.

"Maggie, are you there? Did you hear me?"

"I'm here, and I heard you," Megan muttered.

"Why don't you sound happier?" Keith's tone feigned concern. "I'm offering you the justice so recently denied. Didn't you want such scum taken off the streets?"

"'Off the streets' and 'dead' are a pretty far cry from each other," said Megan. "I'll settle for the beating already delivered. Thanks."

"Unfortunately, it's not just about you, my dear," said Keith. "This is part of a much grander plan."

"What made you target a drug pusher?" Megan asked. She watched the blood leaking from the cut over Gavriel's eye, grateful he was unconscious. At least he wouldn't be in pain. It also spared her from having to deal with his attitude issues. One creep was enough to handle at once. "And how did you escape a lengthy prison term?"

"I wish we had time to catch up properly. I still owe you for interfering in Pennsylvania. Call me sentimental, but I'm saving that pack of cigarettes just for you."

Megan's mind unhelpfully went to a vivid memory of the cigarette burn Keith had given her on one of their last encounters.

"If you want revenge, just kill me," said Megan. "I don't see the point of playing your stupid games. This obsession you have with me isn't healthy."

For either one of us.

"You may not see the point, but Mrs. Cooper would probably appreciate your cooperation."

Megan flinched at the name.

"Shall we ask her? Maybe she'd like a cigarette."

Hot rage and cold despair seized Megan. Her grip tightened on her gun, causing the aim to waver.

"Leave her alone, Keith."

The sound of ripping tape and a small, pained cry preceded a different voice.

"Megan?"

"Beth! Are you all right? Did he hurt you?"

"Not yet," Keith answered, "but I hope you're ready to take me seriously. It's a simple job. Kill Gavriel and wait for the authorities to come get you."

"If it's so simple, why can't you kill Gavriel yourself? Why involve them? Why involve me?" Megan forced herself to breathe.

"The Cooper family is a means to an end. If you confess to the murder, they get to live. As for you, I'm trying to make you into a hero. You can even come up with a scenario where he attacked you first, if you like."

"Tempting, but no," Megan said.

"Really?" Keith sounded genuinely interested. "You'd sacrifice Beth and the kids for a piece of garbage like Gavriel?"

"Even if I followed the instruction, you'd probably kill them."

"Your lack of trust hurts, Maggie." Keith hummed thoughtfully to drag out the moment. "Fortunately for them, I don't need you to really pull the trigger or confess. I just need the bullets to come from your gun, and my people can plant the proper evidence. It would be more satisfying if you actually shot him though. Are you sure you won't reconsider?"

Despair mounted in Megan. She glanced down at her gun almost ready to throw it down in disgust. Keith wanted to frame her for a murder yet to happen. She needed to change this game immediately.

The sleek black metal of her gun glinted in the light. A crazy idea burst into her head. She flipped the gun around and stared down the barrel. It looked a lot larger from this angle.

"What are you doing?" Keith's shouted question alerted her to the presence of a camera. The panic in his voice sounded genuine and gave her a sense of satisfaction.

"Changing the game," Megan murmured. Her palms were sweaty. She concentrated on gauging the angle and adjusted it lower. She didn't want to kill herself, but if she caused enough damage, Keith's scheme of framing her for murder would fall apart.

"Stop her!" Keith barked.

Megan expected the gorilla man in the corner to tackle her, but instead, he fiddled with the phone in his hands. Two pffst sounds filled the room, one right behind the other. Megan felt a sharp pain in her right arm and left shoulder. Her head immediately felt woozy. Her vision clouded, and she stumbled to her knees, dropping the gun in front of her.

"You do keep things interesting." Keith's voice sounded like it was coming to her through a wind tunnel. "Get some rest. I have another task for you to complete before your grand confession."

Megan fought desperately for consciousness and lost.

Chapter 7:
Sidelined

Daniel Cooper woke up when someone shook his right shoulder. Despite his fatigue, he snapped himself to full alertness and worked through the momentary confusion of not awakening beside his wife, Bethany. A mental image of the judge's dead body cleared up any clinging desire to go right back to sleep.

"Hey, sorry to bother you, but I need to talk to you," said Dale Sims.

Staring up at the man quickly got awkward, so Dan sat up.

"What time is it?" Dan inquired.

Sims checked his watch and reported the time.

"3:05." Sims looked apologetic, but he pressed on. "The matter is urgent ... and private. Will you come with me?"

"Where are we going?" Dan asked, standing up. He didn't need an answer, but he liked to be prepared. His mind scrolled through possible topics and came up almost blank. His history with Sims could be measured in hours. That didn't give him a lot to go on. The man was a relatively new face around the Honolulu field office. Once Dan got the assignment to work with Sims, he'd wandered down to the man's isolated office and introduced himself. It's not like they had a chance to sit down and compare life stories.

"My office should be private enough," said Sims.

Dan waved for Sims to lead the way. He felt a momentary twinge of jealousy that the fresh-faced newcomer had a large office all to himself. It didn't seem large due to the obscene amount of electronic equipment occupying every flat surface and most of the floor space. He recalled feeling like he'd stepped into a hoarder's lair the first time he saw Sims's space.

Along the way, Dan debated whether he should call Beth or let her sleep. She would probably bite his head off for calling so late, but she would do the same or worse if he completely failed to check in. After the late dinner with Kai and Megan, the hours had melted by in one case discussion after another. He wasn't always paired with Megan, but the cases they worked together tended to be exciting. He'd warned Beth he would miss dinner and probably be late, but she would be the first to point out that *late* and *3 a.m.* were on two totally different levels of uncool. He started rehearsing his apology as they reached Sims's office.

"Sorry about the mess. I was testing some counter surveillance equipment. The good news is that it works great." Sims threaded his way through the piles of junk to his desk and pressed a button on a black box the size of an old-fashioned encyclopedia. Locating a chair, Sims transferred the equipment to the floor and patted the top of the chair. "You might want to be seated for this."

Dan noticed that once they stepped inside the office, Sims's demeanor shifted. The young man became more confident, almost cocky. Despite slight misgivings, Dan sat down as bid. He was too tired to unravel the mystery of the tech guy right now.

"Is this about the case?" he asked, referring to the one they'd been jointly assigned. "Did Maddox tell you it might have to be put on hold?" Determining where the FBI could improve the equipment available for its agents paled in the public relations category when viewed against the murder of a well-respected judge.

"He did," Sims confirmed. "But this isn't about our case. It's about your new one."

"What about it?" Dan didn't feel at liberty to discuss the murder case with this unknown factor. Techs and other support personnel liked to gossip about certain cases, though he'd never experienced such probes before. It made them feel important to have inside access to the special agents working the glamorous and gruesome cases. "I really can't talk about it with you."

"You'll have to," Sims said with a cryptic half-smile. Slowly, he reached over and plucked a plain burner phone from a box containing dozens of such phones. Tapping out a quick code, he unlocked the phone and held it out to Dan. "Open the photos."

Dan stared at the phone. An uneasy feeling gripped his gut.

"Not until you explain what's going on."

"A picture's always worth more than words," Sims countered.

The two men regarded each other carefully.

Sitting back in the uncomfortable chair, Dan planted his feet, hooked his thumbs through belt loops, and settled in for a wait. This whelp needed to learn the pecking order.

"You're going to take this phone from my hand, and you're going to open to the photos," Sims said. His tone picked up a slightly menacing quality.

"Why?" Dan narrowed his eyes at the man.

"Because Beth would want you to."

Having Sims utter his wife's nickname brought Dan out of the chair and halfway across the man's desk. He gripped the phone in one hand and Sims's collar in the other.

"Careful, Cooper. I'm going to give my boss a report on your behavior, and you really want it to be favorable, for her sake."

Dan let Sims slip free and turned his attention to the phone.

"What's the code?"

"9-9-9-9-9-9," said Sims.

Dan's thumb hurt from jamming it into the tiny keys, but he soon found the collection of photos. His jaw tightened as he flipped through the six pictures. The first image showed Beth and Giggles bound with duct tape and sitting on a thin mattress in a bare corner somewhere. A car seat sat next to Beth, but it faced away from Dan, so he couldn't tell if it held Sweet Pea. The second picture showed the baby sleeping peacefully inside the carrier. The third, fourth, and fifth pictures were similar to the first in context, if not exact content. They clearly showed his wife and daughters being held captive in some sort of bare room. By the fifth picture, the duct tape had been removed, so Giggles clung to Beth. The last image showed only Beth. She looked both frightened and furious as she held a cardboard sign that said: OBEY THEM. Her eyes held a message closer to *kill them*.

"Are you ready to listen?" Sims queried.

Pushing aside the urge to bury his fist in Sims's smug face, Dan nodded stiffly. He didn't trust himself with words, so he poured his frustration into squeezing the life out of the phone.

"It's a lot to absorb," Sims commented. "I don't blame you for being upset, but I need you to focus."

"I want to speak with my wife," Dan declared.

"In due—"

"Now." Dan searched through the phone's contacts to see if there were any numbers to call, but he found nothing. The phone had received the photo packet from a blocked number. "You know I'll listen better when I know they're safe."

Sims said nothing as he weighed the request against his orders. Finally, he shrugged, selected a different phone off the pile, and threw it to Dan.

"Code's 8-8-8-8-8-8. Number's in the contacts. Put it on speaker and get your confirmation so we can have a productive discussion."

Catching the phone, Dan tapped over to contacts and found the entry labeled with Beth's name. The familiarity hit him squarely. As instructed, he switched the phone to speaker mode so Sims could listen in. His heart beat against his chest like a bird wanting out. He didn't breathe until he heard her shaky voice.

"Dan? Who are these people? What do they want with you?"

"I tried to tell him, but he insisted on checking on you first," said Sims.

A strange male voice spoke.

"That'll do, Sims. I'll take it from here." The voice had the confident quality of someone accustomed to being obeyed.

"Yes, sir," the tech guy chirped.

"Agent Cooper, we haven't had the pleasure of meeting in person, but I need your help," said the stranger. "Since I have you both on the line, we can make it a family discussion. Mrs. Cooper, you might want to turn the speaker mode off. No use frightening the girls."

"They're asleep," Beth murmured. The quality of her voice changed enough to tell Dan she'd taken the stranger's advice.

"Good. Yes, I can see that. Oh, don't look so surprised, Mrs. Cooper. There are several cameras on you. I find them more reliable than people sometimes."

"Stop it," Dan growled. He stood up. "You have me, so you have no reason to hold them."

"Ah, but you're not my ultimate target. Maggie is." The man spoke Megan's name tenderly. "One of them anyway."

"Keith, right?" Dan asked, pulling the name from the recesses of his memory.

"Guilty," he acknowledged.

"In case you haven't noticed, Megan's a grown woman," Dan said. "She doesn't answer to me."

"I think you underestimate your worth to her," Keith Danielson noted. "She knows the score already. We told her a few hours before Sims woke you up."

"Then what do you need from me?" Dan demanded.

"Maggie might need a pep talk from you in order to play her part," Keith replied. "And, eventually, I want you to arrest her."

"For what?" asked Beth. "Will you kill her?"

"Not yet," Keith said in a kind, gentle tone. "She too needs to do something for me."

Dan's mind struggled to keep up with the twisted logic.

"You kidnapped my family to control me to control Megan ... to do what? And what would I arrest her for?"

"Murder," Danielson answered.

Beth sucked in sharply.

"Not you," Danielson assured her. "Someone your husband might even say deserves it."

"Who?" Dan wondered.

"Care to hazard a guess, agent?"

"No. I—" Dan cut himself off as a name brightened in his mind. "You're talking about Donean Gavriel. He deserves a prison sentence, not death."

"Who's that?" Beth asked.

"He's a drug dealer," Dan explained.

"He was a drug dealer," Danielson corrected. "It's already done. All that remains is the story to be told."

"Did Megan kill him for you?" Beth's voice pitched higher with her anxiety.

"No, she refused, even with your lives hanging in the balance. That's partly why I need your husband to make her see reason. I didn't need her to pull the trigger, but I still want her arrested for the crime. She needs to know what that feels like."

"What evidence am I going to file against her?" Dan asked grimly.

"You won't need much," said Keith. "She's going to confess, but you have some time. For now, Sims is going to fit you with a device to keep you there until I need you to move against Maggie. As I said, I need her to kill someone for me. I think I can convince her on my own, but if I need you, Sims will give you the details."

Chapter 8:
Rude Awakening

A sharp scent crawled inside Megan's head and yanked her back to consciousness. She jerked away from the offending smell, banging her head against something solid in the process. Her eyes flew open and scanned the surroundings, but the only light source was a dim flashlight lying on the floor near her right foot. Pain zipped back and forth through her head like someone threading a giant needle through the middle of her skull. She groaned.

"Come on, agent. Wake up," commanded a female voice.

Squinting through the semi-darkness, Megan saw the general outline of a figure, but she didn't need to see the speaker to recognize the voice. She tried to move her hands and discovered they were bound in front of her with a plastic tie. Momentary panic gave her the strength to tug hard against the bindings, resulting in sore wrists.

"So that's how it is, assassin," she commented.

"Not at all, and call me Cassandra, please. I needed to haul you into the van myself and binding your limbs was expedient. If you promise to hear me out, I'll cut the bindings and explain what I can. We don't have much time."

"And if I refuse to hear you out?" Megan's inflection turned it into a question.

"Then I'll leave you the knife and be on my way, and by the end of the day, one of us will likely be dead." Cassandra reached down and turned the flashlight to a brighter setting. "I need to know what Keith Danielson's told you so far and what he wants from you."

"Release me first," said Megan. She held out her wrists.

The assassin drew a small dagger from an ankle sheathe and cut the zip tie holding Megan's wrists together. Then, she leaned down and did the same for the ankle ties.

"Where's my gun?" Megan asked. The shoulder holster felt too light to be holding her firearm. She gingerly ran the fingers of her left hand over the deep indentations marking her other wrist.

"Outside the van in a pool of blood," Cassandra answered.

At the mention of blood, Megan noticed that the dark spots she'd dismissed as general grime were far more numerous than she previously thought. She rested her head back against the side of the van and grunted. She'd forgotten about that.

"Let me guess, the blood came from a short Latino guy with bruises all over his body."

"I didn't look too closely, but since Danielson said his plan was to frame you for Donean Gavriel's murder, I'm sure that's him out there."

"You knew about his plan?" Megan's voice contained outrage. "Why didn't you warn me?"

"I tried," Cassandra said, "but it's too late for warnings anyway. We need a new plan."

The blocked calls blazed in Megan's memory. The rest of her horrible night soon flooded back too. She sat bolt upright and patted her pockets to see if she still had a phone on her. The only one she found was the gift from her mysterious tail turned kidnapper. She took it out and stared at it, but didn't make a move to call anyone on it.

"The only reason we're still here is that I think you're being tracked through that phone," said Cassandra.

Megan nodded understanding.

"I've got to call my partner. Do you have a safe phone I can borrow?"

"What happened?" Cassandra inquired, picking up on the concern in Megan's tone.

"Keith happened," Megan muttered bitterly. "He has Dan Cooper's family. I need to talk to him. Do you have a phone or not?"

"I do, but hold on. Let's think about this. Danielson's likely not after your partner, which means the game centers around you. As soon as you call your partner, Danielson's going to know his original plan went wrong."

Megan shook her head.

"I don't think he wants me caught yet. He said something

about a different task for me, but he never explained because I passed out."

"You were drugged with something pretty powerful. It took the smelling salts a minute to work. They're usually faster than that."

"Please. Dan deserves to know."

"All right. But whatever happens, don't let on that you're with me." Cassandra handed Megan a cellphone. "We'll destroy it when you're done."

Megan searched her brain for Dan's number. She'd gotten so used to it being programed into her phone that she almost forgot the number. The time caught her attention as she accessed the keypad. The clock read 4:06. Her finger hesitated a second over the send button.

I hate being the bearer of bad news.

If Dan didn't know about his family's plight, Megan was about to destroy his peace of mind. If he did know, then she needed to do everything in her power to make this right.

"Agent Cooper speaking," Dan said. Tension wrapped thickly around each hoarse word.

"Dan. It's me. I—"

"Megan, he has Beth and the girls," Dan interrupted.

"I know. That's why I'm calling."

"He wants me to arrest you for Gavriel's murder. What's going on? Why is he after you?"

"Pardon the interruption, but I thought I'd answer that myself." Keith Danielson's smooth voice chilled Megan.

She shot an alarmed look at Cassandra who shook her head and put a finger to her lips.

"You're not supposed to be awake yet, Maggie, and you're not using the phone we gave you. That means you have help. Is she there?"

"Who?"

"Don't be coy. If you annoy me too much, I'll hurt them."

"Don't—"

"Stay out of this, Cooper," Keith ordered. "In fact, we're done with you for now. Sit tight. I'll call you if I need you."

A brief click told Megan that Dan had been disconnected.

"She's not here," Megan said, forcing her jaw to move enough to surrender the words. "And as for the phone, maybe you're underestimating me."

"You're lying, but no matter," said Keith. "If she's there, this can be over sooner than anticipated, and you can go to prison with a clear conscience."

"What do you want me to do?" Megan inquired. She met Cassandra's eyes.

The assassin was nodding slowly.

"I'm told you and Cassandra Mirren met on Tantalus Lookout."

"Not true, but close enough," Megan said. Technically, they'd met at a formal dinner before the encounter Keith referred to. "Why?"

"Because I think it's time for a reunion." Keith sounded gleeful. "I'm going to arrange for Cassandra to be at Tantalus Lookout sometime this afternoon. Communicating with her is a little harder than with you, but I'll manage. You should be there. When she arrives, kill her for me. Just be aware that I'm going give her similar instructions. As soon as I get confirmation one of you is dead, the Cooper family is free to go."

"What hold do you have over her?" Megan didn't have to look at Cassandra to know the question would be burning up her insides.

"An old friend; she doesn't have many of those. You don't know him. But even if that fails, she might kill you pre-emptively, so she doesn't have to watch out for you the rest of her life."

"If you can arrange all this, you could have killed me or Cassandra at any point," Megan noted. "Why bring Dan's family into this? Why frame me for Gavriel's murder?"

"The thing with Gavriel is nothing more than a display of power. The lowlifes in this city need a reminder about who's in control."

"Who is in control?" asked Megan.

"I am," Keith declared. "Along with a certain Council. Cassandra used to be a valued employee, but I believe you corrupted her."

"How did I manage that?" Megan questioned.

Cassandra looked mildly amused.

"You made her soft. She wouldn't even kill Judge Jackson for me. I had to do it myself."

Well, that closes that case.

Megan had never solved a murder case in such record time. Now, she just had to live long enough to make sure Keith paid for the crime. The man was turning into quite the thorn in the side.

"I saw," she murmured. "How many times did you shoot him?"

"It was messier than it needed to be," Keith admitted. "Take that as a lesson to be applied here. If you don't want things to get messy, follow my instructions."

"I'll go to the meeting, but I'm not killing for you." Megan heard a tremor in her voice and winced.

"You don't sound sure of yourself, Maggie."

Stop calling me that!

"Let them go," she whispered.

"You know how to purchase their freedom." Keith ended the call.

Megan bowed her head and tapped the phone against one of her knees. Several seconds passed in silence.

"Did you hear?" she asked.

"I heard enough," Cassandra replied. "And I think we can work with this if you're willing, but it's going to take a tremendous amount of trust on both our parts."

The next few minutes were spent listening to Cassandra outline her plan. It was crazy enough to have a chance at working. When she finished, Megan peppered her with questions.

"What about the hostages? Who did he take to control you? How will we find them? How will we get to them?"

"One thing at a time," Cassandra cautioned. She gently took the phone from Megan's hands, took out the battery, slipped the phone into a bag, and crushed it under her booted heel. "First, we need to get you new clothes. You can't run around in public covered in Gavriel's blood."

"If you're right about him having multiple men at both hostage locations, we'll need to work together to free them." Megan felt her throat drain of moisture. "So, who do we go after?"

"We'll have a chat with some of Danielson's men at the lookout for the locations. Then, we'll locate your partner's family first," said Cassandra.

Twin waves of guilt and relief moved through Megan.

"Who does he have?" she asked again.

"I'm not sure, but if it's the 'old friend' I have in mind, Danielson might have made a fatal mistake."

"We can hope anyway," Megan commented.

"Don't worry about my friend for now," Cassandra advised. "Our coordination needs to be perfect, and we only get one try on this. Are you ready?"

Megan blew out a slow breath.

"Not really, but I will be," she promised. A new thought occurred to her. "We should free Dan."

"It's already on my to-do list," Cassandra said. "That's why I'm going to drop you off at one of the safe houses. You'll have to arrange for a ride to the lookout on your own."

"Why didn't you tell me it was on your 'to-do' list?" Megan asked, slightly annoyed.

"Because the plan's a fluid thing," Cassandra answered. "That's how I work. The parts we discussed are still valid, but I might be a little later than originally estimated. You need to get there first anyway, that's important. If you get there too early, try to rest. I'll wake you when necessary."

"How?" Megan wondered.

"With this," Cassandra said, holding up a tiny earpiece. "Try not to let Danielson know you have it. He probably has a way to hack into the frequency."

Megan took the device and slipped it into her ear to test how it would feel. Satisfied she could tolerate the strange sensation, she removed it and placed it in a pocket. She really didn't like having to trust the assassin again, but this wasn't a mission she could simply walk away from. At least three innocent lives rested on this harebrained scheme. She wasn't much for prayer, but for some reason, her mind went back to her Catholic school days. Sister Eliana had told her all the troubles in the world fade behind the power of prayer. Megan hoped some higher power was looking out for the Cooper family because they would need a lot of strength to make it through the day.

Chapter 9:
Recruit

Cassandra dropped Megan off at the cushy safe house about fifteen minutes from the federal building with explicit instructions to change and lay low until showtime. Before leaving, she changed into a business suit. They'd ditched the phone Keith could track, but now that the agent knew of this address, it was burned. Once the Danielson crisis ended, she could worry about that.

She didn't tell Megan the whole plan because the agent wouldn't have agreed with some of what she had in mind. At least they agreed on freeing Cooper. First, Cassandra needed to find him. She assumed Agent Cooper never left the federal building. As it was still around 4:30 in the morning, the building should be mostly empty. The identification badge she'd lifted from Agent Luchek would let her access the building. Hopefully, the night watchman was more interested in a nap or a movie than doing his job, but if he challenged her, she'd deal with it.

Fortunately for her, budget cuts had done away with a live guard in favor of additional electronic measures. One swipe of Megan's badge and Cassandra was in. An FBI cap hid her features from the cameras and a windbreaker let her smuggle in a small black box. Once inside, Cassandra headed for the stairs to check the floor occupied by the FBI offices.

As soon as she stepped into the stairwell, she activated the device. A blinking red light told her it was analyzing her request. Soon, she had a report. Forty nine people, including her, were in the building at this hour. On the assumption that Agent Cooper would have a minder of some sort, Cassandra punched in a command to disregard people who were obviously alone and in groups bigger than four. The parameters eliminated thirty-eight of the people. Of those, one was a group of three. Cassandra mentally disregarded the group of three, which left her with four pairs to investigate. Another command turned these pairs blue and added red dots for everybody else. She'd need to know where people were to avoid them. Three sets of people were above her and one was below in the basement. She decided to check below first because it would be the quickest and easiest choice to eliminate.

Threading her way to the correct door took the better part of five minutes. The lower level seemed to be a labyrinth set up by a deranged mind. Listening outside the door revealed nothing since the sound was too muffled to distinguish voices. If she'd brought a different device, she might have been able to eavesdrop properly, but she couldn't carry everything. Now, she needed to decide how to proceed. If she burst in, she'd have about half a second to distinguish friend from foe. Since Agent Cooper had never met her, he'd likely treat her with hostility. He could be armed or not, she had no way of knowing, though the bits of Megan's phone conversation indicated he was a captive. There were only so many sensors that fit inside her information kit.

One more scan revealed a 95% probability the room's occupants were male. Since it could only measure body mass and height, the machine could be fooled, but Cassandra felt confident about the result this time. Danielson could also have sent a woman to keep Cooper company, but brief encounters with the man said that was unlikely.

Tucking the device away, Cassandra drew her gun and screwed on a silencer. Then, she knocked firmly and pressed her back against the left side of the doorframe.

"Who's there?" The male voice sounded young and defensive.

"Agent Carson," Cassandra said crisply. She didn't know why that name sprang to her lips, but she didn't dwell on it.

"What do you want?"

Cassandra didn't reply. Silence had a way of making the other person go out of their way to counter it. As soon as the door swung open, Cassandra brought the butt of her gun down hard against the man's neck. He collapsed and fell back into the room, clutching at his throat. A short hop over him brought Cassandra into a cramped, crowded office. Agent Cooper stared at her wide-eyed. She confirmed that they were alone before checking on the man she'd felled on her way in.

She recognized him.

"Hello, Dale," she said to the unconscious guy.

Agent Cooper scrambled toward the desk.

Instinct brought Cassandra to her feet. She leveled her gun at Cooper.

"Please don't go for a weapon yet. As I came here to find you, I really don't want to shoot you."

Cooper's blank stare disappeared as understanding entered his eyes.

"You must be Cassandra."

"We're in a tight spot, so forgive my abruptness. Long story short, Keith Danielson's gone out of his way to play a very dangerous game with your partner and me." Cassandra held up a hand to hold back the questions written all over Cooper's face. "I don't know where your family is being held, but you have a choice. A meeting has been set up between Agent Luchek and me on Tantalus Lookout this afternoon. You can come help us flip some of Danielson's men, or you can stay here and wait until we have word on their location."

"There's a problem," said Cooper. He stuck his left leg forward and lifted the pant leg until Cassandra could see the ankle monitor clamped in place.

She thought quickly.

Dale moaned at her feet.

"I have an idea. Come help me with this guy." Cassandra motioned to Dale, tempted to kick him again for being Danielson's lapdog.

Together, Cassandra and Agent Cooper hauled Dale to the chair in front of the desk. A quick search failed to turn up zip ties, so Agent Cooper used some Ethernet cables to bind their prisoner. Meanwhile, Cassandra pulled out her smelling salts and waved them under Dale's nose. Some years she hardly used the stuff, but since meeting Agent Luchek she'd had to resort to them more than once. She followed the smelling salts with a few gentle slaps to bring Dale fully awake.

"How do we disable the ankle monitor?" she asked.

Dale started to curse at her, so she grabbed his left ear and twisted. He tilted his head right to relieve the pressure.

"Owwww!" he whined. "What the—"

Cassandra tweaked his ear to cut off his speech.

Agent Cooper looked ready to lay into Dale.

Making eye contact with Cooper, Cassandra directed him to a place just within peripheral view of their captive.

"Tell me how to disable the monitor and we go away," said Cassandra. She renewed the assault on his ear, twisting enough so he got a good look at Agent Cooper, who needed no prompting to glower menacingly. "Lie or waste my time and I let Cooper beat the information out of you."

"He can't do that," Dale protested. "He works for the freaking government. I got rights!"

"Must I spell this out for you, Dale?" Cassandra knelt, jerking his ear down toward her until he had to meet her eyes. "People with threatened families do desperate things. He might regret his actions later, but right now, what you've got is exactly five seconds before I let him have you. If you want to start buying good will, I suggest you tell us everything you know, starting with where the Cooper family is being held."

"I don't know where they are!" The panic in Dale's eyes told Cassandra there was a good chance he spoke truth on that score.

"Start with the anklet then. How do we disable it?" Cassandra pressed.

"You don't," Dale said sullenly, "but I can. Untie me."

As Cassandra watched, Cooper moved to loosen the bonds.

"You try anything and she won't have to shoot you, understand?" Cooper growled at the young man.

Swallowing the warning she'd been about to utter, Cassandra stepped back so she could cover Cooper.

Dale didn't look happy, but he dutifully disabled the anklet, freeing Agent Cooper.

"Good. Now, put it on and reactivate it," Cassandra instructed.

"What? You can't leave me here. He'll kill me." Dale looked genuinely concerned.

"Not if we kill him first," Cassandra pointed out. "Wish us luck."

"If he knows how to deactivate it, he'll have it off two seconds after we leave," said Agent Cooper.

Cassandra glared at Dale until he reluctantly complied.

"Now what, b—"

Her fist slammed into his jaw, silencing him.

"Tie him up again," she instructed Cooper.

"What if someone finds him?" Cooper wondered.

Shrugging, Cassandra moved around behind the desk to search the drawers again.

"They'll probably let him go and send people to hunt you down, depending on what he tells them, but that might not be all bad." Cassandra rummaged until she found a gun tucked into the bottom left drawer. "Is this yours?" She held the weapon up.

"Yes," Cooper answered. "What do you mean, that might not be bad? I should call my boss and have him rouse the HRT guys."

"Not a good idea," Cassandra said with a firm shake of her head. She suddenly didn't want to arm the FBI man. The tremendous amount of stress and the late hour was messing with his ability to think straight.

Cooper squared his shoulders and balled his fists. In another moment, he'd fly at her and wind up unconscious or dead.

To avoid bloodshed, Cassandra placed both guns on the desk and rested her fingertips near them. She could still reach them faster than he could, but the delay would probably spare his life if he chose to attack.

"I'm sure the Hostage Rescue Team is very good at what they do," Cassandra began, forcing herself to speak slowly. "But they're not subtle, and if Danielson gets even a whisper that they've been called, he'll murder your family and your partner." She winced at having to state it so plainly, but she had no time for delicacy. "The only reason he hasn't killed Megan yet is that he's enjoying the game too much. You take away the game and she dies."

Shifting the focus to Agent Luchek was a calculated risk on Cassandra's part. She needed to get Cooper thinking about the problem rationally. The emotions concerning his family would cloud his judgment. She counted on the fact that his affection for his partner would be strong but detached.

"You're right," Cooper admitted. His stiff movements declared his displeasure with the whole situation.

"Go home and rest. Eat something if you can. The meeting's not for a few hours yet. Try to get to the lookout at least an hour early. I'll send you the final details as soon as I can."

"What about my wife and daughters?" He sounded lost.

Cassandra placed an earpiece on the desk.

"Put this in when you get to the lookout but don't say anything unless you absolutely have to. Megan will be on the line too, and I don't want her distracted." Cassandra picked up her gun, unscrewed the silencer and tucked both away. "After the lookout, we'll go find your family."

Cooper's expression still said he'd like to start combing the city this second.

"I know this is hard, but we need to deal with Danielson." Cassandra suppressed the urge to say more on the matter. "Give me ten minutes to get clear before leaving the room." She spotted a door hanger tossed on top of a box of electronic surveillance equipment. Scanning the goods available, Cassandra pocketed a few small items before handing the door hanger to Cooper. "Put this on the door when you leave."

The Do Not Disturb sign wouldn't hold people out for long, but it might delay discovery for a short time. Finding a cloth used for cleaning dust off the equipment, Cassandra fashioned a makeshift gag for Dale. He'd wake up with a killer headache, but hopefully, he'd have enough sense to disappear without warning Danielson.

The crazy guy had been right about one thing. A few years ago, she would have simply shot the minion. Perhaps she had been *corrupted* by Agent Luchek.

Let's hope I still have an edge when it counts.

Chapter 10:
Tantalus Rematch

The sleep Megan Luchek managed to get was short, restless, yet still helpful. It took the edge off of her exhaustion, enough to let her focus on the tasks at hand. First, she needed to find one of Cassandra's shirts that fit. The woman had broader shoulders than Megan, but her shirts still felt tight. Despite the closet being completely full of clothes, the assassin had been quite insistent about which shirts Megan could choose among. Of these, she selected the white shirt, surprised by how heavy it felt compared to how light it looked. Next, she soaked her own shirt in water liberally mixed with bleach. She found a decent substitute for her suit jacket, as her own was a complete loss. Then, she went to the assassin's gun shop and browsed. As promised, there was a Glock 23 available with several spare magazines. It wasn't her gun, but it would do. Luckily, her shoulder holster had been protected by the suit jacket. Feeling better once armed, she searched the pantry for food.

Dust covered the tops of the cans, but at least their expiration dates still lay in the future. Megan heated some hearty vegetable soup. Since moving to Hawaii, she hadn't indulged in canned soup much. Besides, she was more a frozen entrée connoisseur. The soup wasn't anything like one of her mother's specialties, but it would keep her alive until the meeting. Living beyond the rendezvous required the plan to go smoothly.

The next few hours passed in a flurry of preparations. She'd watched the TV in the kitchen while carrying out more of Cassandra's instructions, but the news wasn't helping her mood. Gavriel's body had been found, and the anchor said the Honolulu Police Department had several promising leads to follow. She said they were trying to get a comment from the FBI due to Gavriel's recent courtroom triumph, but so far, no one had been available to talk to her.

That's right. Keep dreaming. Honolulu will have a four-foot blizzard before Maddox lets somebody talk to you people.

The story was barely a footnote compared to the continuing coverage of Judge Jackson's murder. This time, the anchor looked flustered when she said the FBI's lead investigators on the case were unavailable for interview. Thankfully, thus far, the news people hadn't made the connection between Gavriel and Jackson.

When everything was set, Megan settled onto the couch to wait. Absently, she drew the gun and checked the load. She wanted to make sure the bullets were real. She wished there was more to do. Besides a general loathing for waiting, the extra time freed her mind to start questioning the plan.

What would she do if the assassin betrayed her?

Cassandra had proven reliable while they were in Pennsylvania, but this situation differed from that one by a lot. For one thing, the stakes were smaller. To Megan, they seemed larger because the danger lay closer to people she knew and cared about, but to the assassin, one family of strangers hardly mattered. Keith was probably being straight with her when he said he'd gotten to one of Cassandra's friends, but the assassin seemed to think her acquaintance would be fine. Still, the threats focused on individuals rather than random masses this time.

Is there an advantage to betraying the assassin?

The question disturbed Megan. It went against her nature. In her chosen field, trust kept you alive. She longed to free Dan herself, but she didn't know where he'd been taken. A chance existed that he was still in the federal building under duress, but she couldn't risk showing her face at the office. Maddox had tried to call six times this morning, but Megan had turned off her phone. She'd needed to fight off the urge to call in sick. If she walked into the building, she'd probably not come out for hours, and that would leave Dan's family in a tough spot.

The assassin's plan made some major league assumptions, but Megan admitted they were reasonable ones. Keith's entire team probably consisted of about a dozen operatives, but those might be spread out at two separate hostage locations and possibly a headquarters. This wasn't the middle of nowhere where Keith could house a hundred men and not be noticed. If the main location doubled as one of the hostage locations, that would free up some extra men. Nevertheless, Keith likely wouldn't risk sending more than three to five men to Tantalus Lookout to record the showdown. They would certainly be armed, but observing would be their primary objective until either Cassandra or Megan went down. After that, they might try to capture the survivor and take her to Keith so he could gloat in person. Any more than five men would simply get in each other's way.

Cassandra had dropped vague references to acquiring some extra help, but Megan hadn't had time to question her closely on the subject.

At last, the time came to go to Tantalus Lookout, and Megan realized she still needed a ride. She remembered seeing an obscene number of burner phones near the gun stash. After selecting one, Megan found an app for a local car service and set up a new account with one of the credit cards she found near the boxes of ammo. Apparently being a paranoid assassin required many identities and credit cards. If she wasn't in mortal danger, she might enjoy playing spy. She'd pay the assassin back for the car fare later. In minutes, she had a confirmation number, a car description, a driver's name, and a license plate to look for.

The drive took less than fifteen minutes, but to Megan, it dragged on forever, especially since the driver was a talker. She let him ramble and ask questions. Adept at being vague, she said little during the trip. Upon arrival at her destination, she thanked the driver and got out. It felt weird not to tip the guy, but those details would be calculated through the credit card she'd left on file with the company.

Her new gun was nestled in place and her pockets contained spare magazines. She was as prepared as possible to face Cassandra, but first, she needed to clear the lookout of other people. Megan wished she had her ID badge, but it had gone MIA sometime this morning. It was yet another tiny piece of rope Maddox would use to hang her later, but he'd just have to wait his turn.

As she entered the long path, Megan rehearsed some lines that might sound plausible in explaining why the lookout was suddenly closed to the public. Judging by the cars, she had four groups to roust and send packing. To her surprise, a horde of people approached from the opposite end. From the buzzing chatter, she expected to hear a plague had been unleashed in their midst, but the loudest wails came from a teenage girl.

"My phone! He had no right to take my phone!" wailed the girl.

"You'll get it back," a woman said, looping an arm around the girl's shoulders. She sounded optimistic, but her expression conveyed doubt. "If he works for the government, he probably had good reason."

"He had a gun," piped up a young boy, twisting his head up and back to look at his parents.

The man walking next to the woman shook his head and hurried the boy along.

"Real government agents wouldn't have legitimate business up here," he said, keeping his voice low.

By this time, the horde had reached Megan. Two young couples and an older couple blasted past Megan with furtive glances.

"Your partner's a real piece of work," commented the woman who'd consoled the teenager.

"Yes, ma'am, I'll speak to him about that," Megan said, trying to figure out why the family assumed she was with whoever had confiscated their phones. She decided it must be the suit.

"When will I get my phone back?" demanded the teenager.

"Where are you staying?" Megan asked.

"Why should we tell you?" demanded the man. "We came here to rest, not be harassed."

Megan made a placating gesture.

"I'll see what I can do about getting your property returned as soon as possible."

"The Kahala Hotel and Resort," the girl blurted, earning a glare from her father and a shrug from her mother.

"You better do that because I know some great lawyers who would have a field day with—"

The man stopped talking when his wife cleared her throat loudly.

"Thank you. We appreciate your efforts." The woman seized her husband and daughter's arms and tugged as she headed for the parking lot.

"Where's your gun?" asked the boy.

"Where I need it to be," Megan replied. She nudged the child in the right direction. "Better catch up to your family."

She watched them until they reached their rental car. Once they were safely on their way, Megan turned and walked slowly to the end of the path. As always, the view struck her with its raw beauty. The peaceful image of a thick carpet of green grass sweeping down to meet a thick tree line at the foot of the mountains urged her to relax. Honolulu spread out before her crowned by the Pacific Ocean beyond. It felt wrong to enjoy the beauty while Dan and his family still needed her. The memory of her last trip here returned some of her anxiety.

Megan spent the waiting time carefully scanning the tree line. Somewhere down there, Keith's men would be hiding with their cameras. There was no other place to hide. They would need to draw the men out. If even one of them remained hidden, the carefully laid plan could still fail.

The quiet up here was broken only by the occasional bird call.

"I'm here," Cassandra announced, "but I need another few minutes to coordinate with the help."

Not responding took a lot of effort. Finally, footsteps approached from behind Megan, releasing adrenaline into her system. She tensed and spun around, drawing the borrowed gun. Cassandra already had her gun out, but she didn't point it at Megan yet. The shiny revolver glinted in the early afternoon sunlight. At the current distance, neither of them should have a problem hitting their target. The determining factor now was the will to do so.

"Agent," Cassandra greeted. "Do you mind if we postpone this thing for a moment?"

"By all means," Megan said cordially. They hadn't rehearsed what to say, but since the plan was 99% Cassandra's, Megan opted to take her verbal cues.

Raising her voice, Cassandra addressed their unseen audience.

"You can come out now. We're both here, but we're not doing anything until we get proof of life."

Nothing moved and nobody answered.

Megan stepped to the left corner and searched the trees again, keeping one eye on Cassandra. The assassin drifted to the right corner and did the same.

"We can wait," Cassandra called.

The gun felt heavy in Megan's hands.

An agonizing minute plodded by, but finally, the patience paid off. A man wearing combat fatigues stepped out of the woods midway between the women. As predicted, he held a camera.

"Don't be shy," said Cassandra, waving the man forward. "And call to your buddies."

"I'm here alone," said the man.

Cassandra made a noise that embodied the idea of amused

disbelief.

"Not likely," Megan muttered. "Where's our proof?"

The man slowly reached into his pocket to retrieve two phones. He tossed one toward Cassandra and one toward Megan. Both phones fell short, so if they really wanted to look, they'd have to climb over the railing.

"Do you swear the proof's there?" Cassandra asked.

"Yes," the man answered.

"Do you know where both parties are being held?" she continued.

"No."

Megan detected the lie in the brief hesitation before the man answered. He knew where at least one party was located. Her grip tightened on the gun. The man wore a tactical vest that should stop a bullet, so she could shoot him at least once without killing him immediately.

"Lies are dangerous," said Cassandra, "but lucky for you, I believe you." Although she spoke slowly, her next move happened almost too fast to track. Her gun came up and roared twice. The first bullet struck the man in the center of his chest, and the second bullet hit him high in the left shoulder.

He dropped with a surprised grunt of pain.

Cassandra repositioned and fired once more.

Megan lifted her gun and fired too.

The bullet from Casandra's gun caught Megan full in the chest and flung her back against the railing. The impact left her dazed as warm red fluid slipped through her fingers.

Chapter 11:
Never Mess with Family

Cassandra wanted to go to the agent, but she had unfinished business with the guy on the other side of the fence. Already, he was struggling to reach his sidearm. She could shoot him again, but there was no guarantee of hitting something that would hurt from this lousy angle. Besides, she didn't want him dead until he spilled his guts about Danielson's operation. Tucking the gun into the holster behind her back, Cassandra vaulted the green railing separating the path from the pristine grass.

Pleased to have returned to combat boots, Cassandra stepped up to the fallen guy and pressed a foot lightly down on the wound. If he moved suddenly, she might be in trouble, but it was a risk worth taking.

"Don't move and don't speak until I tell you to." The order was reinforced with a little pressure.

The man gritted his teeth but stayed still.

A search yielded two handguns, a knife, and a pair of handcuffs. Cassandra unloaded the smaller of the two handguns, making sure to check for a bullet in the chamber. She tossed the magazine a few feet left and the empty gun a few feet right. Spotting an earpiece, Cassandra decided to make good use of it. Holding the man's other gun in one hand, she drew her tiny revolver and pressed it to the man's good shoulder.

"Tell your partners to get out here or lose the use of the other arm."

The man's expression remained hard while he considered his

options.

"You have until I lose patience, which is mere seconds away. I'm not going to bother counting aloud."

"All right. You heard her, guys. Get out here."

One man separated from the tree line and advanced toward Cassandra with an assault rifle pointed at her.

The excessive firepower surprised her, but she hid it well.

"One guy's not going to cut it," Cassandra said, digging the revolver's nose into the man's shoulder.

"It was four guys total," reported Agent Cooper, emerging from the trees close behind the man with the assault rifle. "Two were down when I found them. Some sort of tranquilizer. This guy and the one you have are the only others I saw." His service weapon couldn't miss from that range, yet he was just out of the man's reach. "Drop the gun and get on your knees," he instructed the man, shifting so he entered the guy's side vision.

"You're both dead," said the guy with the rifle. "Your family too," he added, speaking to Cooper.

"I don't think so," Agent Cooper countered. "You're having technical difficulties right now. Danielson has no idea what's going on, and you're going to assure him all is well when the time comes. Last warning: gun down."

The man slowly obeyed the order and the previous one to drop to his knees. The FBI man then searched him, removed his other weapons, and handcuffed him. Once certain the man was truly subdued, the FBI man marched him over to where Cassandra and the other captive waited.

"Put him on his stomach and go check on your partner," Cassandra said.

Agent Cooper hesitated.

"I'll get the information," she promised, "but you might not want to watch."

The FBI man turned his attention to Megan, allowing Cassandra to focus on her prisoner. She put the bigger handgun in the space where her revolver once was and switched the little gun to her left hand. Kneeling on the man's chest, she leaned close enough to see his brown eyes.

"All right, CIA man, talk to me," she whispered. The revolver burrowed into the man's right shoulder. "Short, direct answers will have the least painful results. You lie, I shoot you. You refuse to answer, I shoot you. Is any of this confusing to you?"

He shook his head.

Pressing two fingers to the man's neck, Cassandra paused until she understood the rhythm of his pulse. Next, she stared down and started asking questions.

"How many of you are working for Danielson?"

"Eight."

"Is Owen Ramsey one of you?"

A flicker of calculation in the man's eyes told her the next statement would be a lie.

"Yes."

She pulled the trigger.

The blank round slammed into the man's shoulder, jerking it back hard enough to dislocate the joint.

He screamed and arched his back to absorb the pain.

She clamped a hand over his mouth and waited for him to subside.

"That was a blank. The last one in the gun. It'll hurt, but there won't be any real damage. I can even set your shoulder before I leave if you cooperate. The next bullet is very real. That means physical therapy and a new career, assuming my patience lasts." Cassandra moved the gun from the guy's shoulder to his chin. She nodded at the other man. "You have a buddy over there, so I don't really need you. He'll probably be much more talkative if you're dead." She moved the gun back to the shoulder. "Would you like to answer my questions honestly?"

Sweat dripped down the man's face, but he managed to nod. His eyes were clenched shut.

"Open your eyes," Cassandra commanded. She felt for his pulse again and waited a moment while it picked up a new rhythm. "Do you know one or both locations where the hostages are being held?"

"One," the man croaked.

"Which?"

"The family."

"Good. Give me the address and you get to live."

"How do I know you're not lying? Danielson told us all about you," said the man. Righteous indignation made him brave. "You're just a killer for hire."

"The address," she prompted.

His answer made sense but annoyed her, and his attitude brought up a new and disturbing possibility. The CIA men might not be rogues, just working with bad information. If Agent Cooper hadn't knocked out the other two CIA guys, then Owen must have done it. If Danielson had a separate team of Shadow Council operatives, this could get very complicated, but they'd be more likely to kill the CIA men. She didn't have the time to properly mull the possibilities over.

"You don't have much of a choice," Cassandra reminded the man. "And don't believe everything you hear from guys like Danielson." She thought of Agent Cooper's family. "How did he justify kidnapping a woman and two small children?"

"Smoke and mirrors," mumbled the man. "They'd be scared but fine in the end. He said it was for the greater good."

"How was having me kill an FBI agent 'for the greater good'?" Cassandra asked. She stopped kneeling on the man's chest but stayed next to him with the gun at the ready.

"She's a terrorist," he said softly. His gaze was becoming unfocused as the pain built up.

By this point, Cassandra's anger had switched to pity and threatened to turn into paralyzing weariness. She wanted to set him straight on so many things, but if it wasn't too late, she had scant seconds to get a message across.

"Megan's not a terrorist, and take some life advice: never mess with family. They ask you to do this again, you quit."

Not waiting for a response, Cassandra moved to his other side and popped his shoulder back into place. Then, she checked his shoulder wound to make sure he wouldn't bleed out. Cutting some strips off of his pants, Cassandra bound the wound.

The man nodded stiff thanks, knowing she could have just as easily killed him.

"I'm not going to cuff you, but even if help arrives before I send it, sit the rest of this mission out. Find a foreign country to operate in like you're supposed to, and hope we don't meet again."

Cassandra stood up and plucked the earpiece controller from her pocket. She opened a narrow band through the broad jamming signal to contact Owen.

"Owen? Are you there?" She paused to give him a chance to respond, but heard nothing. "Did you know these men were CIA?"

Again, silence answered her.

The question of Owen's true loyalties could drive her mad if she let it.

As she turned to confer with the FBI man, the other CIA assailant caught her attention. He was a pretty bulky guy, but Cassandra managed to roll him enough to look into his eyes.

"Did you hear everything we just said?"

"I did."

"Good. I hate repeating myself. What's your name, and where are the phones taken from the people you guys kicked out of the park?" She'd heard that much through Megan's earpiece.

"Striker, and the phones are in the van."

"What's your real name, and where are the keys?" Cassandra asked.

"Liam. Left pocket."

Cassandra searched until she found the thick set of keys.

"Thank you. I'm going to leave you with the same speech as the other guy. Rethink your career goals, and a get a transfer to someplace where you can do good. Agent Cooper and Agent Luchek are off limits from here on out." She stopped speaking long enough let the message sink into him. "Now, your partner was supposed to convey a message to your boss. If you give him my message, you get to live. Please don't deviate from the message."

"What would you like me to say?" asked Liam.

"Tell him it's done. Agent Luchek is dead, and I want to meet him at the location where he's holding the Cooper family. Tell him he needs to bring what's mine with him."

"He won't believe you," Liam warned.

"Just tell him." Cassandra flicked the switch to temporarily unjam the frequency for Liam's earpiece.

Liam conveyed her message word for word.

Thanking him again, Cassandra stood. Phase one of her plan had largely been a success.

"Where are they?" demanded Agent Cooper, glaring at the prisoner. The muscles in his neck and arms bulged with the desire to smash something.

"I have the address," said Cassandra.

The agent's hard gaze shifted to her. His gun was in his hand but not pointed anywhere in particular.

"You're going to have to follow me there." Cassandra rose so she could make a move should the agent turn hostile.

"Why?" The question cracked through the still air like a

gunshot.

"Because I need you to bring Agent Luchek and I can travel faster alone." Cassandra tossed him a small phone and Megan's ID badge. "Give the ID back to Megan. The phone has an app preloaded with a GPS tracker on my motorcycle. Come as quickly as you can."

"Why should I trust you?" he asked. His gun arm rose a few inches.

"I'm getting very tired of that question, but I'm currently the best chance your family has of surviving."

Chapter 12:
The Devil's Bargain

Megan could hear the murmur of conversations taking place near her, but she couldn't make out many of the words. She thought the earpiece would address that problem, but either hers was damaged or Cassandra had turned it off. Much of Megan's concentration went into breathing shallowly. The nanotechnology incorporated into the shirt she'd borrowed from the assassin kept her alive, but from that range even the blank bullet had packed a punch.

Dan knelt next to her.

"Megan, can you stand?" he asked. His tone bled anxiety. He reached down to help her up, pausing long enough to slip her ID into her pocket.

"How did you get here?" she wondered, accepting the proffered hand. The actual getting up part was pure agony, but she bore it as best she could, making a lot of faces on the way.

"Long story, and we need to go. Cassandra's already on her way to my family. I need to be there. Can you walk?"

"Slowly," Megan answered.

"May I carry you?" The formality thickened his accent.

Megan would have preferred to walk it off naturally, but she figured being carried was better than hobbling along as Dan tried to help.

"Only if you pick up my gun for me."

Soon, they were in Dan's SUV winding their way down from Tantalus Lookout.

"Since you're still alive, I take it that's not real blood," Dan pointed out. "What is it?"

"Ketchup, food coloring, and cornstarch," Megan reported. "I had to thin it down with some water. Did I leave any spare clothes in here?"

"Not sure, but you can check the back."

After trying to turn around, Megan concluded wearing the ketchup mix for another few hours wouldn't hurt as much. It would probably terrify Bethany and the children, but that couldn't be helped. She fervently hoped they were alive long enough to be terrified by her appearance.

"How'd you get free?" Megan asked a few minutes later as they drove down South Beretania Street.

"Friendly neighborhood assassin," Dan replied. "I'm guessing she's also the mastermind behind the ketchup plan. What'd she hit you with?"

"A blank," Megan answered. She slowly drew a deep breath to see if it still hurt. It did, but not as much as before. The improvement encouraged her. "Desperate times, desperate measures and all that. It's like being hit with a bowling ball launched from a cannon."

"Thank you," Dan said quietly.

The thanks caught Megan off guard.

"For what? I haven't done anything."

"For being here. For going to the lookout." Dan struggled to find the right words. "Nothing really made you go. It wasn't your family."

"Dan, they wouldn't be in danger if it wasn't for me." Megan grimaced at how painfully true the words rang in her ears. "Danielson started out as my problem. I need to finish this, and if I have any say at all, I won't let them come to harm."

He stayed quiet.

Megan massaged her temple to ward off a headache.

"If you have something to say, we should clear the air now," she said.

Dan began with a giant sigh.

"This is on me too. Beth was right. I can't keep my personal and work lives separate."

"What will you do?" Megan wondered.

"I don't know, but it doesn't matter now anyway. We have to find them first."

Megan's eyes locked on the phone which he'd placed in the

holder. A blinking red dot showed them their target. She'd heard *GPS* and *motorcycle* and assumed they were following Cassandra. The woman kept popping up in crisis situations. Megan couldn't decide whether to be grateful or hope the assassin stayed gone the next time.

They spent the rest of the short ride lost in their own thoughts.

Finally, they pulled up in front of a rundown building and saw a black motorcycle leaning across one of the doors. Once upon a time, the ground floor hosted retail stores, while the upper floors consisted of offices or apartments. The real estate and construction signs told her somebody wanted to demolish the whole thing and start over. The project probably got mired in red tape, hence the abandoned state of the building.

"That figures," Megan muttered. She waved to the building across the street. "That's where Danielson's man ambushed me the first time. They had Gavriel trussed up in a chair, waiting for me to kill him."

"Did you?" Dan asked.

"No, but they used my gun to kill him," Megan said. "That's going to give Maddox fits."

"Special Agent Oldwick, too. Sims told me he caught the Gavriel case," said Dan. "Are you ready?"

Megan plucked the borrowed gun out of the shoulder holster and nodded.

"Oldwick and Maddox might not be our biggest fans right now, but you should consider waiting here and calling them. We might need the backup."

"What if she got the address wrong?" Dan asked.

A gunshot caught their attention.

"She didn't," Megan said, opening the door before Dan braked to a complete stop. "Make the call. Then, follow the gunshots."

The dreary building reminded Megan of a training exercise. The door looked ready to fall off its hinges. She didn't expect to meet resistance on the perimeter, but she cleared the door anyway. The gunshots sounded distant enough to be coming from an upper room. The wide open emptiness of the room she stepped into was unnerving. She crossed the space as quickly as possible and found a stairwell.

Another gunshot lent speed to her legs. Megan scrambled up the flights of stairs until she came to the fifth floor landing.

"You're wasting bullets, Ms. Mirren," Keith's voice scolded. He sounded very close. "You can't hit me and I can't hit you from this angle, but I have some advantages you don't, including Mr. Smith."

Crouching low, Megan peeked around the doorway. Keith hunkered behind a metal desk. The hostages were positioned at the room's center, directly in everybody's line of fire. Beth and Giggles were unconscious. Sweet Pea's carrier sat next to Beth. Megan didn't recognize the old man, but he sat calmly. The duct tape wrapped around his arms and legs seemed not to bother him in the least. On the far side of the room, Cassandra crouched down behind another ugly desk and fired bullets up into the ceiling at regular intervals.

"Oh, don't count me. I let the little bird fly long ago," spoke the old man. His British accent rendered the words cheerfully. This must be Cassandra's *old friend*. He caught Megan's eye and winked. Shifting a bit, he twisted so that she could see behind his back. He held up two fingers and then pointed to her left. "It was *high* time I got out and saw the world anyway. Too much *down* time makes one dull." His emphasis on the words *high* and *down* gave Megan a message.

She nodded that the message was received. Judging by the room's dimensions, the left wall couldn't be that far. Staying low, Megan inched backwards until most of her body lay just outside the threshold. She hesitated long enough to draw a bracing breath. Then, rolling right, she fired up into the two men huddled there. The desk they'd moved had provided excellent protection from Cassandra, but they hadn't anticipated a threat from the doorway. Megan sent two bullets into each man before rolling left to exit the path of any return fire. As expected, the move caused an explosion of pain in her chest, but at least she hadn't been shot again.

"Maggie?" Keith sounded strangely calm and excited. "I was told you'd been killed. Come join us."

Megan looked to Cassandra for a sign as to what was happening out of her view. The assassin's expression had gone flat and deadly. She shook her head briefly.

The old man clucked in disapproval.

"Ms. Mirren and I were having a discussion about her behavior before you arrived. Did you know she drugged half my hostages?"

"What's that got to do with anything?" Megan asked, mentally kicking herself for playing along with the crazy guy.

"This is her fault," Keith said indignantly. "I would much prefer an adult hostage with me in this moment of need, but that choice was taken away from me."

Finally catching his oblique meaning, Megan forced herself to stand up. This gave her the necessary angle to peek into the baby carrier.

It was empty.

The sharp breath she drew stabbed her in the ribs. She leaned heavily against the doorframe.

For a moment, the only sounds that could be heard were the moaning of the guys Megan had shot. She'd aimed center mass, hoping for any sort of hit from that awkward angle. Their vests probably saved their lives, but hopefully, they'd be down for the duration of the fight.

"You know what I love best about multiple hostages?" Keith asked casually. "Sheer numbers. Still, it would be a shame to remove sweet little Carolina from the equation so early. Won't you join us, please?"

Holding her gun out in front of her, Megan stepped into the room. She immediately focused on Keith Danielson, keeping her aim high so she wouldn't hit Sweet Pea. He held the baby gently, and she slept peacefully. Were someone to take a photo, the only thing out of place would be the gun he'd rested across her chest like a malevolent bottle. When he turned toward her, Megan saw the long gash marking his right forearm. She remembered seeing the letter opener clutched in the judge's cold, dead fist.

"Put her down, Keith." Megan struggled to keep her voice steady. "You want me, you've got me, but that child doesn't deserve this."

Keith looked terrible. His bloodshot eyes held equal measures of lust for vengeance and madness. His hair appeared not to have been combed in a week.

"You first, drop the gun." Inspiration struck and he stiffened. "No, wait!" A malicious grin spread slowly from the left side of his face to the right. "I have a better idea. You're very trigger happy today. Shoot yourself."

"What?" Megan triple-checked the statement to make sure she'd heard him right.

"Maggie." The way he said the name stretched it out. "You never understood me, but I'm a student of human behavior. And like any good student, I enjoy experiments. So, here's the current question. How far does love and loyalty stretch?" He stared at her curiously. "I'm sure at some point you promised dear Agent Dan you'd do anything to preserve his precious little family. So, what's your word worth?"

Megan stood stock-still with her mind racing three thousand

miles per second. She wasn't sure she could move if she wanted to.

Beth stirred and moaned.

Keith looked even happier.

"In another moment, we'll have an important witness," he declared.

A glance back at Cassandra revealed her whispering furiously into a small black object.

"She can't help you this time," Keith said, sounding apologetic.

"Give Beth the baby," Megan said, wishing her voice didn't sound so wispy.

"Double or nothing? I like the way you think." Reaching into a pocket, Keith pulled out a small knife. He tossed it to the floor in front of Bethany. "Mrs. Cooper will be fully awake in a moment. Cut her arms free so she can hold the child."

Megan laid down the gun and picked up the knife. She dragged out the freeing process as much as possible, but the knife was very sharp and the tape's stiffness allowed it to cut away easily.

"Where's Dan?" Beth asked dreamily.

"He's coming," Megan promised.

Hopefully with a ton of help, she added silently.

She dropped the knife behind Beth and peeled away the tape. Then, she pulled the woman's arms out in front and started massaging the fingers and wrists.

"All right, she looks alert now. Pick up your gun and step away from Mrs. Cooper," Keith instructed.

"If I tell you to shut your eyes, you can't hesitate," said Megan, ignoring Keith for the moment. "It's for your own good."

"What's going on?" Beth's eyes pleaded with Megan to explain.

"Don't watch," Megan said.

"Now come get the baby and give her to Mrs. Cooper."

Megan didn't need to look to see his gun had shifted from Sweet Pea to Beth. She turned her left side toward Keith, and he draped the baby across her arm. This time, Megan didn't stall. She delivered Carolina and stayed in front of them, blocking Keith's shot. From this close, a bullet might go clear through her, but she didn't know what else she could do.

Beth met Megan's gaze. Horror and understanding played across her features. She clutched the baby close and turned so more of her body stood between the threat and her child.

"It's all right. Close your eyes. It'll be over soon," Megan promised.

"I honored my part, now it's your turn," said Keith.

The gun suddenly weighed a ton, but Megan tightened her grip on it so it wouldn't fall.

"First, we clarify the terms." Megan didn't bother turning around. "The second I do this, they go free, all of them."

"You only get the Cooper family," Keith told her. "Mr. Smith is Ms. Mirren's to fight for."

Come on, Dan. Come on, Dan.

Megan's options were dwindling fast.

As she started to raise the gun, Cassandra spoke crisply and clearly.

"Agent, duck."

Megan flattened herself on top of Beth and Carolina Cooper. She didn't see what happened next, but a wall of glass to her left shattered, showering her with tiny pieces. A torrent of gunshots rocked the room.

Something thudded to the ground behind her.

Chapter 13:
Free and Clear

Rolling onto her back, Megan scrambled to her feet and stared in disbelief at Keith's body. From the looks of him, she was practically the only one in the room who hadn't shot—or stabbed—him. The sharp pocketknife she'd used to free Beth stuck out of his chest. One bullet had struck his head from the right side and another marked the center of his forehead. A gruesome gathering of bullets outlined the center of his chest like somebody had tried to give him a lead heart.

She became aware of a gentle buzzing noise. Looking out the ruined window, Megan spotted a small flying drone equipped with an automatic pistol. A red beam swept over the room. Apparently satisfied, the machine bobbed left and right, then backed up, turned around, and flew away.

The next thing to pierce Megan's numbness was the sound of quiet weeping. Ashley Cooper had curled herself into a tight ball beside her mother, hands clamped firmly over her ears. Beth stared in Megan's general direction, but her eyes were unfocused, like she'd retreated somewhere deep inside her head.

Dan practically bowled Megan over in his haste to get to his family, but she wouldn't hold that against him.

Movement in her peripheral vision drew her back into the moment as she realized the danger might not be over. One of the guys she'd shot a few minutes ago was crawling toward the door. Megan strode over to the man and knelt in front of him, halting his progress.

"Please don't go anywhere," she said, making sure the man saw the gun still clutched in her hands. "There's a very big mess here, and I need somebody to explain it to my boss. Keith's not going to fulfill that role today, and your colleague will probably be in the hospital a while. That means it's your lucky day. You get to play cut-a-deal first."

The man reluctantly sat back against the wall and raised his hands. His unlucky partner had caught a few more bullets, courtesy of the drone aiming at Keith. The rise and fall of his chest told her there was still some life in him.

"I want my lawyer."

"Really? You're pulling the lawyer card already?"

"Lawyer," the man repeated.

"I'll put that on my to-do list. For now, sit tight."

"Megan, can you help me?" called Dan.

Megan looked to her partner then back to the prisoner. She didn't have handcuffs.

"Throw me your cuffs, and I'll be right there," said Megan.

Dan's handcuffs hit the floor near her and bounced into the prisoner's left boot. Retrieving them from the ground, Megan made good use of the cuffs, leaving the man face down with his hands secured behind him.

"I'm here," Megan announced, kneeling in front of the Cooper family. She slipped the handgun into her shoulder holster.

"Please take Ashley out of the room." Dan's voice was subdued. "I don't want her seeing anything she shouldn't."

The girl had stopped crying, but she looked stricken. Her eyes were clenched shut, and her expression was that of someone expecting to receive a blow. The grip she had on Beth looked permanent.

Megan watched her for a moment, deciding on the best approach. She didn't have much time because the SWAT guys would be here soon with their big guns and loud, scary voices.

Tapping Ashley on the shoulder, Megan waited until one blue eye peered up at her.

"Hey, I could use a hug too. Your daddy says we should get out of here. Close your eyes and I'll take you somewhere safe. Can you do that for me?"

The child burrowed deeper into Beth's side.

"Stay. Mommy."

The words were muffled, but Megan thought she heard them correctly.

"Mommy wants to leave too, but she can't carry you and the baby."

"Leave her!" Ashley wailed.

That's a little harsh, Megan thought with a sigh.

"You don't mean that. You'd be sad if Sweet Pea had to stay in a scary place."

"No!" Ashley shouted.

Megan turned to Dan for moral support.

"Just take her," he advised.

"Sorry, kid, orders is orders," Megan muttered. She pried the toddler's grip loose and held her flailing limbs in place, wishing she had a third arm.

Ashley's piercing scream filled the room, making Megan cringe. She didn't want to risk dropping the child, so she blocked out the noise as best she could. Stepping sideways, Megan exited as quickly as possible, keeping her burden turned away from the worst of the carnage.

Midway down the stairs, Megan heard the SWAT guys enter with their usual lack of subtlety. Not wanting to be taken for a threat, Megan sat down and settled Ashley across her lap. Surprisingly, the girl settled down as the pounding footsteps approached. Taking advantage of the opportunity, Megan turned Ashley so that the child's face stayed fixed in her direction. She wanted to spare her the fright of having a gun shoved in her face again.

"Hands up!" ordered a young man in full tactical gear. The business end of his assault rifle drew a steady bead on Megan.

His team members hustled past them.

Crossing her arms, Megan spread her fingers to show the man she held nothing, but she kept Ashley pinned in place. She met the man's gaze.

"My name is Megan Luchek, and I work for the FBI. My ID badge is in my jacket pocket. Do you want me to get it?"

"Don't move! Keep your hands high!" Her name caused a spark of recognition to ignite in the man's dark eyes.

Great. I'm going to be here for hours.

"I've showed you I'm not holding a gun, but I am wearing one," Megan continued calmly. "If you want to cuff me, go for it, but I'm not letting go of this child until I can place her in her mother's arms. She's seen too many guns as it is today."

The young man hesitated but took her up on the offer and snapped handcuffs in place. Then, he removed the gun from her shoulder holster. He blanched at the large red stain in the center of her shirt.

"Were you hit?" he demanded.

"It's not what you think," Megan assured him. "It's mostly ketchup." She left the explanation there when she saw the man's disbelief. "Never mind. It's a long story."

They waited on the stairs until people started filing out. Megan watched anxiously, hoping to speak with Cassandra before they hauled her away somewhere. Two men escorted the man Megan had cuffed earlier. A pair of paramedics rushed up, presumably to retrieve the badly wounded man. Megan's heart leapt when another man escorted a fully intact Cooper family out of the room. Dan held the baby carrier in one hand and had his other hand wrapped around his wife's back. The last man in the squad stood outside the doorway so the scene wouldn't be disturbed.

The SWAT guy standing with Megan grabbed an elbow and tugged up. Megan craned her neck to see if anyone else would walk out the door. When no one else exited, she smiled. Adjusting her grip, she stood and fell into place a few steps behind Dan's family.

Thinking back to the moments just after Keith went down, Megan tried to recall seeing Cassandra and the assassin's *old friend*. The last sighting of Cassandra had been of her speaking into the mysterious black box.

When they reached the sunshine and fresh air, Megan shut her eyes and paused to appreciate both.

"Luchek!" Maddox's booming voice captured her attention. "Cooper! Where the blazes have you two been? Van! Now!" Special Agent in Charge Bryan Maddox's tone down shifted when he spotted Bethany Cooper and the baby. "Take a moment to settle your family, Cooper, but I do want to see you pronto."

Megan wasn't sure what to do first. The young SWAT guy still had his hand on her left elbow.

Beth Cooper appeared before Megan.

"I'll take her now. Thank you."

"You okay?" asked Megan.

Beth's lips were pressed into a thin line.

"I will be in a while," she promised. "Go help Dan fend off your boss. We can talk later."

"Luchek! What's the holdup?" Maddox demanded.

Megan held up her shiny bracelets by way of explanation.

Maddox muttered something under his breath and marched

over. He removed his dark sunglasses to let the full weight of his glare bear down on the strapping SWAT guy. The SAC was slightly shorter than the man, but his presence more than made up for the height difference.

"Get those cuffs off my agent." He spoke in his deadly calm tone.

Megan rather enjoyed the tone being directed at someone else for a change.

"Yes, sir," replied the man. He quickly released Megan from the handcuffs, looking relieved to turn her over to Maddox.

Her boss eyed her up and down.

"If all that red were real, you'd be dead," he commented.

"It's just—"

Maddox held up a hand to cut her off.

"I'm sure I'll find out how that fits in during the debrief." He turned away and glanced toward the Cooper family. "See if you can pry Cooper away, then meet me in the van. You have *a lot* of explaining to do."

"Yes, sir," Megan said, feeling as meek as the SWAT guy looked.

"And don't ever turn off your phone," said Maddox.

Megan nodded and watched her boss barrel back to his mobile command unit. He didn't take it out often, but the converted van was pretty impressive. She didn't see a point in arguing now, though she mentally admitted she'd probably disobey that order eventually.

Dragging her feet could only slow her down so much. Megan maneuvered to where Dan could see her, but she didn't want to interrupt the serious discussion in progress. She halted a respectful distance away, but still within earshot.

"What do you want from me, Beth?" Dan demanded. "Be honest. Do you want me to quit?"

Their hands were clasped, but they stood about a foot apart, looking ready to start a boxing match. Several emotions flashed across Bethany Cooper's face. Fear, love, anger, and frustration were the only ones Megan recognized.

"What you felt today is a taste of what I feel every day." Beth's voice wavered with the intense effort to control her emotions. A tear slipped out and hit her left cheek on the way to the ground. She brushed at the tear and shook her head violently. Blond hair curled around her face. "But you can't quit!"

The force of the declaration stunned Dan.

"You'd be miserable, and quitting would leave men like that free to hurt others." Beth rested her hands on Dan's neck. "There's nothing else to say, so kiss me and promise you'll be careful."

Dan did both, starting with a long kiss and ending with a solemn promise. He rested his forehead against Beth's for a lengthy moment before pulling away. She broke out of his loose hold and faced Megan.

"I can never thank you enough for what you did today," Beth said.

Megan gave her a puzzled look.

The ghost of a smile formed on Beth's face.

"You may think I was out of it, but I know what he asked of you. And I know you were ready to follow through with it. That kind of loyalty to virtual strangers is rare, so thank you." Beth shifted her gaze from Megan back to Dan. "I'm probably going to have some nightmares from this experience, but I'll feel safer knowing you two will protect each other." Going to tiptoes, Beth kissed Dan's cheek. "After the police station, I'm going home. Try to make it home for dinner."

"He'll be there," said Megan. "Maddox can't hold us forever."

I hope.

She tugged gently on Dan's arm to get him moving in the right direction. The meeting might not be pleasant, but it would be a vast improvement on the last few hours.

Epilogue:
Out of the Shadows

Cassandra Mirren flipped through the three passports in this stash. Clara Dayton was a red-head, Andrea Silven had black hair, and Naomi Allen kept her hair bleached blond.

"I'm partial to this one," Owen Ramsey said from the doorway.

Cassandra whirled, snapping up her gun in the process. Recognizing Owen, she shifted the gun away.

He held his hands up to prove the lack of weapons. The only thing in his hands was a small blue booklet.

"One of these days, I'm just going to shoot you," she said, returning the gun to the bed she knelt beside.

The thing Owen had been holding landed on the bed next to her gun. She knew what it was before she picked it up.

"Where did you get this?"

"It pays to have friends in the State Department," he replied.

Slowly, Cassandra picked up the passport and flipped it open. Next to her picture she read the name: Sarah Carson. The picture was pretty outdated yet still resembled her. She waited to see which emotion would come to the surface, but she felt nothing. She had ceased to be Sarah Carson years ago, and she couldn't go back to that now.

"It's a nice thought," she said, closing the passport with a sense of finality.

"I figured you'd say that," said Owen.

Another passport hit the bed. This one was already open to the main page. It said: Cassandra Mirren. A blue piece of paper stuck out of the right side. Slipping it out, Cassandra saw the paper was a social security card.

"It's completely real," Owen reported. "It's been scrubbed clean, recycled, processed, and made good enough to fool even our own recruiters, though you'll never have to deal with them anyway."

Cassandra got up, sat on the bed, and studied her friend.

"Why do you want this so badly?"

"I don't just want *this*, I want you," said Owen. "And we work well together. This thing with Danielson was touch and go for a while, but you helped me complete my mission where nobody else could."

Cassandra knew she'd tagged Danielson first, but she didn't want to argue about who killed the man. Truth was, they might never know which wound proved fatal first. Owen had controlled the drone that paid out the most damage, but Cassandra, Agent Cooper, and even her mentor got in a good strike. Smith always could work with anything at hand, including pocketknives.

Owen approached slowly, knelt before her, and picked up her hands.

"Cassie, I don't care which identity you want to go with. If you want something completely new, I'll make it happen, but it's time to come out of the shadows. You know what I do isn't pretty, but it's necessary. You don't have to tell me your past, but you're welcome to do so." Owen squeezed her hands. "And this friends thing is killing me. If there's any chance for an 'us' in the future, tell me."

This moment had been a long time in coming. Cassandra had given the matter a lot of thought. She leaned forward and kissed him lightly on the lips.

"People I care about tend to die, but I guess you know what that's like. If you're willing to risk it, so am I."

She could do worse for a second career than the CIA.

One of her numerous cellphones rang. Retrieving her hands from Owen's grasp, Cassandra picked up the correct phone. The number came up blocked. She accepted the call but said nothing.

"Ms. Mirren. We've not had the pleasure of meeting, but I wanted to congratulate you on your performance these past couple of days." The speaker's age couldn't be determined from his voice, but he spoke crisply. "What happened with our mutual friend was unfortunate, but he named you as a possible successor. I'm calling to gauge your level of interest in his unique position."

Cassandra considered the offer. He'd basically handed her a

position on the Shadow Council. If she joined them fully, she could have a hand in directing their path. She could prevent more Keith Danielsons from infesting the ranks. Plans and partial plans tumbled around in her head.

Then, her eyes fell on Owen, and the glimmer of a new future appeared in her mind's eye.

"I'm retired," she said, tapping the button to conclude the call.

THE END

Thank You for Reading:

I hope you liked the Shadow Council series. For more Agent Luchek adventures, check out the Eagle Eyes trilogy.

Please visit my website: **www.juliecgilbert.com** to find a link to the current free works. If you're looking to save money, try the combination books. It's also fun to try a different medium. The audiobooks have fantastic narrators.

Join the Facebook group "Julie C. Gilbert's Special Agents" for monthly book discussions and giveaways.

I would love to connect via email: **devyaschildren@gmail.com; juliecgilbert5steps@gmail.com**

Other Contacts:
www.facebook.com/JulieCGilbert2013
www.instagram.com/juliecgilbert_writer/
https://twitter.com/authorgilbert
www.bookbub.com/authors/julie-c-gilbert

Made in the USA
Middletown, DE
12 July 2024